THE WASHERWOMAN'S DAUGHTERS

Kate Moneymoon's family background is unusual for 1914 — a 'washerwoman' for a mother, an Oxford professor for a father — but she is contented enough until she meets Robert Holker, second son of the Earl of Werrington. Thereafter, her life is never the same again — but then neither is anyone's after World War One breaks out. Kate and her twin sister, Priscilla, serve as VADs in France, where they have many adventures and meet many, very different people.

Books by Pat Lacey
Published by The House of Ulverscroft:

ROSEMARY COTTAGE
SUMMER AT SAINT PIERRE
THE VINTAGE YEAR

PAT LACEY

THE WASHERWOMAN'S DAUGHTERS

Complete and Unabridged

ULVERSCROFT
Leicester

First Large Print Edition
published 1999

British Library CIP Data

Lacey, Pat
    The washerwoman's daughters.—Large print ed.—
Ulverscroft large print series: romance
1. Love stories
2. Large type books
I. Title
823.9'14 [F]

ISBN 0–7089–4110–9

Published by
F. A. Thorpe (Publishing) Ltd.
Anstey, Leicestershire

Set by Words & Graphics Ltd.
Anstey, Leicestershire
Printed and bound in Great Britain by
T. J. International Ltd., Padstow, Cornwall

This book is printed on acid-free paper

To
George

1

'Are you all right?'

'No thanks to you if I am! Dirty, smelly contraption!'

'It's a Harley Davidson, I'll have you know!'

'And this is a mere push-bike, but all I've got, I'll have *you* know.'

'I'm sorry but you *were* on the wrong side of the road. *And* riding with only one hand.'

'The other was holding on to my hat.'

'And much good it did! Allow me!' And the young man in the oily overalls, astride the motor-bike, leaned down to retrieve the straw boater from the gutter. 'It was lucky,' he added, 'that I was doing no more than two miles an hour. She can do fifty, flat out.'

'You don't say!' Kate Moneymoon was determined not to relent. Not while her bicycle was still spreadeagled on the road, a good mile from her home in North Oxford. 'Would you,' she continued, with more than a shade of sarcasm, 'entrust me with holding your precious machine while you inspect mine for damage?'

'I'm afraid,' he said ruefully, 'that I don't need to inspect it. I can see from here that the front wheel's badly buckled.'

'So how am I supposed to get home?'

'That should present no problem. If you can wait

a moment, Miss er . . . ?' And he raised a hopeful eyebrow.

'Moneymoon. Kate Moneymoon. Although, why you need to know . . . '

'Robert Holker,' he said ignoring her protest. 'And may I ask — is your father, Professor Moneymoon, the eminent, social historian?'

She nodded.

'Then I'm in luck. I was just coming to see him to arrange next term's tutorials. So, if you'll wait a moment while I put my bike back in its stable, I'll push yours home. Or better still, why don't you leave it here and I'll take you home on my pillion?'

'Oh, I couldn't possibly!' But her mouth curved into a tentative smile.

It was a pretty mouth, Robert Holker decided. As was the rest of her; tendrils of dark hair escaping from the knot at the nape of her neck, eyes of brilliant sapphire and a small, straight nose above full, lusciously-curved lips. Only the prominence of her cheekbones was out of proportion and even that seemed to accentuate the depth and colour of her eyes. And her figure, or what he could see of it beneath her no-nonsense shirt-waister — high to the neck and reaching to a decidedly trim ankle — was neatly curved. 'I promise I'll drive very carefully,' he assured her.

Now, it was her turn to scrutinise him. Not a handsome face, she decided dispassionately, the nose too craggy beneath the thatch of unruly red hair and the chin jutting like the Rock of Gibraltar, but the mouth was wide and generous and displaying now a smile of surprising sweetness. A face, she decided, that could be trusted.

'All right! I promised Ma I'd be home early, so perhaps I'd better.'

'Good! I'll just put your bike away.' And he picked it up and carried it around the side of the tall, Victorian house in the Iffley Road where he had his lodgings. 'And now,' he came back, his overalls removed, 'to horse!'

Her skirt presented a slight problem and he carefully averted his gaze as she bunched it around her and swung a leg over the pillion. 'Now, hold on to me — both arms around my waist — and lean *with* the bike, not against it, particularly when we go round a bend.'

It was surprisingly easy and exhilarating. Starting slowly, while she got her balance, Robert Holker increased speed over Magdalen Bridge, where a couple of undergraduates leaning on the parapet whistled their appreciation, turned right across the busy traffic of the High Street, sped down Holywell, out into the Parks Road and throttled back under the cherry trees of the Banbury Road, where whistles gave way to shocked stares. 1914, it might be, but whatever next? A young woman on the back of a motor-bike with her arms around the waist of a young man and, what was more, giving every indication of enjoying the experience! For Kate, head back, chin up, hair now completely loose and blowing in the wind, was loving every moment.

'Next left!' she shouted as the Banbury Road reached the open fields. And, as Robert slowed for the corner, she let her body lean with the angle of the bike like an old hand. Really, there was nothing to it!

'Now right!' she instructed. 'And up the little lane on your left, by that pink hawthorn.' And then they were bumping their way down the familiar, rutted lane to her home.

Robert Holker saw an old, grey-stone house, three storeys high and with dormers let into the lichened tiles of its roof. A climbing rose, still in bud, sprawled through the gnarled branches of a purple wisteria, pendulous with bloom. Casement windows were thrown wide to the sunshine.

The house itself, Robert decided, was perfect; beautiful, sturdy, mellowed by time. Inside, he could imagine polished floors, old furniture, bowls of flowers and the scent of beeswax.

But outside was a different story. Where once, perhaps, a green lawn had spread and elegant ladies in pale dresses sat in the shade of beech or elm, there now lay an expanse of bare, stony earth. In the centre of it, and surrounded by an assortment of zinc baths, stood an enormous wooden mangle from which, like the spokes of a giant wheel, stretched lines of billowing sheets and pillowcases, the whole giving an incongruous impression of a fleet of land-locked yachts under sail.

As he brought the bike to a standstill and switched off the ignition, the front door opened to reveal a buxom, rosy-cheeked woman swathed in a snow-white apron. 'Kate! Is everything all right?'

'Fine, Ma! And this is Robert Holker, I — er — bumped into him in the Iffley Road.' And into Robert's ear, 'Welcome to Moneymoon Manor!'

★ ★ ★

'It isn't really called Moneymoon Manor,' Kate told him later, after he'd been regaled with lemonade in a stone-flagged barn of a kitchen and she was leading him out into the garden in search of her father.

'So what is it called?'

'Grubbes! After the man who built it, I imagine. But Ma said what sort of a name was that for someone who took in washing? So Priscilla, who has aspirations, said what about Moneymoon Manor?'

'Priscilla?' he queried, vastly intrigued by this unusual family.

'She's my twin. The beautiful one.' This statement, made so matter-of-factly, left Robert temporarily speechless. And indeed, he conceded, beauty *was* in the eye of the beholder but, even so, no-one, in his opinion, could consider Kate Moneymoon less than beautiful. 'And which one,' he enquired with interest, 'are you?'

'The practical one,' said Kate. 'And mind that bramble!'

The bramble that had threatened to trip him was not the only threat to the unsuspecting visitor to Moneymoon Manor. If the front of it was bare of vegetation, the rear more than made up for it. Here, there was such an abundance of growth, it bordered on the extravagant. Honeysuckle twined itself luxuriantly around hawthorn and clematis which in turn hauled itself upright through branches of lilac and laburnum, and over it all, roses of all varieties grew wherever they could find purchase. At ground level, a rampant periwinkle fought for supremacy

5

with saxifrage and sedum but seemed by no means certain of winning.

'Here's Pa!' said Kate suddenly, and in the manner of a magician producing a rabbit from a hat, drew back a curtain of ivy so that Robert could precede her into a tiny clearing in the forest.

He saw a grey-bearded man wearing a countryman's linen smock over stout, corduroy breeches. Below the knee, his legs were bare and there were thonged sandals on his feet. On his lap was a folded newspaper and beside him on the ground, a pile of books. His eyes were closed, the only sign of movement the gentle fluttering of his beard as he drew breath.

'Pa,' said Kate more loudly, 'wake up! Here's Mr Holker to see you.'

The eyelids lifted to show eyes as deeply blue as Kate's. 'No need to shout, my darling! I'm not asleep. Come and sit down, Mr Holker. I hoped you'd call.' He indicated a rusty iron seat covered with fallen leaves and what looked like the desiccated corpses of an army of caterpillars.

'Really, Pa!' Kate scolded as she swept the seat clean with the palm of her hand.

'Thank you!' said Robert meekly, and sat.

'Tea, Kate?' Professor Moneymoon asked hopefully.

'I'll see what I can do.' And she turned and left them.

'Sweet girl!' said her father fondly. 'Now, tell me about yourself, Mr Holker. You are, I take it, one of the Staffordshire Holkers? Lord Werrington's lot.'

'Afraid so, sir,' said Robert cheerfully, 'but only

the second son, thank God! I think I'd shoot myself if I were in my brother George's shoes.'

Professor Moneymoon glanced down at the newspaper on his lap. 'If today's Manchester Guardian is anything to go by, everyone will be shooting everyone else, before long. However, that aside, I take it you don't entirely approve of the system of inherited wealth?'

'I don't approve of a system that means wealth and power being divided between a few, often degenerate, families. Every man should have an equal chance in life and patently, that is not so as things are at the moment.'

'I wish,' said the professor wistfully, 'that I could have a hundred pounds for every young man I've had through my hands who declaimed the same philosophy. Even one pound would be welcome! But it's extraordinary how their zeal fades once they go down from here.'

'Not this young man, I assure you, sir,' said Robert earnestly. 'I've seen too much misery and poverty in the Potteries alone to let me turn my back on it. Although in a way, I envy those people who live under such conditions. They have a closeness of family ties, a dependence upon each other, that I have never known. Would you believe, sir, that the people to whom I am most attached are my Aunt Bella who is a free-thinker, my father's chauffeur who taught me all I know about engines and my old Nanny who taught me right from wrong, and to keep my mouth closed when I eat! My parents were the merest figureheads in my upbringing. Oh — I have a certain affection for

7

them, I admit. As, no doubt, in their way, they have for me. But it's not the way of the people who work in my father's manufacturies.'

'I have heard,' said the professor drily, 'that sometimes *their* families are so large, they have difficulty in remembering their children's names!'

'And that's another thing,' Robert was not to be persuaded from his argument. 'Birth control! Why ever . . .'

But at that point, the curtain of ivy was drawn aside to reveal a mop-haired lad of perhaps twelve years of age, holding a tray on which had been placed a cloth of immaculate whiteness, a large brown teapot, two mugs of sturdy, but good quality, stoneware, sugar in a blue glass bowl and milk in a matching jug. Large slices of fruit cake had been arranged on a blue glass plate. 'Ma said please to manage without saucers and to give the crumbs to the birds,' said the lad.

'By all means. Thank you, Danny,' said the Professor, 'Please put the tray on . . .' he glanced around vaguely.

'. . . on the seat?' Robert suggested as he got to his feet, 'I am always happier on the ground, anyway.' And he took the tray from the boy. His mission completed, Robert would have expected the boy to scamper off but instead he stood there, gazing at Robert hopefully.

'That motor-bike, sir. Is it yours?'

'It is.'

'A two-cylinder, air-cooled Harley Davidson!' His voice was reverent.

And then, as the boy continued to stand there,

clearly bewitched by the thought of such technical magnificence, Robert asked kindly, 'Would you, when your father has finished with me, and if he is agreeable, of course, like me to take you for a spin?'

'Crikey! Would you really, sir?'

'And in the meantime, Danny,' his father put in, 'it's hands off. No touching, you understand?'

'Oh, of course not, sir. Just looking!' And he was gone before even that privilege could be denied him.

'Danny is your only son, sir?' Robert dared to enquire once he had, at the Professor's request, poured the tea.

'No — we have Edmund, also. Our first-born. Just two years older than Kate — and her twin, Priscilla — and doing reasonably well at Cambridge.'

'At *Cambridge*?' That unmentionable 'other' place!

'It has quite a satisfactory academic record, you know,' said the Professor mildly. 'Especially in mathematics, which is Edmund's forte. Besides, it makes the Boat Race so much more interesting for us. Edmund, Priscilla and their mother shout for Cambridge and Kate, Danny and I for Oxford.'

'Kate has no wish to follow an academic life?' Robert asked casually.

'No. At one time, I thought she might attend St Hilda's, for she has an excellent brain. But she seems more concerned with practical matters. An accurate book-keeper, for instance; her mother's accounts are always in apple-pie order.'

'Yes?' And then, Robert blushed slightly. Had the upward inflexion of the word sounded too inquisitive? He rather feared so for the Professor was

9

giving him a sly glance.

'No doubt, you're wondering why the earnings of an Oxford scholar are not sufficient to support his family. No,' he held up a restraining hand as Robert began to demur, 'please do not deny it. Any intelligent young man would be bound to wonder, especially someone,' he added dryly, 'with your socialist tendencies. The plain truth of the matter is that when my dearest Martha agreed to marry me, it was on the understanding that she be allowed to continue the family business, passed on to her by her mother, and her grandmother before that. For she could not conceive that an adequate living could be made out of books — either by studying or writing them. And the arrangement seemed to me to show such good sense that I agreed without hesitation. Although, if the truth be known, I would have agreed to almost anything, short of downright evil, to persuade Martha to marry me. Her humour and robust attitude to life are exactly what a dull fellow like myself is in need of. Except perhaps on a wet washday when our kitchen resembles nothing so much as Dante's Inferno!'

He took a piece of cake from the tray and munched contentedly, motioning Robert to do the same. 'And her cooking is out of this world! The only fly in an otherwise perfect pot of ointment, is Priscilla. For she would happily consign the Moneymoon Manor Laundry to the bottom of the Isis. But there, that's our Priscilla. And we all love her dearly. Now,' and he drained his cup, 'I mustn't bore you with any more details of my family. Although it intrigues me greatly that you, the son of

10

an earl, and I, the son of a potter once employed by that same earl, should meet, as it were, on common ground.'

'You mean,' and a broad smile now wreathed Robert's face, 'that you and I are both natives of the Potteries?'

'You could put it like that!' said his host.

2

By the end of that day in May, 1914, Robert Holker's plans for the future had changed dramatically. Until then, he had intended to return to Staffordshire at the end of term for a week or two, before accompanying fellow undergraduates on a walking holiday in France. But after meeting the Moneymoons, he knew it would be impossible to leave them so soon; and certainly not until he had established a more meaningful relationship with Kate.

Fortune favoured him. After taking Danny out to Woodstock on his promised spin and thereby making him a friend for life, he found Kate and her mother laying the table for high tea, a meal for which he was clearly expected to stay.

They ate in the kitchen at one end of a long scrubbed-pine table, the other holding an assortment of books, string, packets of starch, a scarlet geranium in a majolica pot and several copies of the Boys Own Paper. Between mouthfuls of delicious, home-cured ham, crusty bread and tomato chutney, Robert made the acquaintance of Priscilla, as unlike her twin as it was possible to be. She wore a lilac silk gown, frilled at throat and wrists, and had tied back her golden curls with a matching ribbon. Only her eyes were like Kate's, but whereas her sister's gaze was direct and uncompromising, Priscilla's was teasing and coy, her eyelashes in a perpetual flutter.

It was her questioning, so thorough it bordered on the inquisitive, that soon elicited the information that Robert's rooms, once term was over, were promised to his landlady's sister, up on a visit from Somerset with her family. 'You'll be going home then?' she asked with every appearance of regret.

'As a matter of fact,' Robert took the plunge, 'I shall probably stay up a little longer. Although where, exactly,' he added ingenuously, 'I don't yet know.' And then he sat in silence and held his breath. Even with a family to accommodate and possibly servants, although he had seen none as yet, Moneymoon Manor must surely have several rooms vacant. An attic would more than suffice.

He was not disappointed. The reaction of those seated around the table was immediate — and highly flattering. 'But you must stay here!' they chorused, all except Kate who kept her eyes firmly on her plate.

'May I really?' And although politeness demanded that he look at Mrs Moneymoon as he spoke, it was at Kate that he glanced immediately afterwards. She raised her head and her gaze was cool.

'We could certainly do with an extra pair of hands.' But don't think, she seemed to be adding, that we're all going to swoon at your feet.

But the look served only to make him more determined. 'I'm truly grateful,' he told Mrs Moneymoon, 'and if there is any way I can be of service . . . ?'

'We'll let you know,' she assured him comfortably. And then the talk turned, as it did so often these days, no matter what the company, to the storm clouds gathering over Europe.

'Prussian Imperialism,' said the Professor, 'must be halted somewhere.'

'We'll halt it, won't we, Robert?' said Danny stoutly, gazing up at his new hero.

'*Mr Holker*, to you, if you please!' said his mother sternly. 'And don't talk with your mouth full!' It was then that Robert realised who it was that this large and kindly lady reminded him of. His old Nanny!

When the meal was over, she showed him the room that was to be his. 'I'm afraid it's right at the top of the house, but the view is magnificent.'

And it was. They stood at the dormer window, gazing out over the ancient roofs, the spires and towers of Oxford to the hazy blue line of the Berkshire Downs. And just for a moment, although he'd thought his mind to be on other, more immediate matters, he thought of Prussian Imperialism and how, if it became necessary, he would do his bit, as Danny had said, to halt it.

And strangely, Mrs Moneymoon seemed to be of a similar mind, for she looked up at him with a sigh and asked, 'How old are you, Robert?'

And when he answered, 'Twentyone, last month,' she sighed again, and said,

'The same as my Edmund.' And then she turned and busied herself with showing him the cupboards and chests he would have at his disposal. 'I hope you'll be comfortable.'

'I'm sure I shall.'

When they were downstairs again and he could think of no further reason for staying and was wondering anxiously where Kate might be, he suddenly remembered her bicycle. 'Would it be possible to see Kate for a moment?' he asked Mrs Moneymoon. 'Her bicycle is at my lodgings.'

'Of course! Indeed, you would have difficulty in *not* seeing her!' And she opened the front door to reveal Kate and two young girls he hadn't previously seen, busily unpegging the washing from the lines and folding it into a large hand cart. Even as he gazed, the last sheet was being folded.

'Danny!' called Kate. And Danny, who had been on his knees in reverent contemplation of Robert's motor-bike, stood up regretfully and came to drag the hand cart away around the side of the house, at the same time telling Robert to be sure and not leave until he had returned. He then left at a run and Robert turned hurriedly to Kate.

'About your bicycle, I'll have it seen to straight away if I can't manage the repair myself. But it may take a day or two. Could I perhaps drive you around in the meantime? Take you wherever you want to go?'

'Thank you, but I don't think that will be necessary. We have a pony and trap for deliveries and I can always use that.'

He was getting nowhere fast! And out of the

14

corner of his eye, he saw Danny speeding back around the side of the house and Priscilla coming out of the front door.

'The river,' he said quickly, 'is very beautiful at this time of year.' Even to his ears, the remark sounded so much like the opening of a stilted, unimportant conversation between strangers, he wasn't surprised when Kate smiled, raised her eyebrows in a whimsical fashion and replied in kind,

'And the strawberry crop, they say, will be exceptionally prolific this summer. Although greenfly, I understand, is also expected!'

And then they were both laughing. But at the same time, he said quickly, 'I wasn't just making conversation, Kate — I may call you Kate, mayn't I? — I was wondering if you would . . .'

But in spite of his almost breathless haste, it was too late. Priscilla and Danny were upon them.

'Leaving us so soon, Mr Holker?' Priscilla laid a dainty, perfectly manicured hand on his arm.

'Robert — I-mean-Mr-Holker,' said Danny, 'could I just . . . ?'

'Danny,' said Kate firmly, 'homework!'

'I was only going to ask Robert — I-mean-Mr-Holker — if I could just sit on the saddle for a minute. Just to get the feel of it.'

'Just for a minute?' Robert, too, gazed hopefully at Kate. Anything to delay his departure.

'Oh, all right! Just for a minute.' And Robert held the bike firm while Danny scrambled aboard.

Priscilla was now carefully inspecting the evening sky. The sun had disappeared in a welter of pink and apricot and swallows wheeled and dipped around

15

the chimneys of Moneymoon Manor. 'Another fine day tomorrow,' she forecast. 'Oh, I do so hope the weather lasts until the end of the month!'

'Why only until the end of the month, Miss Moneymoon?'

'Please call me Priscilla. And I really meant until May Week and the Balls are over.'

His college Ball! Why had he not thought of that before? Probably because he'd had no intention of going to it until now; no particular girl in mind as a partner. But now it was different! His mind leapt ahead. He would hold a small dinner party in his rooms if his landlady was agreeable. Nothing elaborate. Saddle of mutton, perhaps. She was good at that. He'd ask all the Moneymoons, of course, to satisfy the proprieties, even Danny, if he were allowed. And his friend, Sam Bosworth, would do nicely as a partner for Priscilla. And then caution asserted itself. Perhaps he was assuming too much.

'I expect,' he said guilelessly, 'that you will be going to several of the Balls?' He had contrived to include both Kate and Priscilla in his question but it was Priscilla who answered first.

'No, we're quite free at the moment. Aren't we, Kate?'

But Kate was staring stonily at her sister. 'Speak for yourself, Prissy! I'm far too busy to go dancing!'

★ ★ ★

Could it be, he wondered next morning as he wrestled with the damaged bicycle, that it was because Priscilla was so forward in her advances and

16

she, herself, so determined not to be considered the same, that had caused Kate to be so curt towards him? Or could it be — perish the thought! — that she simply didn't like him? And yet, he could have sworn, after she'd recovered from the initial violent impact of their first meeting, that she'd begun to warm towards him.

Well, he tried to be philosophical, he'd know soon enough when he returned her bicycle that afternoon, for his landlady had been most receptive to his suggestion of a dinner party and was already planning the menu.

However, when he presented himself at Money-moon Manor, he was told by her mother that Kate was out with Priscilla in the trap, returning some laundered linen. His keen disappointment was partly dissipated by the warm welcome Mrs Moneymoon gave him and indeed, he conceded, it might be strategically wise, as well as courteous, to extend his invitation to her first, for Kate, in her present mood, would probably refuse it out of hand.

'Have you a moment, ma'am?' he asked after the bicycle had been wheeled into its shed.

'Never too busy to talk to you, Robert! Although I must just have a word with my girls first. Come through!'

So he followed her down the hall, where a copper bowl of crimson peonies stood, cheek by jowl, with a brace and bit on a polished oak chest, through the kitchen and out into an enormous scullery, whose stone-flagged floor and open windows would have ensured its coolness, had it not been for the banked fires glowing in the ranges that occupied almost the

17

whole length of one wall. An assortment of flat irons rested on the surfaces of the ovens and at two long trestle tables, set a respectable distance from the heat, the same two young girls that he'd seen yesterday, stood, pushing their sizzling irons swiftly over the damp linen.

Through an open door, he could see into another vast scullery where several giant coppers were spaced around the walls. Fortunately, for the day was hot, no fires glowed beneath them, although each fire-hole held the makings of one with kindling, and small coal laid across screws of paper. Mrs Moneymoon's gaze followed his.

'In this weather,' she said, 'the coppers are lit early, around five. We aim to have the washing on the lines by nine, and in again before the sun dries it too thoroughly. Yesterday was an exception because we had a rush order. That's what the girls are delivering now.'

'It's certainly a family business.'

'We all pull our weight. Even Priscilla, although she flatly refuses to plunge her hands into hot water. Not that I blame her.' She looked down at her own hands and he saw that the skin was red and coarsened, although there were none of the deep, unsightly cracks he'd sometimes noticed on the hands of the laundry maids at home.

'Glycerine, rose-water and borax,' Mrs Moneymoon told him when he commented upon this. 'An old recipe handed down from my grandmother. I'll make you up a bottle to take home when you go.'

'Thank you,' he said gravely, although he could imagine the expression on his mother's face, if he

18

were to present it to her. 'Not for you, mama, but for Rosie!'

He doubted if his mother even knew of Rosie's existence and even Miss Freeman, the housekeeper, would probably turn up her nose if asked to deliver it. Well, he'd just have to do it himself. And trust Rosie wouldn't consider it a preliminary to something more sinister! It was a telling criticism of the age, he thought wryly, that one couldn't give a bottle of hand liniment to a laundry maid without eyebrows being raised.

'Now,' said Mrs Moneymoon, 'I'll just send Jane and Emma out into the garden for a few minutes to sit in the shade while they cool down, and then we'll have our little chat.' Mrs Moneymoon, he guessed, was an ideal employer. No need for a trade union here!

The chat took place in Mrs Moneymoon's sitting-room; a charming little room whose window faced on to a herb garden at the side of the house. In keeping with the rest of the garden, he saw rosemary, dill and basil intermingling happily with sage and fennel and mint rioting exuberantly over all, but the scent through the open casement was exquisite. But there was another, sharper perfume and gazing around him, Robert saw that practically every flat surface held big bowls of dried lavender. And on a table beside the Victorian sewing chair to which Mrs Moneymoon motioned him, squares of muslin were neatly piled alongside bundles of gaily-coloured ribbon.

'Lavender bags,' Mrs Moneymoon explained. 'Kate's idea. Each returned parcel of laundry has one folded inside. In winter and spring, we import the lavender from the South of France.'

'How very enterprising!'

'My Kate is nothing if not enterprising. And we need the personal touch to compete with the new steam laundries that are springing up. Fortunately, habit dies hard, and many people still consider the old ways best, but it won't be for ever. However, I mustn't bore you with business matters. How may I help you? To decide the date for your moving in, perhaps?'

'No, it was nothing like that. I wanted to invite you and your family to a small dinner party I'm giving in my rooms on the night of my college ball. I should be delighted if you could all come — and to the ball afterwards, of course.'

Her surprise at the invitation was clearly so great that, just for a moment, she seemed almost at a loss for words. 'Why, Robert, I don't know what to say except that you are so very kind. It's years since I have had such an invitation! For my part, I would be delighted to accept. And Priscilla will be over the moon. But as for my husband and Kate,' she shook her head, 'they're both just as likely to plead other arrangements, even though they'll do nothing more than spend the evening with their heads in a book!'

'Perhaps you could persuade them, ma'am?'

'I'll certainly do my best.'

'The invitation includes Danny, too, of course. To dinner, anyway, if not to the ball.'

'Thank you, Robert. At least that means one male to escort us!'

20

Soon afterwards, he took his leave, after Mrs Moneymoon had promised to let him know the family decision as soon as possible.

* * *

The next twentyfour hours were the longest Robert Holker had ever passed; impossible to settle to anything, especially his books. For a while, he contemplated taking a punt on the Cherwell but knew he would risk seeing other young men similarly engaged, but with young ladies gracefully disposed on the cushions of their punts. In the end, he wheeled out his motor-bike and rode out to Dorchester, where he left it in the care of the landlord at the George Inn and took one of his favourite walks across the meadows to the river.

At Day's Lock, the young girl operating the gates reminded him so much of Kate — the same lissom figure, dark-hair and blue eyes, although lacking the intensity of colour of Kate's — that he helped her through with several craft before continuing on his way to the church at Long Wittenham. From there, it was but a leisurely stroll to the top of the Clumps, the two, elm-crowned hills above the village; leisurely, at least, for his long legs but a stiff climb for the elderly gentleman he came upon halfway up, leaning heavily on a stick and with a fat pug panting at his feet.

It seemed impolite to continue at his own, unforced pace while the other was clearly finding it difficult to put one foot in front of the other, so he paused and made a great show of mopping his brow

21

with his handkerchief, although in truth, it was as cool as when he started.

'A lovely day, sir, but we would have been better, perhaps, to have remained on flatter ground.'

'Speak for yourself, sir!' said the other sharply, although his face was as red as a turkey cock's. 'The day I can no longer walk up Wittenham Clumps, will be the day I die!'

And that, Robert thought anxiously, gazing at the choleric countenance, could well be today!

'How old are you, young man?' The old man barked.

'Twentyone, sir.' How frequently that question was being asked of him these days!

'And I'm eightyone! Fought in the Crimea with Cardigan. Wanted to help Kitchener out with the Boers but they said I was too old. So it's not likely they'll let me loose on the Huns. It'll be up to the likes o' you, young feller. And if you break sweat on a molehill like this one, much chance we'll have of winning! Up to the top with you! And wait for me there! Pugsie must have a breather half-way.'

'Very good, sir!' Privately thinking that if left to Pugsie, the expedition would be abandoned then and there, Robert continued on his way. Orders were orders!

Even so, he was considerably relieved, about twenty minutes later, when a scarlet face appeared over the brow of the hill like a rising sun, followed by a labouring Pugsie. Courteously, he rose from the fallen tree-trunk he had been sitting on. 'I think I may have taken your seat, sir,' he thought it safe to suggest. And it was indicative of the other's

22

condition that he said nothing but sank on to it gratefully.

'One of the best views in England,' he said when he'd got his breath back, gazing out over the buttercup meadows to the grey mass of Dorchester Abbey and the wooded slopes of the Chilterns beyond. And Robert agreed.

His object achieved, the old gentleman now seemed more kindly disposed. But his mind was still fixed on the possibility of war, about which he seemed singularly well-informed. 'All began in 1909,' he said, 'when Germany annexed Boznia-Herzegovina with Austria-Hungary's approval. A great Teutonic Empire, that's what they're aiming for — and that's what they'll get if someone doesn't stop them.'

'We'll stop them, sir,' Robert assured him. 'We're not such an effete generation as you might think.'

'I know that, my boy! I know!' And the look the older man now turned on him was almost benign. 'But Europe's like a great tinder-box these days. Just one spark and the whole continent will be ablaze. I have a grandson in the cavalry and it worries me greatly.'

His full title, Robert discovered, was General Sir John Wavertree and he lived now in a comfortable little house in Long Wittenham, looked after by a housekeeper. 'Mollycoddles me almost to death — don't know how I survive!' But indeed, now that he'd recovered from the climb, the General looked remarkably healthy.

'Well,' he said after a few more minutes of conversation, during which Robert told him a little

23

about himself, 'I've enjoyed your company, Mr Holker. Why not come back to tea?'

'I'd be delighted to, sir!'

'Excellent! First back down the hill has the biggest scone! Ready! Steady! Go!' And he was off like a shot, before Robert was even on his feet.

But it was Pugsie who won, his little legs moving so fast they were no more than a blur, with the General coming a close second and Robert a diplomatic third.

Tea extended itself into supper and it was almost closing time when he collected his bike from the George, and rode back to Oxford; to discover a note awaiting him at his lodgings. The Moneymoons would be delighted to accept his kind invitation to dinner and afterwards to the Ball.

3

He saw little of the Moneymoons in the days before the Ball, other than a brief visit to finalise the arrangements. This time, he found Kate leading out a neat, bay cob from the shafts of a freshly-painted, dark-green trap, with 'Moneymoon Manor Laundry' picked out in gold on its side. She had undone the top buttons of her blouse and pushed back her straw boater so that it was like a halo around her dark head. She looked hot.

'Can I help?' he called. For a brief moment, he could have sworn her eyes lit up with pleasure at the sight of him. But then Priscilla came out of the house, saw him and waved.

'Robert! How very nice to see you!'

He lifted his hand to her but turned quickly back to Kate. 'May I take the pony for you? Where does he go?'

'Into the field at the bottom of the lane.' And she indicated a dusty track leading away from the house. 'But we can manage.'

He glanced back at Priscilla and saw white shoes beneath a white, summery skirt that, although slashed from knee to hem for ease of movement, seemed more suited for street wear than a rutted, country lane. 'I'm sure your sister won't mind my standing in for her,' and, with another wave in Priscilla's direction, he took the pony's reins from Kate.

Halfway down the lane, the harness was removed and hung up in a small stable. 'These are Toby's winter quarters,' Kate explained, taking a halter off a hook to slip around the pony's neck.

'Do you have other horses?'

'No horses, but we have a donkey as company for Toby. They're inseparable.'

And sure enough, as they went on down the lane, a furry grey head came over a five-barred gate and Toby whickered a greeting. The gate was opened, the halter removed and he charged through like a warhorse, to circle the field at a full gallop with the donkey, like a grey shadow, running at his heels.

'It's the same every day,' said Kate fondly, as the pair eventually came to a halt and solemnly touched noses. 'They'll stand like that for about five minutes and then wander off to graze, but always together.'

'True love!' said Robert, helping her swing back the gate. 'May we stay and watch?'

She glanced down at the watch pinned to her blouse. 'You may certainly stay for as long as you like. But I should get on. I have the accounts still to do.' But even so, she folded her arms along the topmost bar of the gate, pushed her boater back off her head so that it was suspended round her neck by its strings and let her gaze wander over the vista of fields and hedgerows, frothing now with the creamy blossom of hawthorn. 'I love this time of year.'

'Me, too! Oxfordshire at its best.'

She glanced at him. 'My father tells me you come from Staffordshire. A dismal county, I believe.'

'Not all of it! Parts, I admit, are like a cancerous growth on the earth but many parts are as beautiful as this.'

'The part where you live, no doubt?' The look she gave him was faintly accusatory and he wondered how much her father had told her.

'My family does have that privilege, I grant you. But an undeserved privilege, in my opinion.'

'And yet, whether you like it or not, you've already taken advantage of your favoured position.'

'How do you mean?'

'Did you, like my father, come up to Oxford because of your determination and intellectual abilities or simply because it was expected of you as a matter of course? Forgive me,' she said quickly as he frowned, 'no doubt you have a most agile brain but I feel sure you would have come anyway, even if

26

it had been as slow as a tortoise.'

He thought of his brother George, whose brain was, he had to admit, and in spite of his many excellent qualities, 'as slow as a tortoise' and who had scraped through his examinations only after the most intense cramming. 'That's certainly true but to have refused to have come, to have stayed at home vegetating on my father's estate, just to make a point, would have benefited no-one. Certainly not those people whom I wish to help.'

'You could have attended a technical college; learned a trade, perhaps.'

Goodness! he thought but she's her father's daughter! I'll wager she's a suffragette, too! 'I could have,' he admitted aloud. 'And indeed, I love nothing more than to take an engine to pieces and put it together again. But that would not greatly advance the well-being of the human race. Many can do it faster and better than I.'

'So how *do* you aim to advance the well-being of the human race?' And now she turned to look him fully in the face and there was an earnestness about her that told him her interest was genuine.

'I shall write,' he told her. 'Become a journalist. Perhaps, if I'm thought suitable, stand for Parliament.'

'And what would be your views about women's suffrage? Would you support the Women's Social and Political Union?'

So, he'd been right! In spite of himself, a tiny, self-congratulatory smile curved his lips. But it was a smile that Kate Moneymoon misinterpreted completely.

'So, you're just a typical, male chauvinist, after all! And I had thought . . . ' What she had thought was left unsaid, for she turned on her heel and began marching away from him up the lane.

Within seconds, Robert had caught up with her. 'Kate! Please hear me out! I *do* care about women's suffrage. I think the Pankhursts are the most incredible couple!'

'Incredible, yes! Like — like a gas balloon or — or piped water — but not to be taken seriously.'

'Indeed, I take piped water very seriously!' They were nearly at the top of the lane by now, where Priscilla could be seen waiting, 'Kate,' he said urgently, 'please forgive me if I seemed patronising or insincere. Such, I can assure you, was not my intention.'

'Then why did you smile in that hateful, superior, *masculine* fashion when I mentioned the W.S.P.U.?'

There was no time to dissemble, to try and think up some reasonable excuse.

'Because,' he admitted, 'for once I had correctly predicted what you would say. And that, where someone as delightfully *un*predictable as yourself is concerned, was no mean feat.'

At least, he had silenced her, if nothing more. But was she impressed? Flattered? Pleased? Or displeased even more? He couldn't tell. Perhaps she felt only relief that they had now reached the top of the lane and Priscilla was coming forward, all smiles, to take his arm and lead him, in a most proprietorial manner, into the house.

★　★　★

It was the morning of the Ball and Robert, as his friend, Sam Bosworth put it, was 'in a stew'.

'You've made all the obvious arrangements,' Sam assured him, 'considered eventualities that may never occur, and now all you can do is to pray — that it doesn't rain, that your landlady's cooking is up to standard, that you don't fall flat on your face in the Veleta, that . . . '

' . . . you ensure Miss *Priscilla* Moneymoon is kept by your side all night,' Robert interrupted.

'That sounds a most immoral suggestion, the way you put it! But rest assured that I shall do everything in my power to leave you a clear field with the fair Kate.'

'Actually, its the dark Kate and the fair Priscilla.'

'Good! All women are as wax in my hands, but blondes particularly so!'

In fact, Sam Bosworth was the most normal, unpretentious young man it was possible to meet and Priscilla, Robert was confident, would be treated with the utmost courtesy. He was also good-looking in a rugged, cheery sort of way, which would please Priscilla. And his background — son of a baronet living in the Weald of Kent — should more than satisfy her social aspirations.

'What's happening to the young lad?' Sam enquired. 'Danny, did you say his name was? Not coming to the Ball, surely.'

'No, I've arranged for him to be picked up and taken home after dinner. The same motor car will then return to take us to the Ball.'

'And the Prof and his wife. Are they stepping the light fantastic?'

'Well, *she* is! *He* professes to have two left feet where dancing's concerned. So it will be in order,' Robert relented slightly, 'to circulate to an extent. You may even have the odd dance with Kate, provided you don't monopolise her.'

'Thank 'ee, kindly! And now stop worrying and come and down a pint before lunch.' It was sound advice and Robert took it. For indeed, there was nothing else to be done; a motor car would collect the Moneymoons at eight o'clock precisely and bring them to Iffley Road where he would be waiting; a young girl had been hired to help Mrs Sadler, his landlady, in the kitchen and to serve the meal, and the wine he had chosen was, he felt confident, perfectly matched to the food. Kate had been right, he reflected wryly; scorn his heritage as he might, it was certainly useful to have money in one's pocket!

★ ★ ★

Moneymoon Manor was bustling with activity. It was early evening and the Professor, wearing the rusty black dinner jacket he kept for the occasional university function he was forced to attend, had taken refuge in his study, leaving the rest of the house free to his womenfolk. And, judging by the frantic cries and exclamation, the thudding up and down the stairs, the calling out from one end of the house to the other, they had need of it. Even his sensible, practical wife was behaving like a seventeen-year-old, demanding at the top of her voice if anyone had seen her silk turban with the

30

feathers. Someone, presumably, had for her voice had not been heard for several minutes. It was now Priscilla's turn, accusing someone, presumably Kate, of purloining her gold satin evening shoes. As if Kate would! And yet she, her father had to admit, had been behaving completely out of character all day. He'd had to speak to her three times at the breakfast table before she'd heard, and then had passed the honey instead of the marmalade. *And* poured him tea instead of coffee.

He knew the reason for it, of course. Robert Holker. A nice enough, young fellow, in all conscience, and he hadn't been surprised when Priscilla had sung his praises, because it was a regular occurrence with her whenever her father acquired a remotely presentable pupil. But not so with Kate. She, he considered, possessed a maturity beyond her years, especially when it came to an assessment of human nature. And it had been evident from the day Holker had first come to Moneymoon Manor, and she'd shown herself so against his coming to stay, that he'd had an effect on her; normally, she wouldn't have cared two hoots. And ever since, whenever Priscilla had mentioned him, her lack of interest had been so deliberately feigned, it had defeated its purpose. And only because her mother had told her that no-one else would accept Robert's invitation if she didn't, had she agreed to go tonight. It was as if she were afraid of her own feelings.

Peculiar people, women! thought the Professor. He was quite relieved when the door opened and Danny sidled in. For there was no mystery where he was concerned! Scrubbed and polished to within an inch of his life, he was now wearing his Sunday-best, navy suit with the sailor collar.

'Ma said I was to come in here and sit quietly with you, or she'd flay me alive. What's flaying, Pa?'

'Beating you so hard, your skin peels off in strips.'

'Crikey! She wouldn't really, would she?'

'Highly unlikely, I would say. But you'd better be on the safe side, and do as she says.'

Silence reigned for all of half a minute and then, 'Pa, how old will I have to be to have a motor-bike?'

Really, thought his father, one way and another, young Holker has a lot to answer for! Aloud, he said, 'It's not so much a question of age, Danny, as a matter of achievement. When you've passed all your exams, *then* we might consider it.'

'Oh, *Pa*!' Danny groaned in deep disgust. 'I shall be simply ancient by then!'

★ ★ ★

Upstairs, Kate stood in front of a cheval mirror and tried to assess her appearance dispassionately. Certainly, this particular shade of pale green — the colour of a shallow, in-shore sea — suited her admirably, for her skin seemed to glow and her eyes, by contrast, were made even more vivid. And she'd managed to copy the lines of the Poiret gown that she'd seen in a magazine, well enough; the simple, scooped neckline, the flowing sleeves, the ray of pleats falling straight from the high waistband so that ease of movement on the dance floor would be ensured. Not that she intended to dance a great deal. Perhaps with her father, if he could be persuaded, and *once*, for politeness' sake, with Robert Holker. But no more, unless there was an old-fashioned sequence dance, the Lancers, perhaps. But certainly nothing as intimate as a waltz or a tango where his arms would be around her, his hips touching her's and his cheek, if he so wished, only an inch or two away from her own. The picture was enough to make her want to tear off her sea-green gown and nainsook petticoats that very minute.

But she knew she couldn't do that — for Priscilla's sake, if nothing more. For tonight, as far as her sister was concerned, was like an answer to prayer; the culmination of months of preparation, of countless evenings spent trying out the latest dance craze; the Boston, the rag, the one-step, the tango. The tunes of them all, played on the gramophone, had filled the kitchen on winter evenings when the two girls, with much laughter, had swayed and swooped from one end of it to the other, with Danny beating out the rhythm on an old drum and her mother, who loved dancing, shaking a tambourine.

'But when,' Priscilla had begun to lament of late, 'are we ever going to be able to show people how good we are? When shall we be invited to a *proper* dance?'

Poor Priscilla! Kate thought now, loyally helping with the deliveries, day after day. Part of her, she knew, vastly enjoyed handling the reins in her smartly braided winter skirt and jacket, her neat felt hat turned up at the side over a cockade of feathers and, in summer, her white shirtwaisters and flowery

33

hats; only the boxes and baskets, the piles of gaily striped packages behind her and the lettering on the side of the trap, reminding her that she was 'in trade'.

'If Ma had to work,' she sometimes complained to Kate, 'why couldn't she have chosen something respectable like dress-making or millinery? But taking in washing! I ask you!'

It was greatly to her credit that such complaints never reached her parents' ears. Only to Kate did she confide her disappointments — and hopes.

'We *must* be prepared. If we ever *should* be invited to a ball, then we must know how to dance *and* must have suitable clothes to do it in.' And so Kate, deft with her needle, had spent her free evenings last winter, when she wasn't doing her accounts or out at a meeting, stitching away at evening gowns for the two of them. 'For I shouldn't go anywhere without you, dear Kate!'

With all her heart, Kate wished she did not find so embarrassing, her sister's efforts to persuade the young gentlemen of Oxford that she was as presentable as any of their well-connected, well-bred partners.

'But you *are* the daughter of a professor,' she would sometimes remind her, wondering why she herself should be so proud of the fact, while her twin was not. 'There must be lots of young men who think the world of Pa and would dearly love to have his daughter for a friend.'

'But they never have any money or connections,' Priscilla wailed. 'And they're so *worthy*, Kate! And so *dull*!'

Which was why, Kate thought wryly, Robert Holker had been like an answer to prayer; for it hadn't taken Priscilla long to worm from her father, most of the details of his lineage. Her near certainty that it was herself he was interested in, didn't help at all.

She clasped a string of crystal beads around her neck the exact shade of her gown and wove a similarly coloured wisp of chiffon through the knot of her hair. Tonight, she would just have to hope that he would be swept off his feet by Priscilla's undoubted beauty.

4

It was at nine-thirty p.m., precisely, that Kate realised, against all the odds, that she was enjoying herself enormously. She knew it was half-past-nine because at the moment that she leaned back in her chair, completely relaxed , the little French carriage-clock on Robert's mantelshelf, chimed twice.

They were all seated around a somewhat cumbersome gate-legged table, but the good-humoured jostling at the beginning of the meal as human legs were accommodated to wooden ones, had only added to the enjoyment that had marked the evening from the outset.

Even the frisson of alarm Kate had felt initially at Sam Bosworth's obvious assumption that he was to be Priscilla's escort, thereby indicating that Robert

35

was to be her's, had faded as the evening had progressed. For Robert was the perfect host, equally as attentive to all of them; exchanging technical data with Danny about the Mercedes-Benz that had brought them, complimenting Mrs Moneymoon upon the beauty of her turban with its spray of feathers sprouting from a stone the size, if not the carat, of the Kohinoor, discussing with the Professor the May Balls of *his* day, and trusting earnestly that neither Kate nor Priscilla had been working too hard.

The friendliness of his landlady, especially when she'd recognised Mrs Moneymoon as an old school-friend, and the occasionally inept handling of their dishes by the pretty little serving girl, had increased the easy, intimate atmosphere of the occasion. The food had been delicious and the wine, Kate felt sure, of the highest quality.

But greatest of all her pleasure was in gazing at Priscilla, seated opposite. In her dress of pale gold satin with the insertions of darker gold lace into the long sleeves, her simple headband of ruched, amber velvet, she looked like an angel but recently descended from heaven, as yet untarnished by human contact. The long train which she would carry over her arm when she danced, was now neatly draped over the back of her chair. It was small wonder that Sam Bosworth had eyes for no-one else.

With a sigh of contentment, Kate leaned back in her chair and accepted Robert's offer of more wine without hesitation, even smiling up into his eyes as he poured it, thus causing him to continue pouring until her glass was brimming and, to everyone's delight, she had to lean down to sip it.

And now the evening seemed set to continue in just such a light-hearted manner. A tired but replete Danny had been sent home to the care of Jane and Emma and now his elders were joining the laughing, chattering throng that moved slowly up the steps to the gateway of Robert's college and the illuminated quadrangle beyond.

'Don't be long!' Kate heard Sam murmur to Priscilla as she turned in the direction of the ladies' cloakroom. And in a rush of gratitude, she looked up at Robert and said,

'We're having such a wonderful evening!' And he, for a mad moment, almost cast discretion to the wind and kissed her there and then; if it hadn't been for the feathers in Mrs Moneymoon's turban suddenly tickling the back of her neck as she was swept forward by the throng, he probably would have done.

★　★　★

'Tired?' Robert suggested hopefully. But Kate didn't look in the least tired. Her eyes were sparkling, her cheeks were flushed and several strands of her hair had escaped from its knot to curl, in a most endearing fashion, on to her shoulders. And her foot was already tapping to the habanera rhythm of the tango that the orchestra had just struck up.

He changed his tactics. 'To be honest, I'm not much good at the tango. And I could do with some fresh air.'

Kate looked at him. He had been such an admirable partner until now; whirling her around in the waltz but never too vigourously, gliding smoothly into the Boston, one-stepping until they were both breathless. She couldn't fault him. Nor had he neglected the other members of her family, allowing her mother to lead him through the Lancers with a flattering attention to her every command, making sure that her father was comfortably ensconced with a glass of wine when he was not dancing, even prising Sam and Priscilla apart so that he could partner Priscilla in the Rag while Sam took Kate.

'Although I don't think I'll bother again!' he told Kate. 'She couldn't wait to get back to him.'

'Nor he to her. They certainly do seem to be enjoying themselves.'

'And you, Kate? Are you enjoying yourself?'

'Need you ask?'

Supper had been eaten all together, a gay friendly meal with much cheerful banter and, Robert noticed, many admiring glances directed at Kate and Priscilla, from his friends at nearby tables; although some seemed a little puzzled, as if they were trying without success to remember where they'd seen them before. Robert grinned to himself. The table next to them was particularly noisy. 'Americans,' he explained quietly. 'Nice enough chaps but a bit on the rowdy side.'

After supper, the older Moneymoons professed themselves to be a little weary. 'Although it has been the most wonderful evening, Robert,' Mrs Moneymoon assured him. And the Professor agreed that he hadn't enjoyed himself so much for a long time.

'I promise we'll see the girls safely home,' Robert told them as he put them into a cab.

It was then that the Master of Ceremonies had announced the tango. It was Kate's favourite dance but if Robert really needed some fresh air . . . 'All right,' she relented, 'fresh air, it is.'

'Gardens or cloisters?'

The cloisters were immediately outside the hall, so that the music would still be clearly audible. The gardens were unknown territory, probably full of shadowy corners. 'Cloisters, please!' said Kate.

Robert guided her through the open door with one arm placed lightly around her waist. To his astonishment, once outside, she turned within his arm and stood with her body almost touching his.

'The best of both worlds?' she suggested softly. 'Tango *and* fresh air?' It wasn't at all what he'd intended, but was totally satisfying, even so. When he'd said he was no good at the tango, he'd only been speaking the truth, but it was more because he'd never allowed himself to relax into the sensuous, South American rhythm than because he couldn't perform the steps. Now, with the only light coming through the open doorway and Kate in his arms, he found that his body was magically in tune with her's, knowing instinctively in which direction they should move and what manoeuvre they should make.

The faint, lemony scent of her hair, the closeness of her cheek to his, the feel of her body swaying against him as they abandoned themselves to the music, induced in Robert a feeling of almost

39

unbearable happiness.

'Kate!' he murmured thickly. 'Dear, *dear* Kate!'

What reply she might had made, if any, he was never to know. From inside the ballroom, there came first a shrill cry, followed immediately by a heavy thump. And then the music stopped and for a second there was total silence. And then a sort of wail of anguish.

'Priscilla!' cried Kate and rushed for the door, still holding Robert's hand. In the centre of the dance floor, Priscilla sat in a pool of golden satin, clutching her ankle. Her train, almost completely severed from her dress, lay beside her. Bending over her was one of the Americans who had sat near them at supper, and around the sides of the hall, the other dancers stood staring. As Kate reached her sister, the silence was broken by a loud, female voice.

'Why, if it isn't the washerwoman's daughters! I knew I'd seen them before!' The voice belonged to a tall, red-haired girl whom Kate had noticed in the cloak-room, where she'd been complaining loudly about the lack of space. Kate had thought then that she would have been more at home on a hunting field or addressing an open-air suffragettes' meeting — not that she ever *would*!

Her words were like pebbles thrown into a pool of silence, sending out little ripples of sound; murmurs of astonishment and incredulity, cadences of repressed laughter.

But by then, Sam had pushed aside the American and was kneeling with Kate. And then he had put his arms around the weeping Priscilla and was carrying her off the floor, with Robert going on ahead to clear a way for them. And the music was starting up again; they left the hall to the rhythm of Alexander's Rag Time Band.

★　★　★

It was Sam who explained what had happened; once Priscilla had been taken up to her room by her mother. For so close were they upon the heels of the older Moneymoons, they had found them still getting ready for bed.

'I'm not very good at the tango,' Sam told them, 'too inhibited, I suppose,' — Kate caught Robert's eye but looked away hurriedly — 'but Priscilla wanted to do it. We were just standing there and she was trying to persuade me, when Hank Shelton came by and heard us. And you know what he's like, Robert. Oozes charm when he wants to, and pushy with it. Said something about being delighted to help out a damsel in distress and simply swept Priscilla off. And I must say, the fellow certainly knew how to dance.' Sam stopped at that point to accept a cup of cocoa from Kate for they were all, the Professor included, seated at the kitchen table.

'And so does Priscilla, of course. They danced like one person, almost as if they were glued together. I was quite green with envy. And then everyone else suddenly seemed to notice them and to leave the floor so that they could watch. It was like an exhibition. I don't quite know what happened next. Probably, Priscilla's train had slipped off her arm doing some complicated manoeuvre. But however it happened, Hank must have trodden on it. There was

41

this horrid ripping sound and Priscilla seemed to go one way and Hank the other. And the next minute, poor Priscilla was on the floor. The rest,' he added tactfully, one eye on the Professor, 'you know. But I must say how dreadfully sorry I am that it happened. If I'd taken a firm line with Hank, things might have been different.'

The Professor smiled at him. 'I don't know about this Hank but taking a firm line with Priscilla isn't always easy. I'm quite sure it wasn't your fault, Mr Bosworth.'

'I'm most relieved to hear you say so, sir! Thank you!'

'Well,' said the Professor, 'all's well that ends well! Priscilla's ankle seems to have suffered no more than a sprain. It was just unfortunate that it should have happened when you were all enjoying yourselves so much.'

Clearly, in his opinion, that was the end of the matter and he rose to his feet. 'We mustn't detain you any further. Thank you again, young man!'

So there was to be no way he could have a private word with Kate before he left, Robert thought. But she did at least see them to the front door.

Sam was first out. 'Goodnight, Kate! Thank you for being so understanding.'

And then, as he turned to walk away into the darkness, Kate called out quickly, 'Mind the mangle!' It was the usual, light-hearted warning to unsuspecting visitors leaving Moneymoon Manor at night, but now it seemed to have acquired deeper, more meaningful overtones.

Kate looked up at Robert — and suddenly began

to laugh. 'W-what else would you expect from a w-washerwoman's daughter?' And then, to her horror, the laughter suddenly turned to tears and she was sobbing her heart out in the circle of Robert's arms.

'There, there!' he soothed as if she were a child. 'That woman should have been strangled at birth. She's the most unutterable snob. You're not to let her worry you. And that's an order.'

'I didn't think I *was* worried. I m-must be more t-tired than I thought. It's p-poor Prissy, I'm really concerned about.'

He found he was kissing the top of her head at the same time continuing to pat her back. 'Well, don't be! If he's half the man I think he is, Sam will be back at first light to see how she is — and it's almost that now!' And indeed a streak of primrose light had appeared in the eastern sky and there came the first faint twitter of awakening birds. 'I must take him home now, so that he can come back later. And I'll be back, too.' And he bent down and, very gently, kissed her forehead. 'Goodnight, sweet Kate!'

★ ★ ★

He was back at midday. In time for the afternoon round of deliveries. For there was no way that Priscilla would be able to do them. He found Kate backing Toby into the shafts of the trap, helped by her mother. He went to stand at the pony's head. 'Allow me!'

'That's kind of you, Robert,' Mrs Moneymoon

relinquished her place without complaint.

'And how's the invalid?'

Mrs Moneymoon burst out laughing. 'Thoroughly enjoying herself, ever since young Sam turned up with a great bunch of hot-house freesias. *And* the American with a box of something he called candy! She won't be coming back to work in a hurry.'

'That's why I'm here. I'll have to be told what to do but I'm a reasonably apt pupil.'

Mrs Moneymoon stood with her hands on her hips and studied him. 'Are you serious?'

'Couldn't be more so. I've had plenty of experience handling a pony — my father keeps a couple of hackneys — but I thought perhaps Kate could do the driving while I did the actual deliveries.'

'What do you say, Kate?'

'It would mean you could get on with the lavender bags, Ma.'

'*And* sit with my feet up while I'm doing them. I must say I'm feeling a little tired today.'

Between them, they loaded up the trap with big, wicker hampers. 'Colleges, today,' said Kate. 'A lot of them do their own or use the steam laundries, but we still get the specials they like hand-done.'

With Kate holding the reins and Robert the list of deliveries, they set off. The Banbury Road was busy with young men and women on bicycles, horse-drawn wagons and drays and the occasional noisy motor vehicle. These last, Toby treated with an air of sublime indifference, keeping up a spanking trot and occasionally tossing his head to set his harness jingling. 'He's a terrible show-off,' said Kate.

The sun shone, blossom drifted from the cherry trees on to Toby's broad back and the knot of scarlet ribbons on the end of Kate's whip — which she never used — fluttered bravely in the breeze.

'This is fun!' said Robert, suddenly spotting an acquaintance and bowing regally, thus causing the man to nearly fall from his bicycle.

'Not so good on a wet day,' said Kate.

'Don't you have any form of protection?'

'We have tarpaulin over the laundry and mackintoshes for ourselves and Toby. But Ma always makes us get into a hot bath as soon as we reach home, and Toby has a bran mash.'

'And do you and Priscilla have to man-handle these wicker baskets off the trap yourselves?' It was a question he'd pondered ever since they'd loaded up, with himself taking most of the weight.

'Oh, no! The porters in the lodges always do that.'

'So that means,' he said with mock indignation, 'that I'm superfluous to requirements.'

'W — e — ll,' teasingly, she pretended to consider the point. 'I wouldn't say that exactly, I probably *could* manage without you but it's not really advisable to be on your own. Toby's as good as gold left to himself, but I once came out of Balliol to find him tethered to a lamp-post, at least two hundred yards away.'

'Children?'

'Undergraduates, more like! But one of them did come to my rescue.'

'That was probably the whole point of the exercise!'

'Less painful than being knocked off my bicycle, anyway!'

'Touché! But I didn't really hurt you, did I?'

'Of course not!' she said indulgently.

'So, you don't think too badly of me, now?'

'I never did. But if anyone was going to get involved with a blue-blooded aristocrat — and I know you are! — it had to be Prissy. She's always been a problem where 'town and gown' is concerned. The Moneymoons are such a hybrid lot, anyway; Pa having one of the best brains in Oxford, but coming from a working-class background, and proud of it, too. And Ma, being in trade and having more business acumen in her little finger than most women have in their whole body. And then there's Edmund, following in Pa's footsteps over at Cambridge. Prissy doesn't know where she stands, although she knows where she'd like to!'

'And you, Kate? Where do you stand?'

'On my own two feet! And that's how I like it. Not subservient to anyone. Classless, if you like. And that's the other reason why I didn't want to get involved with you.'

'But Kate, I meant what I said the other day. I honestly don't *want* to be a blue-blooded aristocrat!'

'But you *are* one! You can't get away from the circumstances of your birth and the life you'll be expected to lead, any more than I can. Or Prissy.'

'Then I'll just have to show you that I mean to be different. And I'll begin now!'

For while they talked, Toby had trotted into the wide thoroughfare of St Giles and was drawing up

46

outside St John's College. The porter on duty seemed to be expecting them for he came out on to the pavement. 'Afternoon, miss!'

'Good afternoon, Mr Larwood!'

As Robert leaped down from the box, the man's jaw dropped. 'What the ... ? Afternoon, Mr Holker!'

'Good afternoon, Larwood!' Robert let down the tail board and began to heave down the nearest basket. 'I think this one's yours.'

'Hold hard, sir!' And he turned back towards the college entrance. 'Hey, Fred! Come an' give us a hand!' And Fred who must have been lurking with just this possibility in mind, was with them immediately.

Considerably put out, Robert secured the tail board and clambered up again beside Kate; to find her shaking with laughter. 'I told you it would be impossible!'

'Just you wait!' And indeed he had more luck at Trinity, where he wasn't known, and at Brasenose managed to get away with no more than a puzzled glance. But at Queens, he was recognised again. However, at St Edmund Hall, he slipped on an old coat he'd found in a corner of the trap, turned up the collar and was rewarded with a threepenny bit for his trouble. In great high spirits, and because the trap was now empty, he persuaded Kate to leave Toby in the care of the ostler at the Cape of Good Hope while they strolled through the Botanical Gardens and out into the welcome shade of Broad Walk. There, they sat on a bench and watched the squirrels.

'Kate,' said Robert, 'I have a proposition to make.'

'Indeed?'

'Of the most respectable nature, I assure you! It's this. Assuming that there's going to be a war . . . no,' as she gave an involuntary shake of her head, 'everyone says there will be. And even if it's over in six months, these next few weeks could be my last in Oxford for quite a while. So, I'd like to make them as memorable as possible. Will you help me do that?'

'How?'

'There are many places I want to visit again, things I want to do; listen to the nightingales on Shotover Hill, attend Evensong at Christ Church, visit Dorchester and call on a dear old gentleman I know there, go as often as possible to the theatre, and to concerts. And if I can do all these things with you, then they'll be doubly enjoyable.'

'But I have a job to do.'

'Staying at Moneymoon Manor, I could help you with that. And you must admit with Priscilla laid up for a while, I could be useful.'

She gave him a long look. 'And if I agree, it's understood that there will be no long-term involvement?'

'Absolutely!' he promised, although he hoped it would be otherwise.

'Agreed!' she said then. And put out a slender, brown hand.

He shook it solemnly. 'Agreed!'

5

The Moneymoons were always to remember that summer of 1914 when Robert Holker came to stay for he was a delight to everyone; to the Professor because he could now discuss his reading at first hand; to Mrs Moneymoon because she now had yet another person to care for; to Danny because with Robert came his motorbike; to Priscilla because he took over her duties and to Kate because she now had the companion she had sought since childhood.

For though she loved her twin, Priscilla's mind was not like her's; always probing what it did not understand, continually wondering why? and where? But now, she had someone willing to discuss anything; the merits of a book or poem or even just an idea, and yet was just as willing to suddenly cast discretion to the winds and behave like any impulsive young man with not a care in the world.

Most endearing of all, was the way he threw himself into the routine of Moneymoon Manor; rising at dawn to light the boiler fires, collect the breakfast eggs from the orchard, run Danny to school on the back of his bike and, in the afternoon, help Kate put Toby between the shafts and set out with her on the day's deliveries. Usually, at the end of them, there would be an hour or so to spare when they would stable Toby and stroll through the Meadows or follow Addison's Walk through the leafy glades of Magdalen; and talk about themselves.

'You have no idea,' declared Robert, 'how much I envy you your childhood. It was only when Aunt Bella came to stay that I stopped being miserable.'

'But surely, with all the privileges you enjoyed . . . '

'Like being sent away to school at the tender age of eight?'

'You can't have it both ways! If you were so unhappy at home, you must have been delighted to get away from it!'

'Well, you have a point there and later on, when I was older and made good friends, school did have a great attraction. At least, there I was accepted as what I was and not made to act as second fiddle to George. It's surprising, when I think about it, that George and I got on as well as we did.'

'Tell me about George.' Kate was eager to hear of a childhood that had been so different from her own.

'George is a brick, conscientious and painstaking, doing his level best to reach the high standards our parents set him.'

But often failing, thought Kate shrewdly.

'Left to himself,' Robert continued, 'George would lead the life of a farmer. For he loves everything to do with the earth, the crops that are grown on it and the animals that feed on it. Whenever George went missing, you could always find him at the home farm, helping with the harvest or lending a hand with the milking.'

'But not you?'

'Now and then. But usually, I preferred to wander

50

around my father's pottery, asking foolish questions, getting in everyone's way and even having the temerity to suggest what I considered better ways of doing things. But,' he suddenly took her hand, swinging it as children do, 'enough of me! Let's talk about you.'

'*My* childhood was as haphazard and casual as yours must have been ordered and conventional. But I had the best of both worlds. There was Pa, who would tell us the most wonderful stories and explain why the sky was blue and the grass green. And there was Ma, picking us up when we fell, comforting us when we had a bad dream and not caring at all why the sky was blue and the grass green, except that that was the way God had made them and what was good enough for Him, was good enough for her.'

'And did you ever go to Staffordshire to visit your father's relations?'

'Several times, the last when I was only six just before Grandma Moneymoon died; Grandpa had long gone. I remember little of it now except that the air was dark and difficult to breathe. Grandma's little house was dark, too, and very poky after Moneymoon Manor, but I remember that the brass knocker was so bright you could see your face in it and the doorstep scrubbed as white as Ma's washing. Grandma loved Ma. She was always worried Pa would get ideas above his station, but when she met Ma, she knew he'd be safe! She wouldn't have approved at all of the Earl's son being so friendly with us. And certainly not of our walking together like this.'

For much to Robert's surprise, Kate's hand was still in his. Although he had adhered strictly to the rules Kate had laid down, he had wondered of late if she might be relaxing them a little. Certainly, they were now considered by everyone else, to be a 'couple'. Edmund, home from Cambridge, had naturally assumed it to be so; why else would anyone in his right mind, rise with the lark when he didn't have to, and rush out at the sight of rain to grapple with wet bed-linen?

Edmund, in fact, had he not possessed his mother's generous nature, could have been considerably put out by his sisters' absorption with other men, for Hank was now a constant visitor. With great regret, Sam had had to depart for home as soon as term was ended to be with his parents, but Hank had decided that he could remain in England a few weeks longer.

Often, in the evenings, the four of them would take a punt out on the Cherwell, with Priscilla's injured ankle carefully propped up on a cushion. Sometimes, if the evening was particularly warm, Mrs Moneymoon would pack vast hampers and they would all take to the water, tying up to eat their supper beneath the trailing branches of some enormous willow.

But what Robert — and, he dared to hope, Kate too — liked best of all was for her to climb up on to the pillion and ride out with him to see General Wavertree. Later, after a couple of hours with the old gentleman, they would speed homeward through lanes drenched with the sweetness of honeysuckle, to find everyone else in bed; and so the pleasure of the evening could be prolonged with mugs of cocoa brewed over the dying embers of the kitchen range with himself sprawled on the rug at Kate's feet. It was at times like these that he had the most difficulty in maintaining his side of the bargain; once, indeed, failing miserably to do so.

They had spent the evening as usual with the General, drinking coffee by an open window to enjoy the perfume of the lilies that grew in his tiny garden.

'Been thinking about you two today,' the General said conversationally.

'Indeed, sir?' Robert was intrigued.

'Yes. Feeling damned sorry for you both!'

'*Sorry*, sir?' He was mystified. What possible reason could there be to feel pity for either himself or Kate?

'Yes! Damned sorry!' the General repeated. 'You see, when Isabel and I were engaged, things were so different. The Crimea was behind us, my Colonel had given his consent and I knew the odds were I'd be stationed at home for several months. Even after that, wherever I went, Africa, India, Afghanistan, Isabel would go too. Never any question of it. But now — well,' he shrugged, 'there'll be no chance of Kate going to Europe with you.'

There was a short silence broken only by the shrill squeak of a bat from the bottom of the garden. Kate sipped her coffee in a determined fashion and said nothing.

'They do say, sir,' said Robert eventually, 'that it'll be over by Christmas.'

'Not *this* Christmas!' said the General. 'However,'

53

he bent to fondle Pugsie's ears where he lay at his feet, 'we mustn't make these young people feel gloomy, must we, Pugsie?' And he'd turned the conversation to other, less personal, topics.

But Robert remained thoughtful. Unless he asked her, how would he ever know if Kate's feelings towards him had changed?

That night, his hand on the latch of the door of Moneymoon Manor, he turned and looked at her. Her nose was buried in one of the red roses that now covered the front of the house. 'Can anything smell more beautiful?' she asked.

'Or *look* more beautiful!' Her face was partially hidden by the rose but he knew by heart every angle and contour of it; the curve of her lips, the slender arch of her brows, the dimple in one cheek when she smiled. Suddenly, his feelings were too much for him. Almost of their own volition, his arms went round her and his mouth sought hers. And he hardly knew if it was the petals of the rose he kissed, or her lips, for both had a velvety, yielding softness. But then her head jerked back and the rose shed its petals in a final waft of perfume.

'Robert! You promised!'

'I know! I'm sorry! It was only that what the General said, set me thinking. And hoping.'

'The General,' said Kate, 'is an incurable romantic.'

And so am I, he thought. And so, I think, are you. But he didn't dare say it aloud. Instead, he pushed open the door and she went ahead of him into the dimness of the hall. But that night, by common consent, there was no intimate brewing up of cocoa.

Once she was in her room, Kate pressed her hands to her cheeks. Why had he spoiled it all? Why could he not be content with the moment, instead of trying to force her to face issues she had no wish to face? At least, she admitted, not yet.

6

It was on a day towards the end of July that the morning paper came with the news of the assassination, by a Bosnian Serb, of the Archduke Franz Ferdinand and his wife in Sarajevo.

'Poor man!' said Ma, resting a basket of wet laundry on the kitchen table while she scanned the headlines, but not specifying whether she meant the Archduke or the Bosnian Serb. Both, probably, thought Robert, knowing Ma. He and Kate peered over her shoulder. Could this be the spark that would ignite the great tinder-box of Europe that the General feared?

'Let's go and find Pa,' Kate suggested. 'He'll explain exactly what's happening.'

They found the Professor ensconced in his garden retreat. He took the newspaper and read it in silence.

'This could be it,' he said. 'Just what they've been waiting for.'

'Who waiting for what, Pa?'

'The Austrians — waiting for an excuse to declare war on Serbia. They'll probably bomb Belgrade and then push south to Salonika. That way, they'll have the whole of the Balkans under their thumb.'

'What will Russia have to say to that?' Robert wondered.

'Won't like it at all! Any more than we shall. Or France, or Belgium, because Germany won't stay out of it if Austria-Hungary is involved, and *she*'ll look west as well as east. And once France or Belgium is involved,' the Professor added gloomily, 'we shall be duty bound to support them.'

'Why?' asked Kate. 'Why should we be drawn into something that isn't our concern? We're an island, after all.'

'But an island separated from the rest of Europe by only a narrow stretch of water. And the German Navy has been going from strength to strength of late. No, my dear, I'm afraid we must face it. We shall have to join in.'

'I'm going to find Ma,' said Kate, sounding suddenly desperate. For once, her father's ability to explain things so clearly and concisely, was not what she wanted. She needed Ma's calm, instinctive optimism, her gift of 'making everything better'.

But astonishingly, Ma, too, let her down. Kate found her at the washing lines, but instead of pegging out with her usual vigour, she was just standing there, staring vacantly into space.

'I never thought I would say such a thing,' she sighed as Kate came up behind her, 'but I thank God that Edmund's sight is not all it should be.'

'Oh, Ma!' said Kate and was suddenly in tears, her head pillowed on Ma's broad shoulder, her arms around Ma's ample waist. Ma let her cry, occasionally stroking her hair or murmuring some soothing childhood phrase.

'Sorry, Ma!' said Kate after a minute or two, straightening up and mopping at her eyes with her handkerchief, grateful that Robert wasn't there to see her.

'You cry, my love. As much as you want to.' Ma put back her head and studied her daughter's face. 'Is it Robert?'

'I don't know!' Kate wailed. 'I don't know anything for certain, any more. It's as if the ground's been cut away from under my feet. I'm all topsy-turvy.'

'Give it time,' Ma soothed.

'But suddenly there *isn't* any time. Pa's talking as if we might be at war by this time tomorrow.'

'Well, I doubt that,' said Ma calmly. 'I'm sure Mr Asquith wouldn't be that hasty, let alone dear King George. Anyway,' she gave Kate's shoulders a little shake, 'war or no war, we've got to get this washing dry!'

'Where are Emma and Jane?'

'Gone into town for an hour or two,' Ma said glibly, thinking it advisable not to give the real reason, that their young men had already taken the King's shilling and were to leave for training immediately. 'Can you give me a hand?'

'Of course! And here comes Robert!'

Kate wasn't to know that it was in fact the second time Robert had rounded the side of the house in the last five minutes, the first time drawing back immediately when he saw Kate clasped in her mother's arms. But he had still been within earshot;

had heard Ma's question and Kate's plaintive reply. Extreme caution, he had decided, must dictate his immediate behaviour, certainly normality must seem to be the order of the day; even though there was nothing remotely normal, either about this particular day or about the way he felt at the moment.

With this in mind, he hastily plucked a couple of ripe raspberries from the canes that grew beside the house and hastened towards Kate and her mother.

'Open wide!' he instructed Mrs Moneymoon, and carefully inserted a raspberry into her obligingly opened mouth.

'That reminds me,' she said, licking her lips, 'summer pudding! If you and Kate will pick the fruit, we can have one for lunch.'

'There is nothing,' Robert assured her, 'that I like more than summer pudding.' And to Kate who, at the sight of him, was experiencing yet another absurd urge to cry, 'One for you, too?'

She gave an enormous sniff but obediently opened her mouth. However, Robert, instead of popping in the fruit, made a great performance of gazing earnestly down her throat. ''Pon my soul, madam,' he observed, adjusting an imaginary pince-nez, 'that's an astonishing pair of tonsils, you have! More like twin headlamps!'

'Astonishing, indeed,' Ma agreed, 'considering she had them out when she was five!' And immediately, the tension had passed and they were all laughing so hard, that Priscilla, coming out of the house, demanded to know what she was missing.

That afternoon, they stabled Toby at the Cape of Good Hope as usual, and wandered in to the Botanical Gardens, there to sit on their favourite bench, set within a little glade of shrubs. Kate was calmer now. A morning spent with Robert and Priscilla among the raspberry canes and red currant bushes — for Ma had declared she would make jelly as well as a pudding, if they picked sufficient fruit — had soothed her, reminding her, as it did, of the many childhood hours that she and Priscilla had passed in the same occupation.

'A penny a basin, Ma used to give us,' she told Robert, 'but only a farthing for gooseberries because they were bigger and easier to pick.'

'And two pennies for strawberries,' Priscilla reminded her, 'because that way, we didn't eat so many!'

Now, mistress of her emotions, Kate traced a circle with her toe in the gravel of the path and asked quietly, 'What will you do, Robert, if war is declared?'

'I shall join up straightaway,' he told her, just as quietly, 'as a despatch rider, if they'll have me. If not, as plain Tommy Atkins. George,' he added, 'has already gone. A second lieutenant in the Staffordshire Yeomanry.'

Startled, Kate looked up. 'That was quick!'

'He was in the Reserves. I think,' Robert mused, 'that George might quite enjoy army life.'

'And you wouldn't?'

He shrugged. 'I don't think I shall mind being a

despatch rider. Can't you just see me,' he made a feeble attempt at humour, 'setting out in the teeth of a bombardment, dodging bullets, whipping round shell-holes, facing . . . '

'Don't!' said Kate.

'Sorry!' His hand found hers and squeezed it hard. They were silent for a moment or two, their hands still clasped.

'I'll stay in Oxford for as long as I can,' Robert said eventually, 'if that's all right with your mother. But once war is declared, I shall have to go, Kate.'

'Yes, of course. But you must see your parents first.'

'I know. But they're in the London house until September, so that won't be difficult. What about you, Kate? What will you do?'

'Nurse, I hope. So will Prissy. But we'll stay at home as long as Ma needs us.'

'You've got it all worked out!' He tried not to feel aggrieved that there was no place for him in her plans. 'What about Hank? Where does he fit in?'

'He'll go back to America, I think, because that's what his parents want.'

'Wouldn't he like to take Priscilla with him?'

Kate smiled. 'I'm sure he would. But Prissy wouldn't turn her back on a real, live war, even to sail across the Atlantic! At the moment, she sees it as the most exciting thing that's ever happened to her.' She smiled wryly as she remembered how Prissy had curled up on the end of her bed on the previous night; managing, even with her hair curled up in rags, to look deliciously feminine.

'I shall be like Florence Nightingale, brave and

dedicated, giving my all to the flower of British manhood! Oh, Kate!' she'd clasped her hands around her knees, her eyes shining. 'Won't it be wonderful to be free of the laundry? Much as I dislike her, that dreadful woman was right — we *are* only a washerwoman's daughters.'

'Would you really want Ma to be any different, Priss?'

'Oh, no!' Priscilla was deeply shocked at the suggestion. 'Ma's perfect. I just wish . . . ' her voice trailed away.

Kate laughed. 'I know what you mean, even though I don't share your feelings. But what about Hank?

'Oh, I love him, of course! He's just a darling! But this isn't the moment to tie yourself down to one man, is it? Think what you'd be missing?'

'And them!' said Kate, suddenly dissolving into giggles, in which Prissy had joined. And soon afterwards, she'd gone back to her own room.

But Kate had lain awake for a long time, thinking of what her sister had said; and of how, with her extraordinary naiveté, she'd spoken words of simple wisdom. For the uncertain climate of a war was surely not the right atmosphere in which to tie yourself to any one man; as much for *his* peace of mind as for your own.

Now, she looked up at Robert and saw in his eyes such an expression of naked longing, that she hastily averted her own. One of them, it was clear, must keep a cool head. 'We must be getting back,' she said; and yet seemed powerless to move.

'Kate,' Robert began, his voice thick with

61

emotion. But then a large ball came suddenly bouncing into their corner, followed immediately by its owner, a small boy in a sailor suit who in turn was pursued by an irate nursemaid.

'If I've told you once, Master Henry, I've told you a dozen times. Games must *not* be played in the Gardens!'

'Sorry, old son!' said Robert, fielding the ball and returning it to Master Henry. 'But Nanny's right. Rules must be obeyed!'

Although one, he resolved as he got to his feet, was due to be broken.

* * *

It was just as the Professor had predicted; the Austrians declared war upon Serbia and bombarded Belgrade and the Russians began to mobilise, thus provoking Germany to do the same. On the first day of August, German troops invaded Luxembourg and the British Naval Reserves were called up, and on the following day, Germany seized those British ships unfortunate enough to be docked at Kiel. On the third of August, she declared war upon France and demanded of King Albert that German troops be allowed to pass through Belgium. Naturally, permission was refused; instead King Albert appealed to King George for help. On the fourth of August, Great Britain, while still doing her level best to enjoy a well-earned Bank Holiday, found herself at war with Germany.

'At least,' said the Professor, 'we now know where we stand.'

They were, as usual, gathered in the kitchen. Mrs Moneymoon, her cheeks flushed, glanced around at the faces of her children and saw the quiet resolve on Edmund's and the excitement on Priscilla's; saw how Kate, after one quick exchange of glances with Robert, turned away and busied herself with a sheaf of invoices. It was left to Danny to break the silence.

'So, this is it, Pa?' His eyes were shining with anticipation, his face almost split in two with the enormity of his grin. As if, thought his mother, he was off to camp in Whyteham Woods!

'Danny . . . ' she began, but then stopped. For what was there to say? Like Kate, she felt as if the ground had been cut away from under her feet, that her busy, happy little world was crumbling about her ears. She took a deep breath. 'Danny,' she began again, 'this may be it, but your boots still need cleaning.'

'Aw, Ma . . . '

'Come along, son! I'll help you!' And the Professor put an arm across his son's shoulders and led him away, leaving his wife open-mouthed with shock. She couldn't remember the last time her husband had performed such a menial task. More uneasy than ever, she set about her own tasks; but noticing out of the corner of her eye that Robert and Edmund had begun an animated discussion between themselves, and conducted so quietly there was no way she could overhear. She saw Kate take one look at them and then turn and leave the room. Ten minutes later, Robert followed her.

He found her fondling Toby over the gate of his

field. 'So, you'll be off now!' Her voice was almost brusque.

'Yes — I'm giving Edmund a lift into town to the recruiting depot. And then I'll telephone my parents. Probably go up to London this afternoon, now that Priscilla's ankle is quite better.'

'So soon!' She couldn't prevent the distress in her voice.

Robert put his hands on her shoulders and turned her to face him. 'Kate, listen to me. I've done my best to play the game by your rules. But the war has altered everything. I can't go away without telling you how I feel. I love you, Kate and I want to marry you. Oh, I know,' as she made an involuntary movement of protest, 'I'm rushing things but there's so little time. You do love me, just a little, don't you?'

Desperately, she sought for the right words, tried frantically to remind herself of the conclusions she had reached. 'Robert, of course I'm fond of you. I shall miss you more than I can say. And perhaps,' her voice faltered, 'if things had been different and we'd had more time, — well, who can say? But I'm too fond of you to want to hurt you. To say 'yes' and then discover that we'd both made a terrible mistake.'

'And, that's — your last word on the subject?'

She nodded. 'I'm so sorry!'

She felt his lips on her forehead and the pressure of his hands on her shoulders. But she couldn't look up; not until he'd turned and was walking away from her. And then she watched him through a mist of tears. Suddenly, it was terribly important that he should turn at the top of the lane and wave — to give her a sign that he forgave her and understood, just a little, of how she felt. But he didn't turn and a few minutes later, she heard the sound of his motor-bike starting up.

At lunchtime, Edmund was back — on his own. 'What's happening?' Ma asked.

He gave a rueful smile. 'It'll be a desk job for me, I'm afraid. Maybe the intelligence corps.'

Ma breathed an audible sigh of relief. 'And Robert?'

'Gone up to London,' said Edmund briefly. 'He'll join his regiment from there. He asked me to thank you for everything. And to tell Danny that he'll be writing.'

But no message for me, thought Kate dully. What else could she expect?

7

'Kate! My darling child, what is it?'

Professor Moneymoon, returning up the lane from an unaccustomed walk — how could he possibly concentrate upon the living conditions of the Tudor peasantry when events of such world-shattering importance were taking place at that very moment? — was astonished and distressed to discover his daughter with her arms around Toby's neck and weeping copiously into his mane.

'Oh, Pa! I'm so miserable! And I'm such an idiot!'

She transferred her arms from Toby's neck to her father's but still continued to sob uncontrollably.

'There, there! Tell your old Pa all about it.' It was disturbing to find his normally composed daughter, abandoned to grief.

'It's — it's Robert!'

'I guessed as much. Do you love him, child?'

The head pressed against his shoulder nodded violently. 'And I've a shrewd idea he feels the same way about you?' Again, she nodded. 'So isn't that the important thing? Granted you'll be parted from each other for a while, but there'll be letters and . . . '

'Pa, you don't understand! I've let him go away thinking that I *don't* love him. At least, not enough to marry him. I thought I was being so s-sensible and n-now it's too late . . . ' and the sobs broke out afresh.

He gave her shoulders a little shake and tried another tack. 'Now stop this caterwauling this minute, Kate Moneymoon. You're frightening Toby half out of his wits!' And indeed, the animal was rolling his eyes and tossing his head, and behind him, the long ears of the little grey donkey were twitching in sympathy. Kate's sobs diminished very slightly.

'Now let us assess the situation calmly,' the Professor continued. 'Robert has gone up to London under the impression that you don't wish to marry him. Correct?'

'C-correct!'

'So it's up to you to follow him to London and tell him that you *do* love him and *will* consider matrimony.'

The sobs ceased abruptly and Kate's tear-washed eyes stared into his. 'Pa, I couldn't!'

'Well, of course you could, child. This is no time for false modesty.'

'But the deliveries . . .'

'Damn the deliveries! I'll explain it all to Ma and if necessary do them myself with Prissy's help. But first, I'm going to drive you to the railway station.'

'Oh, Pa! You're wonderful!'

'I know! Now, you go and wash your face and do whatever you have to do and if you see Danny on the way, tell him to come and help me harness Toby.'

★ ★ ★

It is a tall, narrow, porticoed house — one of a terrace built in the Georgian style to accommodate the families of the wealthy and privileged during the Industrial Revolution. Kate, turning from the hansom cab that has brought her here from Paddington Station, refuses to be intimidated.

'Remember,' her father has told her, 'all that matters is for you to see Robert. And remember, too that the Earl of Werrington wouldn't be where he is today, if it wasn't for people like your grandfather. Not, of course, that he'll wish to be reminded of that fact!'

Remembering her father's words, Kate averts her eyes from a notice informing her that tradesmen should use the area steps — she isn't delivering laundry now! — and mounts the flight that leads upward to the imposing, shiny-black front door. But there, she has a problem. Should she lift the large brass knocker, fashioned in the shape of a lion's head, or press the discreet bell-push let into the door frame? She chooses the bell-push and presses it firmly then turns to gaze out at the dusty summer foliage of the gardens around which the crescent is built. Perhaps she and Robert will go and sit there while she tells him of her change of heart.

There comes the click of the opening door and she turns slowly, determined not to be intimidated by some supercilious parlour-maid or pompous butler.

But it's neither. Instead, she finds herself gazing at a tall, elegant woman in a lilac silk, evening dress. Her dark hair, streaked liberally with grey, is arranged in a curling, bouffant fringe above eyes that twinkle in the friendliest fashion.

'Miss Moneymoon?' she enquires.

Dumbfounded, Kate can only nod.

'I saw you coming up the steps and recognised you immediately from Robert's description. It's all right, Boothby,' she turns to dismiss the imposing, dark-suited figure who has now materialised behind her. 'I'll look after Miss Moneymoon.'

'As you wish, m'lady.' Clearly, it is not Boothby's wish.

The woman turns back to Kate, at the same time letting one eyelid droop in a broad wink. 'Come in, Miss Moneymoon. I'm Robert's Aunt Bella. Unfortunately, Robert isn't here at the moment, but he shouldn't be long. An old friend has been called to the Colours. He had to see him.' She holds open the door for Kate to enter.

Kate sees a long, narrow hallway, elegantly tiled in squares of black and white. A huge, formal arrangement of roses and carnations stands stiffly upon a console table, quite unlike the casual bunches that her mother scatters around Money-moon Manor.

'In here,' says Aunt Bella, going to open a door, but before she can do so, another door on the opposite side of the hall is thrown open and a majestic woman, clad in flowing purple, hair coiffeured in the elaborate, upswept style favoured by the young Queen Mary, comes out.

'We're just going in, Bella.' And then she sees Kate. 'Who . . . ?'

'Miss Kate Moneymoon,' Aunt Bella says swiftly. 'A friend of Robert's from Oxford. And this,' she adds, even more swiftly, 'is Robert's mother.'

'I see!' Quite what the Countess of Werrington sees, or thinks she sees, Kate is never to know; because over her shoulder suddenly peers a face that she has good cause to remember, although wishing devoutly to forget.

'Well, I never,' says the tall, red-haired woman who had identified her and Priscilla at Robert's college ball, 'if it isn't the washerwoman's daughter again!' As before the consequences of the statement are immediate; but this time, even more upsetting.

The Countess of Werrington swings round. 'What do you mean, Blanche? Even Robert wouldn't . . . ' And then she swings back towards Kate. 'Or is it, perhaps, an unpaid bill you've come about?'

'I doubt it,' says the woman called Blanche. 'At

least,' she laughs unpleasantly, 'not for laundry. Perhaps for services rendered? Their affair was quite the talk of the town.'

Kate feels her cheeks grow hot. How dare this woman speak of her friendship with Robert in such an insulting manner? She opens her mouth to tell her so but then feels Lady Bella's restraining hand on her arm. 'Just a moment, my dear. Dorothy, allow me to explain . . . '

But even she is not allowed to continue. The Countess, having scrutinised Kate's neat, navy-blue costume and white blouse, her navy straw hat with its crown of daisies, has presumably decided that, either way, she presents no threat. 'If it's a matter of an unpaid bill, Miss Moneymoon, then, if you leave your address, my housekeeper will settle it. But if,' and she allows her voice to rise menacingly, 'it's a question of some — some liaison my son may have formed with you, and which he has wisely decided to terminate, then I'm afraid you will have no satisfaction from me. I suggest you return to Oxford and your — your . . . ' having but the scantiest knowledge of the tools of a washerwoman's trade, she hesitates.

'Soapsuds?' suggests the woman called Blanche with a sneer.

'Exactly so! Soapsuds,' repeats the Countess with satisfaction.

'Really, Dorothy,' Lady Bella moves towards her sister-in-law and thereby releases her grip on Kate's arm. 'You have no right . . . '

But again she isn't allowed to finish. 'My lady,' says Kate crisply, in the tone of voice she would use to discipline Danny, 'I can assure you there is no outstanding account of any description between your son and myself. Nor, as far as I am aware, between him and my mother — who does, indeed provide a professional and competent laundry service — *nor*' and she hesitates very slightly to give weight to her next words, 'between him and my father, Professor Moneymoon, who is his tutor. But I can also assure you that if there were, then Robert and I would settle it between ourselves and certainly not through a third party.'

The statement is not as contemptuous as she would have wished, but it is, she decides, the best she can do at such short notice; once she has left this woman's presence, she will no doubt think of an even more cutting rejoinder and regret that she cannot deliver it. For it is now abundantly clear that the sooner she leaves, the better. She should never have come in the first place. In spite of her love for Robert, she now knows that her first instincts have been right; the pain and anguish that would result from their marriage is not to be considered. She turns to Aunt Bella.

'I think it would be better not to tell Robert about this. Please forget I ever came. But thank you,' she lays her hand briefly on the other woman's arm, 'for your kindness. Robert is right to love you.' And then she turns and makes for the door and knows a moment of panic that she will not be able to open it. But suddenly, gliding unobtrusively into view from whatever dark corner he's been occupying, comes Boothby.

'Allow me, miss!' The door opens and then thuds

71

shut behind her. To Kate, it is like the sounding of a knell.

'My dearest Kate,

Please God, this is the first of many letters I shall write to you during the weeks, perhaps even months, before I see you again. Please forgive Aunt Bella, my darling, for disobeying your wish that I should not be told of your visit. It was more than a romantic soul such as she, could agree to! She cannot forgive herself for not having rushed after you and forcibly restrained you from returning to Oxford.

I will not waste valuable time in apologising for my mother's treatment of you. Suffice it to say that what little love there was between us is now quite dead. I never wish to see her again.

If only I had been able to follow you to Oxford, but Field Marshall Sir John French had other plans for me, alas! I am now under canvas somewhere in the South of England with other members of the British Expeditionary Force. Even as I began to pen these few lines, I was told that our marching orders had come through. Any minute now, we are off to a port of embarkation for France, then Belgium.

Please write to me soon, my darling; unless — and I cannot rid myself of the nightmare possibility — my mother's treatment of you was so cavalier, you consider any further contact with the Holker family to be avoided at all costs. My blood runs cold when I consider what she and Blanche Golding may have said to you; Aunt

Bella refuses to tell me.

I must go now, my dearest Kate. I love you more than life itself and can only pray that I am your own,

Robert

PS   I am assured that my name and number — as at the head of this letter — care of the B.E.F. will be sufficient to find me.
PPS   Please tell Danny that my present machine is like a steam-roller compared with my beloved Harley Davidson! But even so, I'm one of the lucky ones — there are some Don Rs with only push-bikes!'

With a nostalgic sigh, Robert sealed and addressed the envelope, then thrust it into the breast pocket of his tunic. Surely, there would be opportunities for an enterprising Don R to post it, en route to Dover or wherever they were going.

Forty minutes later, the battalion was on its way and Robert was kept busy, either delivering messages from his Colonel riding at the head of the column to the Major at the rear, or holding up civilian traffic to let the battalion through. Often, he had to weave a tortuous path between the marching troops and the cheering residents of the towns and villages through which they passed. Many of the women and children clutched bunches of flowers in their hands, plucked at random from their gardens when the rousing calls of the bugle band had alerted them.

After two hours, Robert began to worry; even if

he'd seen a post office, there would have been no time to post Kate's letter, and the one rest that the men had been given, had been in the middle of a field. When a young girl stepped out almost under his wheels, thrusting a bunch of faded marigolds at him, he decided to take a chance. Stopping his machine, he undid his tunic pocket.

'Would you be kind enough to post this for me? It's very important.'

'Of course! And good luck to you, Tommy!'

'Thank you!' He thrust a coin into her hand along with the letter and was on his way.

When the dust raised by the marching men had settled and the plaintive call of the bugles faded on the breeze, the girl — she was no more than sixteen — turned and began to walk homeward. There was a post office on the corner of her street. Idly, she glanced at the address on the envelope. The soldier's young lady, she reckoned and wished, as she had each day since they'd started marching through, that she had a soldier boy to write to. Her friend Dora had actually had a piece of paper thrust into her hand by one of the Tommies with, 'Please write to me' written on it with his name and number. And Dora *had* written and was now eagerly awaiting a reply.

Just before she reached the post office, the girl was hailed by that same Dora. 'Have you heard? The Jocks are coming through! This could be your chance!'

'The Jocks! Are you sure?' The Jocks, with their kilts swinging above brawny knees, their tam-o-shanters pulled rakishly over one eye, were special;

even if it was difficult sometimes to understand all they said! Writing to one of them would be a feather in her cap, one up, even on Dora!

'Listen!' said Dora. And sure enough there came the unmistakeable wail of the pipes. Without another thought, the girl turned back to the roadside.

Late that night, preparing for bed, she was puzzled to discover a florin in her pocket. It was only then she remembered the letter, and realised she had no idea what had happened to it.

Next morning, she did her very best to find it, retracing her steps, peering into every gutter and down every drain; but it was of no use. Perhaps, she comforted herself, someone had picked it up and posted it. And in any case, the young soldier would surely write again to his girl. To salve her conscience, she gave the florin to the Prince of Wales' War Relief Fund.

★ ★ ★

'Listen to this,' said Mrs Moneymoon, looking up from the weekly War Illustrated. 'A Mrs Collis of Epsom, a soldier's widow, has all her seven sons on active service — two Regulars, four Territorials and one Reservist.' She glanced around the kitchen table at her assembled family. 'I must be one of the lucky ones.' But a note of doubt had crept into her voice. It was left to the Professor, taking his head out of the Manchester Guardian, to reassure her.

'Yes indeed, my dear. Counting our blessings has never had such relevance as it has now.' And he, too, glanced around the table at Edmund, admittedly already in khaki and only home for a few precious hours, but unlikely to be sent further afield than the War Office, and at Danny, still far too young to enlist. And as for the two girls — well, there was no need for them to do anything at all. But even as he considered the possibility, he dismissed it. Did he honestly imagine that Kate would be content to sit at home, rolling the odd bandage or packing comforts for the troops, while the flower of British youth perished on the battlefields of Belgium? Especially the new, tight-lipped Kate who had come back from London, dry-eyed but with two bright spots of scarlet high up on her cheek bones and her chin sticking out like the Rock of Gibraltar and, worst of all, refusing to tell him what had happened; except to say that no, she didn't expect to hear from Robert, ever again. Not that the statement prevented her awaiting every post as if her very life depended upon its arrival, and then trying unsuccessfully to conceal her disappointment when the letter she clearly hoped for, failed to arrive.

Now, she looked up from the ledger she was studying and turned worried eyes upon her mother. 'Ma, there's no doubt that business is falling off. I think it's time we talked about the future.'

Her mother sighed. 'I guessed as much. People are putting away their delicate things and using the big, steam laundries for everything else.'

Priscilla looked up eagerly from the lavender bags she was making, her face wreathed in smiles. 'Don't worry, Ma! The billeting people are looking for big houses, able to take in soldiers.' Two days ago, Priscilla had bade a tearful farewell to Hank when

76

he'd left for Southampton and the next west-bound steamship, and though the tears had been genuine enough, it was clear she had no intention of grieving indefinitely. 'What do you say, Kate?'

'I was thinking more in terms of offering it as a Red Cross Stores Depot,' said Kate. '*If*,' she added hastily, 'Ma and Pa agreed, of course!'

'Well, thank you,' said the Professor drily, 'for including us in your plans! No, it's quite all right, my dear,' as Kate began to mumble apologies, 'it's only fair that we should all consider what is to become of us. And do I take it, that if your Mother and I — and, of course, the Red Cross! — were to agree, you would like to run the Depot yourself?'

'Well, I *had* thought of joining the Red Cross but as a V.A.D. if they'd have me.'

'I'll come with you, Kate!' There was no doubting Priscilla's enthusiasm.

Kate gave her a wry smile. 'It wouldn't be just stroking fevered brows and taking temperatures, you know. It will be emptying bedpans, scrubbing floors and doing as we're told.'

'That's all right,' said Priscilla equably, 'I'm much tougher than you think. And besides,' she grinned mischievously at her sister, 'I should look simply ravishing in uniform!'

Everyone laughed, except Edmund; absorbed in the letter he was writing, he hadn't even been listening. 'Any message for Robert?' he asked suddenly.

The silence was electrifying. Kate spoke first. 'How — how do you know where to write to?'

Edmund grinned. 'Not much point in my being in Intelligence if I can't find out where my friends are!

I promised I'd let him know his precious motor-bike was safe.' Robert's bike, as they all knew, was safely housed in one of the Manor's numerous outbuildings, swathed in sacking. 'Any messages?' he asked again, glancing around the table.

'Give him my love,' said Mrs Moneymoon, carefully not looking at Kate.

'Tell him . . . ' the Professor sought for words. What did you tell a man whom you knew to be in love with your daughter? A daughter, moreover, whose own feelings on the subject were known only to herself. 'Give him,' he amended, 'our very best wishes for a speedy return.'

'Give him a big hug and a kiss!' said Priscilla more precisely.

'Danny?'

Danny's face was a battlefield in itself. He wanted desperately to say that supposing, just supposing, something were to happen to Robert out there, could he, Danny, possibly have the Harley Davidson? But his better instincts — plus the look in his mother's eye, as if she knew exactly what he was thinking — held him back. 'Tell him,' he compromised, 'he needn't worry. I'll keep an eye on his bike for him.'

Edmund scribbled away obediently. 'Kate?'

But Kate's head was back in the ledger. 'No message,' she said curtly.

★ ★ ★

Robert brooded over Edmund's letter for a long time before he opened it. The post corporal had

78

handed it to him outside Battalion HQ after he'd ridden back through the woods and fields that surrounded the little Belgian mining town of Mons, with only an occasional shell crater and burned-out farm building along the way to remind him he'd left behind an army fighting for its life. At first, when he'd seen the postmark, his heart had given a great leap. Kate had written at last! But then he'd seen the hand-writing and known it was Edmund's. At least, he tried to comfort himself, there would now be news of her, perhaps even some explanation for why she hadn't answered his letter.

The longer he put off reading the letter, the longer he could go on hoping. Thrusting it into his pocket, he'd gone to deliver his despatches to the Colonel.

The Colonel knew his father well and, Robert suspected, found it strange that 'young Holker' hadn't taken a commission. He returned Robert's salute with a friendly nod. 'How is it up there, Holker?'

He wondered if the Colonel really wanted his considered opinion or was just being pleasant for old times' sake. Did he really want to hear about the terrifying cacophony of the guns, the incessant chatter of the Maxims, the shriek of German shells landing only feet away, so that he and the other occupants of the front line, were showered with clods of earth? Did he want to know about the shell that had actually landed *in* the trench, so that bits of a human body had rained down on them, along with the earth? A body that, only seconds before, had been peering over the parapet yelling, 'Come on, then, you bloody Boche!'

Did he really want a description of the German infantry advancing out of the woods on the other side of the canal while the British infantry were told, 'Pick your man but hold fire!' Of the seconds that had seemed like eternity before the command 'Fire?' had been given. And of the astonishing accuracy of the marksmen when they had. The Germans had gone down like skittles. But skittles that had seemed, incredibly, to right themselves almost immediately as their places were taken by other, grey-clad men.

'Where the hell are the buggers coming from?' Robert had heard one exasperated infantryman mutter before he suddenly clutched his chest and fell across the parapet, blood spurting between his fingers where the shrapnel had hit him.

'Stretcher bearers!' the man next to him had called and Robert had helped pull the man back into the trench before stepping forward to take his place — for Don Rs, he'd been informed by an extremely articulate Company Sergeant, soon after coming out, were expected to do their bit and not 'sit around on their friggin' arses all day, waitin' for those friggin' bits o' paper!'.

Lining up the sights of his rifle, he'd seen that the Germans were now doing their best to return the British fire.

'Couldn't hit a haystack at fifty yards!' said the soldier next to him with withering scorn. By then Robert himself had lined up his target and pressed the trigger, secretly amazed that he, who had steadfastly refused to join in the annual slaughter of

80

grouse and pheasants on his father's estate, could now aim so dispassionately at a human target. Perhaps that was what war did to a man, coarsening his susceptibilities until he was no more than a destructive automaton.

When he'd eventually been called into the shallow dug-out that was Company HQ, and been given his despatches, there'd been rumours that the cavalry were to be sent in; and suddenly, taking him completely unawares, there had flashed into his mind a picture of Kate up on the box behind Toby, Kate in a white summer dress, her boater tipped over her eyes against the sun as she looked up at him. There was no comparison between Toby and the big, raw-boned chargers of the cavalry, any more than there was between Kate and his present companions, and the picture had faded as quickly as it had come, but it had left him with an almost unbearable longing to see her again, to hold her in his arms and to tell her that he loved her.

Now, as he stood in front of the Colonel, he realised he hadn't replied to his question, rhetorical though it might have been. 'Pretty bad, sir!' he said and stood in silence, awaiting further orders.

The Colonel sighed, but whether because of Robert's reticence or because he knew only too well what it was like up there, it was impossible to judge. 'Come back in half an hour, Holker. There'll be a despatch for Brigade by then.'

So here he was, lying in the shade of a hawthorn hedge, its fruit as yet untouched by autumn scarlet, and opening his precious letter.

For a mathematician, Robert decided, Edmund

had an imaginative turn of phrase. He could see clearly the vast, stone-flagged kitchen, its windows wide to the summer scents of lavender and roses, and the spicy tang of new-mown hay, with the family grouped around the table; the Professor in his linen smock and corduroy breeches, stroking his beard as he pondered the war news in the newspaper, Mrs Moneymoon in her long, white apron, just as eagerly scanning the War Illustrated, Danny absorbed in his Boys' Own Paper, Priscilla at her sewing, and Kate, a tiny furrow of concentration between her brows, totting up the columns in her ledger.

'The winds of change', Edmund had written, 'are blowing even here.' And had gone on to describe the probable conversion of Moneymoon Manor into a Red Cross Stores Depot and of Kate and Priscilla joining the Voluntary Aid Detachment. And of how Danny, having read that the Boy Scouts living near the east coast, were being asked to guard the telephone and telegraph lines, had implored the family to move there immediately!

Then came the individual messages. He scanned them hurriedly, searching in vain for Kate's. Edmund, as if aware of the omission and doing his best to remedy it, had ended by urging Robert to 'look out, old man, for Kate and Priscilla's arrival over there. Not, I trust, that you'll be needing their ministrations.'

Slowly, Robert folded up the letter and put it back into its envelope. No news was not, in this case, good news. Kate's refusal to send him even a simple message — that the squirrels still played in Christ

Church Meadows, that the deer still roamed at Magdalen — was more convincing than any direct statement that she wished to have no more to do with him.

8

'Kate,' wailed Priscilla, 'I think we may have made the most dreadful mistake.'

Kate turned to look at her. '*You* may think so, Prissy, I certainly do not.'

The assertion seemed only to fuel Priscilla's distress. 'It's different for you!'

Kate stopped walking and gazed at her sister in exasperation. It was a bitter November day; far below the grey waters of the Solent surged and tossed; overhead, clouds like tarnished pewter raced across the sky. Clearly, rain was imminent but Nurses Moneymoon K., and Moneymoon P., had been sent out for their daily ration of exercise and exercise they would, even though the wind threatened to treat their voluminous cloaks like balloons and speech was almost impossible.

Kate looked about her then pointed to a flight of steps that led down to the sea and where, in happier times, a bench had been strategically placed to command a view across the water to the ancient, fishing port of Lymington and at the same time shelter its occupants from the wind.

'Oh, that's better!' Gratefully, they pushed back

the wide-brimmed, velour hats they'd pulled down over their ears and blew their noses hard. Then Kate turned to her sister.

'What are you on about, Prissy? I thought you were enjoying life in spite of everything.' By 'everything', she meant their first, soul-destroying encounter with the big, empty house which was to be turned into a convalescent home: the hours spent scrubbing, with water so hot and disinfectant so strong even the lotion of rose water, glycerine and borax that Ma had sent, hadn't prevented their hands growing rough and sore; the endless sweeping up of dead cockroaches and the discovery of more still horribly alive and — perhaps worst of all — the shock of opening a cupboard door upon a rat.

'Is it dead?' Kate had asked after she'd hit it over the head with a broom handle and they had stared, hypnotised, at its still twitching body.

'Of course it's dead!' a stern voice had assured them. 'And if you're like this over a dead rat, what on earth will you be like over a human body?'

The rat immediately forgotten, they'd jerked around like puppets. Sister Hardcastle could have been mounted on castors, the way she was always gliding up behind them, carping and criticising, continually urging them on to even greater endeavours.

'Perhaps,' her voice had boomed on, 'it would be better to give in now, admit that it's all been too much for you and go home to Mummy and Daddy. A maid bringing you breakfast in bed then driving out with Mummy in the carriage to pay calls . . .' but there she'd stopped, for once deprived of the power of speech as Nurses Moneymoon P., and K., instead of hanging their heads in shame, had actually begun to laugh in her face. And not just laugh but actually rock with merriment, holding their sides in almost hysterical abandonment.

'Silence!' she'd roared at last. 'How dare you laugh at me like that?'

'We're — we're not laughing at *you*, Sister,' Kate had tried to explain but in a voice still not quite steady. 'It's just that . . . '

'Silence!' Sister Hardcastle had roared again, her face crimson with rage. 'Take this rodent outside and bury it. And then come back and scrub out the cupboard. In the meantime, I shall speak to Matron.'

'D'you think she really will speak to Matron?' Priscilla had worried as they'd processed through the cavernous kitchens of the house and out into the stableyard, the rat laid out in front of them on a spade, Matron's Jack Russell trotting hopefully at the rear.

'I doubt it.'

'It's not as if we were laughing at *her*!'

'I know! Can you imagine Jane or Emma bringing us breakfast in bed?'

'Or Ma taking us out in the trap to pay calls?'

'Well,' Kate spluttered 'we *did* pay calls in a way, but always at the tradesmen's entrance.'

And they'd laughed so much the rat had fallen off the spade and been seized upon immediately by the Jack Russell. At least, they'd no longer had to bury it.

All this flashed through Kate's mind as she sat waiting anxiously for Priscilla to explain what she'd meant. If she were to lose Prissy's company and support, life 'under Hardcastle' would indeed be difficult to bear. For Prissy, in spite of Kate's fear, had proved herself right; she was tougher than anyone had thought. Kate only hoped the authorities would agree to their remaining together, even to the hoped-for posting to France; if, that is, Prissy didn't decide to throw in the sponge.

Priscilla tucked her hands inside her cloak, with its big red cross emblazoned on the left breast, and stared grimly out to sea. Kate giggled. 'You look like Napoleon!'

'Exactly! That's my point. I *do* look like Napoleon in this hat.'

'But I thought you were looking forward to wearing uniform,' Kate protested.

'I got it all wrong. I thought we'd be wearing sweet little grey bonnets and scarlet, shoulder capes.'

Kate burst out laughing. 'You mean the Queen Alexandra nurses? Oh, Prissy, we'd need more than our First Aid Certificates to be one of those.'

'But even our First Aid isn't being used,' Priscilla grumbled. 'They'll have us sweeping the chimneys next!'

'Don't even *think* it,' Kate warned, 'while Hardcastle is around. But it's my belief that all this is simply to test us. If we can stand up to Hardcastle and survive, then we're probably capable of coping with whatever France can throw at us. And that,' she added soberly, 'could be much worse than we can possibly imagine.'

'All the same,' said Priscilla, 'I do so hope we get there.'

Kate squeezed her hand. 'Me, too!' She grinned affectionately at her sister. 'And don't worry — you won't have to wear your hat when you're on the wards!'

That afternoon, as they entered the main hall, they were told that Matron wished to see them.

'Oh, Lord!' Priscilla groaned, 'I hope it's not that rat.'

'It's nothing personal,' said Megan Jones, a little, Welsh V.A.D. whose husband was in France. 'We've all been called in. You're the last two.' She would say no more — could not, in fact, for tears were suddenly trickling down her cheeks.

Two minutes later, sitting in front of Matron's desk instead of standing to attention as they usually did, they were told that Sister Hardcastle's brother had been killed in France. 'Defending Arras,' said Matron.

They could only stare at her stupidly, 'We had no idea,' said Kate at last, 'that she even had a brother, let alone that he was in France.'

'Sister Hardcastle,' said Matron drily, 'is not given to discussing her private life. Nor to wearing her heart upon her sleeve. And that, perhaps, is one of the reasons why she is such an excellent nurse. Nothing is allowed to detract from her utter dedication to the matter in hand. Even,' and here she allowed a quizzical little smile to play about her lips, 'if that lies in persuading her subordinates that they cannot be selective in what they do. Particularly if they hope to be sent to the Front.'

'Then . . . ' Priscilla raised her head, her eyes shining, 'we will be going?'

'That,' said Matron firmly, 'will depend entirely upon Sister Hardcastle's assessment of you at the end of six months.'

Six months! Kate groaned inwardly. Even with the carrot of service overseas dangling in front of them, that was going to be a long time to endure their present frustration.

'Don't worry,' said Matron as if she knew exactly what Kate was thinking, 'there'll soon be some real nursing to do. But in the meantime, I thought you should be aware that Sister Hardcastle's grief may be channelled into an even greater dedication to duty, with corresponding expectation of the same from her junior nurses. She does not, of course, know that I have spoken to all of you like this.'

'We understand,' said Kate.

'And I would also like to take this opportunity to thank you for all that you have done so far. I know that it cannot have been easy. But then,' she shrugged, 'life is not easy for anyone at the moment. Now,' she reached for a file from the formidable pile at her elbow, 'I suggest you go and have your tea. Unless, of course, there is anything you would like to ask me.'

'There is just one thing, Matron,' said Kate swiftly. 'Could you please give me the exact location of Arras?'

Clearly surprised by the question, Matron rose to her feet and beckoned them to join her in front of a large wall map. 'As you can see, it's in North-west France. Just south of Vimy.'

'So, we've been pushed out of Belgium altogether?'

'By no means,' said Matron crisply. 'Our front line extends right to the Belgian coast.' She turned and looked directly at Kate, 'Do you have anyone out there, Nurse?'

'Oh, no.' said Kate hurriedly. 'At least, only friends.' For Robert could surely be classified as a one-time friend. 'It's just that we don't see the newspapers very often, these days.'

'Good heavens!' Matron was clearly appalled by such a state of affairs. 'Well that, at least, is one thing I can do something about. In future, a current copy of the Times will be placed on the hall table each day. And there, of course, it must remain. No taking it away to read in your quarters.'

'Oh no, Matron! And thank you!'

Late that evening, several V.A.D's gathered on the attic landing around the solitary gas-ring on which they were allowed to brew their bed-time cocoa.

'Poor Sister Hardcastle!' said Megan Jones.

'It's so difficult to feel sorry for her,' Prissy pointed out. 'She seems to be fiercer than ever.'

'I doubt if she wants our pity,' Kate observed thoughtfully.

'The trouble is,' said the Honourable Angela Carstairs, 'that now her brother's gone, it's not likely she'll find another man willing to love her. And I'm not being cruel. Simply stating a fact.'

'She's not exactly an answer to a soldier's prayer,' Kate admitted. 'But I'm beginning to respect her, even like her a bit.'

She was also beginning to respect and like Angela Carstairs, admiring her disarming honesty. 'Ma was one of the parlourmaids when Pa got her in the family way,' she'd informed Kate soon after they'd met. 'Nothing unusual about that, of course. It was when he insisted upon marrying her that the fur began to fly.'

'And are they happy?' Kate had asked.

'Wonderfully so. Ostracised by the county, of course, but with seven children — I'm the eldest, the near bastard, you might say — Ma never has time to notice. She refuses to have Nannies.'

'Have you ever come across the Earl and Countess of Werrington in your travels?' Kate had asked casually.

'Only briefly when they were considering me as a possible match for their eldest son. Dropped me like a hot potato when they discovered my origins. The Earl's harmless enough, but she's an absolute Tartar. Rules the family with a rod of iron, I've heard. Sorry,' she'd added hastily, 'if they're bosom friends of yours.'

'Hardly bosom! We didn't exactly move in the same circles. In fact, I only met her once.'

'Once too often!' Angela had declared and for a moment, Kate had been tempted to tell her the circumstances of that one, unhappy occasion, but then decided it was quite ridiculous that she still remembered it, let alone wanted to talk about it.

★　★　★

It was on the day before the first contingent of wounded was due to arrive, that Kate and Priscilla discovered Angela pouring over the casualty list in the Times. 'Strange,' she said, stabbing at it with a

90

forefinger, 'that we were only talking about the Werringtons the other day. Their son's been killed at Ypres.'

For a moment, Kate thought she was about to faint. The white walls, the polished wooden floor, the flamboyant display of hot-house orchids sent over by some local land-owner, whirled around her. Dimly, she was aware that Priscilla was holding on to her arm.

'There's a photograph, too,' Angela said.

'I'll look,' and Priscilla bent quickly over the table.

It was an eternity before she straightened. 'It's George.'

Kate drew a long, calming breath then leaned forward to study a photograph of a dark-haired, heavily moustached young man in dress uniform. 'Lieutenant Lord George Holker,' read the caption, 'eldest son of the Earl of Werrington, died of wounds while leading his men in the battle for the Ypres canal.'

Poor George! What was it Robert had said of him? 'He loves everything to do with the earth.' But surely that had been English earth and not a patch of foreign soil?

That night, after a frustrating day of polishing and scrubbing surfaces already immaculate, Kate and Priscilla drank their cocoa in the privacy of their cubicle.

'Did you see Robert when you made that mad dash up to London?' Priscilla asked. 'You came back looking so grim, I never liked to ask.'

'Not Robert. But I saw his mother. And that was enough. I can't tell you how rude she was.'

'But did you ever hear from Robert?' Priscilla persisted.

'Not a word. Oh, it was no more than I expected for I'd asked his Aunt Bella not to tell him I'd been. But at the same time, I secretly hoped that she would. Silly of me, because I already knew it was hopeless. And that's especially true now that George is dead.'

'But wasn't he against the law of inheritance? Hank always said he was more American in his ideas than British.'

'Now that he really *is* the heir, he could feel quite differently about it. By the way, how is Hank?'

'Fine. Says he'd be over here like a shot if his father wasn't making him learn the family business from the bottom up.'

'And what is the family business?'

'Beans!' said Priscilla disparagingly. 'I ask you! A bean doesn't even have a bottom!'

★ ★ ★

Partly sheltered from pouring rain by the shattered roof timbers of what had once been the village estaminet, Robert opened his letters; one was from his father, the other from Aunt Bella. As always, he read his Aunt's first.

'Dearest Robert,

Tragic news, I'm afraid. George has been killed at Ypres. Your father received the sad news this morning and I am writing immediately to tell you. No doubt, he, too, will be writing for surely, at a time like this, all hatchets must be buried. I know

92

how bitterly you feel towards your mother for treating Kate Moneymoon as she did but I am sure that you are too big a person not to find it in your heart to forgive. And to write and comfort her.

As yet, we know little of the circumstances of George's death but I am sure that he died as he lived, doing his duty. I know that you, too, dearest boy, also do your duty as you see it and I can only hope and pray that when this ghastly war is over, you will return to claim your inheritance.

Forgive me for this brief note, I will write more fully in a day or two. Your devoted aunt, Bella.'

Unchecked, mingling with the raindrops, the tears coursed down Robert's cheeks. Kind, considerate George, who would never knowingly have hurt another living creature, who even turned aside to avoid crushing a beetle underfoot, had been killed. It was grossly unfair. Or was it, in fact, better for him to have died now at the beginning of this conflict, still believing in its cause, than to have endured the months, possibly years, of senseless slaughter that he feared lay ahead?

Knowing now what it must contain, he opened the letter from his father. It was as brief and to the point as Aunt Bella's.

'Dear Robert,

We have just heard that George has been killed. Your mother, as you can imagine is devastated.

Although you have chosen to ignore the many letters she has written, I hope and pray that you will now see fit to write to her. And then to reconsider your future. For you can no longer shrug off your responsibilities, nor escape the fact that you are now my heir.

In the devout hope that we shall soon hear from you, I remain your ever-loving Father.'

Poor Father! Not a mention of his own grief. Robert folded both letters and put them in his pocket. Tonight, when he was off duty, he would reply to them; to both of them. Although he doubted if he would ever forgive his mother for her callous treatment of Kate, common decency required a letter of sympathy, however brief. As to what his father considered his responsibilities; there would be time enough to consider those if he survived this bloody war.

9

Ranged at the top of the steps between the massive, stone pillars of the portico, they seem to be waiting to review the regiment rather than receive its wounded. Matron, of course is centre-stage, flanked by Sisters Hardcastle and Humphreys — the latter a thin-faced, sharp-eyed woman rumoured to be even more strict than her colleague — with behind them the trained hospital nurses and behind them again, a double row of Red Cross V.A.D's.

Surreptitiously, Kate glances along her row; at Priscilla, bright-eyed and expectant, clearly delighted that at last she is to 'have a go'; at Angela, equally as keen but hiding it under her customary veneer of cynicism; at Megan, moved almost to tears by the occasion and sniffing audibly. Kate wonders what she, herself, looks like. Apprehensive, she decides, although she knows that the worst cases are being sent straight to the big, general hospitals. 'Not that *our* boys won't need all your care and devotion,' Matron has assured them. Kate just hopes her's will be adequate.

Suddenly, a ragged cheer goes up from the little crowd of civilians congregated at the gates, and round the corner of the drive come three Red Cross ambulances.

'Is that all?' Priscilla can't believe her eyes.

The starched white cap in front of her turns briefly. 'Stretcher cases, first!'

They watch in silence as Matron moves to the rear of the first ambulance, Sister Hardcastle to the second and Sister Humphreys to the third, while the drivers and their passenger spring out and run round to swing open the doors. The first stretchers emerge, with large white placards pinned to their blanket-covered occupants. A few words are exchanged while these are read and then the bearers carry the stretchers carefully up the steps; each now accompanied by a staff nurse with a V.A.D. following respectfully behind. The process is repeated until the ambulances are empty.

A hush has fallen over the remaining nurses as they watch; many of the men seem already to have given up the ghost, their eyes closed, their cheeks as white as the bandages that many of them have around their heads. Kate is grateful that her name hasn't yet been called. But then, here and there, eyes open and lips curve into a tentative smile and she wishes it had been.

As the ambulances drive away, big, open-sided army wagons come rumbling up the drive, crammed with men in khaki uniforms; men with an arm in a sling or a leg in plaster, men whose bandages seem to be worn like a Glengarry, rakish over one eye, men who wave arms and crutches, a bed pan even, when they see the nurses now moving in a body down the steps. Some call out a greeting others burst into song, some are unashamedly weeping. Kate feels her own eyes fill and Megan is sobbing quietly.

'Moneymoons! Carstairs! Jones! Over here!' And down the steps they troop, tears knuckled firmly away, smiles of welcome pinned to their faces.

★ ★ ★

Taffy Thomas was from Cardiff. 'Copped me Blighty at Wipers, nurse. Real lucky, I was.' It took Kate over an hour's off-duty studying of Matron's wall map, now re-hung in the main hall, before she realised 'Wipers' was the British Tommy's interpretation of 'Ypres'. 'A Blighty', she already knew was any wound bad enough to require treatment at home; in Taffy's case, pieces of shrapnel lodged too close to his lungs for comfort. Eventually, there'd be an operation but not until he'd recovered from the effects of two days and two nights spent in a shell hole in No Man's Land, steadily losing blood, before they could bring him in.

96

'Thought I was a goner, nurse, an' no mistake. Especially when the bloke I was with died on the second day. But I thought about my old Mam, back in Tiger Bay, an' 'er gettin' the telegram and I thought I'd be buggered — beggin' yer pardon, nurse — if I'd let that 'appen to 'er again. She'd 'ad one already, see, about me dad. Drowned, when the Cressy went down.

His sentiments were echoed by Corporal Joe Bateman in the next bed. Hit in the shoulder by a sniper's bullet while leading a wiring party at La Baissée, he felt an almost pathological guilt that he hadn't finished the job. 'I kept tellin' me mates to let me finish before they carted me off but they wouldn't listen.' Most nights, in his sleep, he continued to tell them — often waking up the whole ward before a nurse reached him with a syringe.

He wasn't the only one. Several of the men cried out in their sleep, although frankly disbelieving when told about it next day.

'Soon have you better!' was the comment made at the foot of almost every bed during the daily round of doctors and nurses.

'And what then, doctor?' some of them dared to ask.

'Not up to me to say, old chap. Certainly a few weeks at home with the family. Then it'll be up to a Medical Board. Can't wait to get back out there, eh?'

'That's about it, doctor.'

But Kate knew otherwise. Often, bringing up the rear of the procession, she noticed how the forced smiles disappeared the moment the doctors had moved on to the next bed, to be replaced by expressions of utter dejection. Sometimes, she wondered if life would be easier for her in a hospital where injuries were so bad, patients either died or were medically discharged. No doubt, she would find out one day, if the war lasted long enough. Meantime, she was grateful that she was coping now, often even enjoying the feeling of being needed.

'Nurse, would you mind . . . ?' was a constant cry in the ward. Usually followed by a request to pick up something that had fallen to the floor, untie the knot of a parcel, open an envelope or even write a letter home. Often, the request was followed by 'Don't like to ask the *proper* nurses, you see!' but even that no longer rankled.

The only difficulty was that the requests had to be fitted in with what the 'proper' nurses had already told her to do. And they weren't requests — they were orders; not to carry them out to the letter would have meant the sharp end of Staff Nurse Holroyd's tongue.

Maud Holroyd was a nice enough woman, Kate thought, with her Buckinghamshire accent and habit of addressing every soldier as her 'duck', but unimaginative too, rigidly disciplined by years of hospital life.

Day duty began at 7 a.m. with bedpans and the taking of pulses and temperatures, followed by breakfast. Then it was bed-making with almost as much attention to their 'corners' as to their occupants. After that came the serious business of wound dressing. The new iodine dressings were always applied by a trained nurse but it was the V.A.D's who had to peel off the old, often from wounds that were still suppurating. No matter how carefully this was done, the winces of pain and hurriedly stifled exclamations were almost as difficult for Kate to bear as for the patient. It was Priscilla who seemed to have perfected the art. Never one to dirty her hands if she could possibly avoid it, the idea of her removing bloody and often stinking dressings, even with forceps, had worried Kate; quite unnecessarily as it turned out.

'Has anyone ever told you,' she heard her telling a patient one morning, 'that your eyes are as blue as periwinkles?'

And while the delighted man was assuring her that no-one ever had until now and would Nurse Moneymoon like to gaze into them for a little longer when she came off duty?, the bandage had been deftly removed and dropped into the bucket, en route for the sluice.

It wasn't, Kate had noticed, a system Priscilla used when a Staff Nurse was actually standing beside her; then, she would merely bend over her patient, but so solicitously that only he could see the enormous wink she was giving him.

It was a method Kate envied but found impossible to adopt herself. However, there were compensations, if they could be so called. When Staff Nurse Holroyd succumbed to a heavy cold just before Christmas, it was Kate who was given the less serious dressings to do on her own while Priscilla helped Sister Hardcastle with the others.

'As different as chalk from cheese, those

Moneymoons,' Kate overheard her telling the Staff Nurse when she was back on duty. 'But both invaluable in their way.'

Kate had almost dropped her tray of dirty mugs in her astonishment but instead had turned and tip-toed hurriedly away, coming back a moment or two later with much clattering and banging, enduring Sister Hardcastle's immediate 'A little less noise please, Nurse. You're a nurse, not a cowhand!' with secret amusement. Sister Hardcastle, she decided, was both chalk *and* cheese!

And never was her dual personality more apparent than on Christmas morning when Joe Bateman dared to kiss her soundly under the mistletoe, to the accompaniment of whistles and catcalls from the rest of the ward.

'Oh, my God!' breathed Angela Carstairs. 'He'll probably be shot at dawn! Court-martialled at the very least!'

But when Joe drew back from the embrace, his eyes rolling, he received no more than a token cuff around the ear and the demand that since he had so much surplus energy, he could help serve the tea; a chore he would have performed anyway.

Later in the day, they heard that Sister Hardcastle had been up most of the preceding night, nursing an amputee.

'An old friend, apparently,' one of the V.A.D's on the ward told Kate over a cup of coffee in the rest room. 'Lost both legs at Arras. Not much hope for him when he was admitted, I gather, but Hardcastle took one look at him and said '*He's* not going to die!' And he hasn't!'

'Too frightened to do otherwise?' Kate suggested.

'That's what I thought at first,' the other girl agreed, 'but it wasn't like that. She just held his hand and talked — about when they were kids and how he had to get better because he still owed her two pence from the last time they'd played Shove Ha'penny. She said that people often hear what's being said to them, even when they're in a coma. Anyway, it certainly worked in this case.'

'I'm beginning to think,' said Kate, 'that if I can be half as good a nurse as Hardcastle, I shall be all right!'

★   ★   ★

Somewhere behind the front line, in the region of Albert, Robert drove carefully down a narrow, rutted lane where the remnants of last night's snowstorm still lingered. Soon, according to his instructions, he should turn left, probably in the village that lay ahead; if it could still be called a village. Captured, then lost, then re-captured, it had been fought over for days with no time for either army to dig itself in.

He slowed and turned left by the remains of a building which a drunken sign proclaimed to be the Gendarmerie, took in with half an eye a cobbled square with a shattered fountain at its centre, and then went back to thinking about his Christmas mail. There had been a letter from Aunt Bella, of course, wrapped around a khaki scarf which he was now wearing, a totally unexpected little note from General Wavertree inside a packet of cigarettes, a more formal one from his father explaining that his mother was still too incapacitated by grief to write herself but would do so as soon as she was able and, most delightful of all, a little parcel from Mrs Moneymoon enclosing a pair of socks and a Balaclava and a letter.

She wrote how sorry they had been to hear of George's death. 'You must be devastated, also your parents.' The Moneymoons were all well and 'doing their bit'; Edmund still at the War Office, Kate and Prissy as V.A.D's on the Isle of Wight, Danny allowing himself to be practised upon as a 'casualty' by a local First Aid Detachment and she, herself, continuing to look after Moneymoon Manor in its new role under the British Red Cross. 'They call me a quartermaster and try to persuade me to wear a uniform but I tell them my apron is the only uniform I need! The Professor sends his best wishes. He still tutors a few undergraduates but finds time to help me with my inventories.'

The letter had filled him with nostalgia. Lost in a delightful dream in which he and Kate were leaning companionably over the gate of Toby's field, he rounded a bend — and came face to face with a German despatch rider.

Unable to believe his eyes, he braked and blinked hard, but there was no doubt of it; the man was in field-grey and wore the familiar, spiked helmet. Like Robert, he had a rifle slung across his back. For a long moment, they continued to stare at each other and then, simultaneously, switched off their engines.

'Fröliche Weihnachten!' said the German.

'Happy Christmas!' replied Robert.

They smiled at each other almost shyly and then the German nodded at Robert's machine. 'You are happy with your B.S.A.?'

'Not as good as my Harley Davidson back home. But all right. And your B.M.W.?'

'It, too, is — all right. But I also have a Harley Davidson — in Germany.'

His name was Franz Muller, he told Robert. He had been at Heidelberg University when war broke out, and had visited Oxford during one of his vacations. Had Robert visited Heidelberg? No? Then he must do so when this silly war was over. Because 'silly' — didn't he agree? — was what it was. 'We must make sure that it does not happen again, my friend.'

Leaving their machines, they stood in the middle of the road and Robert produced General Wavertree's cigarettes. As they smoked, they talked about their previous lives, about their families. Franz had a younger sister, still at school, and his father was a doctor. Robert explained that his older brother had just been killed and that he was now heir to an earldom. 'Not that I shall be any good at it, as George would have been.'

Franz studied him intently. 'I think you could be very good at it. Not, perhaps, as your brother would have been. He was, perhaps a little traditional? But life will never be the same after this war and there will be need of men with vision.' Suddenly, he gave a great whoop of laughter and smote Robert on the back, 'Of men who ride Harley Davidsons!'

Solemnly, they exchanged addresses and then Franz said, 'Now I will take you back to where you should have turned. Ahead, you will find many Fritzes, as I believe you call us, who may not have the good sense to see what a splendid fellow you are!'

But later, Robert discovered that all along the front line fraternisation had taken place, even to the playing of an impromptu game of football. No doubt there'd be hell to pay when the High Command heard about it but Franz had been proved right — war was a silly business.

He hoped that Franz Muller would survive the war. And that they would meet again and continue their discussion. Meanwhile, when he wrote to thank General Wavertree for his present, it might be better not to mention that he'd actually shared it with a 'Hun'!

10

They stand together in the bows of the Cross-Channel ferry as it chugs towards France. It is a beautiful August day but they still wear their long black cloaks, although the velour hats have given way to little straw bonnets. But these are also black, relieved only by white strings tied under the chin.

'We look more like a group of war widows than nurses,' Priscilla has grumbled upon more than one occasion.

But she has soon forgotten her frustrations in the excitement of finally being sent to France.

'It's no picnic over there,' Sister Hardcastle has cautioned. 'There is little comparison between a base hospital in France and a convalescent home on the Isle of Wight.'

'I think Hardcastle was secretly green with envy when she saw us off,' Angela Carstairs says now. 'Even though she'd got Sergeant Hopkins to drool over.'

'We've certainly been proved wrong there,' Kate observes. 'There'll be wedding bells before long.'

'But imagine looking after a man with no legs for the rest of your life!' Priscilla shudders dramatically.

'You wouldn't mind if you really loved him,' Megan is sure about that. 'In fact, I sometimes think I wouldn't mind what injury my Gareth suffered as long as he was alive and out of the fighting.'

Kate puts a comforting arm around her shoulders but says nothing. The Germans have recently started to fire asphyxiating shells into the British lines and the effects of the poison-gas on the lungs of those forced to breathe it in, have been horrendous. Surely death would be preferable to spending the rest of a short life in agony.

'At least,' she says, deliberately changing the subject, 'we're all still together.'

They all nod agreement; for in the last few months they have formed ties that seem set to endure whatever life may now have in store for them.

When a patient has died, they have wept unashamedly upon each other's shoulders; stood up for each other when they've made mistakes and shared their precious parcels from home. They have even formed themselves into an impromptu concert party. Kate and Priscilla's demonstration of the tango has brought down the house at Saturday evening concerts, rivalled only by Angela's interpretation of a company sergeant-major drilling a raw recruit and Megan's heart-felt rendering of 'A Little Grey Home in the West'. Whether through mirth or emotion, there wasn't a dry eye in the audience.

At the moment, they are wondering if it would be proper for them to join in the singing that has started up. For the ferry is packed with troops, mostly the new recruits of Kitchener's Army, coming out for the first time, but with a scattering of old hands among them. A few of them have started to sing 'Oh, you beautiful doll', with saucy glances in the direction of the V.A.D's and this they studiously ignore. But when the first bars of 'Tipperary' ring out, Angela actually turns and conducts those troops standing near them. They love it and follow with 'Hello, hello, who's your lady friend?'

So engrossed are they, no-one notices at first that the coast of France is now visible, with the huge marquees of the Casualty Clearing Stations billowing like giant mushrooms above a rash of smaller tents. When they do, the singing ends on a vociferous 'Are we down-hearted? No!', although Kate observes that it's the uninitiated who shout the loudest.

Soon, the ferry is nudging its way into harbour and they get ready to disembark. To her surprise, Priscilla finds she is searching for Kate's hand, something she hasn't done since childhood. They

106

look at each other and smile. This is what they've been waiting for, even though it does feel rather like the first day at school.

'Dear Ma and Pa,

We have arrived! And although I'm not allowed to say exactly *where*, I can tell you that it's a château — a beautiful, fairy-tale place with pepper-pot towers and battlements and a paved courtyard in front of a massive, iron-studded door which is reached by a double flight of steps. Even Angela, whose own home must be very grand, was impressed.

Because of the steps, the patients are brought in and out by a side door so even the V.A.D's are allowed to use the front entrance; though once inside we have to slink away to the back staircase en route for our quarters up in the attics. Prissy and I are sharing a tiny room where we will have to take it in turns to dress and undress but which has a window facing west across lush French countryside. If it weren't for the troop trains that rattle through a mile or so away, and the rumble of the guns which we can hear if the wind is in the right direction, it would be easy to forget why we are here. But we are at least thirty miles from the lines, so there is no need to worry about us although we are a little apprehensive about tomorrow when we start work; Prissy and I on a medical ward and Angela and Megan on a surgical. We've been told we will be very busy, the result of a second German offensive near Ypres, with heavy casualties at a place called Hooge.

Although we are now at the heart of things, we're less likely to know what's happening elsewhere, so the odd newspaper would be gratefully received.

Prissy will write next time, but don't worry if that's not for a while. Our love to Danny, and Jane and Emma, who must find life very different working in the munition factory after the laundry.

Your loving daughter, Kate'.

What a strange and futile world we live in, Kate thought as she enveloped her letter. Jane and Emma busy making the instruments of war while Prissy and I do our best to patch up the results.

★ ★ ★

About twenty miles east of the château, Robert Holker's thoughts were similar to Kate's. It was now a year since he'd been sent out, a year in which he had turned from an idealistic student into a seasoned campaigner. Now, the sole purpose of each day was to endure; survival was something beyond his control, to be left to Fate to decide. To think of the past had become a luxury that he did not often allow himself. More than ever, now, he was grateful to be a Don R, for it was a solitary existence, and that way he didn't grow so close to other men that their death, if it came, was almost *his* death.

He'd learned his lesson at Hill 60 when the young lad he'd befriended because he was so like Danny, had died in his arms, choking on his own blood. It was as well, he'd reasoned later, that he hadn't taken a commission; better by far to walk alone.

Recently, carrying despatches to Divisional HQ behind the lines, his eye had followed a hovering bird — a buzzard, perhaps? — and he'd noticed a château perched on a rocky outcrop among the trees. A fairy-tale castle, he'd thought, all towers and spires and curlicues, its roofs shining in the sunlight. For a full minute, he'd stopped his bike and gazed up at it, wondering if the owner still lived there, or if he'd fled before the tides of war. A moment or two later, he'd found the answer when he'd passed a convoy of ambulances turning off the road in the direction of the château. Momentarily, he'd allowed his thoughts to turn to Kate. Apart from a postcard from Danny which had told him nothing of what he wanted to hear, other than that 'Kate and Prissy are still on the Isle of Wight, the lucky things!', he'd heard nothing from the Moneymoons. Perhaps it was as well; one less person to worry about and one less to worry about him. Kate had been right, after all, to refuse him.

★ ★ ★

No-one had warned them about the calls. What sounded like a battalion of buglers but was, in fact, no more than four, came to stand on the hillside at the rear of the château and awakened them at six.

'Réveille!' Kate decided, running to the window.

'I thought it was an express train at least!' Priscilla

109

pulled the sheet back over her head.

But Kate remained standing at the window. There was something almost Arcadian about the scene; the men standing straight and tall, god-like, their raised bugles reflecting the early morning sunshine, the clear, pure calls echoing across the valley.

As the last triumphant notes died away, their arms fell and the gods turned into a quartet of soldiers, wiping their mouths on their sleeves, talking, beginning the descent back to the château.

'Wake up, Prissy! I'll wash and dress first and then it's your turn.'

Half an hour later, the gods were back on the hillside. 'Call for breakfast?' Kate wondered.

It was. In their mess, a big, stone-flagged outhouse next to the kitchens, they drank tea and consumed lumpy porridge, but refused bacon; the mere sight of it swimming in fat almost more than their stomachs could stand. Around them, nurses laughed and chattered with the confidence of old hands. Angela and Megan were nowhere to be seen.

Their ward was at the front of the château, a long, graciously-proportioned room with high ceilings, elaborately carved. The walls were stripped down to bare plaster but a huge, marble fireplace, intricately scrolled with gold leaf, remained as a reminder of former glory.

There were so many beds, Kate lost count before she'd walked halfway down it. Breakfast was being served by four V.A.D.'s. Two Staff Nurses were bent over a central table.

'About time, too!' hissed an exhausted-looking

V.A.D., as she rushed past. One of the Staff Nurses looked up and, to Kate's relief, gave them a broad smile. 'You must be the Moneymoons!'

They agreed that they were and hoped they weren't late.

'Don't worry! If it were left to the night staff, we'd have been here at least an hour ago!' Today, she informed them, they would be shown the ropes by the two daytime V.A.D's who would then be on standby. 'Since Ypres, they've worked non-stop so they deserve a break.'

Initially, Sybil Marshall and Eve Grange treated them with the slightly disdainful air of the experienced forced to collaborate with the inexperienced. But as the morning wore on and Kate and Priscilla, obviously eager to learn, plied them with questions, they relaxed into two, desperately tired, normal young women.

'We've had severe bronchitic cases for some months now,' Sybil Marshall told them. 'The result of chlorine gas. Men trying to cough up what remains of their lungs until they're literally blue in the face. And many of them are blinded by it. Apparently, it needs only one minute's exposure to do the most dreadful damage. Can you imagine anything more diabolical? I just hope we've started using it on *them*!'

'At home,' Kate remarked, 'we were told that masks were being made to stop the men breathing it in. That there was no need to worry.'

'Well, they would say that, wouldn't they?' Eve Grange said scornfully. 'Or Kitchener wouldn't get half his recruits. The masks are only cotton-wool pads soaked in ammonia and tied over the nose and mouth.'

'But better than nothing,' Sybil conceded. 'And no doubt they're working on something more substantial. I just hope they'll be quick about it.'

One of the beds at the far end of the ward was curtained off. Inside, the hunched figure of an elderly woman in black crouched beside the bed, holding the hand of a young man who lay propped up on pillows, his face blue, his breath wheezing in painful gasps.

'A cup of tea, Mrs Perkins?' Sybil asked gently.

The woman looked up, her lined face like putty. 'Oh yes, please dear. If only Albert could wake up and have one with me.'

'Albert's her only son,' Sybil told them while she made the tea in the cubbyhole of a kitchen at the end of the ward. 'Her husband was killed in the Boer War when Albert was only five.'

'Poor woman!' said Prissy.

'And poor Albert! He probably won't last the day.'

'I suppose it's something,' Kate pondered, 'that she'll be with him at the end.'

Sybil nodded. 'It will help her to bear her grief. And Albert was still conscious when she arrived, so that's something, I suppose. But she's so grateful to the Army for bringing her out to see him! It makes my blood boil! It simply doesn't occur to her that if it wasn't for them, he'd still be doing his milk round back home in Devon.'

Kate nodded, at the same time wondering how long it would be before she and Prissy became equally as disillusioned. Perhaps it was something she would discuss with the others when they met that evening; if they weren't all too exhausted!

* * *

'To begin with,' Angela said, 'we overslept. Can you imagine a more dreadful start to the day than arriving on the ward half an hour late with our caps askew, our aprons all anyhow and our stockings like concertinas? *And* with no breakfast inside us.'

'But surely you couldn't sleep through those dreadful bugles?' Priscilla protested.

'That's what Sister said. But we're at the front of the château and I suppose we were exhausted after travelling. And the day didn't improve. The trouble was, word had got around that I'm an Hon., so you can imagine how scathing Sister was. In future, she said, Hon. had better stand for 'on time' and not for Honourable, which I clearly wasn't! And I had to endure all this with the other V.A.D's sniggering in the background and the dreamiest M.O. you've ever seen trying not to laugh.'

'I'm sure you managed to rise above it,' Kate soothed.

'I'd hardly call scrubbing out the sluice, rising above anything!'

'Actually, it wasn't as bad as Angie's making out,' Megan assured them, 'because all the men were on her side. They kept calling her 'Honourable Sister', which was like a red rag to a bull when Sister was in earshot.'

113

Angela laughed. 'I had to tell them to stop it, in the end. Anyway, enough about me. How did you two get on?'

They told her about the bronchitics, mentioning Albert Perkins who had died just before they came off duty. 'What were your patients like?' Priscilla asked, not wanting to dwell on the memory of Albert's mother, sobbing uncontrollably but still pathetically grateful that she was to be allowed to stay until tomorrow when he would be buried with full, military honours in the cemetery below the château.

'Much the same as the ones we've been used to,' Megan answered her question, 'but more severe, naturally. And some, like your Albert, will die. Shrapnel all over their bodies. And some of it so deep that the lucky ones who survive will have it in them as long as they live.'

'A lot of amputations,' Angela took up the grim tale, 'mostly caused by gas gangrene.'

'That's where Angie's heart-throb comes in,' Megan chuckled. 'Gas gangrene's his speciality.'

'Tall, dark — and French,' said Angela. 'What more could any nurse want? His name's Pierre. Pierre Montarial.'

'You're on Christian name terms already?' Kate teased.

'Well no, not exactly! To be honest, I don't think he has time for anyone except his patients. He's a brilliant doctor, apparently.'

'Some people have all the luck,' Priscilla sighed.

'Well, get yourself a transfer to surgical. Just as long as I can stay there, too!'

114

11

August gave way to September and the chestnut trees in the little cemetery were tinged with gold when Kate and Priscilla visited Albert Perkin's grave as they'd promised his mother to do. Already, the line of white crosses in which he lay had lengthened and soon there would be more. For rumour had it that an attempt to breach the German lines was to be made before winter. In the wards of the château, steps were taken to accommodate the heavy losses that were bound to ensue; men who'd been considered unfit to travel could hardly believe their ears when told they'd been passed fit for Blighty; extra beds were somehow fitted into wards previously considered crammed to capacity and side wards set up in corridors; senior nursing staff were sent up to Casualty Clearing Stations just behind the lines; and Kate was moved to the surgical ward.

'I see from your records that you are experienced in the dressing of wounds,' said the Sister on her first morning. 'As you may have heard, several nurses are being moved up, myself included. We are leaving this morning. So I am giving you special responsibility for three cases of gas gangrene. There will be a Sister on the burns ward but she is only to be contacted in direst emergency. Is that understood?'

'But . . . ' Kate began.

'But me no buts, nurse! You'll find your specials in the corner at the end of the ward. Good luck!'

She found them without difficulty — marooned at the end of a line of empty beds and utterly despondent.

'Everyone else has been sent back to Blighty and us three are still here. It's not fair.' Their spokesman was a young corporal who looked, Kate had to admit, perfectly healthy, apart from a cradle over one of his legs.

'We could have hobbled to the ambulances, even helped with some of the cases,' complained the man in the next bed who also had a cradle over his legs.

'I couldn't,' the third man admitted. 'There's a piece of shrapnel still in my right thigh. But I could have managed on crutches.' They all glared at her, clearly holding her personally responsible.

Her first thought — that their condition simply wasn't serious enough for home sick leave — she kept to herself; for that would mean them rejoining their regiments in the line. But then she remembered that Sister had mentioned gas gangrene, and all she knew about the condition was that it could sometimes lead to amputation and often death. But these men looked so healthy. If only Angie's heart-throb, Dr Montarial, would deign to appear.

'I'll try and find out what's happening,' she told the men with a confidence she didn't feel. 'Meanwhile, how about some tea?'

That, they agreed, would help a lot and they were sorry, they hadn't meant to take it out on her.

Half an hour later, as she was tidying their beds,

the Cortège appeared.

It was Prissy who'd given the name to the daily round of Matron, Senior Medical Officer (in this case, a Colonel), Ward Sister, Ward Medical Officer and Staff Nurse, 'because they all look so solemn!' This Cortège, however, was rather different. To begin with, the Sister and Staff Nurse were unknown to Kate and probably 'borrowed' from Special Surgical and the Ward Medical Officer, instead of occupying his prescribed place in the procession was actually walking in tandem with the Senior Medical Officer. Only Matron looked as she always did; aloof and inscrutable. Kate, standing to attention beside her three beds, was careful not to catch her eye. In any case, her gaze was riveted on the Ward Medical Officer who was deep in conversation with the Colonel. Angie had been right; he was tall, dark — and undeniably French. And he was also — and her heart gave a sudden, totally unexpected lurch — not only looking straight at *her*, Kate Moneymoon, but actually smiling. And, she, conveniently forgetting the unwritten law that V.A.D's in a military hospital are totally invisible to the upper echelons, was smiling back.

Now, he was turning to the S.M.O. 'These are the men I was telling you about, Colonel. And this is their charming nurse.' They might have been making conversation at a cocktail party, so friendly and informal did he sound. Indeed, the Colonel actually began to extend his hand towards her before remembering where he was. And there was no way he could ignore Matron's hiss of outrage.

'Really, doctor!'

But Pierre Montarial was oblivious to everything except the matter in hand. 'I shall be back shortly, nurse. Please do not go away!'

As if she would — or could! 'Yes, sir! I mean, no, sir!'

'Such obedience!' he murmured softly. And actually winked as he walked past her. When they were gone, Kate dared to glance back over her shoulder; her 'specials' were grinning broadly.

'Taken a proper shine to you, he has, nurse!'

Half an hour later, he was back, beckoning her to join him at the table in the centre of the ward. 'I would like to talk to you about your patients, nurse, but in private. Could you perhaps make me a cup of your excellent English tea in the kitchen.'

This, at least, was normal practice. Overworked medical staff were frequently grateful for a hasty cup of tea or coffee, to save them going back to their mess. She led the way, deeply conscious of three pairs of eyes boring into her back. This would take some living down!

The tea made, they sat companionably either side of a small table. His eyes, she noticed, weren't so much black as a very dark blue. But now, they were unsmiling. He came straight to the point.

'You have heard of gas gangrene, nurse!'

She nodded. 'But I haven't nursed it.'

'It is perhaps the most diabolical method of warfare to date. Chlorine gas is terrible but at least you know immediately that you have inhaled it. With gas gangrene, it can be many days, sometimes weeks, before the symptoms appear. You know of course, about the effects of shrapnel?' Again, Kate nodded. 'But these are special shrapnel bullets with holes in them. Inside the bullet is a phosphorus powder which is highly poisonous. The wound that the bullet makes may be slight. It is when the patient is considered to be well on the way to recovery that the phosphorus — by now in the patient's bloodstream — begins to spread through his body. Before long, the liver and kidneys start to disintegrate and the man is in agony. Death, if he is lucky, will come quickly. If he is not lucky . . . ' he shrugged expressively.

Kate shivered. 'And my three patients . . . ?'

Pierre Montarial nodded soberly. 'They could well be classic examples. But I need to know. I need to observe their wounds.' And now his face was alive with an extraordinary passion. 'Much valuable work has already been done by my French contemporaries and also by those Americans interested in a war so far removed from their own hemisphere. But the English, I fear, are far too busy dealing with their enormous casualties to have time for research.'

'So, am I right in thinking that those three men have been kept back as part of your research?'

'I fear so. But remember, nurse, before you condemn me out of hand for my lack of 'esprit de corps', that such research is vital to future treatment. It's true I could have let them go back to England with the others and *hope* that some English doctor would follow my instructions — to observe and to treat as I suggested. But of this, I could not be sure. And here, during this lull before the battle begins again, you and I can watch over them.' He

119

hesitated for a moment and then leaned across the table, his eyes holding hers. 'What do you say, my little English nurse? Will you help me?'

Kate could only gaze at him, hypnotised by the man's personality and charm. But that was no way, she reminded herself, for a responsible V.A.D. to feel. Of course, she would carry out his instructions implicitly, but because he was the Medical Officer in charge of her specials and not because he was having such a disturbing effect upon her peace of mind. Not since Robert . . . But that was an avenue down which she refused to go. Involuntarily, she shook her head to rid herself of her treacherous thoughts and saw the light fade from his eyes.

'I am sorry, nurse. I should not have asked such a thing of you. To hold back men from seeing their dear ones again, goes much against the grain. The grain of an English oak, solid, strong — and stubborn!'

'Oh, no! I didn't mean that at all! Of course I will help you. I will do exactly what you tell me. I am honoured — yes, honoured! — to be asked.' Fearful that he might withdraw his request, Kate put out her hand to him, across the table; and just as quickly withdrew it. Pierre Montarial burst out laughing.

'My little English nurse! So prim! And so proper!' And then, as he saw the blush steal up her cheeks, added gently, 'And so pretty!' Now it was his turn to cover her hand with his. 'I am sorry, I must not tease you. And I am so grateful. Between us, we shall be an excellent team; you with your English scruples, I with my complete lack of them!'

'You said something about treatment.' Kate was

trying desperately to put the conversation back on to some sort of professional footing. It was as well no-one wanted to take *her* pulse at that moment!

Immediately, he became serious. 'This is the situation. The two men with leg wounds had pieces of shrapnel removed at the Clearing Station. It was near the surface and presented no problem. So I do not yet know what sort of bullet was used. But the wounds are not healing as they should have done. So today, we will begin to draw off the pus and then to irrigate the wounds with a solution of hypochlorus acid. This has been found to be greatly beneficial, if it can be started in time.'

'And the man with the shrapnel still embedded in his thigh?'

'I shall operate this afternoon. If I remove a phosphorus bullet, we shall start treatment immediately. Either way, he has a good chance of recovery. It is the other two about whom we should be anxious. They say that they lay in No Man's Land for many hours before they could be brought in. So the poison may already be in the bloodstream.'

Kate nodded. 'Yes, I see. May I ask what you are going to tell the men? At the moment, they don't understand why they've been kept back.'

'I think we explain that they are to receive special treatment but do not mention that it may be unsuccessful. It is important that they do not lose heart. To give up, is usually to die. Shall we go now, to talk to them?'

★ ★ ★

They lay sprawled on the two beds in the tiny room, cradling mugs of the inevitable cocoa. Angie was disconsolate. 'It was bad enough being moved off surgical without being told I was to nurse the bloody Boche!'

'Language!' Megan reproved automatically.

'Language, my foot! That's one thing you can be sure of — they will be bloody! And as far as I'm concerned, they can bleed to death. In fact,' she brightened visibly, 'perhaps that's what I'll do. I'll peel off their bandages, let down their pulleys and take away their cradles. How about that?'

There was a short silence while they considered the ethics of such a situation. 'You couldn't,' said Kate finally. 'You're too good a nurse.'

'And think how you'd feel if the German nurses treated our boys like that,' Megan pointed out.

'All right,' Angela conceded, for they all knew Megan hadn't heard from her husband for several weeks now and was desperately worried. 'For you, Megs, and for no other reason, I'll look after the bastards. But that doesn't mean I'll be nice to them.'

'Are there any at the moment?' Priscilla asked.

'None! I've spent the day helping to get their ward ready. I've lost count of the number of beds I've made.'

'Me, too,' said Priscilla who had stayed on the medical ward. 'It's certainly going to be a mighty big push.'

'Sorry to have left you on medical on your own,' Kate felt constrained to say. And she *was* sorry to have left Prissy, if not the ward.

'That's all right,' said Prissy equably. 'From what I hear, we shall all be playing General Post before long.'

'What did you think of our Pierre?' Angela asked Kate.

She had been expecting the question. 'He seemed quite pleasant. As you said, very French.'

For a moment, she was afraid Angie would press her further but instead she started to talk about the possibility of a couple of days' standby while they waited for the wounded to arrive. Standby was the last thing Kate wanted at the moment, so she ceased to listen, letting her mind review the extraordinary happenings of the day.

She remembered the care with which Pierre Montarial had explained to the men that they could be suffering the effects of gas gangrene and that the treatment — 'like all treatment that is good for you!' — would be painful. 'But because it is true, as the poet has it, that 'music soothes the savage breast' — although, in fact, none of you are in the least savage! — I have brought my gramophone.'

And it was true! Kate could hardly believe her eyes when she saw that he really had brought in his portable gramophone and an orderly to wind it up and turn over the records, while he and Kate set up the elaborate system of tubes leading into and away from the men's wounds. Although these were not deep, they were suppurating badly and Kate dared not look at the men's faces as drainage tubes were inserted.

'Sing!' Pierre told them. 'Sing as if your lives depended upon it!' And sing they did, even though some of the top notes of 'Tipperary' sounded more like howls of agony.

'Now,' he said, 'we come to the part that will do you the most good.' He turned to the orderly. 'We will have Beethoven's Pastoral Symphony for this, if you please. Something calm, beautiful and inspiring. And proving that some good things have come out of Germany.'

'Are you sure he's a doctor?' one of the men whispered to Kate when Pierre's back was turned. 'He's more like a bloomin' music hall artist?'

Kate grinned at him. 'Believe me, he's a brilliant doctor. Trust him.'

'Don't have much option, do I?' But the man stoically endured the insertion of another tube down which the solution of hypochlorus acid was to be poured. 'It looks like my Alfie's fretwork,' he said with a grimace, when several smaller tubes were added to the main tube.

Pierre laughed. 'You must write and tell him so. Now, I am going to show nurse how to inject this fluid into the tubes and thereby into your wound. Although it will feel very cold and not at all soothing, remember that it will be flushing away the poison. Ready, nurse?' And he filled a large syringe from the enormous container he had placed between the two beds. 'This will have to be done every three hours, I'm afraid.'

Afterwards he told Kate, 'I have arranged for other nurses to administer the solution throughout the night but you will be the one to have overall responsibility.'

She didn't demur. Whatever this man decreed, she

124

now realised, would surely be done.

Before she went off duty, the patient who had had surgery was back on the ward. The bullet that had been removed from his thigh had indeed contained phosphorus poison.

'So in the morning, Pierre told her, 'when he has recovered a little, we shall set up little Alfie's fretwork.'

Kate found she could hardly wait for the morning.

★   ★   ★

At daybreak, like the distant rumble of a giant's stomach, the guns began. Even before Réveille sounded, Kate and Priscilla were awakened.

'It's always like this before a push,' a knowledge-able V.A.D. told them at breakfast. 'Softening up the enemy lines, destroying their barbed wire, generally giving the Boche a taste of what's coming.'

'How long will it go on for?' Kate asked.

The girl shrugged. 'Until the top brass consider they've wiped out enough Germans, I suppose.'

'But don't they bring up reinforcements?'

'They do, of course, but that's where the strategy comes in. The German's don't know where the attack will be and they can hardly reinforce the whole front line. My brother,' she added with an infuriating air of superiority, 'is a Major in the Royal Artillery, so I know about these things.'

'Edmund would know,' Priscilla told Kate. 'He's *our* brother,' she added sweetly, for the benefit of the pompous V.A.D., 'at the War Office.'

'Oh, a *desk* wallah!' said the other girl disparagingly and turned her attention to the V.A.D. on her other side.

Priscilla drew in her breath sharply and Kate put a restraining hand on her arm. The girl had probably got out of bed on the wrong side. But if she had, then so had the rest of the medical staff. Everyone seemed tense and irritable with nerves stretched to breaking point.

'It is always like this when the guns start,' Pierre Montarial told her when she reported for duty and had commented on the atmosphere in the château. 'We know then that it will not be long before we are all rushed off our feet. Part of us wants it never to happen and another part cannot wait for it to start so that we are at least doing something. You and I are lucky, Kate, that we have work to do.'

She couldn't prevent a startled glance at his use of her Christian name.

'Don't worry! I shall be discretion itself when others are with us but when we are alone — well,' he shrugged, 'it is good, is it not, to be friends as well as colleagues? Now,' he became brisk, 'let me tell you about our patients. I have already examined their wounds. One man is doing well, the wound is beginning to heal. The other, Alfie's father,' he shook his head, 'is not so well. I may be forced to amputate the limb and even then recovery will not be certain. But first, we must start the hypochlorus acid treatment on our third man, on whom I operated yesterday. Of him, I am very hopeful that we were in time.'

This time, out of deference to the man whose

126

condition was worsening and who now looked distinctly unwell, the gramophone was not played. But the orderly still remained to help Kate. He was a big, brawny man with feet so flat, they reminded Kate of dinner plates as he paddled down the ward. His name was Bert, he told her, and the Doctor had said he must help Kate in whatever way he could. 'I'm good at lifting, nurse, and there are some things a bloke likes another bloke to do for him.'

That was true, Kate agreed tactfully and introduced him to the sluice with its racks of gleaming white bedpans, while she concentrated upon irrigating the wounds and taking temperatures.

That of the sick man was much higher than it should be and his pulse was weakening. 'Take it every hour,' said Pierre during one of his visits.

Ominously, it continued to rise as the morning wore on and at midday, Pierre decided to amputate the leg 'First, though, I will give him a transfusion.'

Kate looked at him, startled. 'Of blood?'

'Yes. I take it you know little of the procedure?'

'Only that it is essential the donor's blood matches the patient's. And that, even then, there is a danger of the blood clotting and causing a thrombosis.'

He nodded. 'You are right. But now, thanks to those clever Yankees, our knowledge is greatly improved. Sodium citrate, mixed in the correct proportion with the blood, will prevent clotting. I have already discovered our patient's group by using a serum. A transfusion *before* the operation will greatly increase his chances of survival.'

Between them, they set up a drip apparatus above the bed. The man was now so weak, he hardly murmured when the tube was connected into the vein of his arm.

'Watch carefully and before long you should see the pallor of his face begin to diminish,' Pierre told her.

'It will be like a miracle,' said Kate.

He shook his head. 'Not a miracle, just another example of the extraordinary paradox of human behaviour. On the one hand, man devises ever more diabolical methods of killing his fellows, and on the other ever more brilliant ways of rescuing him from the carnage.'

They stood together by the bedside, watching while the level of the liquid in the upturned flask slowly diminished. Kate found that she was holding her breath but when, as Pierre had forecast, a faint wash of colour began to spread across the man's pallid cheeks, she let it out in a long sigh of satisfaction. Pierre glanced down at her.

'It is good, is it not? And indeed, I have seen worse cases than this in the course of my career who have recovered.'

She looked at him curiously. 'What sort of medicine did you practise in civilian life?'

He smiled. 'I divided myself very neatly into two halves. One half ran an expensive clinic on the Right Bank of the Seine in Paris, where I prescribed pills and potions for women who would not have suffered from half their complaints had they not eaten so much rich food. And with the money they were happy to pay me for this simple advice, I ran

128

another clinic on the Left Bank, for those who suffered real illness but could not afford to pay for their treatment. A sort of French Robin Hood, but in this case it was all legal and, as you say, above board. And you, Kate? What did you do? I cannot imagine that you were content to live a life of leisure.'

'Indeed not! My sister and I helped our mother to run a laundry business. And we were quite good at it!'

'I'm sure you were. My mother, too, was a 'blanchiseuse'. But in the laundry of the hospital where I was a student. I owe a great deal to my mother.'

'She must be proud of you now,' said Kate.

He shrugged. 'You know mothers! She would be proud of me if I were a chimney sweep!'

★   ★   ★

Alfie's father came back from surgery looking like a ghost, but there was nothing ghostly about the swathes of bandage over the stump of his right leg. 'Will he make it?' Kate asked Pierre.

'We must hope.'

For the first time, she noticed lines of fatigue about his mouth and dark shadows beneath his eyes. 'Was it a very difficult operation?'

'Not difficult but I had to work quickly. There was no anaesthetist available until much later so I used a spinal analgesic. But I'll give him a shot of morphine now and then we'll put more blood into him.'

'We have plenty?' Kate asked anxiously as they

connected a flask to the man's arm.

'Oh, yes. Always before a push, we are sent gallons of it.'

'And in an emergency, I suppose we could always give it ourselves?' Kate asked thoughtfully.

'Indeed, yes,' he agreed but with his mind now fully occupied with his patient. 'We must still irrigate his stump, I'm afraid, Kate. Every three hours.'

'I can do that,' she said swiftly. 'Just show me what to do and I'll see to it for the rest of the day and night. You get some rest.' She could have been sorting out Priscilla, she reflected, so little notice was she now taking of the difference in their status. And he, too, accepted the suggestion without protest.

'We will do the first dressing together and then you can continue. But I warn you, it will not be a pretty sight.'

She was, she assured him jauntily, as right as ninepence — or nine francs, if he preferred it! But in the event, it took all her self-control not to show her revulsion at the sight of the raw, red flesh. But at least the man was still mercifully unconscious.

'It appears to be clean,' said Pierre with satisfaction, 'but we must still soak lint in our solution and place it over the stump, so.'

After the leg had been loosely bandaged, Kate glanced at her watch. 'I'll renew the dressing at six and again at nine.'

'Thank you!' And barely repressing a yawn, he left the ward.

Kate was due off duty at eight but there was no

ward sister to order her to go and the V.A.D. who was supposed to relieve her raised no objection when told that Kate was staying on. 'I've plenty of other jobs to do and I wasn't exactly looking forward to it!'

When Kate changed the dressing at midnight, the effect of the morphine was beginning to wear off and the man had started to moan, rolling his head from side to side on his pillow as if trying to escape from the pain. Gently, Kate wiped the beads of sweat from his forehead and laid a cold compress across it. As she did so, he opened his eyes and looked straight into hers. 'Hallo, Emily, love!' he whispered and relapsed immediately into unconsciousness.

Kate changed the empty flask of blood for a full one, then felt for the man's pulse. It was little more than a flutter. She frowned. She'd be damned if she'd lose one of her 'specials'!

Suddenly, she remembered how Sister Hardcastle had 'talked' her Sergeant back into life. Swiftly, she looked on the man's chart for his first name, then placed a glass of water conveniently within her reach, drew up a chair and picked up the hand that was lying on the coverlet, and in which the grime of the trenches was still deeply ingrained.

'Hello, Ted, love,' she said, quietly but distinctly. 'this is your Emily. And little Alfie's here with me, falling over himself to tell his Daddy to get better and come home. He talks about you all the time, Ted. He even drew a picture of you in your uniform. Mind you, it wasn't a very good likeness. He gave you a nose the size of an elephant but of course I told him it was just lovely. He's grown a good two inches since you saw him, Ted.'

And so it went on; she talked until the images she had tried to create became real to her; the cottage garden, Alfie's swing hanging from an apple tree, his roller skates outside the back door, his fretwork set out on the kitchen table.

Reaching out a hand to the glass of water, she suddenly realised that Pierre Montarial had come back and was standing in the shadows, watching her intently. She glanced at her watch. Half past two! She'd been talking, with only occasional pauses for a sip of water, for over two hours. But Ted Summers was still alive! And surely it wasn't her imagination that he was now breathing more deeply? She put out a hand to check his pulse but saw that Pierre was already checking it on the other side of the bed. He glanced across at Kate, his face wreathed in smiles.

'He's sleeping normally. You've done it, Kate! You've saved his life!'

She doubted if she would ever hear such thrilling words again, even if they were totally untrue.

'It — it wasn't me!' And now tears of exquisite relief were pouring down her cheeks. 'It was — it was . . . ' She wanted to say that of course it wasn't just her, that they were indeed a team. But the words wouldn't come. Instead, a great sob rose in her throat, making speech quite impossible.

In seconds, Pierre was by her side, kneeling so that he could cradle her in his arms, soothing her with gentle phrases; French phrases she realised later, when she tried to remember what he'd said. But whatever the language, there was no mistaking the tenderness in his voice, the gentleness of his hands as they stroked her hair and mopped up her tears with the enormous handkerchief he'd taken from his pocket.

At last she raised her head from his shoulder and smiled weakly. 'Whatever would Sister say!'

'Why, that you have done magnificent work tonight, that you are tired to the point of exhaustion and that you must now go to bed. But there is one other thing that Sister would *not* say.'

'Which is?'

'That you are even more beautiful when you cry! Now,' he became brisk, 'away with you to bed. But first — listen!'

'To what? I can't hear a thing.'

'Exactly! The guns have stopped. Go and sleep while you can, little one.'

★   ★   ★

All along the front line near Loos, men who had dozed fitfully throughout the night, knuckled sleep from their eyes and knew that it had come at last. The big push that was to settle the enemy's hash once and for all or so they'd been told. And some among them, Kitchener's boys just out from home, believed it. Only the old hands, the diehards, knew better. They were already waiting for their mugs of tea, heavily laced with rum, and with any luck they'd manage an extra swig if the Corporal was a mate of theirs. For they knew that the only way to go 'over the top' was with the fumes of the rum in their nostrils, dulling their senses, but warming the pits of their bellies even if it didn't reach to their freezing feet. Yelling like madmen, they'd stagger across No Man's Lane behind some kid of a subaltern still wet behind the ears. And if Fate was on their side, they'd get a Blighty one on the way, and end up in a shell hole; anything rather than reach the German trenches and have to stick their bayonets into some poor sod before he did the same to them.

A mile or two behind the front line, Robert Holker awoke in a bedroom over an estaminet bar. Quietly, he rolled out of bed and reached for his clothes. And as he dressed, he glanced down· at the girl still asleep under the blankets, her dark hair spread like a web across the pillow. His glance was rueful. If only he'd taken all she'd offered when he'd tumbled into her bed last night. But just when his desire had begun to quicken, as his hands were cupping her voluptuous breasts and his mouth seeking hers, he'd thought of Kate; and his passion had been quenched as thoroughly as if a bucket of cold water had been thrown over him. And now, it was too late.

Leaving some money — the least he could do — where she would see it when she awoke, he crept down the stairs and out into the cold light of dawn.

But, breathing in the freshness of early morning, hearing the sound of bird song in the stillness that always came when the guns ceased their clamour, he knew he had no real regrets. If he lived to be a hundred, — or died that day — he'd never forget Kate; nor cease to want her.

12

They have seen nothing like it before. Compared with this torrent, this Niagara, of wounded, the arrival of the convalescents on the Isle of Wight was like a gently flowing stream.

First came the ambulances and lorries, and even some horse-drawn carts, carpeted thickly with straw, all bumping down the track from the railhead with the stretcher cases. And just when they were beginning to think that would be all they would have to accommodate until the arrival of the next train, a seemingly never-ending column of walking wounded starts to hobble into the coutryard. Most of them come in pairs, one supporting the other, but some are in threes, with one man who should surely have been a stretcher case, being almost carried by the other two. One badly wounded private has even been placed in a hand cart and is being pushed by a sergeant who has but one serviceable arm, the other supported in a filthy, blood-stained sling. Many have bandages over their eyes and are led by their comrades. Many are retching violently as they stagger along and many have faces blackened by burns.

Fortunately, it is not such a shock as it might have been for the nurses have been briefed; if such a term can be applied to the hasty instructions the Colonel has given them before the convoys begin to arrive.

'Apparently, casualties are so heavy, the Clearing

Stations have been swamped. Many men are coming straight from the battlefield, with only the dressings put on them at the First Aid Posts. Few will have had their uniforms removed. The first priority with these men will be to clean them up before their wounds can be examined. Many will have been so badly wounded, there will be little we can do other than to make their last hours as comfortable as possible. These men will be nursed separately from those for whom there is still hope. Medical Officers, as usual, will decide to which ward the wounded are to be taken, assisted by senior nursing staff. Junior nurses, V.A.D's and orderlies will work under their supervision.'

But in spite of their briefing, Kate and Priscilla are aghast as they gaze across the courtyard, now completely covered by the stretchers they have just helped to unload. Then they see, just as the S.M.O. has said, that the Medical Officers, Pierre among them, are working their way along the rows, inspecting each man and pinning a label to his chest. The walking wounded clearly grateful just to have arrived, sit propped up against the walls, or whatever solid structure they can find, patiently awaiting their turn.

Bert, standing at Pierre's elbow, beckons to the girls and stepping carefully between the stretchers — no mean feat in itself, so closely are they packed — they help him and other orderlies to carry 'their' men into the bath-house. They do this many times before a Sister tells them to leave the orderlies to carry in the rest and to begin work on those already inside.

'Call me in an emergency!' she says before disappearing into an adjacent ward.

Fortunately, Bert is still with them. 'Right, missies! It's off with their uniforms and then a quick wash before getting them to bed.'

Many of the men are unconscious but those who are not wince in agony as their uniforms are removed. And clearly, many of them have reservations about being undressed by a strange young woman.

'Shut your eyes and pretend I'm your wife,' Priscilla advises one embarrassed man as she pulls off his trousers.

'I ain't got no wife, nurse, but I reckon *you'll* have to marry me after this!' And then his face twists with pain as she wields an enormous pair of scissors to remove the sleeve of his tunic. Peeling it away, she reveals a dressing to which half the mud of Flanders seems still to be clinging. Carefully, she sponges around the dressing with the warm, soapy water Bert has brought by the bucket-full.

'That could be . . . ' Kate begins to comment hopefully to a man whose leg is peppered with shell splinters and whose trousers and puttees she has just removed. She had been about to say 'a Blighty one' but hastily changes it to 'a little complicated!' For a man's hopes must not be raised on the say-so of a mere V.A.D., even if she and Prissy are temporarily in charge of so many wounded men she cannot bring herself to count them.

Hastily, for he's still lying on the floor of the bath-house, she swabs the rest of his body down and covers him with a blanket. 'Soon have you tucked up in bed!'

'As long as you're in it with me!' he suggests cheerfully.

Once again, Kate marvels at the courage of these men; and at the way in which this war is sweeping away so many of the social barriers and conventions she has grown up with. At home, in civilian life, this man would never have dreamt of making such a comment. Please God, she thinks, the snobbish values of pre-war England are gone for ever. And suddenly, quite without warning, she remembers Robert Holker enthusing over such a possibility as they leant on the gate of Toby's field, breathing in the sweet scent of May blossom, feeling the sun warm upon their faces. Where is Robert now? she wonders. And does he ever think of those halcyon days?

But this is neither the time nor the place for treacherous memories. And her resolution is strengthened by the sudden discovery that lice are crawling out of the discarded uniforms awaiting removal to the fumigators. Her revulsion at the sight of the bloated, maggot-like creatures is far greater than any she has felt since she began to nurse. Immediately, her head begins to itch and she has to force her lips into a ghastly travesty of a smile as she moves on to the next man.

Eventually, all are lying in or on their beds, awaiting treatment. Kate eases her aching back and glances down the ward. Surely Sister won't have too much to complain of here!

A few minutes later, as Pierre begins his rounds with herself and Prissy in attendance, she learns that she is to be in charge.

'Although Sister will be on hand,' Pierre tells her, 'to be . . .'

' . . . called in an emergency!' Kate finishes for him. The words are beginning to sound familiar.

'I told her,' Pierre insists, 'that you could manage!'

★   ★   ★

'Angie, you look stunning! Short hair really suits you.' Kate drew back her own cropped head, the better to study her handiwork, scissors poised to snip off even more of Angela's chestnut locks if she wished. On the other side of the tiny room, Megan circled Priscilla, her already shorn head anxiously cocked.

'Have I got it equal on both sides, Prissy?'

Priscilla peered into the hand mirror. 'I'm sure you have. And any way, I don't care! It just feels so marvellous to have the weight of it off my neck.'

'We still have to wash it,' Angela pointed out.

'I brought plenty of Lysol up with me from the ward,' Kate told her. 'And it won't take long to dry now that it's so short.'

They took it in turns in the bathroom and half an hour later they were all back, free of lice and rubbing dry each other's hair. Kate began to brew the inevitable cocoa. 'Talk to each other!' Sister had advised when she'd made a hurried tour of the ward just before they came off duty. 'Don't just lie in bed, going over in your mind all the dreadful sights you've seen today. And if you can't talk to each other, come and talk to me.'

139

Since she looked as exhausted as they felt, they were duly impressed by the offer. And it certainly wasn't her fault that the number of wounded had far exceeded what was expected.

Now, even though it was eleven o'clock and they were all on duty again at seven next morning, Kate was resolved to follow Sister's advice. She knew Priscilla was all right but she was worried about Megan who had been put with the terminally ill; privately, Kate wondered if the choice had been a wise one for soft-hearted Meg, who still hadn't heard from her husband. 'How did you get on, Megs?' she asked.

'I just can't believe they're all doomed to die,' Meg said. 'There's one lad in particular — he's only eighteen — with a piece of shrapnel in his head. He's lost so much blood already, they say they daren't risk a major operation. But surely it would be worth a try if he's going to die anyway? And to make it worse, he's delirious and keeps calling me Annie and telling me he loves me!'

'Perhaps they will decide to operate, after all,' Kate tried to comfort her, 'when things have calmed down a bit.' She wondered if she could have a word with Pierre about the lad. But Pierre was still in the operating theatre and likely to remain there until the small hours. The lad would have to wait.

'How about you, Angie?' Priscilla asked. 'Did you still feel like finishing off your patients?' For they'd all noticed the ambulances that had drawn up apart from the others so that the men in field-grey could be carried unobtrusively to the ward at the back of the château.

140

Angela shook her head. 'Once their uniforms were off, they were just like our own men. And a darned sight more polite! Mind you, they could have been saying the most awful things about me behind my back, because my German's practically nonexistent but I doubt it. They just seemed pathetically grateful to be out of the fighting, although there was one man who just lay there and refused to open his mouth. However . . . ' she shrugged, 'with luck and my brilliant nursing, they'll all survive!'

'What did you do with the one who wouldn't speak?' Kate asked curiously, for Angela was renowned for her resourcefulness.

'Said 'there, there it could be worse' or words to that effect, because he's only got a fractured ankle. But I could have been talking to myself for all the notice he took. Tomorrow, if he's still silent, I'll tell him just what I think of him, the arrogant bastard!'

'That's my Angie!' said Kate.

★　★　★

Next day, the pattern was set on Kate's ward that was to continue non-stop for many weeks. At least, the routine tasks of blanket baths and bedpans could now be left to Bert with the help of another orderly. It was the daily dressings that took up most of Kate and Priscilla's time and the setting up of the special treatment needed for the gas gangrene patients, but at least the treatment was working. Pierre, on his rounds and looking ever more exhausted as day followed day without respite, was delighted at its success.

141

'But there is now yet another horror to contend with. Liquid fire. The Germans have begun to carry canisters of petrol on their backs which they ignite and spray over our men through a rubber hosepipe. The results are diabolical. Now and then, of course,' he grinned sardonically, 'the wind changes and it is blown back over themselves!'

Kate shuddered and resolved not to tell Angela of this latest horror, lest it disturb the delicate balance of the relationship she had managed to achieve with her patients; at least, with most of them. For each night, before they dragged their weary bodies to bed, they continued the practice of talking about their day, and each night, Angela reported on her German who still maintained his dreadful, brooding silence, in spite of all her efforts to involve him in the life of the ward.

Each night, too, Megan related how yet another of her patients had died and that she doubted if she could carry on much longer. But each morning found her back on the ward, doing her best to comfort and sustain those who still hung on to life, albeit by a thread. But at least Pierre had found time to visit and to decide that there were those for whom an operation could be risked, provided a blood transfusion could be given beforehand — and her young lad with the shrapnel in his head had been among them.

Sometimes, the call to 'Fall In' would be sounded in the middle of the night and they would all tumble sleepily from their warm beds to meet yet another convoy.

It was after one of these nocturnal call-outs, when

142

the new intake had been settled for what remained of the night, that Kate discovered Priscilla in tears in the tiny kitchen of their ward. 'Prissy, darling! What is it?'

But Priscilla could do nothing but sob. Words, although she clearly did her best to form them, were impossible. Kate eased her on to a chair and crouched beside her.

'Prissy, love, please try to tell me what it is.' But Prissy's sobs grew even more uncontrolled.

Kate tried to think coherently. What could have upset her so? Death was something they were all accustomed to by now, so it was unlikely to be that. In any case, none of their old patients had died that night. Nor had any among the new arrivals on their ward. Or could it be — and the thought was like a knife-thrust to her heart, causing her breath to catch in her throat in a terrible rush of fear — Prissy had recognised someone among the stretcher cases out in the courtyard before they had been carried inside. Her hand flew to her mouth.

'Prissy, just nod if I'm on the right track. Is it someone you know?'

Prissy's head nodded violently. 'Someone we both know?' Again, Prissy nodded.

'Robert — Holker?'

The relief when Prissy shook her head was almost too great for her to bear. Her head began to swim and she came perilously close to fainting as Prissy stammered, 'Not — not Robert. Sam — Sam Bosworth.'

'Oh, Prissy darling, I'm so sorry! I'm so very sorry!' And now she was rocking her sister in her

143

arms. 'Is he — dead?'

'Not — not yet! In Meg's ward!' Prissy could only manage monosyllables.

'I see.' So at least they'd be able to visit — if Prissy could bear it. 'Now listen, love. Try to stop crying or you're going to be ill. Would you like to go off duty for a bit? No? Then bathe your eyes and put the kettle on. Apart from a couple of the new patients who are allowed a drink, I could do with a cup — and so could you. And Pierre will be along in a minute. All right?'

Priscilla nodded and did her best to quell her tears. With a heavy heart, Kate went back to the ward. They should be sent off soon for a few hours' rest and then they would both go to see Sam.

★ ★ ★

Slivers of steel from an exploding shell had torn his liver to shreds, Megan explained as she led them down the ward. 'He's not expected to last more than a few hours.' And indeed, his bed was ominously close to the central table.

'He's just had a shot of morphine,' Megan whispered as they went to sit either side of the still figure, 'but he's still conscious.'

Priscilla put her hand over the one that lay, motionless, on the cover. 'Hello, Sam!'

His eyelids flickered and then opened wearily, as if the simple, spontaneous action were taking all his strength. His eyes were deep, dark pools in the gaunt pallor of his face. But then he saw her. 'Prissy! By all — that's wonderful!' And turning his head a fraction. 'And Kate! I don't — believe it!'

'The proverbial bad penny! That's us!' Kate managed to say.

He smiled weakly, fighting the morphine. 'Robert said . . . you were . . . nursing. But thought . . . still at home.'

The temptation to lean closer, to ask urgently. 'How is Robert, Sam? Where is he?' was almost irresistible. Instead, she forced herself to say lightly. 'Couldn't let you two have all the glory!'

'Some — glory!' But his eyelids were already beginning to droop. Kate rose swiftly.

'I'll leave you to talk to Prissy. God bless you, Sam!'

She went and sat at the table with Meg, watching anxiously while Priscilla leaned closer to whisper into Sam's ear. He smiled radiantly and Priscilla sank to her knees and placed her lips gently over his. And then, still with that radiant smile upon his face, he drifted into unconsciousness. Priscilla sat for a moment, fighting tears, his hand still in hers, then she laid it carefully back on the cover and tiptoed back to Kate. Hand in hand, they left the ward.

That night, after the others had gone to their own room, they lay and talked. Meg had already told them that Sam had died a couple of hours after they had seen him and without regaining consciousness.

'I feel so guilty,' Priscilla, dry-eyed now, said sadly.

'But why, Prissy? If he cared for you more than you cared for him, it was hardly your fault.'

'In those days,' said Priscilla, as if it were a lifetime away, 'I didn't care for anyone except myself. I played the field — isn't that the expression? And when Hank came along, with all his talk about the new world, he was so different and exciting, I forgot Sam.'

'As I remember it,' said Kate loyally, 'you divided yourself very neatly between the two of them. I was full of admiration.'

'And there was I, thinking how wonderful it must be to care deeply for just one person, as you seemed to.'

'But dangerous,' said Kate. 'In the end, it can be very painful.'

'But you're over Robert now, aren't you, Kate? I mean, Pierre . . . well, it's obvious he thinks the world of you.'

'But he's like that with all the nurses,' Kate pointed out. 'Even Sister goes bright pink when he appears on the ward.'

'Well, *I* don't, I can assure you! But, more to the point, how do you feel about him?'

'I wish I knew! Oh, I grant you, working with him is fascinating. Sometimes, I wonder if I could cope with it all, if I didn't know he was there. But this morning, when Sam suddenly mentioned Robert's name, I would have given anything to have been able to ask him where he is and how he is.'

'Couldn't you write to that aunt of his?' Priscilla suggested.

'Oh, no!' Kate was quite sure about that. 'If Robert had wanted to keep in touch, he would have written. It's much better the way it is.'

Next day, they followed Lieutenant Sam Bosworth's funeral procession into the cemetery that was now spread over a wide area, and stood to attention, their cloaks billowing in the chill breeze, while the coffin was lowered and the Last Post sounded.

'He was just a friend,' they told the padre when he enquired if they were family. 'But a very special one.'

13

'Now listen here,' said Angela sternly, 'stop sulking like a spoiled child and give me a hand. You're mobile, for heaven's sake, not stuck in your bed like most of the other poor devils. You could help me shave them for a start.'

'I'm not a bloody barber?' said the man in the wheelchair, who had the lower part of his right leg in plaster.

The silence was electrifying. Those nearby stopped what they were doing and stared at the man who had just spoken. For it was the first time he'd done so since they'd arrived at the château over a week ago. And what's more, he'd spoken in impeccable English, as if it were his mother tongue.

Angela, a bowl in one hand, a razor in the other, recovered first. 'D'you mean to tell me you've let me say all the dreadful things I have, because I didn't think you understood, and all the time you *did*?' It was a somewhat confused sentence but there was no doubt that the man understood it. He nodded but with his eyes staring fixedly down the ward.

'Look at me when I'm talking to you!' Angela snapped, beside herself with rage and embarrassment.

And the man did just that, turning his head to give her a long, appraising stare, from the tip of her shoes up over her long white apron, with the red cross emblazoned on its bib and where her breasts swelled invitingly, to her face, scarlet with fury, to her white cap tied at the nape of her neck and from which locks of chestnut hair had escaped to curl about her ears. 'You look marvellous when you're angry!' he said and now there was no mistaking his English, public-school accent.

'I was so furious,' Angela told the others that night, 'I actually lifted my hand to hit him, but fortunately Sister chose that moment to come bustling in. Even so, I thought I was for it, but Ernst — that's his name, Ernst Schreiber — said, quite loudly so that she'd hear, 'Thank you, nurse, but I don't feel sick any more.' I think Sister was so astonished at hearing him utter, she'd hardly noticed my hand. But it was decent of him to try and cover up for me.'

'The least he could do,' Kate commented, 'considering it was his fault in the first place.'

'That's what he said afterwards. When Sister had gone, he asked if he could be pushed out into the garden — it's quite sheltered and the sun was out — and once there, he talked non-stop as if he were making up for lost time. Can you believe that he went to the same school that my brothers are at now? His father's a banker in Munich, but his mother's English. He was actually at Art College in

England when war broke out but he'd gone home for the summer. At first, because he had so many friends in England, he flatly refused to join the army. But in the end, he volunteered as a stretcher bearer. And that was fine until he fell into a shell hole in No Man's Land and broke his ankle. He would have tried to crawl back to his lines if it hadn't been for all the dead and wounded lying on top of him. Fortunately, they were mostly British so when our stretcher bearers brought them in, they picked him up as well.'

'But why wouldn't he talk?' Kate asked.

Angela grinned. 'It was like a game, he said, watching me get more and more frustrated, making bigger and bigger threats that I didn't think he understood. I actually threatened to cut off his willy, at one point?'

'Angie, you didn't!' Megan was horrified.

'I did! In the end, he said he had to find out what I was really like.'

'And?' Priscilla leaned forward, her eyes sparkling.

'He said I was even more fun than I looked! Oh, I know,' as Kate studied her thoughtfully, 'I probably broke all the rules in fraternising with him. But, what the hell?'

'You don't have to justify yourself to us,' Kate told her. 'It's Sister you'll have to watch out for.'

'Don't worry! It's just a bit of fun!' Suddenly, she pretended an enormous yawn, wanting the conversation to end there. For it wasn't just a bit of fun; she and Ernst both knew it.

* * *

149

In spite of the bitter conflict raging between their two countries and the knowledge that Ernst would, inevitably, recover and leave the château, their relationship, as the days passed, seemed to evolve naturally and without haste, as if they had all the time in the world.

'We have so much in common,' Angela told Kate one afternoon during a precious hour off duty when they were pacing the grounds, enjoying the crisp, pure air after the wards, where Lysol fought a perpetual battle with the rank odours of dysentery and decay. 'Like me, he's a mongrel. His German friends have always accused him of being pro-British and his English friends of being pro-German. He could never win.'

'What puzzles me,' said Kate, 'is how on earth you manage to discuss these things.'

'It's easy! He couldn't be more cooperative now, on the wards. He helps me shave the men, make the tea and hand out the meals and all the time nobody understands what we're saying to each other. Except Sister, of course. We have to watch out for her, but she thinks the sun shines out of his arse, now he's so helpful.'

'Angie,' Kate cautioned, 'try not to get too involved. When the next big push comes, he'll be moved on, if not sooner.'

'I know, but with a bit of luck he'll be sent to a P.O.W. camp in England and then anything might happen.'

'Well, take care! And don't ever arrange to meet him off the ward and on your own.'

'Fat chance, more's the pity!'

But in fact, and this she wasn't even telling Kate, she had found paper and pencil for Ernst and each afternoon, weather permitting, she would push him out into the little garden so that he could sketch; ostensibly, the ragged bushes of myrtle and japonica that grew there but in reality, a head and shoulders study of herself.

'For me to have something of you to remember when I have to go away,' he pleaded. 'So take off your cap, liebling, just for a minute.'

And she, knowing full well that Sister might come looking for her at any moment, did so, running her hand through her hair to loosen it so that it drifted about her face in a tawny cloud. But even that wasn't enough.

'Don't stop there, my little, English prude! Loosen your blouse, just a little.'

'I'm *not* a prude! But I *am* a nurse and sister will have my guts for garters if she sees me.'

But she had still undone the top buttons of her blouse and leaned forward as Ernst had asked, fully aware that she was now revealing the lace of her bodice and the deep, shadowy cleft between her breasts.

'Good! That's better!' And he had sketched with quick, decisive strokes while her heart had fluttered like a caged bird: but whether through fear of Sister's sudden appearance or because of Ernst's gaze as he, too, leaned closer, she couldn't have said.

★ ★ ★

Sister never did discover them in the little garden. The sketch was safely finished and another begun and they began to feel they lived in their own safe, little world, far from the perils of human interference, so that the end, when it came, was unbearable in its harshness.

'I must see you alone,' Ernst said one rainy morning soon after Angela had come on duty. He was pushing the early morning, tea trolley down the ward.

She guessed what was coming. For a week now, he'd been walking with only the aid of a stick.

'The M.O. came round last night after you'd gone off duty,' he told her when they eventually met up in the kitchen. 'I'm considered well enough to be discharged tomorrow.'

'*Tomorrow?* Oh, Ernst!'

They gazed into each other's eyes, fraught with the anguish of parting.

'I love you, liebling!'

'I love you, too, my darling!'

Their hands met and held as, for the first time, they kissed. It was no more than the briefest pressure of his lips upon hers before she drew back, amazed at her daring. But it was enough for them both to realise — that it was not enough.

'I must see you before I go, liebling. Alone.'

They both glanced through the window; the rain was merciless, the skies grey and overcast. The garden would be out of the question for today.

'Is there somewhere?' Ernst asked. 'An old barn? An outhouse? Anywhere . . . ?'

Angela, caution thrown to the winds, thought

152

quickly. 'There's some sort of potting shed. You reach it at the end of the little garden if you turn right along the wall. But it would take too long . . . I'd be missed.'

'I don't mean now. I mean when you're off duty. Tonight, after lights out.'

She hesitated for a fraction of a second. This was precisely what Kate had warned her against. But it was an emergency. By this time tomorrow, Ernst might have gone, and when would she see him again? 'All right! About ten o'clock?'

He nodded. 'I'll pretend I need to go to the lavatory. There's an old coat someone's left hanging in the sluice. I'll slip it on over my pyjamas.'

It was so like planning a midnight feast at school, she almost giggled. 'Till tonight, then!'

'Till tonight!'

Several of the patients, she discovered, were to be discharged; to where they had no idea. But they hoped it would be England for rumour had it that life for a P.O.W. over there could be quite amazingly pleasant with local landowners being more than cooperative about allowing them to fish their rivers, or even hunt their foxes if they indulged in such a practice. Angela's father, considering such behaviour cruel and barbaric, didn't, but she knew that he had German prisoners working on the estate. Wouldn't it be wonderful if . . . ?

The day passed in a dream.

★ ★ ★

153

The rain has stopped but ragged clouds still stream across a pale moon. Angela pulls her cloak around her and keeps to the shadows as she hurries through the little garden. The ward, when she has glanced in, has been quiet with only a single, shaded light over the central table and not a nurse in sight. There may be an emergency in the adjoining ward and the care of the German prisoners, though the Geneva Convention is strictly adhered to, will certainly not take precedence over British requirements.

She reaches the potting shed. Its door is ajar but she still hesitates, not knowing if Ernst is already inside. Tentatively, she moves into the darkness and immediately, a hand comes out and grabs her.

Although she has been half expecting it, she gives an involuntary squeak of terror. Immediately a hand is clamped firmly over her mouth. 'Quiet, my darling!'

'Oh, Ernst, it is you!'

'Who else were you expecting? Matron? The Colonel?'

For a moment, they shake with hysterical laughter and Angela guesses that Ernst's nerves are as taut as her own. Except, of course, that he has little to lose. Or could they, perhaps, shoot him as an attempted escapee and herself as an accomplice? Why hadn't she thought of that?

'Come here!' Ernst wraps his arms around her and draws her close. The borrowed coat falls apart and through the thin fabric of his pyjamas, she can feel the wild thudding of his heart. And now they are kissing, their tongues frantically exploring each other's mouths. She feels his hardness as he presses against her. Suddenly, some small, professional part of her brain thinks how strange it is that she, to whom the male organ has now become so familiar, has never seen it as anything but soft and pliable. This one thrusts against her like an animal, huge and demanding.

Now, his hands are cupping her breasts and she arches her back so that they fall easily from her blouse, already unbuttoned under her cape, and she moans softly as he caresses her nipples.

His hand has begun to fumble at the waistband of her skirt when the door is suddenly flung back on its hinges and the powerful beam of a torch shines directly on to them.

'Take your hands off her, you bloody Kraut! And then you're for it!'

★ ★ ★

Dry-mouthed, she faced Matron in her office. Clearly, she had already retired for the night, for she wore a thick dressing-gown of navy serge, buttoned high to the neck. And yet it was over an hour now, since the guard had disturbed them; since Ernst had been frog-marched away and she had been taken without ceremony to Matron's office.

No doubt it was part of her punishment to be kept on tenterhooks, allowing her imagination to conjure up all manner of dreadful consequences. To be sent home with her tail between her legs? To be sent to another hospital? To be deprived of all privileges — not that there were many — for an indefinite period? But it wasn't her own future she

155

was worried about. It was Ernst's. Or had he already been . . . ? Her mind baulked at the dreadful possibility.

For what seemed an eternity, Matron remained silent, turning an ivory paper-knife over and over on her desk. Angela wondered if she was supposed to sink to her knees, to babble apologies and to entreat forgiveness. But when she did eventually speak, Angela could hardly believe what she was hearing.

'Clearly, nurse, you were the victim of a man so unscrupulous, so bestial in his desires, that he took advantage of the devoted care you had lavished upon him since he came here. For such despicable behaviour there can be no excuse. It is just one more proof — if it were needed — that the Hun is a barbarian. I can only thank a merciful Providence that sent the guard in time.'

She paused for a second and Angela drew breath to tell her that it was not like that at all; that Ernst was no barbarian, that he loved her as she loved him and that she had gone willingly to meet him. But Matron carried on as if determined to nip the possibility of such a confession in the bud.

'As I understand it, the guard arrived before the man could achieve his foul purpose. You were not raped.'

It was more a statement than a question but Angela could not contain herself any longer. 'Oh no, Matron, it wasn't like that! There was no question of . . .'

'Good! I am greatly relieved to hear it.' Matron swept on, 'Now,' her voice softened slightly, 'you must be exhausted after your ordeal. So you are

156

excused duties for the next twenty-four hours. Try and put this dreadful experience behind you. But nurse — and I must make this *quite* clear — you are never, ever, to allow yourself to be put in such a situation again. Do I make myself clear? Now, you may go.'

But she couldn't go! Not without asking . . . 'Ernst,' she quavered, 'has he . . . ?'

'The German,' Matron interrupted coldly, 'has already been dealt with. You need have no fears on that account. And now, I must insist that you go to your bed.' And she actually walked to the door and held it open herself, a concession quite unprecedented in Angela's experience.

She was halfway up the back stairs before she realised what must have happened. That hour she had been forced to spend on her own, wondering and worrying, Matron had spent with the Colonel, devising a way in which, no matter how damning the evidence against her, a curtain could be discreetly drawn over what had happened so that the reputation of her nurses could remain untarnished and, perhaps most important of all, without the loss of a trained nurse at a time when medical resources were already stretched to the limit. And what easier way than to place all the blame upon Ernst — who would never be allowed to plead his case?

Crouched on the stairs, Angela put her head upon her arms and wept bitterly.

★ ★ ★

157

Only to Kate did Angela relate the full story. Megan, never one to suspect intrigue was happy to accept that she had been given a rest-day after working so hard. But Kate, who had known of her attraction to Ernst and had detected a thinly veiled air of excitement about her during the last few days, wondered. During her half-hour lunch break from the wards, she sped up to Angela's room; to find her sitting on the bed, staring bleakly into space.

'Kate! Thank God you've come! I'm going mad up here on my own, not knowing what's happened to Ernst.'

'Tell me what's been going on.'

As briefly as possible, Angela told her everything. Kate wasted no time in recrimination; who was to say she would not have done the same in similar circumstances? 'I'll make it my business to have a word with Mary Barnes in the Orderly Room,' she promised. Mary was a V.A.D. on the admin. side. That evening, Kate managed to sit next to her at supper-time.

'Busy, Mary?'

'Hectic! Some lucky fellows going home and some poor devils going back up the line. The fortunes of war, I suppose, but it seems so sad when you think of the P.O.W's being sent to England,.'

'Lucky blighters! Did they all go'

'All except one chap, Ernst something or other. He was sent off on his own with a couple of heavily-armed guards. Don't know why. Spat in the Colonel's eye, perhaps! I say, I don't think much of this macaroni cheese, do you?'

'Dreadful!' Kate agreed although in fact, she'd

158

hardly tasted it. Doggedly, she returned to the subject. 'I suppose you'll know more about this German when the guards come back?'

'Well, no, that's another strange thing — the guard isn't coming back. Replacement's due tomorrow, I gather. So we shall never know what happened to our Ernst! Shot at dawn, maybe!' She pushed back her plate. 'I'm giving up on this. Can I get you any afters? Plum duff or sago.'

Feeling suddenly sick, Kate shook her head. 'Neither, thanks.'

14

It was tempting not to think about the world outside; to simply fall out of bed each morning and slog through each day with its interminable routine of dressings and treatments and fall back into bed at night. Fortunately, there were letters from families and friends to keep them in touch, including, miraculously, one for Meg from her husband.

'But where can he be?' she demanded of the others. 'He talks about the heat and the flies and how he'd give anything to feel English rain on his face, but in the next sentence he says how pleasant it is to see the sea.

'Gallipoli, I should think,' said Kate. 'Pa said in his last letter that the Allies had landed at Salonika.'

They went to pour over an old atlas they'd found in what remained of the château's library.

'There it is!' Angela pointed to the long, narrow peninsular jutting out into the Aegean Sea with the straits of the Dardanelles between it and the main bulk of Turkey.

'What on earth are we doing in such a God-forsaken place?' asked Priscilla.

'According to Mr Churchill,' Kate said, 'if we can capture it, we shall be halfway to taking Constantinople, and that would mean Turkey out of the war. Then we could carry on to help poor little Serbia and that would make the Germans divert some of their troops from France and Flanders. From here, in fact.'

Angela shuddered. 'And when you consider that 'here' is just a few hundred yards of bare earth that we've been fighting over for months, well . . . I think the human race is going mad — stark, staring mad.'

Ever since Ernst's ominous departure, Angela had grown more and more depressed. 'Something will happen,' Kate tried to cheer her. 'Something always does.'

'Yes — like another big push!'

'Well at least Megs now knows where her husband is,' Priscilla pointed out. And that, they all agreed, was a definite advantage.

By the same post, came a packet of newspapers and magazines from which they learned that the British were now using mustard gas against the Germans, that there'd been a Zeppelin raid on London in which fifty-six people had been killed and that British casualties, so far, totalled nearly five hundred thousand.

'Isn't there anything nice?' Priscilla wailed.

'King George has been to France to visit the troops,' Kate read. 'And there's a recipe here for Christmas cake using cod-liver oil instead of butter. Ugh!'

Angela raised her head. 'Wouldn't it be heaven to go home for Christmas? I'd willingly eat cake made of sawdust if I could just sit by a big log fire. And take the dogs for a walk.'

'And have a really hot bath.'

'And stay in bed till ten o'clock.'

'And have muffins for tea.'

'With honey. Oodles of honey.'

They were silent for several seconds while they contemplated paradise.

'Actually,' said Kate at last, 'I'd settle for a seventy-two hour pass. Here, in France. And why wait for Christmas?'

★ ★ ★

At first, they didn't believe it. Wishful thinking, thought Kate when Priscilla came rushing in with the news that a leave roster had been pinned to their notice-board and that, incredibly, they were all on it.

'Come and see!' Priscilla invited, twirling around like a humming top. 'Oh, I'm so excited!'

It was true. 'Due to the imminent arrival of additional nursing staff, seventy-two hour passes for the following V.A.D's will be granted once the new intake is familiar with the routine of the hospital.' And all their names were on the list. They could hardly wait to discuss where they should go.

'Paris?' Priscilla suggested.

161

'Not in this uniform!' said Angela firmly.

'Too far, anyway,' Kate considered.

'And we'd be sure to lose ourselves,' cautious Meg pointed out.

It was Pierre who decided for them. 'It's good of you to let Prissy and me go together,' Kate thanked him.

'*C'est rien!* I am confident that you will fully instruct the new nurses before you go.'

'Of course, sir!' He raised his eyebrows at that 'sir' but didn't comment. Since Angela's dreadful experience with Ernst, it had seemed more than ever important to Kate to maintain a discreet professional distance between herself and Pierre. Fraternisation between doctors and humble V.A.D's was almost as '*verboten*' as that between nurses and prisoners. But now and again, she would catch his eye and detect a distinctly *un*professional twinkle — before she looked hastily away. For she was still perilously aware of him as a man as well as her superior officer, still felt her heart beat faster if their hands touched in the course of their work.

'And where will you all go for your well-deserved rest?' he enquired now.

'Well, there's a list of army hostels and service organisations that would have us, but we can't decide which one.'

He was horrified. 'Except that you would not have to work — and I would not discount *that* completely! — the conditions would be similar to those you have now. No, you must go somewhere warm and welcoming, with food prepared by a

162

proper 'chef' who will not massacre it, discipline it, force it to become what it does not want to be!'

Kate thought of the desiccated cabbage, the underdone potatoes, the shrivelled meat, and knew what he meant.

'You need a sympathetic 'patron',' he warmed to his theme, 'who will not turn you out into the cold simply because it is ten o'clock and the rules say you must 'vacate the premises' at that hour. Premises!' he spat out the word. 'You want a house — a home — not premises! And I think I know exactly the place; if Madame Furneau is still there, of course, if she has not been forced to turn her lovely house into one of your — your *premises*! Or even,' he gave her a particularly outrageous wink, 'a brothel!'

'A brothel?' Priscilla, coming up to them at that moment, had heard only the last two words. 'What's this about a brothel?'

Pierre chuckled. 'Your sister and I were simply discussing where you could spend your little holiday. *Mon Dieu!*' as Priscilla gazed at him in alarm. 'What have I said now?' He backed away, his hands raised in protest. 'I will leave your sister to explain just what I did say.' And to Kate, 'I will make a telephone call. I will enquire.'

★ ★ ★

'Once upon a time,' Pierre had told them, 'it was a simple farmhouse. But then the farmer became ambitious. Or perhaps it was his wife! In any event, a new wing was added with a pepperpot tower. In

163

France, no house of consequence is complete without its pepperpot tower! But then, the farmer's son became even more ambitious than his parents and decided that he must have a moat. To do that, he merely had to divert a river! But if you have a moat, you must also have a drawbridge. So now you have this quaint, incongruous house, half cottage, half fortified manor. In fact, it's called 'Le Petit Manoir'.'

They stood and gazed, while the obliging workman who had given them a lift from the station on his cart, disappeared down the track that led to the village. It was as Pierre had described it. The façade was half-timbered with its first storey overhanging the shining expanse of the moat, its roof a jumble of ancient tiles, twisted chimneys and latticed dormers. At one end, a slender tower, capped with slate, rose above an iron-studded door, now thrown open to show a cobbled courtyard where white doves circled about a stone well-head. As they watched, a pair of swans floated into view around the side of the tower, their wake rippling in the pale winter sunshine.

'Perfect!' Angela sighed. 'All we need now is mine host bustling out to greet us!'

'Mine host is away at the war, I gather,' said Kate. 'But this could be his wife.'

A tall, dark-haired woman wearing the sort of voluminous black skirt favoured by peasant women with what looked like a man's grey woollen pullover, had appeared in the doorway. On her feet were sturdy wooden sabots.

'Surely not!' said Angela.

164

But the woman was crossing the drawbridge towards them, hands out-stretched, face wreathed in smiles. 'Welcome to Le Petit Manoir! I cannot tell you how pleased I am to see you. Nowadays,' she gestured at her skirt, its hem, they could see now, mud-stained and torn, her ankles beneath it in thick, home-spun stockings, 'I dress like a peasant because that is how I live, working on the land. To have guests to stay — especially those on whom I can practise my English! — is like old times. Now, my name is Marie-Claire Furneau and you must call me Marie-Claire. And you are . . . ?'

They introduced themselves as she led them across the drawbridge and into the courtyard. 'Ah — you are the one called Kate,' she said softly and Kate blushed, hoping the others hadn't heard yet secretly pleased that Pierre must have mentioned her by name.

The courtyard was as enchanting as the exterior of the house. The gnarled, grey branches of a wisteria softened the classic proportions of the 'new' wing with its double row of long sash windows and along the opposite side, a large stable block had been built; but now, only a couple of shaggy black ponies peered over the loose-box doors.

The fourth side of the square had been left open — and commanded a view that had them gasping. Immediately below, where the moat rejoined the main river, the ground tumbled away into the terraces of a vineyard, now sadly overgrown, and the river tumbled with it in a series of torrents and waterfalls, to lose itself eventually in a vast patchwork of fields and dykes and the poplar-lined roads that ran, straight as arrows, across Northern France.

'We are looking west,' said Marie-Claire, 'away from the battlefields. But you have come to escape from the war, not to remember it, so we will speak of it no more. Now, I will show you your rooms. One looks over the moat, the other on to the courtyard.'

It was pure chance that Angela was immediately behind Kate and so followed her into a room where the ripple of the water was reflected through the lattice on to the low ceiling, and brass bedsteads flaunted enormous white eiderdowns like huge puff balls.

'Prissy won't mind?' Angela asked.

'She'll be as delighted to have a change as I am!' For Kate guessed that Angela would welcome an opportunity to talk freely about Ernst.

That evening, they ate what Marie-Claire called, somewhat disparagingly, 'rabbit stew'. A delicious concoction in which herbs and spices had clearly played a major part. It was followed by a sponge pudding that bore as little resemblance to the château's plum duff as the Camembert that rounded off the meal did to mousetrap Cheddar.

They ate at a scrubbed oak table in the enormous, stone-flagged kitchen of the original house and in the company of Marie-Claire's two children, Denise, a girl of thirteen and Phillipe, a boy of fifteen.

'I hope you do not mind such informality,' Marie-Claire apologised, 'but wood for the stoves is hard to come by these days. However, tomorrow we shall be 'en fête' as it's Saturday and the children will be at home, so we shall dine in the salon — roast pheasants! The birds have been hanging for several days, awaiting your arrival.'

'Already, I am drooling!' said Angela. And already, you are looking more like your old self, thought Kate. And she blessed Pierre for having arranged such a wonderful holiday. A pity, she found herself thinking, that he could not be here to share it with them but that, of course was a sentimental notion, proof, if it was needed, of the magical influence of Le Petit Manoir.

Soon after they'd finished their meal, Marie-Claire having refused all offers to wash the dishes — 'I have a little maid who comes up from the village each day to help me' — they went up to their rooms.

'Tired?' Angela asked once she and Kate were under their eiderdowns.

'No,' said Kate valiantly, although she could feel every tiny muscle relaxing into what was surely a feather mattress. 'How do you feel about Ernst these days?' she asked, coming directly to the point.

'Still trying to come to terms with what happened.'

'But no regrets?'

'Only if . . . ' Angela's voice trembled slightly, 'something dreadful has happened to him. My worst fear is that he may have been taken away and shot.'

'Far more likely that he's been sent to a French P.O.W. camp. After all, the Red Cross had been notified that he was a prisoner. The authorities would hardly . . . '

'The authorities,' Angela snorted, 'will do just as

they please! My blood still boils when I think of the way they twisted what really happened. It was so unfair on Ernst.'

'Just as well for you, though,' Kate pointed out.

'I suppose so. But Sister watches me like a hawk, these days. I'm never allowed to be in the ward on my own, and I swear all my mail is censored. Incoming, as well as outgoing.'

'But you're still glad you met Ernst?' Kate asked drowsily.

'Oh, *yes*! I'll never forget him.'

'Nor I,' said Kate fighting sleep. But she didn't mean Ernst, of course. She meant Pierre. Or was it . . . ? She slept. And dreamt of a man who had Pierre's face but spoke with Robert's voice.

★ ★ ★

They woke to sunlight slanting between the curtains. Kate's little travelling clock informed them it was just gone ten.

'Good heavens!' But Kate still lay there, cocooned in soft, luxurious warmth.

'No rush,' said Angela. 'Marie-Claire told us to stay in bed as long as we liked.'

'So she did.' Kate lay back, remembering the previous evening, and then she raised herself on one elbow to peer at the white hump that was Angela. 'Angie, I'm so sorry. I seem to remember I went to sleep on you last night.'

'Don't worry! I soon followed you. And you were so right. I *was* lucky not to be sent home — fancy missing all this! So, I'm going to look on the bright side from now on and start learning German! Ready for after the war when Ernst and I will find each other again. And that's not as unlikely as you might think. He knows where my family live in England.'

Clearly, such optimism, such certainty that their love would survive the enormous odds stacked against it, must be encouraged. 'Angie, you're brilliant!' Kate told her. 'And there are sure to be books that will help you in the château library.' Privately, she feared her friend was building her hopes too high.

The conversation was interrupted by a knock on the door. Priscilla, still in her dressing gown, peered around it. 'Good, you're awake!' She was followed by Meg, similarly clad and carrying a tray that held four bowls of steaming coffee. 'Compliments of Marie-Claire!'

All four of them now under the massive eiderdowns, they sipped, sighed with contentment and planned the day.

'Marie-Claire says two of us can ride the ponies,' Priscilla explained, 'with Phillipe on his bicycle to show the way. So Meg and I thought you and Angie could do that, because she doesn't ride and I'm not keen, while we walk down to the village with Denise. Imagine — real shops *and* a café!'

'But we can't ride in our skirts,' Kate pointed out.

'Marie-Claire says you can borrow a couple of pairs of her breeches. Miles too big for you, of course, Kate but you'll just have to reef them in.'

And reef them in she did, with a piece of garden twine, so that they ballooned around her like a clown's pantaloons. The addition of one of

Monsieur Furneau's massive pullovers did nothing to add to her chic, but what did it matter? Angela looked quite smart enough for the two of them.

They set off down the lane at a sedate trot with Phillipe free-wheeling beside them until they reached a broad, grassy ride across common land. Kate felt her pony gather itself for action and, for one terrifying moment, found that her own unused muscles refused to respond, but then her thighs tightened around the saddle, her hands took up the reins and she was thundering after the broad rump of Angela's mount. They reached the end of the common, neck and neck, with Phillipe pedalling furiously in the rear.

'That,' Angela gasped, 'was purest heaven!' And Kate, breathless, could only nod.

They rode for miles through a forest of sweet chestnuts, its floor soft and springy with empty husks, then beside a shallow stream that flowed through fields where Charolais cattle scattered before them, and so, eventually, back across the common for one final, breath-taking gallop before clattering across the drawbridge and into the courtyard of Le Petit Manoir. With the westering sun shining straight into their eyes, the figures that came to greet them were vague shapes against the brightness.

Kate slithered to the ground. But there, as if in protest at the treatment they'd been subjected to, her legs buckled beneath her at the same moment that the twine holding up her breeches gave way.

'Allow me!' said Pierre Montarial, holding her very tightly indeed.

* ★ ★ ★

'Under the circumstances, what else could I do,' Pierre Montarial enquired of the circle of laughing faces around the table, 'but pick her up and carry her indoors. Surely even an Englishman would have done the same?'

'An Englishman would have simply looked the other way,' said Angela, wiping the tears from her eyes.

'And let her breeches fall to the ground? That would have been most ungallant!'

He smiled down at Kate, seated beside him, and noticed her blushes. 'Forgive me, Kate! I should not tease you like this.'

'I must have looked such a clown!' she said. 'I certainly felt like one!' Would she ever forget her embarrassment as Pierre, realising immediately what had happened, had swept her up in his arms and carried her up to her room? But along with embarrassment, had come a deep, sensual pleasure at lying there against his heart, his eyes smiling down at her as he'd laid her gently on her bed. 'Better now, 'chérie'?'

Had Megan not been hot on his heels, clearly concerned for Kate's modesty, anything might have happened. As it was, he'd straightened up, murmured something about seeing Marie-Claire about a hot bath for Kate and left the room.

Now, to Kate's relief, the whole affair was being treated as a great joke. And at least, after such an unconventional start to his visit, there'd been no place for formality on anyone's part.

171

'There was an ambulance coming this way,' he'd explained, 'so I thought I'd come and see how my four little nurses were enjoying themselves. And,' with an affectionate smile in her direction, 'see my old friend, Marie-Claire, and her family. I have arranged to be picked up again early tomorrow morning.'

Kate glanced around the table and sighed with pleasure. Candlelight from a silver candelabra glowed on the crystal goblets, the carafes of red wine, the bowls of scarlet apples and the sprigs of mistletoe that Phillipe had climbed the orchard apple trees to gather. The meal was nearly over but the conversation, along with the wine, continued to flow.

'I can hardly believe,' said Pierre, 'that these are the same exhausted, war-weary nurses who left the château yesterday morning. Whatever you've done to them, Marie-Claire, has worked wonders.'

So then they all had to tell him about the delicious food, the hours of blissful sleep and the relaxations of the day; with Megan and Priscilla giving a description of the little general store in the village that sold this wonderful ribbon, so wonderful they'd bought yards and yards of it to trim their blouses which could, perhaps, explain why they all looked so different.

But it wasn't just that, Kate decided, noticing how the lines of strain had faded from Meg's anxious little face, and how Angela's eyes held their old sparkle, and as for Prissy — well, she just wished Hank could see her now, for he'd have defied his father without a moment's hesitation and been over on the next boat!

172

Suddenly daring, she banged on the table and raised her glass. 'A toast! To Marie-Claire and Pierre!' For it would have been unthinkable in present circumstances, to have called him 'Dr Montarial'.

'To Marie-Claire and Pierre,' they all chorused. And then Angela proposed,

'Denise and Phillipe!' to their delighted confusion.

And after that it would have been churlish not to have mentioned Yvonne, the little maid who had sat at table with them.

After all that drinking, it was inevitable, essential even, that they should gravitate to the sofas and easy chairs set around the big log fire and where Pierre distributed tiny glasses of Calvados.

'Happy?' he whispered to Kate as he sat beside her. And when she murmured that she couldn't be happier and that she couldn't thank him enough for bringing it all about, he squeezed her hand and said something about gratitude not being exactly what he had in mind. But since, by then, they'd all begun to sing Christmas carols in a somewhat boisterous fashion, she couldn't be quite sure what he'd said. In any case, her eyelids had suddenly grown heavy.

She woke to silence, broken only by the soft hiss of a smouldering log and the gentle purring of a cat that had come to crouch on the hearth. Beside her on the settee, Pierre leant forward, gazing into the flames. Apart from the cat, they were alone. She stirred in alarm. 'Where . . . ?'

He turned his head quickly. 'Don't alarm yourself, *chérie!* You looked so peaceful it was decided not to disturb you.'

'Goodness!' She pushed herself upright. 'Angela will be wondering . . . '

'Angela will be wondering nothing at all! Angela will be fast asleep!'

'But I must still . . . ' she tried to rise but really it was all such an effort and Pierre was doing nothing to help her. She sank back against the cushions.

'Good! Personally, I think it would be a wicked waste to leave this wonderful fire. But is there anything I can get you? A glass of water, perhaps?'

'A glass of water would be most acceptable.'

'I will get it.' He went out to the kitchen and she could hear the opening and closing of a cupboard door, the running of water.

'You are very much at home here,' she said when he'd come back and she was sipping gratefully.

'We came here often before the war. I was at school with Claude, Marie-Claire's husband. He is away at the front now, near Verdun, I think.'

Kate looked at him over the rim of her glass, her eyes troubled. 'We came here often,' he had said. Did he mean with his parents? But then she remembered that his mother had worked as a laundrymaid in order to put him through medical school. It was hardly likely there'd been money to spare for journeys into the countryside. But if not his parents, then who? And if it *was* another woman, then surely he should not be sitting beside her at — she glanced at her watch — two o'clock in the morning, with an expression in his eyes that was causing her heart to race uncontrollably. And now he was leaning forward to take the glass from her and put it safely on a side-table before putting his hands on her shoulders, and bringing his face down to hers, his lips . . .

Abruptly, she twisted her head away. 'Kate, Kate!' he chided. 'We are not in the hospital now.'

'You said 'we',' Kate said in a flat voice.

Puzzled, he stared down at her. 'What . . . ?'

'You said 'we' came here often before the war. If you have a wife or a fiancée . . . '

And now he smiled, a gentle, teasing smile without rancour. 'You mean, my little English rose, that if that is the case, then I should not be sitting here with you like this? And perhaps you would be right. But it does not arise for I have no wife, my Kate. Nor a fiancée. Heloise was a friend — a true and loving companion of whom I am still very fond — but that is all.'

'Where is she now?'

He shrugged. 'Somewhere in France. Like you, she is a nurse. But now, *chérie*, it is my turn to ask questions. Did *you* not have a loving companion before the war? I cannot believe that someone so beautiful, so charming, did not.' His lips brushed her forehead and for a moment, she was tempted to say no, that apart from the briefest of flirtations with some of her father's pupils, her experience of love had been virtually nonexistent. But Robert, even after all this time, should not be denied.

'There was one,' she admitted. 'But only one.'

'And where is he now?'

'Like your Heloise, somewhere in France, I suppose.'

His lips had begun to explore her face, planting

tiny kisses upon her eyes, her chin, the tip of her nose. 'So you see,' he said softly, as his mouth found hers, 'we are both free.'

The kiss was like nothing she had experienced before. The first gentle persuasion of his tongue to separate her lips seemed to titillate her whole body to a fever pitch of longing; although for what, she had no clear idea, except that her own tongue was now playing a ridiculous, tantalising game with his, that her hands were caressing the thick mass of his hair, that her breasts were straining against the yielding fabric of her blouse, that there was a yearning ache in the pit of her stomach. She felt Pierre's hand between her thighs and groaned softly.

'Sweet Kate!' he murmured. 'My sweet Kate, I want you so!'

If only he hadn't called her his 'Sweet Kate'! If only Robert hadn't used the same endearment! For it was enough to break the spell, to cause her to pull away from him before it was too late. For she wasn't *his* 'Sweet Kate'. Not *yet*, at any rate. She looked up into his eyes. 'I'm so sorry, Pierre!'

He shook his head as if to clear it, his eyes unfocused as he fought for control. And then he smiled ruefully as he drew back. 'I'm sorry, too! But I'm a patient man, Kate. In the end, I get what I want!'

Only later, under her eiderdown, listening to Angela's steady breathing, did she remember Pierre's exact words. 'I want you!' Not, as Robert had said. 'I love you!' But what, after all, did that signify? For clearly, Robert no longer did.

15

After all, it was a mixed blessing to know exactly where Meg's Gareth was. Books in the château library, translated laboriously with the aid of a French dictionary, told them that Gallipoli was a bare and barren place, rocky and precipitous, hostile to mankind.

'In a way,' Angela tried to look on the positive side, 'if you *must* have a war, it's the right place to have one. At least, there won't be many refugees. Not like here.' For they'd all seen the columns of dejected women, children and old people who'd stumbled along the road below the château after the autumn push, their meagre possessions piled high on makeshift carts, old perambulators or, more often than not, their own backs.

Soberly, they agreed that this was true although the fact didn't exactly improve Gareth's lot; a viewpoint that was given extra credence when newspapers from home told of the dysentery that had ravaged the troops during the heat of August, of the lack of fresh water and, worst of all, medical supplies, although hospital ships were standing off-shore in the Bay of Mudros.

'D'you think they'd let me go out there to nurse?' a distraught Megan asked.

'When was Gareth's letter dated?' Priscilla, ever

practical, looked up from the geography book she was consulting.

'September,' said Meg. 'September 19th. Two days,' her voice wobbled dangerously, 'before our wedding anniversary.'

'Well, in that case, I should think he's survived the worst. According to this, it'll be growing much colder now.'

In such small ways, did they try to comfort her; until another newspaper article told of the November storms that had flooded the Gallipoli trenches, bringing untold misery to the soldiers trying to exist inside them. They knew by now what happened to men in such conditions. Already several severe cases of frostbite and trench foot were being treated in the wards. In extreme cases, toes had to be amputated, if not the whole foot.

'He never would change his socks when they got wet,' Megan mourned.

No-one liked to point out it was highly unlikely he'd have a dry pair to change into, anyway.

Eventually, Megan could bear it no longer. Just before Christmas, she requested an interview with Matron. If the army wouldn't send her out there, she'd find some other way. It was no use pointing out there was no other way.

Matron's reaction surprised them. She quite understood Nurse Jones's anxiety but soon, she prophesied, there'd be nothing to worry about.

'I am not, of course, privy to Mr Winston Churchill's exact intentions, Nurse, but I think it probable there will soon be no British soldiers left on Gallipoli.'

Megan stared at her, speechless with terror. Was she prophesying the massacre of the entire British force?

'Evacuation,' said Matron crisply. 'Reading between the lines, that is my sincere expectation. My advice to you, Nurse, is to wait as patiently as possible until after Christmas. And then, I promise you, if Gallipoli is still occupied, I will forward your application immediately.' And with that, Megan had to be content.

Unlike the previous year, the Christmas of 1915 provided little in the way of respite. General Sir Douglas Haig had taken over from Field Marshall Sir John French as Commander of the army in France and Flanders and a new War Cabinet had been formed at home, with Lloyd George as a new and enthusiastic Minister of Munitions. Fighting still continued around Loos and just before Christmas the Germans launched a vicious gas attack north-east of Ypres. Although it was repulsed and in spite of the improved gas mask, the medical ward at the château was inundated with coughing, wheezing men.

'This lot won't be joining in, that's for sure,' said Priscilla on Christmas morning as the little group of nurses who had volunteered to sing carols, congregated outside the ward.

'So we'll have to sing even louder,' said Kate, 'though I wish we had a little male support.'

'Let's press-gang Dr Montarial, then,' suggested one of the group, as Pierre came out of the ward.

Kate didn't join in the chorus of approval. Since coming back from Le Petit Manoir, Pierre had maintained a certain professional distance and she was anxious for it to continue. So part of her wasn't sorry when he laughingly pleaded 'another appointment' and walked on. But another part was wickedly delighted when he wished them all 'Joyeux Nöel' but gave her an almost imperceptible nod so that she felt it was meant for her ears alone.

'What about the Germans?' someone asked outside their ward. 'Shall we serenade them?'

'Why not?' said Angela. And so the haunting strains of 'Silent Night' floated up to the ceiling, to be taken up immediately in their own language by the prisoners. Angela, Kate noticed, was near to tears.

After the carol singing it was time for the best present of all, the collection of Christmas mail. They hurried to the post-room for an eager inspection of their pigeon-holes.

'Good old Pa!' Kate seized a fat envelope addressed to herself and Priscilla.

'And good old Hank!' Priscilla picked up one bearing an American stamp.

'A letter from Gareth's parents? I wonder if . . . ' Megan was tearing open the envelope.

'One from Ma, bless her! And one,' Angela consulted the postmark, 'from Cousin Annie in Scotland. That's all.' Clearly, she felt it wasn't enough. 'I don't know what I expected,' she added for Kate's ears alone, 'a Christmas card with 'Fröhliche Weihnachten!' on it, or something equally as impossible!'

'You'd be sent home so fast your feet wouldn't

touch the ground, if that were to happen!' Kate reminded her.

'Suppose so! But it would be worth it!'

Slowly, they walked away from the post-room, reading their letters as they went. Seconds later, Kate felt a hand grasp her shoulder in a grip that made her wince. She turned quickly. Angela stood there, her eyes shining, her cheeks flushed. When she spoke, her voice was an incoherent gabble.

'Lis-listen to this from C-Cousin Annie! Or — bet-better still, read it yourself!' She pointed to a paragraph in her letter.

'The other day, I had a very pleasant surprise. I met your old friend Ernest. Do you remember him? Very good at art — he said he once drew *you*, sitting in the garden. Well, he asked after you and sent his love. He'll be in Scotland for quite a while, he said. So, if you want to send him a message . . . '

'I can hardly believe it! The coincidence!' Angela's voice still trembled with excitement. 'He must have been sent to work on Uncle Ian's estate outside Inverness. His name is Carstairs, too, of course. So Ernst would have guessed . . . '

'Keep your voice down,' Kate cautioned. 'You don't want anyone to suspect . . . '

'No, of course not!' Angela dropped her voice to a whisper so conspiratorial it would have aroused as much suspicion as a shout had anyone been listening. 'But, oh Cousin Annie — I love you!'

'What about your Uncle Ian. D'you think he knows?'

Angela sobered a little. 'He's a stickler for what he calls 'the done thing' so I doubt it. It took him all his time to forgive Pa for marrying Ma. But Cousin Annie's always been a friend. Oh, I'm so excited, I shall burst!'

'Go and get your cloak and we'll go for a stroll,' Kate suggested. 'I'm not on duty until after lunch.'

'Brilliant idea! At least then, I can tell the trees!'

★ ★ ★

In an abandoned barn, some way behind the front line near Loos, Robert Holker was also eagerly scanning his Christmas mail. Would there be . . . ? Yes! A letter addressed in Mrs Moneymoon's characteristically large and flowing hand. It was as well, thought Robert affectionately, that Kate had been the one to keep the books for no ledger could have accommodated Mrs Moneymoon's numerals. He tore open the envelope.

In the event, it told him little of what he really wanted to know; Moneymoon Manor was still a hive of industry; the clothes line area had been ploughed up for vegetables; his motorcycle was being meticulously cared for by Danny, and ever since a way had been discovered of using newspapers instead of hay as a means of generating heat for cooking, the Professor's Manchester Guardian had been constantly whipped away from him before he'd read it — much to his annoyance! Almost as an afterthought came the information that Kate and Priscilla were now 'somewhere in France'.

'It would be so nice,' Mrs Moneymoon had added, as if the Western Front were some enormous garden party, 'if you happened to bump into each other!'

Well at least, Robert thought as he put the letter back into its envelope, we are now in the same country. But there were so many places where a V.A.D. could serve, so many Casualty Clearing Stations, so many Red Cross trains, so many Base Hospitals under canvas, so many big houses commandeered for the wounded — like the fairy-tale château he'd once seen. He turned to the rest of his mail.

His father wrote of the difficulties of running the estate; of grass put under the plough, of woodland uncoppiced and birds untended — 'we only shoot for the pot, now' — of cottages abandoned when tenants were called to the colours and their wives to the nearest munition factory. 'I long for the day when you will be here to help me lick it all back into shape'. More and more, his father seemed to be taking it for granted that Robert would fill the role that tradition demanded.

'Your mother,' the letter ended, 'is doing her best to carry out the duties expected of her, attending meetings of the Red Cross, and visiting the old people on the estate. But she misses George dreadfully. And yourself, of course,' he'd added dutifully.

Aunt Bella's letter, too, spoke of deprivations but, with her unfailing sense of humour, managed to put them firmly in their place.

'Fires are kept to the bare minimum so that we sit around in our outdoor clothes to keep warm and visitors think we are about to go out! This can be extremely useful if the visitor is not particularly welcome!

However, for the first time in my life, it is perfectly acceptable for me to do manual work. And I revel in it; digging away in the vegetable garden as if my life depended upon it — as indeed, it does! I am becoming an authority upon which type of vegetable grows best in our soil and every morning it is a race between old Mathews, our one remaining gardener, and myself as to who reaches the stableyard first in order to shovel up the droppings from our single carriage horse, now demoted to pulling the dogcart. *He* — Mathews — says he needs it for his asparagus bed and I plead for it on behalf of my tomatoes! So far, the honours are roughly even!

Look after yourself, my dearest boy; if that is not too foolish a sentiment under the circumstances. I know that things will never be the same after this dreadful war is over but please God, *some* things will be improved.'

There speaks a truly sensible woman, Robert thought, turning to his next letter. It was addressed in a hand he didn't recognise; cramped and ill-formed as if the writer was unused to holding a pen. It was from General Wavertree's housekeeper and informed him, with little preamble, that the General had died in his sleep at the beginning of December.

'He had never been the same after his grandson was killed — at some place called Awdrenny.'

— Audregnies, Robert corrected automatically, he'd heard of the Lancers' magnificent charge there in August —

'And soon afterwards, the boy's parents also died — in a motor-car accident. Inventions of the devil, the General always called them — and he was right.

Anyway, when Pugsie had to be put to sleep because of the weakness of his heart, that was the end of it as far as the General was concerned. He just gave up.

He never told you any of this, sir, because he said you had enough to put up with where you were. But he always liked to read your letters. He's a good boy, he used to say, bothering with an old fogey like me. And he was fond of that nice young lady of yours, too.

I am sorry to be the bearer of such sad news at Christmas time but I thought you should know.

God bless you, sir. And keep you safe.

Ada Crawley (Miss)

P.S. Before he died, the General arranged that I could continue to live here as long as I wanted. And this I shall do until such time as the new owner tells me otherwise.'

Poor old boy! thought Robert, dying on his own like that. I wish it could have been otherwise. But I'm glad I wrote to him.

He picked up his last letter; a large, stout envelope bearing the address of a firm of London solicitors. Estate business, perhaps, that his father had requested be sent to him — but it wasn't from the family firm. He opened it; to discover that 'according to instructions issued by our late client, General Wavertree' he was now the owner of the deceased's house in Long Wittenham, Oxfordshire and an income, once probate was granted, of approximately £5,000 a year, most of it derived from stocks and shares. His instructions as to what, if anything, he would like done with his property, were awaited. Meanwhile, General Wavertee's housekeeper, Miss Ada Crawley, was happy to remain in residence and was, indeed, entitled to do so, under the terms of the General's will, for as long as she wished.

His first thought was that Kate had loved that little house. 'It's like a child's drawing,' she'd declared. 'A straight path up to the front door and that set squarely between big, sash windows, bay trees in half-barrels either side and three windows in the floor above. And just two tiny attic windows let into the roof exactly between the chimneys!'

The perfect little house, he found himself thinking now, while his mind tried to come to terms with this extraordinary piece of good fortune, for a newly-married couple setting up house for the first time. Here, surely he could be plain Robert Holker, Esq., finishing his studies at Oxford University while his pretty young wife busied herself with all manner of house-wifely duties. They'd have a dog of course, perhaps two, and a horse at livery in the village for Kate — *he'd* have his Harley Davidson! On £5,000 a year, they could manage all that.

Freedom, he thought, freedom from the yoke of an inheritance that I bitterly resent and the chance to ask the girl I love to share an ordinary man's life. Was it too much to ask?

'Holker!' a voice broke into his thoughts. 'Put your letters away and come and have your Christmas dinner. Cook happened to see a couple of chickens sauntering down the road so he commandeered them for the pot. Scrawny old birds, but they're an improvement on bully beef.'

He got to his feet, shaking his head to rid himself of his impossible dream. For the odds were stacked too heavily against it; in the first place, would he survive the war, would his luck hold? and in the second, would Kate, even if he were to find her, want to marry plain Robert Holker any more than she'd wanted to marry the future Earl of Werrington?

★　★　★

Just before New Year, Megan was called to Matron's office; there to be told that the evacuation of Gallipoli, as Matron had predicted, had begun on the 20th of December, under cover of darkness. Due largely to the troops themselves who, with great cunning, had managed to convince the Turks that their numbers remained constant even while they slipped silently away into the night, it had been a glorious success. Nurse Jones's husband should now be on his way home, on board one of the troop ships that had waited out in the bay. Almost delirious with relief, Megan came out of the office and hurried to find the others.

Just one hour later, when she was in the middle of writing to Gareth's parents, she received a second summons; and this time was given a chair. A telegram had just arrived from the War Office informing her that Lieutenant Gareth Jones had been wounded during the evacuation of Gallipoli and had been disembarked at Malta where, it was feared, his condition was critical.

'Malta?' Megan quavered. 'Why . . . ? Where . . . ?'

'We have a garrison there,' Matron explained. 'And a hospital. But it is, of course, a long way from here. You would have to travel back to England and from there go by troop ship. And I should warn you, Nurse, that the German U-boats are active in the Bay of Biscay and the Mediterranean. And there is always the possibility, as you well know, that when you arrive, it could be — too late.'

But Megan was already on her feet. 'When may I leave?'

'Immediately, of course, if you're sure . . . ' But Megan was very sure.

By then, Angela and Kate were back on duty. It was Priscilla who helped her pack her valise, request sandwiches and coffee from the kitchen, collect her travel warrant from a sympathetic Mary Barnes in the Orderly room and accompany her to the station in the truck that the Colonel had authorised.

'I felt so sorry for her,' she told Kate and Angela later. 'So tiny and defenceless as she waved goodbye. And yet so brave. She'll write, of course, as soon as she has any news.' And with that they had to be content. But the conditions in the hospitals in Malta, they learned from one of the Sisters who had a friend who had served there, were primitive in the extreme.

16

January brought no news of Megan; but did bring, to Angela's fury, her replacement.

Adelaide Fanshawe was from London's East End where her father kept a public house and her mother a pie shop. She had red hair, a temper to match and a heart as big as her size seven boots. Strangely enough, it was the boots that caused Angela's fury. They lay on her bed when she came off duty one evening, all three pairs of them, highly polished and of good-quality leather.

'Like great, shiny, black beetles,' she told Kate and Priscilla indignantly when she arrived in their room, mug in hand, for their customary bed-time cocoa. 'They were even polished *underneath*!'

'So they should be,' said Kate. 'Ma always makes Danny polish his soles as well as his uppers. *You* wouldn't know. The boot boy probably did yours.'

Angela glared. She always hated any reference to the privileged, peace-time position she'd undoubtedly enjoyed. 'I couldn't help that!'

'Any more than Adelaide Fanshawe could help *her* birthright. Anyway, what did you say?'

'I told her to look smart and take them off my

bed. And she spat at me like a stable cat and said she'd do it when she was good and ready. *She* wasn't taking orders from another V.A.D., even if that V.A.D. did happen to come out of the top drawer. And talking of drawers, she reckoned she was entitled to half the chest, so would I please move my stuff out. The trouble is it's not my stuff, it's what poor old Megs left behind. That's the real trouble,' she added ruefully, 'I still hoped Meg would be coming back.'

'We all hoped that,' said Priscilla.

There was a short silence while they all thought about Megan. Then Angela said thoughtfully, '*She* wouldn't have been such a selfish cow, would she? *She'd* have made Adelaide Fanshawe welcome, boots and all.'

The others nodded but said nothing. They knew their friend. 'So,' she got to her feet, 'I'll go and get her, shall I?'

'I'll come with you,' Kate offered, 'while Prissy makes the cocoa.'

They talked far into the night, far longer than they should have done but it was important that Addie Fanshawe should be made to feel at home, to understand that she really was wanted. And in return, she told them what was happening in England now; how any young man not in uniform was liable to be handed a white feather in the street by some cruel, insensitive woman — for how did *they* know he hadn't some perfectly good reason for not fighting, like asthma or flat feet?

But even so, 'some old geyser', Lord Derby, Addie thought it was, had discovered there really were too many single men not pulling their weight, so it was likely something called conscription would start up.

'And when you think,' Addie pointed out, 'that those bloody Germans have had the cheek to start bombing Kent — yes, honest! the very place we used to go hop-picking in the summer — it's hardly surprising, *nine* bombs they dropped the night before I came away. And actually killed a bloke!'

When she and Angela finally left, sometime after midnight, Addie thanked them politely for 'having' her but made it quite clear that while she hoped to come again, she didn't expect charity. 'My Uncle Bernie — he's a pawnbroker in Houndsditch — he's been ever so generous, so I'm not short of a bob or two. And Ma will be sending me parcels.'

Any contribution, they assured her, would be gratefully received. And they were delighted to have her company.

'*My Ma*,' they heard Angela relating as she led Addie away, 'was a parlour-maid. So I'm only half 'top-drawer' as you call it. The other half's more a sort of bargain basement!'

★   ★   ★

Addie Fanshawe settled in to her new life with amazing swiftness. She was, it soon became clear, a law unto herself. 'I'm not putting up with this!' she declared on her first morning at breakfast, when the porridge was more than usually lumpy and bacon fried to unrecognisable, leather-like strips. And she picked up her plate and carried it through to the kitchens that served both Other Ranks' and Officers'

Messes, her chin jutting at an alarming angle, her eyes flashing blue flames.

'Ye gods and little fishes!' Angela — who was with her — was appalled. 'Stand by to collect the pieces!'

But there were no pieces. In fact, there was no Addie, in any shape or form.

'What d'you suppose has happened to her?' Angela fretted when it was time for them to go on duty.

'Hauled up before the Colonel, at the very least,' said Mary Barnes who'd arrived just as Addie had made her spectacular departure. 'Don't worry, it won't matter if I'm a few minutes late. I'll hang on.'

In the end, she'd gone in search of Addie and found her busily instructing an army private in the art of porridge-making while a bemused Sergeant scratched his head and wondered what to do next. Addie, however, suffered no such indecision.

'Red Cross workers are allowed to turn their hands to anything, aren't they?' she enquired of Mary. 'So why don't I help out here instead of on the wards? Could you fix it for me?' She allowed one eyelid to drop in an enormous wink. 'I'll make it worth your while!'

Mary scurried away, not at all sure of her ability to 'fix it'. But, amazingly, everyone from Matron downwards had welcomed the suggestion. 'What a relief!' she was even overheard to comment to the Colonel.

It was a sentiment soon echoed by everyone in the château. The porridge became smooth and creamy, the bacon was done to crisp perfection and before long Addie's beef pies were almost fought over at dinner-time.

'Don't know how you do it, m'dear,' said the Colonel on one of his routine visits of inspection, now undertaken with increasing frequency.

'You should taste my Ma's eel pies!' said Addie unperturbed. 'They're out of this world.'

But the Colonel wasn't so sure about eels. 'Best left in the river, m'dear!'

'She's so different from Meg,' said Angela, 'I don't feel I'm betraying a friendship when I say she's a great room-mate. Although I still wish . . . '

They all did. But their hopes were finally dashed when Kate opened the letter with the unusual stamp that was addressed to all three of them.

'My dearest friends,' Meg had written, 'I know that you will all be greatly saddened to hear that my beloved Gareth passed away soon after I arrived here. But at least I was with him when he died, something for which I shall always be grateful. The Sister on the ward was kindness itself and I know now just how those relatives felt who came out to be with *our* boys — so keep up the good work.

I am very fortunate, too, in that one of Gareth's friends, a John Corben, was also wounded at Gallipoli but not as badly as Gareth, so he was able to tell me exactly what happened. Apparently, they were both among the last to leave because they'd been detailed to blow up the powder magazines still remaining on the beaches.

John was hit in the leg by a splinter from a Turkish shell and Gareth went back for him. *He* was hit in the chest as they reached the boat waiting to take them out to the troop ship. John says that had Gareth not gone back for him, he would have been safely on the previous boat. There is talk of a posthumous decoration, which I hope will be of some comfort to his parents, although it is of little to me.

And now for a piece of news that will surprise you. The name of the Sister I mentioned who was so kind to me, is Sister Hopkins, née Hardcastle! I couldn't believe my eyes! She married Sergeant Hopkins — you remember him? the man with both legs amputated whom she nursed? — but they then decided that while he went to a special hospital at Roehampton to learn how to use his artificial legs and perhaps to help others similarly afflicted, she would continue to nurse. And she was sent out here.

In many ways, it is a beautiful island — John showed me a little of it before he was fit enough to go home — but the conditions in the hospitals are really grim. So I have decided I will stay out here and do what I can to help.

I cannot tell you how much I miss you all, but I hope you will understand that I feel I am needed more here. It means, too, that I will be able to tend Gareth's grave. And Sister Hopkins will keep an eye on me. Believe it or not, she sends you her love! As I do, of course. I could never have got through the last year without your support. I shall never forget you.

God bless you all, I am as sure as I can be that we shall meet again one day.

Your loving friend, Meg.

P.S. In a way, life is easier now. At least there is no more worry.'

They wept unashamedly upon each other's shoulders; for Gareth, for Meg, for the sheer futility of it all.

★ ★ ★

On the 24th of March, the cross-channel steamship, Sussex, was torpedoed as it neared the French coast. Among the hundred or so feared lost, were two V.A.D's from the château. The consequent pall of sadness that descended over the wards was so great it even obliterated, for a short time, all thoughts of the war. Except, of course, that it *was* the war.

'But it was a civilian boat!' Kate raged. 'What's the point of the Hague Convention if both sides don't stick to it?'

She was venting her fury in the sluice while preparing yet another container of hypochlorous acid solution for the gas gangrene patients.

Pierre, supervising the operation, was unexpectedly slow to agree with her. Kate glanced up in surprise; he was usually even more vehement than she in condemnation of the enemy. His face, she now noticed, was unusually pale, his eyes troubled.

'Pierre, are you all right?' It was an indication of

her concern that she used his Christian name without thinking.

He smiled at her. 'I am all right. But my news is not, I'm afraid. Or perhaps,' and his smile grew rueful, 'I am presuming too much. Perhaps you will not be at all disturbed to hear that I have decided to leave the château. For a while, at least.'

'But . . . why . . . ?' She knew, of course, that he was only seconded to the British army, that, theoretically, he could at any time go back to the French hospital from whence he'd come. But she had never entertained it as a serious possibility.

'Quite simply, because I am needed elsewhere. At a place called Verdun.'

Briefly, he told her of the devastating bombardment by the German long-range guns of the city that lay at the end of the deep valley in Lorraine, and was now mercilessly exposed to the enemy massing on the hillsides around it.

'The shells are huge, both in size and quantity. And, as so often happens, our army is hampered by the tide of refugees going in the other direction. The casualties are enormous, both among the civilians and the 'poilus'. So you see,' he shrugged expressively, 'it is a matter of all patriotic Frenchmen rallying to the cause.'

'But you're needed here,' Kate protested.

Again, he shrugged. '*Chérie*, I know! But how would you feel if London, or your beautiful city of Oxford, were under siege? Would you not want to help your fellow countrymen?'

There was only one answer. She nodded. 'But we shall miss you.'

'More to the point, will *you* miss me, Kate?'

'Of course! You're one of the best Medical Officers in the hospital. It's been a privilege to work . . . '

'Kate,' he chided her gently, 'you know that is not at all what I meant. Will you miss *me*, not just as a doctor?'

She was silent for a moment, collecting her thoughts. No-one was safe in this war. Only the other day, a Zeppelin had been sighted droning steadily eastward and shells could now be fired with greater and greater accuracy. Even going home on leave, after the tragedy of the Sussex, could no longer be considered an escape from danger. And Verdun was clearly a most dangerous place. The least she could do was to send Pierre on his way with an honest answer. 'Yes, I shall miss you, Pierre. Very much indeed.'

He put down the measuring spoon he'd been playing with and seized her hand. She was astonished to see that there were tears in his eyes. 'Oh, Kate! If only we had met many years ago! If only . . . '

'Many years ago,' Kate interrupted with a little, deprecatory laugh, for she hadn't intended to unleash such a flood of Gallic emotion, 'you had your friend Heloise for company.'

He frowned slightly. 'I have told you. She was a good friend. Nothing more. Otherwise why did I not marry her?'

Perhaps, she almost suggested, because she did not want to marry you? But instead, she asked. 'And what am I, if not a good friend?'

'*That*, of course! But I want you to be more

197

— much more! When this war is over — perhaps, before — I want to marry you. Just think of it, *chérie!* Between us, we could achieve so much — I as a doctor, you as a nurse. You are — how do you call it? — a natural. You could become qualified without difficulty.'

In his enthusiasm, he was now holding both her hands. Sister, Kate calculated swiftly, would soon be returning from lunch. She tried to disengage herself but he held her hands even more firmly. 'Please, dearest Kate, promise me you'll think about it while I am away.'

'You'll be coming back, then?'

'Oh, yes! If not in an official capacity then unofficially for your answer. And if it is yes, then . . . ' he paused significantly, 'I think it will be time to visit Le Petit Manoir again. And this time — alone.' And before she could draw back, he had leaned forward and kissed her on the mouth. And she, for one glorious moment of madness, kissed him back.

* * *

She missed him. Oh, how she missed him! On many days she had caught only a fleeting glimpse of him and then usually in Sister's presence, but she had always known that he could appear at any moment, to smile at her, to exchange a few words, sometimes to drink a quick cup of coffee.

It was Priscilla who put it into words. 'Life's not so much *fun*, now Pierre's not here!' But as Kate was swift to point out, while secretly agreeing with her, they hadn't joined for fun!

'I will not write,' Pierre had told her. 'There will be no time and, in any case, I think you would feel compromised if a letter should arrive with Capitaine Montarial as the sender!'

'But what if . . . ?' She had stopped there, unable to put her fear into words. But Pierre had felt no such inhibition.

'If I were to die? Don't worry, *chérie*. My mother would be informed and I shall write to her now and ask that she inform you also.'

Kate had derived a tiny grain of comfort from the thought that telling his mother of her existence, somehow implied that she was already part of the Montarial family. For the more she thought about it, the more she liked the idea of marriage to Pierre. And the thought sustained her through the April days, along with the bird song that began to cheer the early mornings, when the windows of the wards could be opened wide to the soft, spring breeze.

The news from Verdun was not good. Although the city had not fallen, it remained under heavy bombardment and casualties, Kate had heard, were severe. It was a relief to share Priscilla's delight when she heard from Hank that he was hoping to join the American Red Cross.

'He says Uncle Sam's still dragging his feet,' Priscilla explained, 'but apparently many Americans feel guilty about not joining in the war, especially since the Germans sank the Lusitania. Even his parents are coming round to that way of thinking and since Hank can drive an automobile, there'd be nothing to stop him.'

'It's just possible,' Kate cautioned, 'that he

wouldn't be sent to France.'

'Oh, he would!' Priscilla was confident. 'Just think, Kate — forty-eight hours in Paris!'

'Just think!' Kate echoed. And wouldn't it be wonderful, she thought, if it could be a foursome, with herself and Pierre? Only occasionally, just before falling asleep, would she remember Robert Holker.

Priscilla was not the only one to be pleased with the way life was treating her. Angela, since receiving her cousin's letter about Ernst, habitually wore a tiny smile on her face.

'We have a very simple system,' she explained to Kate. 'When I write to Cousin Annie — which I do much more frequently than I used to! — I always enclose a note for her little brother. Of course, she has no brother, little or otherwise. They are for Ernst.'

'And what do you call this little brother?'

'Angus! A good Scottish name! Of course, I cannot write what I want to — that I love him and long to see him again. But I do talk about how I hope to see him when the war is over, perhaps before, if I get leave. And how he must keep up with his art.'

'And does he reply?'

'Oh, yes! In a round, schoolboy hand with many smudges and crossings out! But I am becoming adept at reading between the lines!'

Addie Fanshawe, too, was pleased with life. She was 'walking out' with the Mess Sergeant — 'although sometimes, I think it's only my recipe for rabbit pie he's after!'

17

May is a month of mixed fortunes for the Allies. The fighting around Verdun continues unabated but the city is not taken. At home, Mr Asquith introduces his Bill for the compulsory service of all men between the ages of 18 and 41. At Jutland, off the Danish coast, Admiral Jellico sees off the German fleet; no matter that the loss of British ships is nearly as great as that of the Germans, it is the enemy cruisers that finally slink away.

But in June, as if Neptune is keeping the balance, H.M.S. Hampshire is hit by a mine off the Orkneys and sinks, with Lord Kitchener among the casualties. Quite what his lordship was doing on board isn't clear, but rumour has it he was on his way to consult his brave Russian allies. Whatever the reason, it is a bitter blow to morale.

In Picardy, on the marshy banks of the River Somme, around villages like Albert, Bapaume and Gommecourt, the push to cap all previous efforts is coming to the boil. For weeks, Robert Holker has known something was afoot. Like several of his companions, he's been transferred south to Picardy from his old regiment in the north and once there, despatches between Battalion, Brigade and Division have come fast and furious with rarely more than an hour between his journeys. Rapid communication has always been of the greatest importance but now it isn't only he and the other Don R's who provide it. There had been a time, in fact, when they'd thought themselves obsolete, for apart from the network of telephones installed by the sappers, there are heliographs, Morse lamps, semaphore flags — how Danny would have enjoyed that! he'd thought when first he'd seen the signallers at their practice — and even carrier pigeons.

Everywhere they go behind the lines, they see men being drilled. Mostly, they are Kitchener's Boys, fresh out from home and more determined than ever, perhaps, since the untimely death of their hero, to fight for their country. But their numbers are strengthened by 'old soldiers' from crack regiments like the Rifle Brigade and the Guards and the Territorial Forces who've been in it from the beginning. Melded together, they are clearly becoming an army to be reckoned with. Surely, this time, they would break the German might and sweep on to victory? Even the most cynical admit to a little hope.

And the beauty of the countryside in which they now find themselves seems to add to their optimism. It could almost be the gently undulating landscape of Oxfordshire, Robert reflects, as he rides between apple orchards pink with blossom and hedges laced with briar. When, one day he passes the turning to the château he'd seen on a previous journey and notices the white caps of nurses fluttering around it, he almost concocts some trumped-up excuse to turn off, in order to discover if, by any chance . . . ? Had he not had a companion with him — and he a sergeant! — he might well have done so.

★ ★ ★

Now, Robert and thousands of other men know that the waiting is nearly over. Bombardment of the enemy lines has been going on for days but now the muzzles of the guns have been lifted so that their fire concentrates upon the German support lines, leaving the front line to the mercy of the British infantry. And mercy is something *they* have no intention of showing.

For over a week, working parties with faces blackened so that they resemble a troupe of seaside minstrels, have crawled out across No Man's Land to cut the enemy wire, devoutly grateful for dark and cloudy skies. Night after night, troops have been quietly moving up to fill the trenches behind the front line and behind them again, men are now occupying every available barn and building. Now, on the morning of July 1st, it is all coming together.

Robert, standing in the front line outside the deep dug-out that is Battalion H.Q., is aware that the atmosphere is subtly different from the morning of the Loos offensive, perhaps because so many of the troops around him are new to the game, perhaps even because the slight haze over the sun promises a fine day ahead. Whatever the reason, there is an almost tangible air of excited expectancy in the trench as men stand, bayonets fixed, their eyes already focused on the sandbagged parapet over which they will scramble as soon as the command is given by their Colonel. Robert is suddenly reminded of the atmosphere before the first school cricket match of the season, when teams, as yet untried, prepare to play; although today, he reflects, only one of the teams is aware of the fixture. Or that, at least, is how it should be; but he's too much of an old campaigner to be completely confident this is so.

Suddenly, the haze over the sun becomes thicker and anxiously the men glance up to the sky. But it's a man-made cloud; a smoke-screen drifting away over No Man's Land into the German line, to blind and confuse its occupants. It won't be long now.

The Colonel, standing at the foot of the firing step, checks his watch, blows a whistle and mounts the step, his revolver held high. 'Advance!'

'Good luck!' Robert feels constrained to say to those nearest him, although he doubts if they even hear. They certainly don't reply as they surge forward to scale the ladders and heave themselves over the parapet, pushed forward by those behind. He feels the now familiar pang of guilt as he watches them go, although his turn will come when the runners are sent back to report success or failure. Please God, this time it will be success.

He uses his periscope to check on the progress of the advance, hears the Colonel, now within yards of the German line, give the command to 'Charge!', sees the glint of sunlight on bayonets now poised to lunge. And then, suddenly, it is all obliterated by clouds of smoke rolling *towards* him. The wind has changed! The German line will now be bathed in bright sunlight, offering no cover to the advancing men. A corporal who has come out of Battalion H.Q., begins to cough and turns back into the dug-out. And as the trench fills up with the second wave of troops from the support lines, Robert follows him.

Inside, a Captain is speaking urgently into a telephone and a private bends over a spirit lamp, making tea. Tea, thinks Robert, while men are being slaughtered only yards away! But he knows, even so, that he'll be grateful for a cup when it's brewed. Suddenly, a man practically falls down the steps leading from the trench and Robert goes to help him. Incredibly, it's a German prisoner. Already! White-faced, babbling incoherently in German, he is led away for interrogation.

'Gave himself up without a murmur,' says the private sent back with him. And Robert feels a rush of optimism. If they're all like that . . . !

But it soon becomes patently clear that they are *not* all like that. At first, when the smoke clears sufficiently for them to see the coloured markers carried by the British troops, now hoisted in the German lines, they are quietly confident. Very soon, the runners should be back to report a splendid victory. But then — and at first, they can hardly believe it — the German bombardment starts. A crippling hail of shells rakes No Man's Land and the British lines with devastating thoroughness. Not only does the opposing side seem to have known of the fixture, they are responding in the most discourteous manner. When a bomb lands immediately outside H.Q., Robert, standing too near the entrance is blown off his feet. The runner, when he eventually staggers in, clutches the upper part of his left arm with his right hand, and blood oozes between his fingers. But his leather satchel is intact.

'Well done!' says the Captain taking it from him. And the man, his face contorted with pain, still manages a tiny appreciative smile. 'Well done, indeed!' Robert echoes as he helps an orderly to apply a field dressing to the man's arm.

A few minutes later, as he leaves the dug-out to make for his motor-bike, he is still trying to come to terms with the news, gasped out by the runner before he has keeled over in a dead faint, that the Colonel has been killed. But the shock is obliterated by the fresh horror that awaits him. The front line is now a travesty of the well-built, fortified construction it had been. Sandbags lie everywhere but on the parapet, their contents spilling out over the bodies of the men who lie among them, some clearly already dead, some whose condition is so pitiful it would be better if they were. One man lies sprawled over what remains of the parapet, both legs blown off, his mouth open in what was surely a final scream of agony. But as Robert edges past, aware that he must not be deflected from his duty, for the telephone lines have been severed in the bombardment, the man suddenly twitches violently and one fearful glance shows that he is still alive. His lips move and Robert is unable to stop himself leaning towards him.

'Fag!' The word is no more than an expulsion of breath, hardly audible against the cacophony of the guns.

Hurriedly, Robert pulls out a packet of cigarettes, lights one and gently places it between the man's swollen lips. And he, inhaling deeply, takes in his last, dying breaths. Robert, now staring fixedly ahead, goes on his way, taking no notice now of the pitiful bodies he walks between and sometimes, unavoidably, over.

Even in the support trenches, chaos prevails. Men, wounded but still able to walk, try to make their way to the First Aid Posts, hindered by the stretcher bearers whose burdens give little or no indication if they are alive or dead. And fighting against this never-ending tide of wounded, and clearly appalled by what they see, come those whose purpose it is — or was — to sustain the original advance; the ration parties, the ammunition parties and the sappers. Their resolve to continue with their objectives, no matter how pointless, is not helped by some of the advice they receive.

'Bloody shambles!' 'Hell on earth!' 'You'll never get back alive!' are some of the milder comments Robert hears. And the confusion is not helped by those who do not appear to be wounded but are deeply shell-shocked and who have now given up the struggle to survive; faces expressionless, eyes staring vacantly, they simply lean or sit against the sides of the trench, their out-stretched legs a further obstacle for others to stumble over.

As if all this is not enough, the German bombardment continues relentlessly. Even as Robert comes in sight of his bike, a shell lands nearby and he sees it keel over on to its side. He'll be lucky if it's still rideable.

He is destined never to know. The whine of the approaching shell seems louder than all the others and instinctively he ducks. But it's of no avail. He actually sees the bright orange flash of the explosion before a dense shower of shrapnel rains down upon him. He knows no more.

Several hours later, a stretcher bearer turns his body over, feels for a pulse, then straightens wearily. 'This one's a gonner, poor sod. Best leave him till dark.' And he and his companion move quickly on towards those for whom there is still hope, whose cries and groans at least show they're alive. The dead must wait.

* * *

Not many miles away as the crow flies, Kate and Priscilla know exactly what is expected of them. This time, they have been given Meg's old ward for the 'no-hopers'. But the same care must be taken, the same reassurance given, although there are some on whom reassurance is wasted; already deeply unconscious, they will remain so until they slip away into eternity.

At least, Kate tries to console herself, for she dreads the hours ahead, Pierre is back. Even Verdun has taken second place to the battle of the Somme. So far, there's been only time for a brief exchange of greetings before the wounded begin to arrive but she knows that eventually he will seek her out, be it hours or, more likely, days ahead. And she longs for that moment.

It is now well past midnight, but still the ambulances arrive. Wearily, she goes out into the courtyard to greet what is surely the last, for the château must already have reached bursting point. The driver is swinging open the doors. 'No need to worry yourself over this lot, nurse. They're all for the morgue as soon as they're certified.'

'I'll get back inside, then.' She has already turned away when the sound comes. It is no more than a whimper from the body lying nearest to the doors, and bodies, as Kate well knows, can produce the most extraordinary noises long after life has left them. Even so, she pauses. The driver, who has heard it, too, flashes his torch on to the man's face. And Kate, her hand to her mouth, almost faints as she recognizes him; and then is galvanised into immediate action.

Minutes later, Pierre gazes down at the mud-plastered features of Robert Holker. Not that he knows then who he is; only that he is someone so important to Kate that she has just broken every rule in the book. Instinct has sent her to find the one person, in her estimation, who can save him. If Pierre cannot, then no-one can.

18

'Tidy him up,' Pierre told Kate, 'and I'll be back as soon as I can. The morphia will keep him under.'

But for how long? The agony he would be in if — *when?* — he regained consciousness was dreadful to imagine. His body was literally full of shrapnel. And some, judging by the state of his uniform, had gone deep. It would take hours on the operating table, she guessed, to locate and extract all the jagged fragments of metal; hours that he, in his present appallingly weak condition would surely not survive. A transfusion? Would that be in part, at least, the answer?

As she removed the tattered shreds of his uniform and began to swab away the blood, she blessed the fact that in a ward where generally there was little cause for urgency, other than to sedate, it was acceptable for a nurse to concentrate upon any patient who might have the remotest chance of recovery. And Priscilla, after her first horrified appraisal of the situation, had been wonderfully supportive. Kate's principal fear was that Pierre would become so involved in the other wards that he would be unable to return. And why, in fact, should he? What was Robert Holker to him? And what, indeed, was he to her other than an old friend?

But she knew the answer as, with Priscilla's help, she transferred him to a central bed in the ward and then felt for a barely discernible pulse. He was more, much more, than an old friend. Suddenly, it was an enormous relief to admit it; to face the fact that all her effort over the last two years to put him out of her mind had been an utter waste of time. Gazing down at the haggard face on the pillow, she knew that she still loved him — and that he must not die.

'He is a sick man, Kate, You must appreciate that his chances of survival are remote.' Pierre, to her huge relief, had come back, but now seemed determined to kill all hope.

She knew that it would be wrong to try and influence his professional judgement, to use his feelings for her as a means of persuasion, but she still heard herself asking, 'D'you remember little Alfie's father? It was touch and go with him but in the end, we were successful. Could we not try again?'

He answered with another question. 'He is important to you, this man?'

'Very important.'

'Then we will try. But first,' and he stroked his chin reflectively, 'there must be transfusions. And at this moment, that is difficult. Stocks of blood are very low, the demand has far exceeded the supply. I can get some — but not enough.'

'But can't I give it?'

'Certainly that would be possible, provided your group is the same.'

Greatly relieved to see from the gleam in his eye that he had accepted the challenge, she smiled at him. 'Thank you, Pierre!'

'For you, anything!'

'Even to squaring it with Sister?'

'Even that!'

Quite what he did say to Sister, Kate couldn't hear, but it was clearly sufficient. 'Provided,' she told Kate, 'that you are able to rest afterwards. Your sister has assured me that she will cover for your duty.'

Once it was established that Kate's was a compatible blood group, Robert's bed was wheeled into a side ward and another placed beside it.

'Quite a simple affair,' Pierre told her when she was lying down and he had swabbed her left arm, made a small incision and then carefully inserted the end of a tube. 'First the blood will go into this bottle and then, by way of this other tube, straight into your friend's arm.'

'His name's Robert,' she said with a tiny smile.

'And is he, perhaps, the friend of whom you once spoke?'

'The same.' She wondered if he really wanted to know or if he was merely trying to relax his 'patient' with small talk.

'Now, I am going to put this roll of bandage into your hand and you will squeeze it and then relax. Squeeze and relax. Splendid!' He stood back and watched while Kate's blood dripped steadily into the bottle.

She was lying on her back, her eyes closed, fearful to gaze into Robert's face, only inches from her own. Squeeze and relax. Squeeze and relax. And then, after a few minutes, Pierre said softly, 'Look!'

She opened her eyes and saw, just as with Alfie's father, how the colour was slowly coming back into Robert's cheeks. 'But we must not be over — confident,' Pierre cautioned. 'The worst, for him, is still to come.'

But now, Kate thought exultantly, he has some good Moneymoon blood in his veins! And she thought how indignant his mother would be if she were to hear of it. The blue blood of the Holkers diluted by that of a washerwoman's daughter!

She closed her eyes again and felt Pierre withdraw the tube, felt the sharp prick of a needle as he stitched the small wound and heard him ask Priscilla to bandage it, before he walked quietly away. And then, still exultant, almost light-headed with relief, she pretended a dramatic wince as

Priscilla began her ministrations. 'Ouch!'

But Priscilla knew her too well. 'Kate! You're pulling my leg!'

She grinned. 'Hardly that!' And then they both suddenly dissolved into near-hysterical laughter.

'We'll do it, Kate!' Priscilla promised. 'Between us, we'll do it!'

★　★　★

Late that night, Robert went down to the operating theatre. 'They brought him back about three o'clock,' Priscilla reported next morning when she took a cup of tea to the side ward where Kate had remained since the transfusion. 'It's too soon for a prognosis. But Pierre didn't want him under for too long at a stretch so he's only removed half of the shrapnel. He'll have more surgery this afternoon.'

'And more blood?'

'Yes — but not yours this time. Now, how are you feeling? I'm going off duty now but Sister says you are not to get up until you feel like it.'

'Oh, I'm fine now. Arm's a bit stiff but it's my left, so I shall manage.'

And manage she did, although with some difficulty, forcing herself to concentrate upon the routine tasks of the ward when she wasn't monitoring Robert's pulse and temperature or adjusting the drip from the bottle above his head or, as she had with Alfie's father, doing her best to keep up a one-sided flow of conversation. But this time, she had no need to use her imagination; this time she knew just what to remind him of — Christchurch Meadows and the squirrels, Magdalen with its fallow deer, secluded stretches of the Cher where willows trailed their skirts and punts could moor unseen. It all came flooding back — to her, at least, for there was no response from the still figure on the bed.

When lunchtime came and she asked permission to spend it at Robert's bedside, Sister agreed without hesitation, provided that sandwiches and coffee were sent in. It was Addie who brought them and who told her, 'The whole hospital knows about you and your fiancé fighting for his life, and we're lining up to give our blood — my Fred's the next. It's just like a story book!'

'He's not . . . ' she began but then stopped herself, for that must be the reason Pierre had given to ensure Sister's co-operation.

Early in the afternoon, Pierre came back. 'It's still touch and go, Kate, but I shall have to risk taking out the remainder of the shrapnel now, or it will turn septic.'

Not for the first time, Kate wondered what Pierre's own personal feelings about Robert were. Did he, beneath his mask of professionalism, resent his presence, seeing it as an intrusion upon his own plans for Kate's future? And yet to start the rumour of Robert being her fiancé was hardly the action of a man intent upon filling that role himself. It was puzzling.

★   ★   ★

Robert's return to the ward coincided with Priscilla's return to duty. 'Go and have a hot meal,

Kate. Angie's in the mess and longing to see you. And Robert won't come round for ages yet.'

If at all, Kate found herself thinking as she gazed down at the gaunt face. Surely the cheekbones were more prominent now, the skin paler, the breath even more shallow? She didn't want to leave him, even to have a word with Angela.

'Trust me,' said Priscilla gently, knowing what she was thinking. And not to do so would have been a denial of Priscilla's competence. She went.

'Well, you're a dark horse and no mistake!' said Angela cheerfully, making room for her in the mess. 'How many more fiancés have you got tucked up your sleeve?'

'Oh, just the odd half-dozen,' said Kate, deciding that flippancy was the best course. 'There's nothing like a war for clarifying the mind,' she added more seriously. And Angela nodded, clearly accepting this simple explanation at its face value.

When she got back to the ward, she found to her horror that Robert had become delirious.

'He keeps muttering away about some school cricket match,' Priscilla told her. 'Pierre's been back. Apparently, there's still some shrapnel in his head. He says there simply isn't the equipment here for removing it safely, so the plan is to get him well enough to travel back to England. The trouble now, is that I've had to start changing some of his earlier dressings and the pain has set him off.'

'It'll be quicker if we both do it,' said Kate.

The figure on the bed suddenly became very still. 'Kate?' asked Robert urgently. 'Is that you, Kate?'

Instantly, she was beside him. 'Yes, Robert, I'm here.'

Unfocused, his eyes seemed to bore into her. 'There's no hope, you know. We shall lose the match.'

'There's always hope, Robert,' she tried to keep her voice steady as she took a dampened cloth from the bowl beside his bed and gently wiped his forehead. It was very hot.

He frowned. 'You don't understand, Kate. We just haven't got the men.'

Desperately, she drew on her meagre knowledge of the game of cricket. 'We'll just have to train more, then. How about some practise at the nets tonight? That might help.'

And for a few moments, miraculously, it seemed to work. 'Good idea, Kate! Will you come, too?'

'Of course! And Prissy! And Danny! And Pa and Ma if we can persuade them! Now, Robert, this may hurt a little. Prissy and I have to change your dressings but the pain won't last, I promise you.'

This puzzled him. 'What dressings?' And then enlightenment came. 'You mean the pitch? Something to feed the grass and make it grow?'

'That's it!'

'And then we must roll it, you know. That'll take some doing.'

'We'll all help.'

'Even Toby! We'll harness him to the roller,' Priscilla contributed as, gently and methodically, they began to work down the length of Robert's body, replacing the old dressings. Most of the wounds, they were relieved to see, were clean.

Robert gave a kind of manic chuckle, deep in his throat. 'Good old Toby! And that little donkey friend of his. I never knew his name.'

'Flurrie,' said Kate.

'Nice name. Nice little chap!'

'Girl,' Priscilla corrected automatically, as she peeled off an old dressing.

'Can't be a girl,' he objected. 'Girls don't play cricket.'

'We do!' said Kate stoutly. 'You should see our googlies!' She had heard Edmund use the expression, although she had no idea what it meant.

And so the crazy, inconsequential conversation continued, until Pierre arrived and administered more morphia. 'The next few hours will be critical. Call me if there's any change.'

But there was no change — other than that Robert was now silent. They changed dressings and fixed up another bottle of blood — Fred's? Kate wondered — and then Priscilla brought fresh water to moisten Robert's cracked lips and a cup of coffee for Kate. 'I'll get on with the other jobs. You sit with him for a while and then I'll take over.'

For the rest of the day and far into the night, they took it in turns to sit beside the bed with occasional brief interludes to rest but rarely to sleep. Sometime before dawn, Priscilla came back to find Kate staring, wide-eyed, at Robert. 'Prissy, he's stopped breathing!'

Priscilla picked up the seemingly lifeless hand lying on the cover. 'No! There's a definite pulse.'

And at that moment, Robert opened his eyes and looked straight at her. 'Hello, Prissy! As pretty as

217

ever, I see!' Then he closed his eyes again, gave a tiny, contented sigh, murmured, 'Almost as pretty as Kate!' and fell immediately into a deep sleep.

'Cheek!' Priscilla pretended indignation. 'Everyone knows I'm the p-pretty one. K-Kate's the one with the b-brains!' She could hardly finish the sentence for the sob in her voice.

'Oh, Prissy!' Kate was similarly afflicted. 'We've done it!'

* * *

Robert had no idea of time when he awoke several hours later, and only a confused idea of place — except that it must be a hospital of some sort because there were two nurses standing at the foot of his bed, deep in conversation with a tall, dark man with a stethoscope around his neck who must be a doctor. Then one of the nurses turned her head and he saw that it was Kate and he remembered at least part of what had gone before.

His body felt as if red-hot nails were being hammered into it and his head throbbed unbearably. He closed his eyes, making the pain fractionally more bearable, but then couldn't see Kate so he compromised by peering through his lashes.

The other nurse, and she wore a more complicated sort of bonnet, so she was probably a Sister, then said, quite distinctly, 'Your fiancé is a man of great courage and determination, Nurse Moneymoon,' which shocked him so much that he opened his eyes fully and saw that Kate was gazing at the doctor with a look on her face that he had

218

only ever seen there in his imagination. A sort of dreamy, far-away, *loving* look.

'Pierre — Dr Montarial — was wonderful!' she said.

And that, Robert decided, feeling utterly devastated, said it all. In view of what he was now remembering, he thought it likely that Kate and this Pierre — and hadn't Prissy been there, too? — had between them saved his life. So he supposed he had much to thank them for — although, indeed, life now seemed singularly devoid of purpose. Later, when his headache had eased and the hammering of the red-hot nails had ceased, he must pull himself together and thank them. But just now, he really hadn't the strength — or the inclination. In fact, he wished they hadn't bothered.

★   ★   ★

Kate was being sent to bed for a good night's sleep. But first she had to make sure that Robert's progress was continuing. Standing at the foot of his bed, she gazed hungrily at his sleeping face, committing to memory how one eyebrow grew slightly higher than the other, the way his hair curled into the nape of his neck in the most disarming fashion and how the scar on his chin — caused, he'd once told her, when he'd fallen from a tree as a child — had the shape of a tiny star.

Tomorrow, she promised herself, she would throw false modesty to the winds and tell him that she loved him. For time was limited. As soon as possible, Pierre had told her, he would be sent home. Perhaps, her mind raced ahead, she could get leave and visit him in the London hospital where the delicate brain surgery would be performed. Not even the disapproval of that old martinet of a mother of his would stop her!

'Making sure that all is still well?' Pierre had come softly up behind her.

She nodded. 'I shall never be able to thank you enough, Pierre.'

He gave a small, deprecatory shrug. 'I was only doing my duty. But for you, I think, it was something much more?'

'Much more,' she agreed.

'So — will you marry eventually?'

'If he'll have me!'

'Of that, there can be little doubt.' And now, she thought, she could detect a note of envy in his voice.

'Pierre, I'm so sorry if I've hurt you. Perhaps, if Robert hadn't been wounded. If he hadn't come to *this* hospital . . . '

He shook his head. 'We must not argue with Fate, *chérie*. And you must not worry about me. I, too, now see things differently, since Verdun. When we had more time, I was going to tell you . . . ' he hesitated as if seeking the right words.

'What? What were you going to tell me?'

'You are not the only one whom the long arm of coincidence has touched. In the hospital at Verdun, I met Heloise again.'

'Pierre!' Involuntarily, her voice rose a fraction.

'In spite of the horror — perhaps even because of it — we were drawn *very* close together. Much closer than before.'

'Oh, Pierre, I'm so glad!'

Robert, disturbed from sleep by Kate's exclamation of delight, opened his eyes; to see her rise on tiptoe and put her arms around the neck of the man she had called Pierre and kiss him soundly upon the mouth.

Well, that proved it! he thought savagely, and feigned sleep until he heard them walk away. Opening his eyes, he saw that they were holding hands — and that, somehow, seemed an even more telling sign of intimacy than the kiss. He lost all hope.

★   ★   ★

Next morning, Kate woke from a deep sleep to find that she had slept through Réveille. She glanced over to the other bed and felt a twinge of guilt when she saw that it was empty. Why hadn't Prissy woken her? But then she remembered that Sister had told her to 'take her time' and for one delicious moment, she allowed herself to lie there and think of Robert, planning the conversation they would have.

She would wait until his dressings had been changed and he'd been made as comfortable as possible and then, while the screens were still in place around his bed, she'd take him the mid-morning cup of tea.

'Robert,' she'd say with due solemnity, 'I've something to tell you. Something very important to me. But before I say it, you must understand that I fully realise my feelings may not be reciprocated.' She didn't like the formality of 'reciprocated' but could think of no better way of putting it. And perhaps by then he would have interrupted her, would have said, 'Let me be the one to say it first, Kate. I love you.'

Suddenly aware that she was very hungry, and that if she didn't hurry, breakfast would be over, she dressed hurriedly and went down to the mess. It was almost deserted but Addie made her fresh coffee and fried her bacon and a precious egg. Fred, his arm in a sling, gave her a cheerful 'good morning' and looked inordinately pleased when she thanked him for giving his blood. 'The least I could do, miss. And there's plenty more where that came from.'

When she reached the ward, she saw Priscilla at the far end with a dressings trolley and raised her hand in greeting before going straight to Robert's bed, meaning to do no more at that moment, than to wish him a brief good morning. At the same time, she was surprised to see that Priscilla had left her trolley and was walking quickly towards her, almost running, in fact. They reached Robert's bed at the same moment. Except that — it was no longer Robert's bed. A stranger lay in it — a man with fair hair and a cage over his legs. Panic-stricken, she turned to her sister.

'He's not . . . ?' But she couldn't finish. For how often had she come on duty to find that someone who had been making an excellent recovery, had suffered a relapse during the night? But then she saw that Priscilla was shaking her head.

'No, Kate, he's all right. At least, as far as I know he is. But there was an emergency in the night. A Clearing Station behind the lines had a direct hit and the men that weren't killed had to be evacuated right away. So it was a case of those not on the danger list, being sent home immediately. And Robert was one of them. Apparently, a V.A.D. on duty was actually going home on leave later today so she went with him. He's in good hands.'

But not *hers* — where he belonged. 'Did he — leave any message?'

Priscilla shook her head. 'Afraid not. But I'm sure he'll be in touch, Kate.'

She tried to take comfort from Priscilla's words. Because, surely, *this* time, he would write. And soon.

★ ★ ★

She took to haunting the Post Room; to no avail. 'Give him time,' Priscilla cautioned. 'He won't feel like writing until the op's over.' But that was another worry. It would be a difficult operation, Pierre had said. And what if he had never reached England in the first place? The V.A.D. who had gone with him was still on leave so could not be asked for her report.

But that worry, at least, was soon removed. 'You two are wanted in Matron's office when you come off duty,' said Mary Barnes, coming to find them on the ward. 'Nothing to worry about,' she added as they automatically checked back over the last few days but could think of nothing sufficiently heinous to justify a 'carpeting'. 'She looks like a cat that's swallowed a gallon of cream!'

'Please sit down,' Matron invited them when they

eventually presented themselves in front of her. 'I have just received a letter. It is rare, in wartime, for a patient to write and express his appreciation of the care he has received. But one,' here she consulted the writing paper she was holding, 'a Private Robert Holker, has taken the trouble to do so. And has mentioned you both by name.'

She glanced up and smiled briefly. 'Were it not that Private Holker indicates that he knew you both in civilian life, I would find it more than a little worrying that he calls you by your Christian names. However, that is by the way. The gist of his letter is that he wishes me to know of the care and dedication with which you nursed him. Without it, he is convinced he would have died. He would be grateful, he says, if I would pass on his gratitude and appreciation.' She paused and they mumbled *their* appreciation of her so doing. And then Kate said,

'May I ask, Matron, if Private Holker mentions if he's had his operation? Dr Montarial said that one would be necessary.'

Matron consulted the letter. 'He makes no mention of it. But the letter is written from the East London hospital so he could either have had it, or still be waiting for it.'

'Thank you, Matron.'

'There is one other thing,' Matron consulted a file on the table in front of her. 'I see from your documents that you have been here for over a year now. So you are more than due some home leave. As soon as the present offensive has achieved its objective, you may have seven days, at least. I'll speak to Sister.'

'Thank you, Matron.'

It was Priscilla who dared to say, 'Excuse me, Matron, but Nurse Carstairs has been here as long as we have. Would she be eligible, too?'

'Ah yes, Nurse Carstairs!' Matron pursed her lips. Clearly, nurses who dallied with German P.o.W.s were in a different category from those about whom grateful patients wrote letters of appreciation. But then she nodded. 'If she can be spared, then she may go with you.'

Outside Matron's office, Kate gave Priscilla a hug. 'Well done! Angie will be delighted.'

Priscilla drew back to study her sister's face. 'And you, Kate? You're pleased, too?'

'Of course!' And she tried to put from her mind the near certainty that now there would be no personal letter from Robert for her. It was as well, she reflected wryly, that they had both been spared the embarrassment of her declaration.

19

'The treat's on me,' Angela said. 'If it wasn't for you two, I'd still be pounding the wards.'

They were taking tea at one of London's fashionable hotels, greatly enjoying the comfort of their surroundings and the luxury of being waited upon, even by a somewhat elderly gentleman. Matron's promise of leave 'when the present offensive has achieved its objective' had proved an ambiguous offer. It was now nearly a hundred days since the Somme offensive had been launched with such high hopes. And certainly, if the advance of one, single mile could be deemed its 'objective' then it had certainly been achieved, but it was doubtful if Sir Douglas Haig and Mr Lloyd George considered it to be so and certainly not the soldiers themselves; nor Matron whose nursing staff had continued to patch up the survivors as best they could.

Rumour had it that one final effort was to be made before winter closed in, with the Anzac Corps from 'down under' strengthening what remained of the British battalions. 'Go now,' Matron had told them towards the end of September after a fresh draft of V.A.D.s had been 'broken in'. 'I have a feeling this winter is going to be the worst on record.'

They had travelled up from Dover to Victoria together and, still in uniform, had automatically lent a hand with the unloading of the stretcher cases from a hospital train that had drawn up at a platform nearby.

'D'you know, I wouldn't mind doing that job,' Angela said when the last ambulance had been loaded and they were repairing to the station buffet for a cup of tea. 'At least you'd be on the move. And maybe get home for a hot bath occasionally. Now, how about us meeting up in London halfway through our leave? No-one will have far to come.' For Angela's ancestral home was buried deep in the Kentish countryside.

A brilliant idea, Kate and Priscilla had agreed; Kate because she had decided to visit the London hospital from which Robert had written his letter to Matron, although she knew it was unlikely he would still be there; and Prissy because, since receiving Hank's letter telling her that he had at last joined the American Field Ambulance and would be over in France as soon as he could 'wangle it', she had been so happy, she would have agreed to anything. Now, she was allowing her eyes to wander contentedly over the men and women seated around them.

There had been a big Zeppelin raid on London only a few days previously in which thirty-eight people had been killed and over a hundred injured, but clearly, this had not affected morale, perhaps because two Zepps had actually been shot down and the crew of one taken prisoner. Most of the men drinking tea and toying with tiny, cucumber sandwiches while they chatted with their women-folk, seemed cheerful enough. Many were in uniform, some with crutches lying beside them, some with an arm in a sling.

'Just think,' Prissy said, 'we may have nursed some of these men.'

Angela chuckled. 'I'm not sure that their wives or girl friends would want to know that! But if you go on gazing around in that enquiring fashion, Prissy, that naval officer sitting by himself over there — yes, the one giving you the glad-eye like no-one's business — will be over to claim your acquaintance. And you certainly couldn't have nursed *him*!'

Priscilla had the grace to blush. 'It's so long since I've looked at a man as a man and not as a patient!'

'Your Hank had better look out, then!'

'You're looking pretty good, yourself, Angie,' Kate observed.

'Stunning!' Priscilla agreed generously. For she had never seen Angela in mufti before and greatly admired the three-quarter length coat in cinammon-coloured wool she was wearing over a matching, hobble skirt, daringly slit to the knee. She, herself, wore a pre-war, tailored costume whose skirt she had shortened to a good eight inches from the ground while Kate, knowing that she would be walking through London's East End had donned a sensible navy coat and skirt and stout shoes which she was now trying to keep hidden.

'I'm on top of the world!' Angela agreed and then, lowering her voice. 'Shall I tell you all about it?'

'Ernst?' Priscilla, who was now privy to Angela's liaison, forgot all about the naval officer who had been gazing at her with such open admiration, and leaned forward. 'You've seen him?'

Angela didn't answer directly but continued to look mysterious. 'I knew that travelling up to Inverness the moment I got home, would be difficult to explain, so I decided to tell my parents all about him. Well,' she gave a wry grin, '*almost* all! Pa was a bit put out at first — he's very patriotic, you know — but as Ma reminded him, no-one could be happier than they are and theirs wasn't exactly a marriage made in court circles! However, that made Pa bristle like a porcupine and ask who was saying anything about *marriage*, for heaven's sake, and I wasn't *pregnant*, was I? Because if so — he'd be off to Inverness himself on the next train! That was the cue for Ma to burst out laughing and say he sounded exactly like *her* father had when he knew *she* was pregnant by Pa! Which rather took the wind out of his sails. Am I making sense?'

The two rapt faces opposite nodded their complete understanding; they were adept by now at unravelling Angela's complicated sentences. The naval officer, having called for his bill, lingered by their table for a brief second before leaving, but went unnoticed.

'So the upshot was,' Angela continued, 'a telephone call was made to Uncle Ian asking if I could come and stay for a couple of days. Pa mentioned the Zepp raids — there've been quite a few on Kent, you know. He said that coming home on leave from the Western front, the last thing I needed was disturbed nights. The result was that Uncle Ian and Cousin Annie met me at Inverness with a pony and trap, half-a-dozen hot-water bottles, a mountain of rugs and a flask of best malt whisky. Uncle Ian, at least, thought I was on the verge of collapse. Cousin Annie, of course, knew my real reason for coming and helped me drink the whisky! We were quite a merry party by the time we reached Uncle Ian's castle. Just as well, because it was cold as charity.'

Here, Angela paused for breath and to take a sustaining sip of tea and then signalled to the waiter to bring a fresh pot. 'I thought our old place was cold enough,' she continued, 'but Uncle Ian's was like the grave. At bed-time, they distributed the dogs as foot-warmers, along with the candles — they haven't got electricity because Uncle Ian thinks it would encourage sloth, no matter that Auntie Doll

229

would give her right arm for it. Anyway, *they* went off with the two wolfhounds, Annie had her own spaniel and I was given Sandy, the Highland terrier. And off we trooped up the stairs looking like a turn at the circus.

Obviously, Annie and I had a lot to talk about, so we decided to pool the dogs and share the same bed. We woke up in the morning, sticking to each other like postage stamps, with the spaniel on our feet and Sandy wrapped across our necks like a ruff. But at least we were warm.'

She paused again while she poured fresh tea. Kate and Priscilla exchanged broad grins.

'I thought our family was unusual,' said Kate, 'but yours beats ours into a cocked hat.'

'You don't know the half of it,' said Angela. 'After the war you must come and stay. Although come to think of it,' her voice grew soft, her eyes dreamy, 'I won't be there, will I?'

'Angie,' said Priscilla in a threatening voice, 'if you don't get on with it, I shall hit you with this teapot. Did you get to see Ernst? Yes or no? Or did Uncle Ian discover all and shoot him with his twelve bore?'

'If Uncle Ian had discovered all, I shouldn't be sitting here, talking to you like this. *I* would have been shot! Cousin Annie and I had to be extremely careful. It took us half the night to work out our plan of campaign and even then we were doubtful if it would succeed.'

Priscilla raised the teapot threateningly and the eyes of the elderly waiter threatened to pop out of his head as he hastened forward. They had looked such a *nice* trio of young ladies!

230

But Angela was raising her hands in a gesture of reconciliation. 'All right, Prissy, you win! Yes — I saw Ernst!'

'Thank you!' Priscilla put down the teapot and the waiter relaxed but still hovered. 'Now tell us how you managed it.'

'Well, Annie knew roughly what the P.O.W.s did each day and, of course, she had often managed to talk to Ernst, but that was usually when they were working near the castle. They were billeted in a row of cottages on the estate with just a couple of soldiers looking after them. I suppose they thought escape wasn't really a possibility. Each day, the soldiers would march them to whatever part of the estate they were needed and stand around while they got on with the job. Extremely boring, as you can imagine. *Any* diversion was welcome. And Cousin Annie can be quite a diversion when she puts her mind to it! But our first problem was finding out exactly where the prisoners were working, Uncle Ian wouldn't know, even if we'd dared ask him, because he left all that to his factor. And by the time we'd tracked *him* down, a whole day had been wasted. But we did manage to find out where they'd be on the following day; clearing out a burn about a mile to the north of the castle. So early next morning we set off before Uncle Ian and Auntie Doll had even come down. I was so excited, I could hardly breathe.'

And indeed, as if she were re-enacting the whole scenario, Angela's breathing was now rapid, her cheeks glowing and her eyes sparkling with anticipation. To his extreme annoyance, the waiter

231

was suddenly summoned to the other side of the restaurant and stomped irritably away. His wife, who was an invalid, did so enjoy any little titbits of conversation he might happen to overhear during the course of his day, not that he could make much sense of this one!

'It was one of the longest miles I've ever walked,' Angela continued slowly, 'and most of it across moorland. Tangles of heather and something Cousin Annie called whin. I tripped over so many times, I lost count. And then we saw them — a line of men silhouetted against the skyline, bending and reaching and sometimes getting down on their knees. I tried to imagine Ernst's face when he saw me. And then I began to panic. Perhaps he wouldn't recognise me! It was nearly a year, after all, since we'd seen each other. And perhaps *he* had changed and I wouldn't recognise *him*! By the time we reached them, I was in a muck sweat.

The plan was for Cousin Annie to stroll over to the guards — we'd brought the dogs so that it would seem as if we were just out for a walk — and to engage them in conversation while I sauntered over to the prisoners and pretended an interest in what they were doing.

Well, Cousin Annie started doing her bit and I began to walk along the edge of the burn towards the prisoners. At first, they all looked exactly the same in their drab uniforms and I was so busy trying to decide which one was Ernst, I didn't look where I was putting my feet. And the next moment, I was flat on my face — again! — and my hat was sailing away down the burn!

I was so embarrassed, I just lay there with my mouth full of heather, and then I heard Ernst's voice in my ear. '*Liebling*, are you all right? Have you hurt yourself?' And I lifted my head and there he was, crouching by my side. I nearly fainted with joy.'

Priscilla, dewy-eyed, managed a tremulous smile while Kate, whose own day had been far from joyful, nodded her understanding.

'And then he just took over,' Angela continued. 'I started to whisper that I was perfectly all right and that it was wonderful to see him again but he interrupted me. 'Your ankle, *fräulein*?' he said in a voice loud enough for the guard to hear, 'You say you've hurt your ankle? I'm not surprised!' And then he was unlacing my boot — oh, the delight of feeling his hands caressing my foot! — and I was pretending to wince with pain.

And then he was shouting to the guard that 'the fraulein could not possibly walk' and that he would carry me to wherever I wished to go. I whispered in his ear, 'in that case, what about Paris or New York?' and he hissed back that even *he* couldn't walk on water and to shut up and behave myself and leave it to him! It was all I could do not to giggle!

The upshot was, he and another prisoner who couldn't speak a word of English carried me back to the castle between them, with one of the soldiers and Cousin Annie bringing up the rear. The other soldier stayed with the other prisoners. Cousin Annie did her best to chat away to our soldier and keep him as far behind us as possible. And as Ernst and his friend couldn't hurry for fear of dropping me, it took us well over two hours!'

She paused, reliving those hours.

'Did he say what happened to him after he was taken away from the château?' Kate asked at last.

'He was in solitary confinement in a French prison for several weeks,' Angela told her, 'but was eventually shipped to England. He thinks the authorities have it in mind for him to be an interpreter so he told me not to be alarmed if he should suddenly vanish without trace. Because . . . ' her voice trailed away.

'Because?' Priscilla prompted.

Angela blushed — a rare occurrence. 'Because whatever happened, he would always love me,' and her cheeks dimpled at the recollection. 'And you are *not* going to get any more from me than that, Priscilla Moneymoon!'

'But how's the ankle now?' Priscilla asked cheekily. 'I didn't notice you limping!'

Angela laughed. 'Once we reached home, Cousin Annie had her work cut out persuading Uncle Ian and Auntie Doll I didn't need a doctor. But she managed it and since I came home next day, I didn't have to hobble for too long. Shall we have more tea?' she suggested, glancing around for the waiter.

'I think,' Kate said, 'that we may have already outstayed our welcome.' And indeed, most of the other tables were now empty and while their waiter was certainly hovering, it seemed to be more in order to present their bill than to bring more tea.

'But I want to hear how your Robert is,' Angela protested, but at the same time reaching for her handbag.

'There's nothing much to tell,' Kate stalled. And

Angela, after one swift glance at her face, didn't pursue the matter. But outside, as they stood in Piccadilly, scanning the traffic for a cab, she put her arm around Kate's shoulders and gave her a quick hug. 'Sorry to have droned on in such a boring way.'

Kate hugged her back. 'Angie, you couldn't be boring if you tried. And honestly, I'm fine. See you next week.'

But later, sitting opposite Priscilla in the Oxford train, she leaned back wearily against the stiff, prickly fustian of the cushions and admitted to herself that she was by no means 'fine'.

It had been a long day. Refusing Priscilla's offer to come with her, not because she wanted to be alone but because she knew her sister was eager to visit the American Embassy to enquire if there was news of Hank's unit, she'd travelled to the East End on the open top-deck of an omnibus. As the bus had trundled through the crowded streets where many children ran bare-foot, some clad in little more than rags, or hung in groups around the doors of the public houses, she noticed little shrines set up on some of the street corners, with bunches of flowers and evergreen stuck into jamjars and placed beneath the photograph of a soldier or sailor. And over the photographs would be a simple, heart-rending message; 'in loving memory' of 'dear Jack' or 'Thomas' or 'William'. Sometimes there were several photographs as if many families in the same street all mourned a loved one.

One day, no doubt, their names would be carved in stone upon a memorial but in the meantime,

Kate thought, the simple reminders must help wives and mothers without the comfort of a grave to visit, to come to terms with their loss. At least, she remembered thankfully, Robert had not been killed, although he could still, unbeknown to her, have died on the operating table. And that, she told herself, was the only reason why she was visiting the hospital. If he was still alive, there wasn't a snowball's chance in hell, as Angela would have put it, that he would still be there. But all the same . . .

Outside the hospital, she clattered down the winding staircase of the bus, responded with a grateful smile to the conductor's cheerful, 'Here we are then, missy!' as he helped her off and, clutching the bag of hot-house grapes she'd brought — just in case — mounted the broad flight of steps that led to the cavernous, marble-floored entrance hall. Men in hospital blues, some in wheelchairs and many on crutches, moved from one door to another or stood patiently in line. Many were accompanied by a nurse and for the first time, Kate regretted she had not worn her uniform. But the temptation to 'dress up' for Robert — just in case — even if only to wear a daintily ruched, white blouse under her navy coat and to pin a silver filigree brooch to her lapel, had been irresistible.

A formidable woman in mufti, with a mouth like a steel trap and eyes like boot buttons, sat behind a desk in the middle of the hall. Kate took up position behind a tearful young woman with two small children clinging to her skirts, and waited.

'But I saw 'im only yesterday,' the woman was protesting. 'And 'e was right as ninepence then.'

'No-one admitted to a hospital,' the other pointed out severely, 'can be — right as ninepence, as you put it.'

'Well, you know wot I mean! 'E was sittin' up in bed an' askin' me to bring in the kids. Which I 'ave. Orl the way from 'Oundsditch! So — what you done with 'im?' The woman was growing belligerent but at the same time, Kate could see, very worried.

'*When* I have a moment, I'll look into it. Meanwhile, take a seat. Next, please.' And Kate was fixed with a grim stare.

Swiftly, she made up her mind. 'I have come to enquire,' she said in what Priscilla would have recognised as her 'you will take your medicine and no nonsense' voice, 'about Lord Robert Holker.' She hoped she was giving him his correct title. 'The son of the Earl of Werrington,' she added to make sure. 'He was admitted a couple of months ago, with severe head injuries.'

The woman's expression altered immediately from aloof disdain to fawning respect. I was right, Kate thought. She's a bully and even worse, a sycophantic snob.

'Er — we don't usually give out information except to close relatives or friends. You are . . . ?'

'I am a *very* close friend,' said Kate firmly. 'And I'm just back from an inspection of hospitals on the Western Front. Otherwise, I would have called before. Now,' she glanced at her watch, 'I am expected for tea in the West End in a couple of hours,' — that, at least, was true — 'so I would appreciate a speedy answer to my enquiry.'

Her bluff worked like a charm. Without

hesitation, the woman extracted a massive, leather-bound book from a drawer in her desk. 'I'll just check. Holker, you say?'

She consulted an index and turned the pages swiftly. 'Ah, here he is! Except that . . . there must be some mistake.' She raised an astonished eyebrow. 'It says here that he's a *Private* — and no mention of a title.'

'Lord Robert,' said Kate crisply, 'is a great believer in democracy. Now, is he still here or has he been discharged?'

The woman glanced back at the records 'He was discharged over a month ago to convalesce at Holker Hall.' She was silent for a moment while she read on. 'Now isn't that nice!'

'*Nice?*' Kate queried, trying not to show her acute disappointment.

'It says here that Holker Hall is a Convalescent Home. Didn't you know? So he'll receive expert medical attention and be with his family at the same time.'

'As you say, very nice!' The woman was still simpering at her, still delighted with herself for providing such satisfactory information. 'While you have your book out,' Kate continued, 'you can check the whereabouts of that lady's husband, can't you?' And she indicated the woman with the two children who was now sitting forlornly on one of the benches lining the walls.

'Oh, very well!' With ill-concealed impatience, the woman turned the pages once again. 'Discharged,' she said after a moment. 'Sent home this morning.'

'Couldn't his wife have been told that yesterday?'

238

Kate made no effort to keep the exasperation from her voice.

'Nothing to do with me, I can assure you!'

Any more, Kate thought wearily, than it is to do with me. Except that we are all supposed to be united in a common cause.

'It's good news,' she told the dejected woman. 'Your husband was discharged this morning. He's probably waiting for you at home even now.'

The woman stared at her for a long moment and then suddenly began to cry; dreadful wailing sobs that threatened to tear her thin frame apart. Her children, after one startled look, joined their sobs to hers.

Kate put her arms around the hunched figure and rocked her gently. She had seen a similar reaction from other wives who had travelled to France convinced they were going to the death-beds of their loved ones, and been unable, at first, to accept that they had miraculously recovered.

But already this woman's natural resilience was asserting itself. Already, she was on her feet, grinning hugely at Kate, wiping away her tears. 'Best get back then. 'Cos 'e ain't got no key! Come along, 'Liza, 'Enry. And thank *you*, miss. I'd still be waitin' if that old cow 'ad 'er way!'

'Please take these for your husband,' and Kate pressed the bag of grapes into the woman's hand. 'I won't be needing them now.'

Riding back inside the bus — not caring, now, where she sat — Kate chewed her lip. So — Robert had gone home to Staffordshire, possibly to await his discharge. She would never try to visit him there.

The future seemed bleak, indeed.

It had taken all her concentration to listen attentively to Priscilla's description of her visit to the Embassy. 'They wouldn't tell me a thing. Except to remind me that the United States is a neutral country and that if Hank was on his way over, there'd be no guarantee he'd be with the Allies. It could just as well be the Germans.'

'True, I suppose.'

'I don't think Hank would stand for that. Anyway, enough of me. How did you get on?'

Briefly, Kate told her what had happened at the hospital. 'At least,' Priscilla tried to console her, 'Robert's still alive.'

'I know. That's the most important thing.' But oh, how she envied that woman with her two children!

20

As if Lloyd George's appointment as Prime Minister had turned the tide of German resistance, the Allies began to advance, north of the Somme battlefield and the French claimed a glorious victory at Verdun. Pierre broke all the rules by smuggling in a bottle of wine to toast the 'poilus'.

'And Heloise,' Kate reminded him. 'Will she have leave now?'

'I hope so. We may manage a few days at Le Petit Manoir. Perhaps you and Priscilla could come, too? I would like you to meet her.'

Kate, remembering how she had so nearly succumbed to Pierre's advances at Le Petit Manoir, envied his capacity to move happily, and apparently without regret, from one emotional entanglement to the next. When she'd come back from leave, he had shown a professional interest in Robert's condition. 'All is well with your fiancé?' he had asked.

And Kate had told him all she knew. 'You visited him at this Holker Hall?' Pierre had persisted.

And because Pierre was her good friend and because, above all else, she wished to avoid further enquiries, she had explained that she had not visited him, that it was unlikely she would ever do so and that her brief 'engagement' was over. 'After all, Pierre, it was *you* who arranged it in the first place!'

And he, seeing the pain in her eyes, had probed no further, contenting himself with a muttered, 'Oh, you English! I don't know what to make of you.'

As for the remainder of the medical staff, they had all been too busy, once they'd established that Robert's operation had been successful, to enquire too often or too deeply. Fortunately, Addie Fanshawe was so excited over her own engagement to her Sergeant, she had little time to concern herself over Kate's affairs, except to notice that she seemed to be working harder than ever and had more need, therefore, of the nourishing little titbits Addie smuggled out of the kitchen. That it was Priscilla who usually ate them, passed unnoticed.

'We might have won the war already, Prissy looks so happy,' Angela observed to Kate. For Hank was now in France and serving with the Allies; at the moment, in Paris, but 'working on' his superiors to move him nearer the château. Or at least give him a few days' furlough to 'hitch a ride' that way.

'Just stay put, honey,' he wrote, 'and I'll be with you just as soon as Uncle Sam allows it.'

The knowledge lent wings to Priscilla's feet as she skimmed about the ward, sparkling with happiness and hope and causing the most war-hardened of her patients to fall a little in love with her. Even when she and Kate had to break the ice in their bedroom ewers each morning before they could wash, her cheerfulness never flagged.

For Matron's prophecy was proving correct — it was rapidly becoming the coldest and wettest winter they had known. It was no surprise when the three V.A.D.s were moved on to the Medical ward to help with the increase in bronchial and rheumatic cases.

'Never thought I'd get the screws at my age,' complained a young man still in his teens, but no longer able to straighten his spine.

'Hardly surprising,' Kate commented when he told her how the mud in the trenches was now knee-deep and how the men on guard duty supported each other back to back, like book-ends, in case they slipped and suffocated in the mire. In a way, he was fortunate, although she didn't tell him so, that he'd succumbed to 'the screws' before falling victim to the worst scourge of all — trench foot.

'It's the stench I find so difficult to bear,' Angela said. 'I'm going to suggest we go back to Tudor times and carry posies of flowers and herbs around our necks when we go on duty.'

242

'And I'm sure Matron would be happy to pick them for you!' Kate scoffed. 'Meanwhile, I suggest a piece of gauze soaked in Lysol.' For something was certainly needed to combat the dreadful smell that rose when the wet, tightly-bound puttees were cut away from the men's legs to reveal the black and putrid flesh beneath. Few who suffered the agony of returning circulation could bear to look down at the cause of their pain. Only the macabre thought that their toes might eventually drop off and they would be sent home, cheered them a little.

'At least,' Priscilla was still determined to look on the bright side, 'the oil we rub in keeps our hands soft and smooth.'

'Getting ready for that diamond solitaire, are we?' Angela teased and Kate grinned. Somehow, they were getting through the days; Priscilla in joyful anticipation, Angela in a sort of limbo, for there'd been no letter from Cousin Annie since they'd returned from leave, and herself in a state of suspended animation, unable to contemplate the future but determined not to dwell on the past.

Meg's letters from Malta brought both pleasure and envy. 'I'm thinking of you all,' she wrote, 'and wishing with all my heart that you could be here to lie in the sun and gaze out over a sea that changes from sapphire to turquoise to jade even as I watch.' With all their hearts, they wished so, too!

★ ★ ★

It had taken Robert Holker several days to accept that he wasn't going to die; and many more to

243

decide what he should now do with the rest of his life.

The doctors in the London hospital had not shared the optimism of the French doctor whom Kate Moneymoon was to marry. They had shaken their heads and murmured about the difficulty of operating so near the brain, of how there was still so much to learn about surgery in that area, and would he not consider the option of 'leaving well alone'? If he did so, there could be many years of life ahead of him, as long as the shrapnel embedded in his skull did not move. Admittedly, they would be of a fairly sedentary nature; undue excitement would have to be avoided, as also any form of sustained, physical activity. Perhaps a gentle game of croquet or a round of bridge, provided he was not too concerned about their outcome, too depressed if he were to lose. They understood he was now heir to a considerable estate, but provided he employed a good bailiff, the running of this should not be beyond his capacity.

When he had declared, without a moment's hesitation, that the life they had described would be quite unbearable and that he would be grateful if they would operate without delay and be damned to the consequences, they had gone, muttering, away, leaving him convinced of his early demise. Even the Sister's cheery comment that 'they're always like this! Full of gloom and doom but brilliant surgeons for all that!' hadn't cheered him greatly. He had even decided to dispose of his unentailed property and had written to Danny telling him that he was now the owner of his Harley Davidson, and to the

244

solicitors who had managed General Wavertree's affairs, declaring that, in the event of his death, the house in Long Wittenham was to pass to Miss Kate Moneymoon of Moneymoon Manor, Oxfordshire — for Frenchmen, he understood, were not always constant in their affections and she could well have need of it in time. He was not at all sure that the declaration was entirely legal, even after it had been witnessed by the obliging Ward Sister and one of her nurses, but there was something about the matter-of-fact way they appended their signatures that made him suspect that such a request often came their way, so perhaps all was in order. The Sister even assured him, without his even asking, that both letters would remain in her safe keeping until after the operation and that she had no doubt she would soon be returning them to him.

When she did so, twentyfour hours after he had come round from the anaesthetic, her triumphant, 'I told you so!' had been the first indication that he was out of danger. But the medics had still been cautious when he'd asked about his future in the Army. It was far too soon to say, they'd told him, and in any case, he'd do well to remember that the muscles of his right leg were now considerably shorter than those in his left so that he'd always walk with a limp. A return to active service was definitely out of the question. Why did he not go back to his ancestral home to convalesce and at the same time, consider life as a landed gentleman?

When the ambulance had finally disgorged him at the entrance to his ancestral home, he'd remembered their words with a certain wry amusement. To begin with, there was hardly any land to be seen; a multitude of huts and tents had sprung up on what had once been stretches of smooth green sward, dotted with flowerbeds and shrubberies, pergolas and paths. And the house itself had the slightly dilapidated air of a society beauty, rather the worse for wear after a night out on the tiles. Robert had never liked it, thinking that the flamboyance of the spires and turrets with which the Victorian architect had embellished it, served no useful purpose other than to distract the eye from a façade of uncompromising yellow brick, even now only slightly mellowed by time and the determined efforts of the British army.

For even as he stood on the weed-grown gravel outside the open front door, two young subalterns in wheel chairs tried to propel themselves through it simultaneously and cannoned into the door frame, causing the already battered wood to splinter even further.

'Steady on!' remonstrated the little nurse who had helped him from the ambulance and now stood at his side.

'Sorry, nurse!' said one, but with no obvious regret. 'But we've got a bet on, you see. First one to the lake gets to help Nurse Frobisher with the tea.' And turning their chairs, they skimmed, with amazing dexterity, towards the ornamental lake that had been the pride and joy of the first Earl. Now, the lake itself was hardly visible beneath swathes of bright green algae, the pair of swans that had once sailed so majestically upon the silver waters, clearly long gone.

'I would have thought,' said Robert to his nurse, 'that the one who *lost* the race would have to help with the tea.'

'Ah, but you haven't met Nurse Frobisher!' the little nurse laughed, without rancour. 'I sometimes think if they'd fought the Germans like they fight over her, the war would have been over in six months!'

'Even with the likes of you around?' Robert asked gallantly, secretly amazed to hear himself make such a remark after so many years without practise.

'Thank you, kind sir!' She sketched a mock curtsey and then straightened hurriedly. 'Here comes Matron!'

'Robert! My *dear* boy!' He turned quickly to see Aunt Bella bearing down upon him, her arms wide in welcome. But a vastly different Aunt Bella from the fashionable lady he had last seen three years ago. Now, she seemed to be swathed from head to foot in dark grey serge, with an enormous, starched coif of pristine whiteness upon her head.

'But you look like a nun!' was all he could say before she hugged him to her.'

Her laugh, the same, slightly raucous peel of spontaneous mirth that had enchanted him since childhood, rang out and he knew, in spite of her appearance, that she was still his beloved Aunt Bee.

'Thank you, nurse,' she said to his little escort. 'I'll look after Lord Robert now. But would you please ask for tea to be brought to my office?'

And then she was leading him across the hall to the door that led to what had been the morning room. Now, its walls were covered with charts and maps, its only furniture a large desk, a couple of sturdy, straight-backed chairs and several steel, filing cabinets. She motioned him to one of the chairs and he sat down carefully, grateful to be able to take the weight off his legs, for the short walk from the ambulance had proved unexpectedly tiring.

'I've arranged for you to be in your own room,' Aunt Bella told him. 'But first you must tell me all the news.'

Robert smiled at her. 'I've really nothing to tell, except that I had a brief encounter with a German shell and came off rather the worse for wear. But thanks to excellent nursing — and I'll tell you more of that later — I'm well on the way to recovery. It's *you* that things have obviously been happening to. *Matron*, indeed! It took you all your time to bandage a cut finger without fainting, when George and I were small!'

'Oh, I'm not that sort of a Matron! Purely administrative, I assure you. But when they requisitioned the Hall, I insisted upon being requisitioned with it. Especially since they erected their huts all over my garden! So, just to humour me, they said I could help with the administration. They had the shock of their lives when I turned out to be quite good at it. So did I!'

She leaned closer to Robert and almost whispered, 'I've never admitted this to another living soul and may God forgive me for saying it now, but there's a bit of me that's really enjoying this war. And that's a dreadful thing to say to someone who could so easily have been killed in it. As, indeed, poor George was. Your parents, I'm afraid, have quite given me up. Come in!' For a knock had come at the door. A rosy-cheeked, buxom woman entered, carrying a tray of tea. 'Ah, Emily! Look who's here!'

And the next moment, Robert was trying to rise, delighted to see his old nurse-maid.

'Master Robert! Now — stay just where you are! Don't you dare move another inch!'

'Dear Emm! As bossy as ever, I see!' But he allowed himself to be hugged and kissed and generally made much of before Emily eventually went away, at the same time promising 'to tell Cook you're here!'

'Mrs Barcock?' he asked his aunt. 'She's still here, too?'

'That was another thing I insisted upon. That all the house staff, at least, should be kept on, if they wished to be. Many of them didn't, of course. They were off to the munitions' factory before you could say 'knife' but Emma didn't because of her elderly parents.'

'My parents?' he prompted. 'You were telling me about them when Emm arrived.'

Aunt Bella's face became serious. 'They're quite comfortable in the Dower House, living in their own little world. But it's no longer the real world. They talk about the war as if it's happening to other people, Dorothy, particularly. Lately, I've thought her mind has become a little confused. When I told her that you were coming, she grew very excited but then I heard her telling your father that it was George who was coming.'

'How is Pa?' Robert asked.

'He's quite compos mentis. But so busy

humouring your mother he often gets things muddled himself. You'll have to go very carefully with both of them, Robert. But now, I've talked enough. I'm tiring you. Drink up your tea and then I'll show you to your room. You've got Nurse Frobisher to look after you, so you'll be all right.'

'Who *is* this Nurse Frobisher?' he asked.

Aunt Bella twinkled at him. 'You'll soon find out!'

★ ★ ★

'Of course I remember you, Robert!' said Alice Frobisher.

It was more than he could say of her. For, once met, no-one would ever forget this beautiful creature. He could quite see, now, what all the fuss had been about. She was like a wood nymph minted in gold; golden hair, coiled neatly now beneath her cap but reaching to well below her waist, he would have thought, when unbound, eyes of tawny amber, deep-set in the perfect oval of her face and a skin that glowed like a ripe peach.

He decided to be honest. 'I am quite sure,' he told her, 'that I have never met you before in my life, because there is no way that I could possibly have forgotten you.'

She laughed; a glorious sound like a peel of muted bells. 'Think back! To when you and George were home for the holidays. I used to pester my mother to drive over from Bellwood to visit *your* mother and to take me with her. And sometimes your mother would insist that you let me play with you. You must have hated it because you once put me up a tree and left me there for the whole afternoon!'

And now he, too, was laughing. 'I don't believe it! Little Fatty Frobisher! You were like a barrel with pigtails and a brace on its teeth!'

She shook with laughter. 'That was me!'

'It's as well I'm lying in bed,' he told her, 'or I'd have fainted from shock. As it is, my temperature must be soaring.'

'Well, we'll soon find out!' And she popped a thermometer into his mouth, at the same time picking up his wrist. And while she stood there, seemingly intent upon her tasks, he allowed his gaze to travel — discreetly, he hoped — over her delicately pointed breasts, her hour-glass waist and slim hips. For her uniform was nothing like the serviceable, shapeless affair worn by most of the nurses he had met so far. This one was a dress, cleverly designed to mould and accentuate her figure. The sort of dress he would have expected to be worn by the only child of possibly the wealthiest man in the county. His mother, he remembered with amusement, had been faintly scathing in her attitude towards a member of the 'nouveau riche' who had made his money in the Potteries, quite forgetting that her own husband's grandfather had done exactly the same a mere century or so earlier.

'Are you living here?' he asked once the thermometer had been taken from his mouth.

'No. Manners drives me over each day in the trap and comes for me each evening. Daddy insists upon it, although sometimes, of course, if there's a concert or something, I'm allowed to stay.'

251

Unbidden, there flashed into his mind a picture of Kate and Priscilla Moneymoon working all the hours that God gave them and at the most menial of tasks, with no hope of going 'home to Daddy' each evening. He was tempted to set the cat among the pigeons and request a bed-pan!

'The lavatory, as you may remember, is down the corridor,' said Alice Frobisher suddenly, as if divining his intention, 'and if you require a bed-pan or bottle, they're in your locker. There's also a male orderly, if you'd prefer one to a nurse.' She indicated the bell-pull over his bed. 'You ring twice for him and once for me. Although,' she glanced at the watch pinned to her breast, 'I shall be going off duty in five minutes and it will be Nurse Jenkins you'll get.'

'Thank you!' he said meekly and now thinking that perhaps there was more to Alice Frobisher than the sheer perfection that met the eye.

★　★　★

'Of course she's not just a pretty face,' said Aunt Bella. 'She had the devil's own job persuading her parents to let her come over here every day. She's not twentyone yet, you know.'

'What will she do when she is? Leap over the traces altogether and go off to France?'

Aunt Bella looked at him shrewdly. 'I'm not privy to her intentions and I wouldn't tell you of them, if I was. But don't judge everyone by that erstwhile lady friend of yours. Kate Moneymoon is an exceptional person, as no doubt her sister is also.

From what you've told me, they probably saved your life in France. But there are plenty of other worthwhile people 'born to blush unseen upon the desert air', as someone or other once put it.'

'I wouldn't say little Fatty Frobisher was exactly born to blush unseen. Look at her now!'

They were sitting in the late autumn sunshine in the shade of an ancient cedar that grew in the small portion of the lawn that had remained untouched. A few hundred yards away, on the terrace that fronted the house on the south side, Alice Frobisher was dispensing afternoon tea to a swarm of young men.

'You know what I mean,' said Aunt Bella testily. 'And for heaven's sake, stop calling her by that revolting name. George, you know, was extremely fond of her.'

'I'm sure he was. George was fond of everyone.'

'I mean he'd asked her to marry him, before he was sent to France.'

'Good God! That really surprises me.'

'Alice Frobisher,' said his aunt calmly, 'would have made a wonderful Countess of Werrington. Still would, of course,' she added with an assumed air of innocence.

And now, he saw it all. 'You mean my parents wanted George to marry her?'

'I think they may have put the idea into George's head in the first place. But he certainly wasn't averse to the suggestion.'

'And what did little Fatty — I mean, Alice — think about it?'

Aunt Bella sighed. 'We never knew. George went off to France and Alice's third finger remained bare, but they may have had plans. Certainly, she was very upset when we heard he'd been killed. But she was young, she soon seemed to get over it. But there's more to Alice Frobisher than you might think, Robert. Still waters run deep, they say, and I, for one, am never sure what she's thinking. But I can tell you this much. Your father would be delighted if you were to marry her. It would solve many of his problems.'

'Problems?'

'Well, you must see for yourself how run down the estate has become. There'll be compensation from the War Office, of course, when it's all over, but I doubt if it will be nearly enough. Alice's dowry, which would be considerable, would make all the difference.'

'But we still have the Pottery,' he pointed out.

'True, but it's not the money-making concern it was in your grandfather's day. Unlike Frobisher's. Alice's father is a much younger man than yours and he's invested his capital in other concerns. Munitions, mostly, they say.'

'Pa hasn't said anything about financial problems to me,' Robert said.

'Not yet. But I know it's in his mind to. That's why I'm mentioning it to you now. Forewarned is fore-armed. I don't want you to worry about it, particularly in your present state of health, but I thought you should know. You're dining with them tonight, aren't you?'

He nodded. 'Thank you, Aunt Bee.' His gaze fell once more upon the little group on the terrace, now even larger as more men gathered around the tea trolley. 'Little Fatty wouldn't have *me*, anyway,' he said.

'Little Fatty,' said his aunt crisply, 'has adored you since the day she was born!'

★ ★ ★

'It is so good to have you home, George,' said the Countess of Werrington.

Robert caught his father's eye and gave an almost imperceptible nod of understanding. As on previous occasions, his mother had greeted him as 'Robert' but later, as her concentration diminished, had called him by his brother's name and gazed at him with the special fondness she had always shown towards the son who had conformed so admirably to whatever she had expected of him.

'Not quite the woman she was,' his father had tried to explain her condition when Robert had first visited the Dower House. 'Knocked her for six when dear George went. Pinned all her hopes on him, d'you see.'

'I'm afraid,' Robert had felt constrained to say, 'that I've always been a sore disappointment to you both.'

The Earl hadn't attempted to deny it. 'Main thing is — you're home now. Some time, when you're feeling more your old self, we must talk about the future.'

And now, after dinner on the evening of the day of his conversation with Aunt Bella about Alice Frobisher, he guessed that 'some time' had arrived.

'I think I'll go up now,' his mother said. 'A busy

day tomorrow, you know.'

'I'll ring for Florence, my dear.' And her husband crossed to the bell-pull, while Robert helped his mother to her feet and gave her his arm to the door, there to deliver her into the somewhat doubtful care of her elderly maid.

'I don't know which is in the most need of assistance,' he told his father after the door had closed behind them.

'Florence understands your mother. Body may be crippled with arthritis but mind's clear as a bell. Plays along with your mother's little foibles like a Trojan.'

'Has she really got a busy day tomorrow?' Robert asked.

'Only if you count a few more stitches in her tapestry! And ordering impossible meals from the cook. Sirloins of beef and haunches of venison — stuff we never see nowadays, unless Bella sends us something down from the house. Fortunately, she's forgotten long before the meals are served what she's ordered.'

'No Red Cross meetings these days?'

The Earl shook his head sadly. 'Bella's taken all that over. Your aunt,' he added dryly, 'positively revels in her new responsibilities.'

'And what about you, father? Do you have much to do?'

The Earl shrugged. 'This and that. But with no men to do the work anyway, it's best to turn a blind eye to what needs doing. However,' he turned suddenly from the fireplace where he had been staring down morosely into the dying embers of the fire, and faced Robert, 'it won't always be like that. Soon, we shall drive the Hun back to where he belongs, the young men will come home and we shall pick up where we left off.'

'I doubt,' said Robert gently, 'that things will ever be quite the same again, father.'

'They could be!' And now the older man was glaring ferociously at his son. 'If everyone is prepared to do their bit, to pull together, accept their responsibilities.'

Robert shook his head. 'Those men lucky enough to survive won't want to go back to the old ways.'

'What's wrong with the old ways? Free board, free uniform, a job for life if they behave themselves.'

Robert sighed. His father's attitude hadn't really changed over the years and nor would it, now. He felt a sudden rush of compassion for the man. It was hardly his fault that the old order was crumbling.

'You'll see,' his father promised, apparently taking his silence for agreement. 'They'll soon find out which side their bread is buttered. As you may do yourself, before long.'

Robert raised his eyebrows at that. Was he to be threatened with being cut off with the proverbial shilling? But that would be too simple a solution. Before irretrievable damage could be done to their already precarious relationship, he must change the subject. 'How is the Pottery doing?' he asked, remembering Aunt Bella's fears.

The Earl's expression changed abruptly from pugnacity to boredom. 'Some time since I've visited it,' he admitted. 'But Bennett sends me regular reports. Good chap, Bennett!'

Bennett, as Robert recalled, had been nearing retirement even before the war had started. 'Perhaps I could go over and take a look at it when I'm a little more mobile?' he suggested.

'Please yourself! But if you're thinking of improving the family fortunes, you'd be better occupied looking nearer home.'

'How do you mean, father?'

The old man straddled the hearth-rug, his hands clasped behind his back as he gazed down at his son. And now there was a tinge of nervousness in his voice. 'Entirely your own affair, of course, my boy. And no doubt there've been other things on your mind, the last couple of years. But even you with your peculiar views on life, must think about women sometimes. A wife? Children? Wouldn't be averse to dandling a grandchild on my knee, I can tell you! Had great hopes, at one time, of George and that little Frobisher girl. But . . . ' he shook his head sadly, ' . . . it wasn't to be.'

He brooded in silence for a moment but then looked up quickly. 'She's still around, you know. Still fancy free, still got her head screwed on the right way. And comes over to dine with us, from time to time. You might care to join us, eh? Talk over old times.'

Here we go! thought Robert. Just as Aunt Bee had foretold! But there would be no harm in enjoying a little feminine company while he was at home. It might even take his mind off the picture of Kate Moneymoon and that confounded French doctor, standing in each other's arms at the foot of his bed, that so often haunted his dreams.

'You're tired,' Pierre said to Kate as he sipped a cup of tea in the ward kitchen.

'I can't be! I had home leave in September.'

'Which I think perhaps you did not enjoy as much as you should have done,' he surmised shrewdly.

'How is Heloise?' Kate deliberately changed the subject. Sometimes, she wondered what would have happened if she had accepted the offer of marriage Pierre had made before he went off to Verdun. Would she now be contemplating a fulfilled and satisfying future with a man with whom she could have lived in great contentment if not consuming passion? Or would Pierre's feelings for her have faded when he re-met his old love?

'Heloise,' said Pierre softly, as if answering her unspoken question, 'is in Verdun. But *you* are here with me now and looking, although very tired, very beautiful, too. I am sure that it could be arranged for you to spend a night or two away from the hospital.'

His meaning was clear. Even as she took a precautionary step backward, Kate thought with a flicker of amusement that if she had married him, she would never have had a moment's peace! But in one respect, he could be right. She had heard that sexual satisfaction, even without love, could be a rejuvenating experience. So who could tell? Perhaps, one day . . .

Meanwhile, she put back her head and grinned up at Pierre. 'I'm certainly not asking for a pass before Christmas. Prissy, Angela and I have decided to make this one a Christmas to remember! You'll see!'

21

It was strange, Robert thought later, that 'little Fatty Frobisher' should be the one to influence a decision that could so easily change the course of his life.

Until now, his path had been directed for him; in childhood by his old Nanny and his tutor, and afterwards by masters at preparatory and public school. Then had come a pre-ordained course at university and finally, the strait-jacket of the army. It was something, he supposed, that he had kicked over the traces sufficiently to refuse a commission and become a Don R., although even that had been greatly influenced by his passion for motor-bikes.

But now — 'The choice is yours,' he was told at the medical board he attended just before Christmas. 'Active service is definitely out of the question but you could still serve elsewhere in the army; in a commissioned capacity if you so wished. On the other hand, you may prefer an honourable discharge in order to serve your country on the home front. This would be equally as acceptable to us.'

What, he had asked, would serving 'elsewhere in the army' mean exactly? He had little enthusiasm for a desk job.

But that was an avenue down which they were not empowered to go. All they could do was to recommend. But they understood that the brigadier of his old regiment thought most highly of him. A position on his staff might be arranged by the War Office.

So service in France was still a possibility? A wild wisp of an idea was beginning to eddy through his brain.

They would certainly have no objection to France, as long as he remembered his limitations. As he'd been told, the index finger of his right hand would never straighten, he would always walk with a limp and might need the help of a stick when he was tired. But there was certainly nothing wrong with his mental faculties. So, if he wished to be recommended for what was described, somewhat ironically in his case, as 'a commission in the field' — thereby avoiding exhaustive training at an Officer Cadet Training Unit — they would set the ball rolling.

Could he, he had asked, think it over for a few days? Perhaps until after Christmas? Weigh up the pros and cons and discuss it with his family?

But, of course! And they would like to congratulate him upon his patriotism. Most men in his position would have jumped at the chance of a discharge.

But most men, he'd reflected as he'd left the board, didn't have a ghost to lay. And the compulsion to see with their own eyes if a certain marriage had taken place.

★　★　★

Priscilla sat on her bed, hugging herself with glee, Hank's letter open beside her. He'd been given Christmas furlough.

261

' 'Only for Christmas day,' ' she read out to Kate and Angela, ' 'but my officer's a great guy. He's fixed for me to deliver medical supplies to your château on Christmas Eve — so expect me some time that day. Oh, boy! I can hardly wait!' '

Priscilla paused for a second, then looked up, her eyes sparkling. 'He says he'd be entitled to a lot more furlough if we were to be married! So, how about it?'

'Is that you asking us, or him asking you?' Angela asked.

'Both! He's asking me and I'm asking you what you think.'

'You'd certainly have *my* blessing, although your more level-headed sister might have other ideas.'

'What *do* you think, Kate?'

'Let's just wait and see.'

'You think we might change our minds when we see each other again, don't you? But we shan't!'

'Don't worry!' Angela tried to reassure Kate. 'That's exactly how I felt before I met Ernst again.'

'Any news of him?' Kate asked, for Angela had also had a letter.

'Yes and no. Cousin Annie says he's definitely gone from the estate, but she doesn't know where to. It's probably as he warned me — he's acting as an interpreter, somewhere. So, as little as I want to leave you two, I may apply to work on the trains. There's a sporting chance he might be in London.'

'Well, you can't go before Prissy's wedding, if she *is* going to be married,' Kate pointed out, privately thinking that looking for a needle in a haystack would be child's play compared with searching for

Ernst among London's teeming millions.

'And I would definitely want you and Kate as bridesmaids,' said Priscilla.

'And Matron as Maid of Honour?' Angela suggested, tongue in cheek. 'And what about the Colonel and Hank's officer holding up the Union Jack and the Stars and Stripes outside the church?'

They shrieked with laughter.

'The most important thing,' said Angela, 'is to make sure Prissy looks so ravishing when Hank arrives at Christmas, he goes down on one knee and proposes, there and then. So how about us dressing her up?'

'What in, for heaven's sake?'

'Let's have a browse in the box room at the end of your corridor. My family was always dressing up for charades, before the war, and I doubt if the French were any different. If there's enough, we could all do it. After all, we're allowed to borrow books from the library, so why not clothes from the attics? We'd put them straight back after Christmas. Sister's such a good sport, I'm sure she'd let us wear them. And the men would love it.'

'Let's go and look now,' Priscilla suggested. 'It's only ten o'clock and I'm far too excited to sleep.'

* * *

In England, it is the coldest winter in living memory. The lake is a sheet of ice and the branches of the cedar tree under which Robert and Aunt Bella had sheltered from the September sunshine are now heavy with snow. But everyone has been greatly cheered by a Christmas message sent by King George V and his queen. Each man has received an embossed card expressing sympathy for the suffering they have endured and wishing them a speedy return to health.

Now, on Christmas morning, Alice Frobisher and Robert stand in the window of what was once the drawing-room of Holker Hall. Behind them, the ward is decorated with swags of evergreen and a spruce tree, brought in from the estate, stands in the corner. An even larger tree can be glimpsed in the main hall where a great log fire is burning and where Christmas festivities will take place that evening. Both trees are festooned with paper chains and brightly-coloured baubles.

'It looks far more festive,' Robert claims, 'than it ever used to. As I remember, Christmas was a rather solemn affair with the servants lining up for their statutory goose and plum pudding. And George and I, longing to get back to our tin soldiers and model railways, having to shake hands with them all, as if we'd never met them before in our lives!'

He glances down at Alice, trim and pretty in her uniform and remembers how she has spent the last few days up step-ladders, patiently trailing ivy and paper chains over windows and door-frames, with a circle of admiring officers urging her to go 'higher, nurse! Just one step higher!' while they admire the neatness of her ankles. And she, knowing quite well what they are about, has still done her best to oblige. 'You're a good sport, Alice,' Robert says now.

Alice looks up at him, one eyebrow lifted. 'Just a good sport?' She smiles ruefully. 'I'm still little Fatty

Frobisher to you, aren't I, Robert?'

'What a suggestion! You're a gorgeous butterfly delighting everyone with your brilliance!'

'But as far as *you're* concerned, I'm still a plump little caterpillar! Just like the ones you and George used to try and put down my neck!'

'They would have been Cabbage Whites, collected from the vegetable garden. And even in that uniform, Alice, you're no Cabbage White!'

'No uniform tonight!' Alice declares. 'Our best bibs and tucker, Matron says.'

Over the last few weeks, when he has met Alice several times at the Dower House or at Bellwood, her own home, he has often seen her in evening clothes. 'The men are in for a treat, then.'

'Even you, dear Robert, may find me faintly attractive!'

'But I always do! And not *faintly*!' And indeed, he does, but he is also acutely aware, as in childhood, that Alice is the pursuer and he the pursued, even though he often chides himself for not reversing the roles. For his mind has become a sort of battlefield, one half maintaining that Alice belongs to a background that he has sworn to reject; the other reminding him that, even so, he is still a man and that Alice Frobisher would make a wonderful bedmate.

Just at this moment, standing together at the 'drawing-room' window, it is for all the world as if they are already married and are planning what they will do with the day. He bends to plant a light kiss on her forehead. 'Whatever you wear, dear Alice, you will look enchanting.' And realises, even as he speaks, that he could not have sounded more like a doting husband, if he'd tried. He feels a faint throb of foreboding.

★ ★ ★

Aunt Bella has surpassed herself. Turkey — perhaps a little tough and lacking the plump perfection of yester-years, but mouth-watering, for all that — followed by plum pudding laced with precious brandy, has been served to everyone. Now, the more mobile of the patients have congregated in the main hall with a pile of records and a gramophone; or, to be exact, two gramophones in the charge of two men. Urged on by their friends, they have done their best to synchronise their timing so that identical records will sound as one augmented whole. But their efforts have been so disastrous, they have now given up the idea altogether and begun to play totally different recordings, one half of their audience singing 'Pack Up Your Troubles' while the other half roars out 'Tipperary'.

'Equal firsts!' declares Aunt Bella when it ends, and begins to ladle punch from a giant tureen. She is helped by nurses who have exchanged their uniforms for pre-war, party clothes. Some have also let down their hair, in both senses, and are almost completely unrecognisable.

Alice, Robert reflects, had been right to assume he would find her attractive. She is wearing a black velvet gown — but no funereal garment, this. The bodice is cut in a plunging V that reveals the creamy whiteness of neck and shoulders, and the velvet

266

moulds her breasts and thighs so closely there seems little doubt there is no other garment beneath. It is a possibility that every man present, he suspects, would give a year of his life to explore. Certainly, his own pulses quicken alarmingly as he looks at her and, just for a moment, he ponders on the advisability, the morality even, of so flagrantly displaying her charms before men for whom the sexual act may now be difficult, if not impossible, to achieve.

But such thoughts fade rapidly when 'ragtime' takes over and Alice presents herself before him. With a mock curtsy, she asks him to dance.

'With my gammy leg? You can't be serious!'

'Indeed, I am! Just put your arms around me and sort of wriggle your upper body in time to the music.'

And indeed, swaying his torso in rhythm to the beat while his feet remain firmly rooted to the floor, as Alice does the same, is a most pleasurable experience. Feeling the thrust of her breasts against him, the pressure of her thighs, he is embarrassingly aware that if they continue, his arousal will become patently obvious to everyone. He suspects that this is her purpose.

With a Herculean effort, he holds himself away from her until the record ends and is then delighted to see the little nurse who had 'welcomed' him to Holker Hall, standing nearby. He excuses himself from Alice but not before she has given him a quick, proprietorial hug and murmured. 'That was wonderful!' in his ear.

And so the festivities continue with solo

performances alternating with the music. Aunt Bella, to her nephew's astonishment, brings the house down with a dramatic rendering of The Road to Mandalay.

'Where and when did you learn that?' he demands.

'This isn't the first war in my life, remember!' And just for a moment, a nostalgic far-away look comes into her eyes and he wonders, as he often has before, why she has never married. But this certainly isn't the time to ask. And in any case, Alice has begun to sing, accompanied at the piano by a soldier whose fingers must know their own way about the keyboard, because his eyes never leave her as she stands there with her hands clasped modestly over her breast. And, as she sings, her gaze sweeps over her rapt audience, so that every man present must be convinced it is he with whom she yearns to travel that long, long trail a-winding into the land of her dreams.

Towards midnight, Aunt Bella calls out, 'Time for bed, I think. Thank you everyone, for a wonderful party!'

As the men scatter to their wards, accompanied in some cases by attendant nurses, and Robert begins to limp up the stairs, he is aware that Alice is just behind him and Aunt Bella is behind her. He turns. 'I'll be all right, Alice. No need to help me.' And indeed, he is perfectly capable, nowadays, of putting himself to bed.

'Of course not!' she says swiftly. 'But I'm sleeping here tonight. Special dispensation for Christmas.' And when he stops outside his own door, she continues on down the corridor.

He breathes a sigh of relief that Aunt Bella is still behind her. It has been a good evening and one he has no wish to spoil by denying Alice what she may now consider 'her rights'; or, worse still, capitulating to her charms. Just to be on the safe side, he locks his door.

For about one thing, he is now quite clear. He is not going to be 'rushed'. The thought of marrying Alice Frobisher is no longer an absurdity; his body would even welcome it. But it must be in his own time and certainly not while there is the remotest chance that Kate Moneymoon remains unmarried. He has no doubt now, what he will tell the Medical Board.

★　★　★

In France, too, the wounded have received their Christmas message from the King and Queen and now, just at the moment when Alice is serenading the men at Holker Hall, Priscilla, Kate and Angela are singing to the men at the château; but there are differences. Their song — 'There's Something About a Soldier' — was first sung during an earlier war and their clothes, too, are from another age. Rummaging through the attics has produced an astonishing miscellany of antique garments; not only garments but wigs.

'I've always wanted to be a sultry brunette like you, Kate,' Priscilla has confessed and now sports a luxuriant mop of jet-black curls that peep out provocatively from beneath a floppy, artist's beret. An enormous black bow tied beneath her chin and a paint-smeared smock over close-fitting, black velvet trousers, complete her outfit.

Kate is deliciously feminine as a school-room miss with two flaxen pigtails swinging down her back and white, lace-trimmed pantaloons peeping from beneath a blue, striped dress.

Angela has been unable to resist a Pompadour gown complete with hooped and panniered skirt and flowing sleeves. She has topped it with an elaborately curled Pompadour wig.

That none of them look in the least like a soldier detracts not at all from their audience's enjoyment of the song. Those men who are able to, join in the chorus and call vociferously for an encore.

'How about some carols?' one of them calls out. And Priscilla leads them into 'Come All Ye Faithful'. She is radiant with happiness and her gaze moves constantly towards the door through which Hank is expected to appear at any moment. For his carefully-laid plans have gone awry and his visit has been postponed; but only by a day and since early morning, Priscilla's excitement has been mounting. Now it is at fever-pitch as, bright-eyed and flushed, she moves slowly down the ward, her light soprano voice supported by the tenor and bass of the two ambulance drivers who have brought wounded men to the château earlier in the day and have been persuaded to stay on to help. One of them, a brawny, sandy-haired Scot, has barely left Priscilla's side since the festivities started and by now is firmly convinced he has found the love of his life.

'You're a bonny, wee lassie and no mistake,' he murmurs into her ear as 'Come All Ye Faithful' gives way to 'Good King Wenceslaus'. 'Just the wee lassie I've been looking for.'

And she, oblivious to everything except Hank's impending arrival, smiles radiantly and murmurs back, 'You're not so bad, yourself, Jock!' And 'Jock' dares to slide an arm around her waist and to wonder, not for the first time, how he can inveigle her out of the ward and into some secluded corner.

Kate, going to the kitchen to put the kettles on for bed-time cocoa — for there is a limit, even on Christmas night, to what sick men can endure — notices what is happening and fears the situation is getting out of hand. This particular 'Jock' has a reputation for hot-headedness. However, before she can fill even one kettle, the singing suddenly stops and she hears a door swing back on its hinges. She turns and practically runs back into the ward.

A tall figure clad in olive-green breeches, yellow leather jacket and a flying helmet, a scarlet neckerchief at his throat, stands in the doorway gazing, open-mouthed, at Angela. 'For Pete's sake, what is this? A fancy-dress ball?' He seems oblivious of his own bizarre appearance and she, for once, is speechless with surprise.

'Hank!' Priscilla, unaware of Sister hovering at her elbow, launches herself forward.

'Prissy! Sweetheart! I didn't recognise you!' He picks her up in his arms and swings her high. Then clasps her to him in a great bear-hug before putting back his head just far enough to allow him to kiss her soundly on the mouth. Over her shoulder, he suddenly sees Sister. 'Hello, honey! Are you for real? Or dressed up like the others?'

271

With the greatest difficulty, Kate manages not to laugh. Sister has been warned, of course, of Hank's impending arrival, but certainly hasn't expected such a colourful character. None of them have! The men are agog with curiosity and several have begun to whistle and cat-call.

Sister catches Kate's eye and thanks heaven that at least one of the Moneymoon girls seems to be showing some sense. And Nurse Carstairs can always be relied upon in an emergency even if she does look like Marie Antoinette. Really, she should never have allowed such a performance. It's as well Matron is dining with the Colonel. She beckons Kate and Angela to her. 'My office, I think!'

The next moment, Hank is being shepherded out of the ward and into the minute cubicle that is Sister's office. But not before Kate and Angela have been soundly kissed and Sister herself bussed heartily on the cheek. She raises her eyebrows as she shuts the door firmly upon Hank and Priscilla. 'I've seen everything now! The sooner we get the men settled for the night, the better. It may be Christmas, but . . . '

The other two murmur agreement and Kate looks around for the two ambulance drivers but sees only one. 'Where's Jock?'

'Scarpered!' his mate says succinctly. 'And don't ask me to repeat what he said, nurse, because I couldn't. That Yank certainly put *his* nose out of joint and no mistake!'

'That Yank,' says Angela, taking off her wig, rolling up her sleeves and tying on an apron, 'would put anyone's nose out of joint!'

22

'It's all fixed,' said Priscilla on Boxing Day after Hank had gone. 'We're getting married.'

'When?' Kate, Angela and Abbie spoke as one.

'April. Hank says he daren't ask for leave before then.'

'Does Matron know?'

'Yes. She's writing to Ma and Pa for their approval but I've told her there won't be a problem.'

'And it's going to be here, at the château?'

'Yes. We want it to be as quiet and informal as possible.'

Angela exploded into laughter. 'Informal — yes! But *quiet*? Not with your Hank around!'

Priscilla chuckled. 'Well, you know what I mean. No fuss. Just you lot and Mary Barnes. And we shall both wear uniform.'

'Does Hank *have* a uniform, then?' Kate asked with assumed innocence.

'Oh, yes! But it's such a drab affair — almost like a German uniform — none of them wear it.'

'And what about a honeymoon?' Abbie wanted to know. 'A couple of nights at the Coq d'Or?' The Coq d'Or was the estaminet in the village.

'No — it'll be a morning ceremony and then we shall be off to Le Petit Manoir. If Marie-Claire can have us.' A sudden thought struck her. 'Abbie, why don't we have a double wedding? You and Fred, Hank and me.'

But Abbie shook her head. 'Thanks for the suggestion, Prissy, but mine's got to be at home. Mum's already started making over her own wedding dress for me and my two little sisters will be bridesmaids. They'd lynch me if I got married out here.'

'Ma and Pa will be a bit sad, too, I expect,' Priscilla admitted. 'But it does mean they won't have the advantage over Hank's parents. What do you think, Kate?'

'They'll understand,' Kate agreed. 'And they know Hank and like him.'

'At least *your* wedding will be at home,' said Abbie for Kate had never disillusioned her about Robert. 'How is your Robert, Kate?'

'Still convalescing,' said Kate and left it at that. For the first time, she wished that Robert was commissioned, for then there would be every chance that either Ma or Pa would read of his discharge in the London Gazette. As it was, she would probably have to wait until after the war for news of him when, no doubt, the heir to the Earl of Werrington would be mentioned from time to time in the glossy, Society journals.

She tried not to think of him too often but seeing Hank again had brought memories flooding back. What happy carefree days those had been in the summer of 1914 before this dreadful war had turned their lives upside down. What a high-minded, scrupulous *idiot* she'd been! At least, Prissy was having the good sense to grasp happiness with two

274

hands. She forced herself to listen to Abbie apparently taking on the catering arrangements for the wedding breakfast.

'D'you think you could manage those hamburger things, Hank's so darned crazy about?' Prissy was asking her, apparently determined to adopt not only the American way of life but its phraseology, too.

'Sausage sandwiches, that's all *they* are!' said Abbie scornfully. And they all laughed. This wedding's going to be just what we need to take our minds off the war, Kate thought.

★ ★ ★

They had need of some light relief as 1917 dragged itself on to the calendar. Not only did the temperature drop to below zero but snow fell heavily and then froze so that the château resembled an enormous iced cake glistening in the thin sunshine that rarely lasted long enough to thaw the icicles. The nurses yearned for their off-duty time, not to rest in their rooms, but to seize their cloaks and rush out into the open air, there to stamp their way through the icy woods and fields until the circulation returned to their frozen bodies. For the British coal-miners — and perhaps with good reason — had chosen to go on strike and heating the vast wards of the château became increasingly difficult.

At night, Kate and Priscilla huddled into one bed so that their blankets could be distributed to their patients and Angela and Abbie soon followed suit. 'And it's much warmer,' Angela reported, 'even if I

275

do wake up with my mouth full of Abbie's hair!'

Matron, to her astonishment — but not to the Colonel's, for he had recommended her — was mentioned in despatches. But the honour, as she was quick to point out, was given on behalf of all her nursing staff. When she called them together to tell them so, they cheered her to the rafters.

At least, during such conditions when the trenches were either rock-hard or knee-deep in mud, there were no major offensives. But the cases of frostbite and trench foot increased; as did the cold. In early February, Kate fainted on the ward and was put to bed. At first it was feared she had pneumonia but then a severe chill was diagnosed and rest and warmth recommended.

'I'll ring Marie-Claire,' said Pierre immediately and twentyfour hours later Kate was installed at Le Petit Manoir. Her bed was in a tiny sitting-room that led off the kitchen its door left open so that she could feel the warmth of the wood-burning stove and smell the appetising aroma of the 'potage' that simmered constantly on the hob.

Nor was she short of professional care. When she'd been lifted from the ambulance and carried across the drawbridge, the short journey had been supervised by a French woman with an abundance of jet-black hair coiled around her head and a voice that, although low and husky, still possessed the quality of command. 'Like iron filings coated with honey', Priscilla was to describe it later.

'This,' Marie-Claire introduced her once Kate was settled, 'is Heloise Deneuve.'

A cool hand was placed gently on Kate's brow.

'Rest now, *ma petite*. Tomorrow, we will introduce ourselves properly.'

Next day, once Kate had received as competent a blanket-bath as any she'd ever given herself and been fed a bowl of bread and milk, laced with brandy, Heloise perched on her bed.

'A minute's conversation and then you must rest! But it is a pleasure to meet you, Kate. Pierre has told me so much about you.'

But how much? Kate wondered.

'He told me,' Heloise continued with a twinkle in eyes the colour of damp wood violets, 'that you were an excellent nurse and looked like a wild rose. But that, like the rose, you could also be very prickly. Which means,' her mouth widened into a broad grin, 'and knowing my Pierre as I do, that you probably repelled his advances. Am I not right?'

Kate's blush was sufficient reply.

'And having met you,' Heloise pursued, 'I can quite see why he likened your appearance to a rose. Now,' she rose to her feet, 'when you are feeling stronger we will talk more, not only about Pierre but about other things.'

Kate put out a detaining hand. 'Before you go — please don't feel obliged — just because you're here . . . ' her voice trailed away weakly.

Heloise chuckled. 'I need something to keep my hand in! And you are a delightful change from the cases I've been nursing just lately.'

That evening, everyone ate supper together, the family and Heloise at the big kitchen table and Kate propped up in bed with her door open. Denise and Phillipe, home from school, took it in turns to wait on her, bringing her soup, followed by a creamy, apple mousse that slid effortlessly down her throat. Afterwards, they all sat around her bed, drinking their acorn coffee, until Heloise shooed them away.

'We must get Kate better soon because in a few days, I think there will be visitors.'

And she was right! Pierre, Priscilla, Abbie and Angela, hitching a lift on army trucks, reached Le Petit Manoir in time for lunch on a day of glorious sunshine. 'But we'll have to catch the last train back tonight,' said Pierre. 'The British have attacked at Arras. Successfully, they say but there will be many casualties.'

'But Matron says you are not to think of coming back until you are quite well,' Priscilla told Kate. 'But I must say, you look tons better already.'

'How could I not?' asked Kate. 'With Marie-Claire providing such appetising food and Heloise such professional care.' It had amused her to notice how Pierre had greeted both herself and Heloise with no trace of embarrassment, kissing each soundly upon both cheeks.

After lunch, Kate was swathed in rugs, tucked up securely on a big, wooden sleigh drawn by one of the ponies, and taken for a sedate ride across the common. Pierre held the reins and everyone else ran or walked by her side. There was much cheerful laughter and throwing of snowballs.

Just like any ordinary, family outing, thought Kate. It took a French biplane droning overhead towards the front lines to remind her that none of them, except for the Furneau family, would have been there had it not been for the war. So at least some good had come out of it, she reflected, for in what other circumstance could such deep and diverse friendships have been forged? Please God, she thought, we never go back to the old way of life, with its rigid class structure and hidebound conventions. And she wondered, as she so often did in spite of her determination not to, how Robert was and if, now that he was back with his family his principles would remain the same. She feared they would not.

Her reverie was shattered by a snowball whizzing past her head far too close for comfort, and Pierre urged the pony into a trot so that the others were left behind.

'You are really feeling better then, little one?' he called over his shoulder, slowing the pony to a walk.

'Oh, yes, Pierre, thank you!'

'You like her, my Heloise?'

'Very much!'

'I knew you would!' he said with irritating complacency and Kate scooped up a handful of snow and hurled it at the back of his neck. Such smugness!

Later that evening after the visitors had gone and Heloise was taking Kate's temperature, she said, 'It was good to see Pierre again, was it not?' Kate nodded vigorously. 'He is so lucky to have you as a friend and colleague.' This time, Kate managed a deprecatory shrug. 'When we are married,' Heloise continued, 'I shall be both wife and mistress to him and in return, I shall expect fidelity. But until then, when we are apart like this,' and now she was the one to shrug, 'Pierre is a passionate man — that is partly why he attracts me — and it would not worry me at all if he were to seek consolation with someone I knew and *liked*.'

Her meaning was clear. Kate waited until the thermometer was removed from her mouth, then said firmly, 'Well, it would worry *me* very much indeed, and precisely *because* I knew and liked his fianceé!'

Heloise looked at her for a moment and then they both burst into laughter.

'*Vive la difference!*' said Heloise and bent to kiss Kate lightly on the forehead.

★ ★ ★

Kate returned to the château refreshed in body and spirit; and with her relationship with Pierre on a new footing. For Heloise was now her friend.

'You mean I am now, as you English put it, 'beyond the pale'?' Pierre enquired when her new-found confidence prompted her to explain how she now felt about him.

'In my book, at any rate,' Kate assured him.

'There speaks my little English nurse! As prim as ever!' And then he put his hands on her shoulders and studied her intently. 'Dear Kate, there is something about you — a quality of innocence that I think you will never lose. But be careful of it, for it makes you very vulnerable.'

Afterwards, Kate thought hard about what he had said. Perhaps she *was* a naive innocent, especially in a world at war, but 'to your own self be true' someone had written and that must be her philosophy. One day, another man might mean as much to her as Robert had done, but until then, she would guard her innocence.

Feeling more content than she had for many months, she concentrated upon plans for Priscilla's wedding. Not that there were many. The padre was asked to keep free the morning of the first of May, Priscilla's leave was booked, the duty roster was arranged so that Kate and Angela would both be free on the morning of the wedding and Abbie went into a huddle with Fred to arrange the best wedding breakfast ever to be held on the Western Front — a claim that was unlikely to be challenged! The steady advance of the British on the Somme and the French in Champagne added to the feeling of optimism that, once again, was beginning to spread through the château.

And then, on the 3rd of April, 1917, the United States of America entered the war. Excitement rose to fever pitch; for everyone except Priscilla.

'This alters everything,' she wailed to Kate and Angela after speaking to Hank on the telephone. 'He says he's off to Paris to join the American army.'

'But he's not trained,' Kate objected

'You know Hank! He says the sooner he joins, the sooner he can get to grips with the Germans and the sooner it will all be over.'

'You mean Hank versus the Hun, single-handed?' Angela lifted an eyebrow.

'Not quite! His friends are all doing the same thing. I can quite see how they feel.'

'So what's happening?' Kate asked.

'He'll be down in a day or two and will I fix it

281

with the padre? I'm on my way to see Matron now. He says there'll be no chance of more than twentyfour hours, so it will have to be the Coq d'Or after all. I shall have to telephone Le Petit Manoir.'

So Priscilla and Hank were married very quietly in the tiny chapel of the château but there was still room for drama. The bridegroom and his best man held up by an unseasonal blizzard, arrived with only minutes to spare, and the couple's vows were exchanged against the sinister rumble of the guns. For at Arras, the British were acting as decoys to lure the Germans away from a big attack by the French in Champagne.

Afterwards, toasts were drunk hurriedly in Matron's office before everyone except the bride and groom went back on duty.

'But it won't last long now,' Hank's best man, Jamie Coleano, predicted. 'We'll soon have the Boche on the run, you'll see! Over by Christmas, I'd say.'

Matron and the Colonel exchanged glances but refrained from comment. Just so had the youth of Britain spoken in 1914.

The happy couple were waved away from the château with due ceremony, as if heading for a fortnight on the Riviera instead of the Coq d'Or for a one-night stay. There were unexpected tears in Priscilla's eyes as she clung to Kate. 'D' you realise . . . ?'

Kate hugged her back, 'I know! The first time we've been separated since I caught chicken pox and you didn't. But Ma always said you'd be the first to marry. Good luck, Prissie!'

Later, when the party was breaking up, Kate turned to Jamie Coleano. 'What are you doing now, Mr Coleano?' she felt obliged to enquire. 'You'll wait until tomorrow for Hank, I suppose?'

'Jamie, please! Yes, we're driving up to Paris in the morning and the Colonel's allowing me to stay here overnight. But what to do in the meantime is a problem. Normally, I'd head for the nearest bar, but knowing that's where Hank is, puts it straight out of bounds. I don't suppose . . . ?' He looked hopefully at Kate.

She hesitated. 'Well, I have to go on duty now, but I'll be free this evening. Perhaps . . . ' she turned to Matron. 'Would it be in order, Matron, for me to meet Mr Coleano when I come off duty?'

Matron pondered. Fraternisation with the military was not to be encouraged but this young man wasn't in the army — yet. 'I think that will be in order, Nurse. Provided, of course, that you entertain Mr Coleano in the communal sitting room.'

'Thank you, Matron.' Kate turned back to Jamie, saw the astonished look on his face and barely repressed a smile. 'I'll meet you in the main hall at six, Mr Coleano.'

★ ★ ★

'You'd have thought I was suggesting a night of lust and debauchery,' said Jamie Coleano, his blue eyes alight with laughter. 'Not sitting two feet apart in a morgue!'

'Oh, come,' said Kate, 'it's not as bad as that!' But in fact, the V.A.D.'s sitting room was a cheerless place, full of drab, standard-issue furniture.

'My sister's in the American Red Cross,' Jamie told her. 'And they're allowed to throw parties in their mess. With real men!'

'I'm afraid it's not like that with us. Officially, we're not allowed to be seen outside the hospital in the company of a man.'

'Then how come that cute little Abbie is so friendly with her Sergeant?'

'That's rather different,' Kate tried to explain. 'To begin with, they work together and the kitchen staff are a law unto themselves. Matron tends only to worry about the nursing staff.'

'I don't get it,' Jamie was genuinely perplexed. 'You spend all day and half the night doing unmentionable things to men's bodies that even their wives would think twice about, and off duty you're supposed to live like nuns!'

'Believe you me,' said Kate, 'when we come off duty, we're so tired we don't think about anything but bed.'

'That's just what I'm saying!' said Jamie Coleano.

His frankness was refreshing. By ten o'clock, Kate felt there was little she didn't know about him and his family; his father in real estate in Boston, his mother on innumerable War-Aid committees, his 'kid sister' knitting him a scarf so long he'd be able to share it with two other men at least, and a dog called Ike that he was missing 'like crazy'.

When they eventually said goodnight in the main hall, it seemed perfectly natural for him to kiss her lightly on the forehead. 'Goodnight, Kate! I hope we meet up again before too long.'

'Goodnight!' As he bounded lightly up the main staircase and she turned towards the back stairs, Kate found herself hoping very much that she would soon meet Jamie Coleano again. He was better than any tonic.

★　★　★

In the bar of the Coq d'Or, Captain Robert Holker eases his right leg into a more comfortable position and raises his glass to his driver. 'You say you've been here before, Corporal?'

'Aye, sir! Last Christmas, up at yon castle. I was roped in as an ambulance driver and stayed to help.'

'On the wards?'

'Aye! Helping the nurses hand round the tea. That kind o' thing.'

'I was here myself, last July,' Robert indicates his leg. 'Wounded on the first day of the Somme offensive. Thought I might call in there tomorrow. Seems a pity not to say thank you to the nurses while I'm here.' He hopes he's making it sound as if pure coincidence has caused him to pass this way.

'Well, I can tell you one o' them won't be there, sir. Popped up myself, I did, while you was having your dinner and was told one o' them had just got married. Spent her wedding night here, by all accounts.'

The whisky in Robert's glass slops over as he puts it down on the bar. Take it easy! he tells himself. There must be well over fifty nurses up there. He forces himself to appear only mildly interested.

'Indeed? What was her name, d' you know?'

The Corporal frowns. 'Funny name! Money *bags* I called her but it weren't quite that.'

'Moneymoon, was it?'

'That's it, sir! Fancy you rememberin'! Money-moon. Nice girl — should'a had more sense.'

Robert licks lips grown suddenly dry and forces himself to react naturally. 'Nothing wrong with getting married, surely, Corporal?'

'To a bleedin' foreigner, there is! Beggin' your pardon, sir, but there's Scotsmen a'plenty would ha' gi'en their right arm for a girl like her. Well,' he grunts disconsolately, 'I would ha', anyway?'

Robert clears his throat. 'I seem to remember,' he says carefully, 'that there were two Moneymoons. Sisters. Priscilla and Kate. Which . . . ?'

'Oh, I didn'a get as far as Christian names, sir. No such luck?'

'Was she dark-haired, or fair?'

'Oh, dark, sir! Black as your hat!'

So there is no doubt. Robert reaches for the stick that leans against his stool and rises stiffly to his feet. 'Forgive me for the inconvenience, Corporal, but I think, after all, we should push on to Brigade tonight. Finish your drink while I settle the bill.' And he limps away towards the reception area. Fate may have dealt him the cruellest blow in her repertoire but she can't force him to sleep under the same roof, perhaps even in the same bed, as Kate and that damned doctor had on their wedding night.

Next day, he writes to Danny Moneymoon, telling him that he is to consider himself the sole owner of the Harley Davidson. He can think of no cleaner way of severing all connections with a family he had once hoped to be part of. And now there will be no need ever to go back to Moneymoon Manor.

23

Priscilla was pregnant; and no-one more astonished than she.

'I can't believe it!' She sat cross-legged on her bed, a boyish stripling more than a married woman, albeit of such short standing.

'What d'you mean, you can't believe it?' Angela scoffed. 'The marriage was consummated, I take it?'

'Oh, yes!' Priscilla's cheeks went bright pink. 'Several times!'

'Well, then?'

'It just hadn't occurred to me.'

'Daughter of a university professor you may be, but in some fields your education has been sadly neglected. It's like this, Prissy. Boy meets girl. Girl . . . '

'Oh, shut up!' And Priscilla threw a well-aimed pillow.

'Ma will be pleased,' said Kate.

'Hank, too, I hope?' Angela, with the skill of long practice had fielded the pillow.

'Oh, yes! Apart from anything else, I'll be going home now and able to see him.'

For Hank and Jamie, contrary to all their

expectations, were languishing in London, awaiting the arrival of their commander-to-be, General Pershing, and growing steadily more and more frustrated; especially since the Canadian army, many of them Americans who'd crossed the border to enlist, had acquitted themselves so well at Vimy Ridge.

'Well,' Kate looked across at Angela, 'this settles it. With Abbie getting married and no doubt pregnant too, I'm not staying here on my own. It's the hospital trains for me, too.'

'Whoopee! We'll go and see Matron in the morning.'

★ ★ ★

'I shall miss you, Kate,' said Pierre.

'And I, you. But we'll meet again one day.'

'Of course! Heloise will see to that.'

'Thank you, Pierre, for everything. You've taught me so much.'

'But never what I wanted to! Now it will be left to some clumsy Englishman who won't know his arse from his . . . '

'Thank you, Pierre!'

★ ★ ★

'It's no good, Angie! You'll have to cut my hair again. A louse actually fell into my porridge this morning!'

'Lucky old louse! *I* had to make do with bread and jam!'

Nothing was quite as they'd expected. To begin with, their official journeys went no further than Boulogne, sometimes Le Havre. Only if they had leave was it possible to 'organise' themselves on to a boat for England. But even if only for a seventytwo hour pass, it was worth it and Kate had twice managed to reach Moneymoon Manor and a few glorious hours of home comforts. Once, Angela had come with her and immediately adopted Ma and Pa as her 'reserve' parents.

Now, towards the end of September, Kate had decided to spend her next pass — due in a couple of days — with Priscilla who was staying at a small hotel near Hank's camp, not far from London. First, though, there were more pressing matters on her mind; like the three hundred or so casualties of the battle for the Menin Road that they had just taken on board under cover of darkness.

Tanks were now being used by the British in ever-increasing numbers but already the Germans had produced an anti-tank howitzer and many of the wounded were suffering from terrible burns inflicted when the gasoline tanks had been hit. The lucky ones, Kate considered, were those who had died instantly; during a journey that could easily take up to two or three days, depending upon the number of times they were shunted into sidings to allow a troop or supply train to rumble through, many of the survivors could easily die, too, and in great pain if the morphia didn't last.

There were medical officers on board who would administer it where necessary but even so, she and Angela would be kept busy for most of the night, moving — with practised ease by now — up and down the corridors, swaying to the motion of the train, giving sips of precious water where needed, sometimes easing a bandage hurriedly applied at a First Aid post behind the lines and now too tight for comfort, applying fresh dressings where necessary.

'It's just a patch-up job,' Angela had decided soon after they'd started. 'Not at all what we've been used to.'

'But necessary, all the same,' said Kate.

And the men's optimism, their relief at knowing they had a 'Blighty' and were on their way home, was almost tangible. Facetious comments — 'Tickets, please!' 'All change!' 'Put me off in Piccadilly, please nurse!' invariably greeted the opening of a compartment door.

With luck, either she or Angela would be able to snatch a couple of hours' sleep in the small hours — separately, of course, which was just as well because it was difficult for both of them to stretch out comfortably in the narrow compartment they shared, first class though it might once have been.

Tonight, Angela was to have first 'kip' but decided to postpone it in favour of a wash in their tiny hand-basin. 'With luck, I'll get a hot bath in Boulogne, while you're skiving off home,' she told Kate. 'And do I need it! I stink!'

For they had only exchanged one set of smells for another. On the wards, the odour of Lysol had clung to their clothes and lingered in their hair. Now, it was the stench of unwashed bodies, of uniforms stiff with blood and faeces — and crawling, more often than not, with lice — that filled their nostrils. But there was no way they would complain, other than to each other and in the privacy of their tiny 'room'.

'Just bring me back some soap,' Angela implored. 'Oodles and oodles of lavender soap! That's all I ask!'

★ ★ ★

'It's so good to see you, Prissy!' said Kate, hugging her twin as well as she could over the hump of her stomach. 'And Hank! And Jamie!'

'Not half as good as it is to see you, honey,' said Jamie Coleano.

To her surprise, all three had come to meet her at Victoria. Too late, she wished she'd spent more time at Dover having a wash and brush up, but that would have meant missing her train and time was precious. With luck, there would be hot water at Prissy's hotel. But the others had different ideas when she suggested going there.

'No time,' said Jamie. 'We're off tomorrow.'

'Tomorrow?'

'Yep!' Hank confirmed. 'We're going at last. Destination unknown but I guess it's where you've just come from, Kate.'

'So it's a night out on the town for all of us,' said Jamie.

'Seats at the Alhambra and supper afterwards.'

'Don't worry, Kate,' Priscilla reassured her. 'We're all booked in at a hotel just around the corner. We'll go there now.'

'Fifteen minutes,' said Jamie when they arrived. 'If you're not down by then, I'm coming up to get you.'

'He would, too!' said Priscilla as she and Kate went up in the lift. 'He's talked of nothing else but seeing you for days now. He was desperately worried they'd have to go before you arrived. Now, here's your room. I'll run a bath while you undress.'

Oh, the bliss of it! Kate wallowed in the hot water, drawing in deep breaths of the scented steam, curling up her toes in ecstasy. 'Prissy, I've simply got to wash my hair, too. You can't imagine . . . '

'Oh yes, I can! My memory isn't that short. Don't worry. I'll rub it dry.'

'Prissy, how are you? How's the baby?'

'We're both fine. Hank's over the moon. Oh Kate, I can't tell you how happy I'd be if it wasn't for this dreadful war. What if Hank doesn't come back? What if . . . ?'

'Now come on, Priss! That's no way for a seasoned campaigner to talk.'

'I know! It's just that I keep remembering poor Sam Bosworth.'

'Think about all the men we've nursed who *did* survive.'

'But at what cost! But you're right, Kate. I mustn't think this way, especially on their last night.'

Only a few minutes late, they were back in the foyer. Kate's hair was still damp but she was gloriously, squeakily clean and wearing one of the dresses Priscilla had outgrown — a pre-war concoction of frills and lace and layers upon layers of misty white tulle.

'You look a million dollars,' said Jamie Coleano, linking her arm through his. 'Good enough to eat!'

They'd sung 'Yankee Doodle Dandy' until they were hoarse, tried to pick up the words of 'Over There', the new marching song brought across the Atlantic by the 'dough-boys', and shed tears over the old favourites. And through it all, Jamie had sat with his arm around Kate's shoulders, his free hand holding hers, occasionally leaning over to kiss the lobe of her ear. It was all a far cry from France and the troop trains with their sombre cargo; and from the trenches where Jamie must soon be going.

She had no way of telling if he thought of the future with anything but cheerful optimism. Glancing at him from time to time, she saw only his flushed face, the sparkle in his eyes, the way that his sandy hair, dark with sweat, clung to his temples. Suddenly, although he must be about the same age as herself, she felt old enough to be his mother.

Now, sitting in the lounge of their hotel, sipping coffee, she realised that the excitement of the evening was still with him. But now there was something else: a wish, perhaps, that their 'night on the town' should never end. But there was no way that Priscilla and Hank were going to stay up much longer. Already, in the glances they were exchanging, the close entwining of their fingers, they had begun to withdraw into their own private world. Now, Hank was on his feet, pulling Priscilla up with him.

'See you sharp at six, Jamie! Back at base by seven!' Jamie sketched a mock salute of agreement.

Priscilla bent to kiss Kate. 'No need for us to rush

in the morning. Breakfast around eight and then the Oxford train.'

'More coffee, Kate?' Jamie asked when they'd gone.

She shook her head. 'I think I'll go up, too, Jamie. It's been a wonderful evening but I'm a bit short of sleep.'

'I'll come with you.'

She wasn't at all sure of the propriety of their mounting the stairs together. But perhaps a free and easy American wouldn't see it that way. And surely Jamie wasn't the sort of man who . . .

But when she reached the door of her room, he was still beside her. She looked up at him. 'Thank you again, Jamie, for a wonderful . . .' And then she stopped abruptly. For now she could easily give a name to the emotion that was gripping him. It wasn't excitement, it was fear — stark, naked fear, easily seen in the grimace that was stretching his mouth into a pathetic rictus of a smile, turning his eyes into dark pools of sheer terror. She had seen it before on the faces of men passed fit to go back to the line. And in Jamie's case, he could only guess at the horror; his imagination fuelled, no doubt, by the tales he would have heard.

'Kate — could I? Just for a while? A few minutes only . . .'

To deny him would have been like turning away a frightened child. With no clear idea of what was to happen next, Kate opened her door and held it wide. 'Come in, Jamie!'

★ ★ ★

Next morning, Kate sat in the lounge of the hotel, idly leafing through a magazine, but with her mind on other matters. Should she tell Prissy that Jamie had spent last night in her bed; that she'd cradled him in her arms while he sobbed out his fears, not only of the battle field itself, but of letting his 'buddies' down.

'I met up with these Canadians in a pub. They'd come back from somewhere called Hill 70. Captured it in the end, but oh boy, the stories they told! The more they drank, the worse they got. In the end, I had to leave them to it and come away.'

'You were on your own?'

'Yes, that was probably half the trouble. Hank was with Priss, of course. That's when I really wished you were there, too, Kate.'

She'd pulled the eiderdown more closely about their shoulders, for the room was cold. 'And you hadn't felt that way before?'

'Not really! Mind you, I've always been a soft-hearted sort of guy. Dad took me fishing once but I never went again — couldn't stand the sight of him bashing their brains out with a stone. But war's different. We didn't need the fish but there are good reasons why the Germans have to be stopped.'

Kate thought briefly of the 'German ward' in the château and of those men who must once have thought that the British, too, must be stopped. But this was hardly the moment for a discussion on the ethics of war.

'Perhaps that's what will get you through in the end, Jamie. The knowledge that you're fighting for a cause.' How difficult it was to choose the right words. Especially when your feet were freezing and you longed for sleep.

But perhaps all that Jamie had required was for her to listen while he talked because, towards dawn, he fell asleep, his head pillowed on her shoulder. Gently, she had eased herself off the bed, tucking the eiderdown around him and then, finding spare blankets in a wardrobe, had stretched out on the bed beside him, to doze fitfully. But after he had gone to join Hank, leaving her with a hasty kiss and a few muttered words of gratitude, she had slept. At least one good thing had come out of the life she now led — it had taught her to snatch sleep how and where she could.

Now, as she continued to flick in a desultory fashion through her magazine, she decided that if Prissy didn't come down soon, she'd have to go and wake her or they'd miss their train. How good it would be to see Ma and Pa again! There were still fortyeight precious hours before she need be back at Dover.

And then she froze, her fingers poised over the magazine, her attention riveted on the photograph she was gazing at. Not a particularly good photograph — it had been taken at a garden party held to raise money for army comforts and there was a blur of tents and stalls behind the man and the woman standing, arm in arm in the foreground. But Kate had no need of the caption to recognise the man: 'Captain Lord Robert Holker and Miss Alice Frobisher, taken at Holker Hall, seat of the Earl of Werrington, Lord Robert's father. Miss Frobisher is a nurse at the Hall and Lord Robert is, of course, a regular visitor when his duties as a staff officer permit.'

Kate put down the magazine, her cheeks flaming. So much for the principles of the Oxford undergraduate who'd been so determined to turn his back upon inherited privilege! Here he was, commissioned and clearly back in the bosom of his family, the conforming heir.

But she knew that wasn't the real reason for the utter devastation she was now feeling; it was the proprietorial manner in which Alice Frobisher was gazing up at Robert and he down at her. The camera, they said, could never lie.

★　★　★

By the greatest good fortune, Edmund was on leave. He met them at the railway station with Toby and the trap.

'Oh, this is really like old times!' Kate threw her arms around Toby's neck and hugged him while the pony tossed his head and whickered softly. 'How are you, old boy?'

'Typical!' said Edmund, putting their suitcases into the trap. 'More pleased to see an animal than a mere brother! Don't I get a kiss?'

'Of course!'

It was good to jog along the familiar streets. 'Oxford never changes,' Priscilla exulted as they turned left out of Beaumont Street into the leafy expanse of St Giles. 'There are even students still.'

'But very young, you notice,' said Edmund, 'and out-numbered by service men. Not to mention all the patriotic housewives. I was actually handed a white feather by one when I was in town yesterday. I was in mufti, of course.'

'You weren't? Oh, Edmund!' Both Kate and Priscilla were horrified.

'Oh, I quite enjoyed it! I took it from her, bowed politely and said, 'Thank you so much, madam! And do you have one for my Colonel, I wonder? And what about Sir Douglas Haig? I shall be seeing him next week.'

'Oh, Edmund! How priceless! What did the poor woman say?' Kate asked.

'She didn't know whether to believe me or not — but at least it made her shut up and think.'

'And will you really be seeing Sir Douglas Haig next week?' Priscilla wanted to know.

'I'll be *seeing* him all right. Frequently do — around Whitehall. But we're not exactly on speaking terms!'

They were clopping up the Banbury Road by now, the sunlight sifting through the trees on to Toby's rump. 'May I take the reins?' Kate asked. 'See if I can still manage him?'

Obligingly, Edmund drew Toby to a standstill and changed places. Kate picked up the reins, enjoying the feel of the leather sliding across her palms. It was as if she'd never been away; as if wicker baskets and boxes of laundry were still piled high behind her — and Robert Holker was by her side, boasting that no-one would recognise him and that he'd pass, any day, as an ordinary delivery boy. But there could be no going back. It was only because she'd so recently seen Robert's photograph in the magazine that her treacherous memory had betrayed her. Nothing more. It was poor Jamie Coleano she must think about now.

Later, after they'd reached home and been hugged rapturously by Ma and Pa and even received a perfunctory kiss from Danny, and Priscilla had been taken off by Ma to inspect the room that was to be the nursery, she sat with Edmund in the garden behind the house. This was still exactly as it always had been. There was no way, except with a plough and a team of shires, that the jungle of vegetation could be subdued. Now, she and Edmund were surrounded by a Russian vine that had completely hidden the rose trees to which it clung.

For a while, they talked about the general progress of the war; or, in Edmund's opinion, lack of it. 'It's inevitable with trench warfare,' he explained. 'One day, the British advance a hundred yards, the next, the Germans take it back. Heaven knows how it will end. If both armies would agree to draw stumps and take the entire shooting match off to the Sahara desert, or somewhere equally as spacious, the whole bloody battle could be over in a week — maybe two!'

'Perhaps, now the Americans are in, the thing will speed up,' Kate ventured.

'Not for some time, I'm afraid. General Pershing doesn't want to commit the comparatively small number of his regular troops until they've been strengthened by the new National army. And that will take time. I doubt if we'll see much action from the Yanks until next year. Maybe a spring offensive.'

'So Hank's lot won't be fighting for quite a while?'

'They'll just have to be content with plunging their bayonets into sawdust dummies, I'm afraid, digging pretend trenches and getting as fit as possible. It's the French who will train them — the crack Chasseurs Alpins, I believe — and they'll make a good job of it.'

So Jamie Coleano should be safe from his fear for a little while longer. It was useful to have a brother at the War Office! On a sudden impulse, Kate turned to him again.

'Edmund, do you ever have any contact with German prisoners of war? Or at least know where they are?'

He glanced at her quickly. 'Why do you ask?'

Kate blushed. 'It's not for myself. It's for another nurse who is a very good friend of mine. She was nursing the P.O.W.s in France and became quite friendly with one of them. Difficult not to, sometimes, although we're not supposed to become involved with our patients. She occasionally wonders what's become of him.'

'Occasionally wonders' was a flagrant understatement for the way Angela would sit on her bunk in her rare moments off duty and give herself up to worrying about Ernst. However, Kate's attempt at nonchalance didn't seem to be helping her enquiry. Edmund was shaking his head.

'There's no way I'm going to pinpoint exactly where a certain P.O.W. is, even for you. I don't know if you've read it in the papers yet, but twentytwo German officers escaped from a camp in Nottinghamshire the other day. Many of them have been recaptured and the rest soon will be but you can see how careful one has to be. And I know you nurses! All tender loving care on the surface but absolutely ruthless when it comes to getting what you want! No — hear me out!' for Kate had opened her mouth to disagree. 'It's probably what makes you so good at your job. But I'd bet my last shilling that if I were to tell you where your friend's friend was, she'd be off to find him like a shot.'

Since this was so exactly what Angela would do, Kate could only bite her tongue, contemplate her toes and murmur, 'I had no idea my little brother was so familiar with the wily ways of women!'

'Growing up with you and Priss was quite enough to educate me! However,' he grinned suddenly, 'it also taught me the gentle art of compromise. Tell me this German's name and I'll look him up and at least make sure he's still in the land of the living. If he is, I'll tell you but *not* where he is. Understood?'

'Understood!' said Kate meekly.

24

The life of a Staff Officer was not as tedious as Robert had feared. Much depended upon the personality of his Brigadier and his was an exception to the 'blimpish' characters that many of them were.

Brigadier Terence O'Murphy or 'the Brig' as he was called by his staff, came from an impoverished Irish family and, unlike most of his colleagues, had to exist almost entirely upon army pay. This gave him a refreshingly down-to-earth outlook on life. Apart from his wife and three daughters, to whom he was devoted, he had one consuming passion — horseflesh. Contemptuous of the motorised transport put at his disposal, he invariably chose to ride everywhere and usually took Robert with him.

Often he was in reminiscent mood — his stories usually about horses. 'When the O'Murphys hunted,' he confessed, 'it wasn't a question of reserve mounts but of reserve people! Couldn't afford to mount three daughters, a wife *and* myself, d'you see? So we'd hand over our one poor beast like a baton on a relay race. Very confusing for the Master — and for the horse, too, no doubt!'

He was a receptive listener, too, in whom Robert found it easy to confide his unease about the future. 'I think you'll find,' the older man told him, 'that you'll be overtaken by events. There simply won't be the money and resources to maintain an estate like yours after the war. Or the men. I doubt if Tommy Atkins is going to accept a return to the old ways. Between you and me, Robert, I'm sometimes amazed that he continues to accept our orders now. Army discipline, I suppose. But I'm pretty damn sure, it won't be 'Yes, sir! No, sir! Three bags full, sir!' once he's out of uniform. And I can't say I blame him. Play it by ear, Robert, that's my advice. Compromise. Be prepared to change.'

There was much good sense in what he said, Robert decided. Why not appear to conform, assume the mantle of heir and perhaps even persuade his father to relinquish the reins of command, but do nothing dramatic? Perhaps, after all, marry Alice Frobisher, if she was still interested. Now that Kate was lost to him, it mattered little with whom he spent the rest of his life, provided, of course, that they had sufficient in common to share both bed and board in an amicable fashion. The more he thought about it, the more sensible the idea became; although to actually put his theories into practice might be another matter.

On this particular day, the Brig drew rein at the top of a slight rise and surveyed the stretch of Northern France and Belgium that lay below. In the immediate foreground rooks circled lazily above trees that still held a vestige of autumn foliage; below them, the ground fell away sharply, bleak and bare but for occasional farm buildings, now little more than rubble. Beyond them again, a forest of blackened poles was all that remained of a wood that had once been bright with bud and blossom, where birds had sung and lovers lain in bosky shade. It was there that the front lines stretched their sinuous lengths. 'Who do we think we are,' asked the Brig bitterly, 'that we expect men to endure such conditions? Before long, Robert, we shall go down and see it for ourselves.'

Robert couldn't hide his alarm. The safety of 'top brass' was of the greatest importance. 'Er — yes, sir!'

'You don't sound very enthusiastic,' the Brig accused. 'If you'd prefer not to go with me . . . '

'Oh, no sir! It's not that! I was just wondering what Major Matheson would have to say about it.'

'Fuck, Major Matheson!' said the Brig crisply, to Robert's horrified delight. But all the same, he knew

303

it wouldn't be the Brig who would receive the force of the Major's disapproval; it would be the junior officer who hadn't been able to dissuade his superior from risking his life in an unscheduled inspection of the battlefield — otherwise, himself. However, there was no immediate need to worry. Tomorrow, both he and the Brig would be going on leave.

As they turned their horses away from the devastated landscape and headed back to Brigade, he began to work out what he would say to Alice.

★ ★ ★

She was pleased to see him, there was no doubt of that, even standing beside Aunt Bella to welcome him as he got out of the cab he'd managed to find in Stafford. 'Drive round into the stable yard,' he instructed the driver. 'Ask for Mrs Barcock and say Robert has asked her to give you a cup of tea and something to eat.'

The driver seen to, he turned to embrace his aunt. 'Good to see you, Aunt Bee!' It seemed natural then to turn to Alice and hug her, too. And she certainly hugged him back but the way in which she turned her face away so that his lips brushed her cheek and not her own mouth surprised him. But after all, he reminded himself, they were standing in a public place and she could hardly throw her arms around his neck and cover his face with kisses in the presence of her Matron, even if it was only Aunt Bee. He thought no more of it.

'I'm so sorry,' his aunt was saying. 'You're in your

own room but I'm afraid you're having to share with a Major Gethin for a couple of nights. We've simply nowhere else to put him. However, you could always go to the Dower House, if you'd prefer?'

'No thanks, Aunt Bee. Tomorrow will be time enough to see the parents.' And she nodded her understanding.

Alec Gethin was a likeable character. Badly wounded at the 3rd Battle of Ypres, his right arm had been amputated above the elbow. In a couple of days' time, he was due to leave Holker Hall for a special rehabilitation unit where he would be assessed for an artificial extension to his arm.

'I shall manage,' he assured Robert over a cup of tea in Aunt Bella's sitting room. 'It's my wife I'm worried about. She's finding it very difficult to come to terms with having a cripple for a husband. Some women are like that. While others . . . ' he left the sentence unfinished but his gaze settled upon Alice as she came into the room, and his eyes were openly worshipping.

Nothing changes! thought Robert wryly. I wonder if the poor devil knows that most of the other patients are in love with her, too?

But this time, he was soon to realise, it was rather different; Alice loved him back. Not, perhaps, with the same intensity as Alec's feelings for her but with much more than the casual regard she showed for her other patients. When she examined the stump of his arm, Robert was usually in the vicinity and he could not help but notice how their eyes would hold each other's gaze and once, Alice leaned swiftly down to brush Alec's cheek with her lips. He was relieved that Aunt Bella wasn't around. Family friend though Alice was, such unprofessional behaviour would never have been tolerated.

His own reaction surprised him. He was actually jealous! It was nothing like the bitter resentment he'd felt when Kate had embraced her French doctor, and he suspected that it was really little more than wounded pride — for had he not decided, in a most chauvinistic manner, that Alice should become his wife? — but if he was right in his surmise, the laugh was on him.

Two days later, jaw grimly set, eyes full of despair, Alec Gethin left for the next stage of his rehabilitation. 'I'm sorry for that poor man,' Aunt Bella confided to Robert after she'd waved him off. 'Not because of his arm, but because of his wife's attitude towards it. He's been here three months and she's never visited him once. Some nonsense about not being able to leave her war work. The only war work she's ever done,' Aunt Bella snorted, 'is to serve cups of tea to officers in some posh canteen or other. She doesn't even make the stuff — just pours it out — with her finger delicately crooked, no doubt!'

Robert saw little of Alice during the next two days. 'Off-duty time,' Aunt Bella explained, 'but I'm surprised she hasn't been over to see you.'

However, on the following day, Alice was back and with an invitation to Robert for dinner at Bellwood that evening. 'Your parents are coming, too.'

After he'd accepted the invitation, he studied her more closely. 'Alice, are you feeling all right?' For the pallor of her cheeks was intense and accentuated by the dark hollows beneath her eyes.

She nodded briskly. 'Yes, of course! Just a little tired. I went up to London yesterday and the trains were so crowded I couldn't find a seat.' He waited, in case she was going to elaborate but when she simply bent her head once more over the bandages she was rolling, he asked gently, 'Missing Alec?'

Her head snapped up and for a second, she glared at him fiercely. 'Of course not! Why on earth should you think such a thing?'

He was astonished at her reaction; not so much because of her denial but because he could have sworn that her eyes, just for a moment, had held not anger but fear.

But then she quickly put out a hand to cover his. 'Sorry to snap, my dear! But I certainly didn't want you of all people to think there was something special between Alec Gethin and me.'

The inference was obvious. So perhaps he *had* imagined the depth of her feeling; perhaps she *had* felt only deep compassion for a man who had lost not only a good right arm but his wife's affection also. Anyway, what did it matter now? Alec Gethin had gone and it was unlikely Alice would ever see him again. Deliberately, he changed the subject. 'I'm amazed that you've persuaded my parents to actually go out at night.'

'Well, Daddy insisted. He said he wanted it to be a very special dinner party. He's actually using some of his precious petrol to drive over and collect them. I thought you could come back with me in the trap. Your aunt, too.'

'You mean Aunt Bee's coming as well?'

'I told you! It's Daddy's special night!'

And he was right, Robert decided later. Mr Frobisher excelled himself; as had his cook. Course followed course in a meal of peace-time proportions, and with each course came liberal quantities of the appropriate wine. By the end of the meal, Robert, out of practice with such excess, was feeling distinctly merry. When Alice, following the older women into the drawing room, turned her head and gave him a tiny, conspiratorial wave, he had no hesitation in waving back.

Her father circulated the port. 'Very good to have you with us!' he told Robert.

'Very good!' his own father echoed.

'And now that we're alone,' Mr Frobisher continued portentiously, 'I hope you'll forgive me for mentioning something very dear to my heart. To both our hearts, I think you'll agree, sir?' He turned courteously to the Earl.

'Very dear!' repeated the older man, as if playing a well-rehearsed part. And it was then that Robert, in spite of his intoxication, began to see where the conversation was leading; what, in fact, had been the purpose of Mr Frobisher's 'special night' in the first place. Cunning old fox! he thought without rancour.

'You and my daughter,' his host continued, 'have known each other all your lives. Childhood friends, if not sweethearts. They say that familiarity breeds contempt but in your case . . . ?' he paused, gazing expectantly at Robert.

'Certainly *not* contempt!' Robert obliged 'Very fond indeed of your daughter sir!' He had a horrible feeling he was about to let loose a mighty belch but managed to restrain it.

'As she is of you, Robert! I'm delighted to hear that our minds are running roughly along the same lines.'

'Delighted!' echoed the Earl of Werrington dutifully.

Mr Frobisher charged all their glasses. 'So I give you the toast — Alice and Robert!'

'Alice and Robert!' echoed the Earl.

Robert chuckled to himself. They could use this man at Brigade HQ! How to persuade a reluctant suitor to marry your daughter in one easy lesson! He, too, raised his glass. 'Alice and Robert!' he murmured thickly. Why not? The way he was feeling at the moment, he'd have toasted the Kaiser.

The rest of the evening passed in a haze. He distinctly remembered being offered a bed for the night and was equally aware of his own insistence that he return to Holker Hall with Aunt Bella and, somewhat to his surprise, Alice. Something about an early duty next day and not wanting to get up in the morning.

'Thank you so much,' he murmured to his host, 'for a memorable evening.'

'My pleasure!' Mr Frobisher assured him.

★   ★   ★

The hands on Robert's travelling clock are pointing to two when he is awakened by a naked body lying on top of him.

'Who . . . ?' But there is no need for him to

continue. It is Alice, her arms around his neck, her body pressed hard against his.

'Darling, darling Robert!' His legs are thrust apart by her own demanding thighs and he lies spreadeagled beneath her.

'Alice, for God's sake stop! You don't know what you're doing!'

'Oh, but I do, my darling! I know just what I'm doing!' And indeed, it is more than obvious that she does; one hand now pulling at the girdle of his pyjama trousers, then going unerringly to his groin. He thanks Providence that his intake of alcohol on the previous night makes an erection well nigh impossible.

It is her competence that shocks him the most. How many times has she done this before? Confused memories race through his mind — of menservants who have left Bellwood under a cloud, of a gamekeeper who was considered 'forward' and dismissed on the spot. And George . . . ?

He sits up in bed so abruptly, she almost falls out of it. 'Did you do this with George?'

She misconstrues his reason for asking. 'Compared with how I feel about you — how I've *always* felt about you — George meant nothing to me. It's always been you, Robert.'

'But did George allow you,' he persists, 'to . . . ?'

'Oh, yes! George could deny me nothing. And he wanted it, too.'

Robert breathes a sigh of satisfaction. 'Good!'

Now it is Alice's turn to be startled. 'Why do you say that?'

'Because I'm grateful that dear old George went

to his grave, at least thinking that you loved him. He would never have known . . . ' Again, his sentence remains unfinished. For he can hardly add, ' . . . that you were a promiscuous whore'. For that, surely, is what she is.

Now, however, all that matters is to get her back to her own room. 'Alice, where are you sleeping?'

'Here, my darling! With you!'

'You most certainly are not! Now, come on, put my dressing gown on.'

'But dearest Robert, now that Daddy's had a word with you and you've agreed . . . '

So he'd been right to think the whole evening carefully orchestrated.

They are halfway along the corridor towards the next flight of stairs, with Alice still protesting, when a nearby door is flung open.

'Just what,' demands an outraged Aunt Bella, 'is going on?'

⋆ ⋆ ⋆

He would never have thought he would be so grateful for a telegram recalling him from leave.

'Sorry about this, my boy,' the Brig told him when they met at Dover. 'Some important do in the pipeline, I understand. Spoiled your leave, no doubt?'

Robert grinned wryly. 'Not exactly! Got me out of rather a hole, in fact.'

The Brig glanced at him shrewdly. 'Want to talk about it?'

'Not at the moment, sir, thank you. I'm still trying

to collect my thoughts.' And that, he decided, was the understatement of all time. For he knew he would never forget the bitter hurt and disappointment in Aunt Bella's eyes when he and Alice had faced her that morning in her office.

'I would never have thought this of you, Robert. I know that I have no jurisdiction over you, that as a grown man you have your own standards of what is right and wrong, even if they are not mine. But even so, in *my* hospital, to seduce one of *my* nurses . . .'

'Forgive me, Matron,' Alice had dared to interrupt, 'but it wasn't like that at all. Robert and I are engaged, you know. I went to him of my own free will.'

'Is this true, Robert?'

'That she came of her own free will — certainly. But that we're engaged . . .'

'Oh, come now, Robert! After you've actually spoken to Daddy!' Alice's arm was through his, her eyes gazing appealingly up at him.

What could he say? That he'd been too drunk to know what he was saying or doing?

'And there's another thing,' Alice began but was interrupted by a sharp knock on the door.

'Come!' called Aunt Bella. When Emily had entered, carrying a telegram, Robert could have hugged her.

'For Master Robert!' said Emily, seeming to forget in her obvious astonishment at finding him so clearly at loggerheads with his aunt, that he was no longer in the nursery.

He'd given her a broad smile before scanning the contents of the telegram, 'I'm recalled! Dover as soon as I can make it! Aunt Bee, forgive me for dashing off. Forgive me for everything! I'll write and explain.' And he'd followed Emily out of the room. Outside in the hall, she'd turned to face him.

'You in trouble, Master Robert?'

He'd bent and kissed her cheek 'Yes! But this time, I'm not to blame Em. At least, not totally. Now, you're not to worry!' But it was abundantly clear that she did — and would continue to do so.

Now, as the steamer nosed its way out of Dover harbour into a choppy sea, Robert admitted that he, too, was worried. To marry Alice Frobisher because he wanted to, was one thing. To be press-ganged into it, was quite another.

★　★　★

Wouldn't it be wonderful, Kate sometimes thought, if the trains were occasionally only half-full, as if would-be passengers had decided against making the journey. As it was, she doubted if she would ever again board a peace-time train without remembering the station platforms of France and Belgium, crowded with wounded men who somehow must be accommodated.

In the last weeks, it was as if the Allies had been determined to show the Americans — still in training, still not committed to battle — that they could beat the Germans single-handed. Could there be one brick still standing upon another in the town they called Ypres? She doubted it.

But on this particular night, it was the wounded survivors of the battle for Cambrai that they were

313

picking up; the Hindenburg Line, so they'd heard, had been breached along a ten mile front and tanks had been used on a vast scale. But now, as she and Angela stood in the empty train as it clanged into the station, and stared down at the sea of men waiting for it to stop, there was only one thing she could be sure of — the cost had been high. It would be several hours before all the men were on board and accounted for, and they could start working their way down the train.

They were about halfway along it, picking their way carefully through those carriages that had been gutted to accommodate the stretcher cases, going separately into the individual compartments that held the walking wounded, when Kate came to a sudden standstill. Angela, close behind, nearly cannoned into her.

'What's the matter, Kate?'

Kate raised her hand for silence, at the same time peering intently around her at the rows of stretchers. 'I thought someone called me.'

And then it came again. 'Kate!'

It was little more than a whisper and it came from a man lying in the corner. She went to crouch at his side, shining her torch to see him more clearly.

'Jamie Coleano!' She gazed at him in bewilderment. 'What's happened? We thought the Americans . . . '

He nodded weakly. 'I know! I'm the odd ball, as usual. Me and Hank . . . '

'Hank's here as well?'

'No!' He paused. 'Long story, Kate. Could I have some water first?'

314

'Of course!' As she poured it for him, she made a decision. 'Jamie, I'll come back later.' She glanced down the length of his body and saw the makeshift splints on both legs. 'Is there anything more I can do for you at the moment?'

'Not right now! Just — come back before the doc puts me out again.'

'I will — as quickly as I can. Just tell me one thing before I go. Is Hank safe?'

Jamie didn't answer. He didn't have to. The expression in his eyes was enough.

★ ★ ★

A long story it might have been, had Jamie Coleano been well enough to relate it in detail. But by the time Kate was able to come back to him, morphia had already been administered by one of the medical officers. However, the few graphic phrases he was able to utter before he sank into unconsciousness were enough to paint a tragic picture.

'Small groups of us were being taken into the front line. Just for a few hours. Part of our training. I wanted to go — get it over with. Hank didn't. Said it would come soon enough. But wouldn't let me go without him.'

He stopped to draw breath and take a sip of water from the cup Kate was holding. 'Should have been all right. Quiet, just like the Frenchies said. And then — Boche raiding party. They wanted prisoners for interrogation. I was wounded in the cross fire.'

'And Hank?'

315

'Blown sky-high. And the Boche with him. One of our own shells, I think. Saw it with my own eyes, Kate. Had no chance. And all — my fault.' His voice trailed off into incomprehensible mutterings and his head fell back on the pillow.

Kate continued to squat by his side, deep in thought. She could imagine how it had been; Jamie, determined to conquer his fear, insisting upon being one of the first to volunteer; Hank, conscious of his family commitments, but also of his responsibility to his friend; and the sheer bad luck of being in the line when the German raiding party had come over.

Rising to her feet, she went to find Angela. As soon as they reached Boulogne, she must request an interview with the Commandant there. Prissy — now within days of her time — must be told about Hank before the official telegram arrived. It was the least she could do.

25

The Christmas of 1917 passed with little cause for celebration on Robert's part. Two days before the old year ended, he received a letter from Alice. It came immediately to the point.

'Dearest Robert, This letter will come as a great surprise. I am expecting a baby — our baby! I had suspected it since your last leave and now the doctor has confirmed it.

So, my darling, we must be married as soon as possible for the baby's sake. Can you arrange leave? I'm sure that nice Brigadier will do all he can to help. After all, you were recalled before your last leave was up.

I have told Daddy and Mummy and your parents about the baby. While professing to be shocked, it is obvious they are secretly delighted. An heir, we hope, for the title. Your father is positively rejuvenated; as is your mother, although she is still convinced it is George's baby!

Write soon, my darling, and tell me that you are as thrilled as I. All my love, Alice.'

The audacity of it took Robert's breath away. Without a doubt, it was Alec Gethin's child she was expecting. He, Robert, could still deny paternity, of course, but in view of the incriminating circumstances in which Aunt Bella had discovered him, he doubted he would be believed.

Sunk in gloom, desperately trying to think of a way out of his dilemma, it was hardly surprising that the Brig noticed his preoccupation. 'I need some fresh air, Robert. Shall we ride?'

When they'd gone a mile or so from the manor house where Brigade was currently accommodated, he drew rein. 'Now, my boy, tell me what's on your mind. And don't say 'nothing', or I'll have you hung, drawn and quartered!'

Robert smiled wryly. 'That might not be a bad idea!'

'Stop talking poppycock and dismount!'

Their horses grazing peacefully, the Brig and Robert seated themselves on a fallen tree-trunk.

'Cigarette?' the Brig proffered a battered, silver case.

'Thank you, sir.' They lit up.

'Begin!' ordered the Brig. 'At the beginning, if it's not asking too much!'

It was a good half-hour before he spoke again. By then, Robert felt drained but strangely peaceful. By sharing it with another person, his despair had lifted. The Brig was a wise old bird.

'You're quite sure,' the older man asked, 'that the child isn't yours?'

'Oh yes, sir! Quite!'

'Then you've been properly cuckolded, my boy. A feminine trick as old as the hills.' He paused, considering. 'Two options, as I see it,' he continued after a few moments. 'One — knuckle under, marry the girl, please your parents. Two — cock a snook, thumb your nose and take the consequences. Unlikely she'd take you to court. And you can't be disinherited for conduct not befitting an officer and a gentleman. You'd be ostracised, of course, but who cares a twopenny damn about that?'

Robert thought longingly of the little house in Oxfordshire and so, inevitably, of Kate. If there'd been the slightest chance of marrying her, he'd have called Alice Frobisher's bluff without a second thought. But as things were, refusing to marry her would have the most dreadful effect upon his parents. Finish them completely. And what of Aunt Bella? Would she believe him if he were to explain what had really happened? Or would there always be that nagging suspicion?

There was no doubt about it; life would be easier

318

for all of them if he were to 'knuckle under' as the Brig had put it. So tomorrow, he'd write to Alice; tell her that he could only manage seventytwo hours at the most but with a special licence, that would be sufficient. The future he would let take care of itself. Once the baby had been born without the stigma of illegitimacy, the situation could be reviewed. There was always the possibility of divorce for he doubted if Alice Frobisher would ever be content without a lover. And he certainly didn't intend to fulfil that role.

He turned to the Brig. 'Thank you for listening, sir.'

The older man studied him intently. He could guess what his decision would be. Silly young fool! But honourable young fool, too, he supposed. With a sigh, he rose to his feet.

'Tomorrow, young man, we shall go down and wish the troops a happy New Year.'

Oh, God! And he'd thought the threat long forgotten, a passing whim. 'Major Matheson . . .' he began feebly.

'Bugger Major Matheson!' said the Brig predictably.

★ ★ ★

At least their 'jaunt' as the Brig described it, took his mind off Alice. Major Matheson had, as expected, hit the roof. 'Don't I have enough on my mind without an irresponsible Brigadier to look after? He must know the Germans have been sending over raiding parties — even in daylight. Surely you could

319

have dissuaded him, Holker?'

'I did try, sir. But he was adamant.'

'I'll give him adamant! Well, at least I shall warn the Colonel that he's coming.'

'I don't think he'd want you to do even that, sir!'

'Sod what *he* wants!'

'Yes, sir!' He was almost beginning to enjoy the situation!

But his light-hearted frame of mind lasted only until the next afternoon when he and the Brig met the Colonel at the entrance to the support line. He looked like a cat on scaldingly hot bricks. Over his arm, two ground sheets were draped and the straps of two steel helmets swung from his wrist. 'I wonder if you'd like to slip these on, sir. You, too, Captain.'

But the Brig would have none of it. 'The purpose of this exercise, Colonel, is to boost morale. I am hardly going to do that looking like Tommy Atkins in person!'

'Er — no, sir!' But the Colonel's discomfiture was so apparent, Robert took pity on him. 'I'll wear a ground sheet, sir. If the Brigadier doesn't mind.'

'Wear the bloody lot!' said the Brig with heavy sarcasm. So Robert slipped on a ground sheet and replaced his cap with a helmet. He relieved the Colonel of the remaining ground sheet and steel helmet and crammed his cap firmly under his arm. Thus adorned, he followed his superior officers into the trench. No-one was going to look at *him*, anyway.

There was no doubt of the good the Brigadier was doing by paying this impromptu visit, Robert soon decided. The men in the support trench, busy cleaning their rifles, filling sandbags, even in a couple of instances, writing letters home, were transparently glad to see him. Startled though they were at first by the sudden appearance of a high-ranking officer in their midst, there was admiration and respect on their faces as they answered his questions.

'You're doing a bloody good job,' the Brig told them when the little entourage had reached the end of the support trench. 'Let's hope 1918 will see the end of it all.'

If they'd been further back in the lines, they would have given him three hearty cheers. As it was, they contented themselves with muttered expressions of good will. 'Happy New Year to you, sir!' 'Good to see you, sir!' 'Good luck to you!'

'And now,' the Brig turned briskly to the Colonel, 'the front line, if you please, Colonel.'

'The — er — *front* line, sir?'

'Colonel,' said the Brig patiently, 'even I know that that was a *support* trench. Shall I find my own way or . . . ?'

'No, sir!' the Colonel resigned himself to the inevitable. 'I'll take you. But I must insist, sir, that you at least wear a helmet.'

Grudgingly, the Brig agreed. 'Here, Captain Holker, carry my cap for me, if you please.' And Robert found himself juggling with the Brig's red-banded cap as well as his own.

Little had changed, he noticed, since his days as a Don R. The same lookouts on the fire-steps, snug in their sand-bagged embrasures, gazing fixedly out across No Man's Land; the same men on stand-by, leaning against the sides of the trench, or squatting, their rifles between their knees; the same buzz of activity around the dug-out that was Battalion HQ.

'Tea, sir?' suggested the Colonel, suddenly seeing a way of getting the Brig under cover, at least for a while.

'Delighted!' said the Brig. 'I'll have a mug of the men's. Sure to be a brew-up going on somewhere.'

He was right. Even as he spoke, a man came out of a dug-out, carrying two steaming mugs, both of which he nearly dropped when he saw the red tabs on the Brig's jacket and the crossed swords and baton on his shoulders.

'May I?' The Brig took one mug. 'And Captain Holker will have the other.' Hastily Robert jammed both caps under one arm and took the other mug from the goggle-eyed man. It was just as he remembered — hot, strong and sweet.

A Sergeant appeared around a corner of the trench and immediately noticed a look-out gazing back over his shoulder. 'Eyes front, man! You're not a fuckin' fairy on a fuckin' Christmas tree!' And then he saw the Brig and came quiveringly to attention. 'Sir!'

'Point taken, Sergeant!' said the Brig mildly, then glanced at the Colonel who was practically puce in the face. 'Perhaps, after all . . . ?' And regretfully, he allowed himself to be ushered down the steps into Battalion HQ. There, to his great delight, he found a runner who hailed from the same part of Ireland as himself. And the runner, as articulate as the Brig, made the most of his moments of glory. Hurricane lamps were being lit when Robert at last managed to prise them apart.

'May the Holy Mother of God and all the Saints preserve yer honour until we meet again — in Joe Mulligan's bar,' said the runner reverently. 'Sir!' he added, catching the Colonel's baleful eye.

'Amen to that!' agreed the Brig, while the Colonel rolled his eyes to heaven, no doubt in a silent prayer of his own.

They emerged into a starry twilight. The Brig turned to the Colonel. 'Thank you, Colonel. I much appreciate . . .'

He never finished his sentence. There came a steady pounding of feet, the staccato burst of a machine gun and a brief command — in German. The stars above the parapet were suddenly obliterated and Robert felt rather than saw the Colonel hurling himself on top of the Brig. But then he, himself, was floored by at least two burly figures jumping on him from above. And back came the stars but this time brilliantly green as they exploded inside his head, making the blackness that followed even more complete.

★   ★   ★

'I don't care, Mrs Barcock, I'm not going to let Master Robert take the blame for something he didn't do.'

'But Em, you can't be sure he didn't,' Mrs Barcock passed a floury hand over her brow where perplexity was writ large. 'You know what men are!'

'Master Robert never was and never will be! Anyway, what chance did he have? Major Gethin was sharing his bedroom right up until the time he left.'

'It doesn't always have to happen in a bedroom, Em.'

'And where else then, in a perishing cold November in a great barn like this, tell me that? It's certainly where that Alice and Major Gethin did it. I *saw* her, Mrs Barcock, with my own eyes, coming out of the Major's room. Not once, but twice.'

'And *that's* going to take some explaining,' Mrs Barcock pointed out. 'How you happened to be down on the first floor landing in the middle of the night.'

'You know as well as I do, the closets on the attic floor weren't working the whole of November.'

'So why didn't you use your chamber pot, same as the rest of us?'

'Because I'd have to have carried it all the way down the back stairs to empty, that's why! And my legs ain't . . .'

'All right! All right!' Mrs Barcock knew when she'd lost an argument and this wasn't one she particularly wanted to win, anyway. 'Go and tell her Ladyship now, then, Em. If you're sure, the sooner she knows, the better.

★ ★ ★

The first thing Robert sees when he comes round, is the Brig's cap lying beside him. He knows it's the Brig's because of the insignia on the band. By some fluke of circumstance, it must have been scooped up when . . . when what? Hazily, the events that have

324

led up to his present uncomfortable position on a hard, stone floor in what appears to be some sort of farm outbuilding, begin to come back to him.

Old Matheson has been proved right. It must have been yet another raiding party to establish which regiments the Germans are facing across No Man's Land. Clearly, they are preparing for a big push. With Russia's virtual withdrawal from the conflict because of her domestic problems Ludendorff has no doubt switched his troops on the Eastern front to reinforce those already in the West. By now, the build-up must be formidable. What a time to be captured! The sooner he's back where he belongs, the better.

As he is alone, he presumes no other prisoner has been taken. But what a catch they must think they have! A brigadier, no less! Unless the pips on his epaulettes have already given him away? But the ground sheet so thoughtfully provided by the Colonel is still draped around his shoulders, although his revolver has been removed from its holster.

A door in the wall opposite opens and he hitches the ground sheet more closely around him. A young German officer comes in and smiles at him nervously. He can't be much more than nineteen. He comes to crouch at Robert's side. 'Herr Brigadier . . . ' he begins.

Robert breathes a sigh of relief. His next move is now clear. He scowls fiercely. 'A Brigadier is not accustomed to conversing with a pip-squeak young officer like you.'

The man seems to understand what he has said.

'Herr Brigadier,' he tries again, 'the Major will soon be here.'

Robert brings his face closer to the other's. 'A General,' he demands. 'Bring me a General and I will speak to him but to no-one else. Certainly not a mere Major. You understand?'

The German nods unhappily. 'I understand. But I think it will be easier, Herr Brigadier, if I take *you* to the General.'

This is reasonable, of course. But Robert has no wish to go further away from the British front line. 'I trust you have a vehicle suitable for my transportation?'

'We have the vehicle in which you were brought here, Herr Brigadier.'

'Show it to me!' Robert gets to his feet with difficulty and immediately his head begins to throb. He staggers slightly and the young officer clutches his arm. Deliberately, Robert allows himself to lean heavily on the man's shoulder and they walk slowly to the door which the German opens with his free arm. Outside, two guards spring to attention. Beyond them, Robert sees a cobbled yard, lit by a solitary hurricane lamp, and upon which a small army wagon is drawn up. The back is open but there is a tarpaulin cover over the driving area. It is similar in style and comfort to that which the Brig has at his disposal. However, Robert sniffs disparagingly. 'I will inspect!'

The German officer at his heels, he walks slowly around it. And then he pauses, his heart thudding. A motor-cycle is parked just beyond the wagon, in front of some bushes. It is a B.M.W., a model that he knows well. Like a man in a trance, he drags his eyes away from it, aware that the German is speaking to him. 'Real leather, Herr Brigadier! The seats are real leather!'

'So I see!' Robert peers into the wagon at what is undoubtedly a real leather seat, while his mind races. He straightens slowly. 'Well, since this is all there is . . . ' he shrugs. 'But first, I must obey the call of nature.'

His hand goes to open his flies as he begins to walk towards the bushes. The young German is horrified. 'Herr Brigadier, there is no need! We have a privy.'

He waves the man away. 'There is no time!' As he goes, he checks the rest of the yard. There are no other soldiers in sight except for the two guards, but there must be others in the buildings, the despatch rider for one. If only he knew when the machine was last used. If recently, the carburettor won't need priming. But if it's cold . . . .

Pretending to stagger slightly, he rests a hand lightly on the machine and feels warmth rising from the engine. He's in luck! Impossible to check the contents of the fuel tank but it's unlikely to be low.

Hardly able to believe his good fortune, he lurches into the bushes at the same time waving away the hovering German. 'Big shit!' he threatens fiercely, beginning to take down his breeches. He grins to himself as the man retreats hastily and even turns his back.

He relieves himself, does up his flies, hoists up his breeches and takes a deep breath, then quietly creeps from the bushes and leaps for the machine.

He has let out the clutch and jumped the engine into life before the German realises what is happening. By then, it is too late; he is roaring away into the night. But not, as he believes, in the direction of the front lines but even deeper into the Belgian countryside.

26

Kate gazed down at the tiny, crumpled face of her niece and marvelled. The blue eyes glared back at her, the rose-bud mouth opened on a furious howl and star-fish hands beat the air. 'You're a fighter, Rosie May!'

'A hungry fighter!' said Priscilla, pushing herself up on her pillows. 'Give her to me, Kate.'

So the week-old morsel that was Rosie May Shelton was handed back to her mother and attached firmly to her breast.

'How are you feeling, Priss?' Kate perched on the bed.

'Loads better now. Just a bit sore. I shall get up soon.'

'Ma will have a fit if you do!'

'Then she'll just have to have one! I've got to be doing something, Kate. Lying here, I think too much.'

'I can imagine.'

'If only we *knew*! Sometimes, I almost wish there was proof that he'd been killed.'

'Jamie does seem pretty sure,' Kate pointed out gently. 'When I visited him the other day, he spoke as if there was little hope.'

'Shot to smithereens!' was what Jamie had actually said.

'Then how come the authorities have said 'missing, believed killed'? Why haven't they sent back his identification disc?'

'It may have been difficult to find.'

In fact, it was a question she'd asked Jamie. 'Kate, you must be crazy. There was no way in that morass of mud and blood and bits of bodies they would have found a disc. Even if it were there. It could have been blown yards away.' He'd groaned aloud as he'd sunk his head into his hands. 'And it was all my fault, Kate. If I hadn't been so crazy to prove myself . . .' Jamie Coleano's legs might be healing nicely, but the same couldn't be said of his mind.

'I'll go up and see him myself as soon as I can,' Priscilla said now.

'We'll see!' A visit to the depressed young soldier was the last thing Kate would advise at the moment.

Leaving Priscilla gazing adoringly at Rosie May's downy head, Kate went slowly downstairs to talk to Ma. She'd been given special leave to see Priscilla through her confinement and she'd soon be going back. At least, she'd have good news for Angela; Edmund, down for fortyeight hours, had told her, 'there's no need to worry about that German P.O.W. you mentioned. Tell your friend he's landed on his feet and no mistake. And don't ask me any more because I'm not telling you!'

But that should be more than enough to make

Angela very happy indeed. What a mad world we live in, Kate thought as she went through the hall to the kitchen; Prissy's husband missing, probably killed, Angela in love with a man she hasn't seen for months and is unlikely to for many more, and herself still hankering after a man who didn't care for her and anyway, was going to marry another girl. For she had seen the announcement in the paper; 'The engagement is announced between Miss Alice Frobisher and Captain Lord Robert Holker. Captain Holker is away on active service but we understand the marriage will take place on his next leave.'

This time, Kate had been ready for it; ever since Robert had written to Danny, giving him his precious Harley Davidson, she'd known it was the end. It had been a generous gift and Ma had stood over Danny while he'd written his thank-you letter, but to Kate it had been a symbolic act. She'd felt no surprise when there'd been no reply to Danny's letter.

★   ★   ★

Robert can go no further; not because the fuel tank is empty, although it must be nearly so, but because the pain in his right leg is now excruciating. Jump-starting the machine had done it no good at all and during the miles he has covered since then, the pain has settled into a nightmarish throbbing that he can no longer ignore. Also, he is soaked through to the skin from the icy water of a ditch in which he has taken refuge from a troop of marching

Germans. He has long ago accepted the unpalatable fact that he is riding away from the front lines.

But what, he has been asking himself for the last hour, had he hoped to achieve anyway, by that mad dash for freedom? To sail, majestically, over No Man's Land like Pegasus, then to drop snugly into the British front lines?

Far more sensible, he now thinks, if he'd stayed where he was, misled the Germans as much as he could and allowed himself to be incarcerated for the rest of the war. In fact, a small voice whispers, wouldn't that have been the easiest way out of your own problems? You could hardly be expected to marry Alice Frobisher from behind the barbed wire of a German Stalag!

The voice grows more vociferous. So why not give yourself up next time you meet a German convoy? Resign yourself to the inevitable? But even Germans have now become thin on the ground. He has seen no-one at all for the last half-hour. When he spies the glimmer of a whitewashed wall and realises he is approaching a farm, he stops and dismounts stiffly. He has just about enough energy to push the machine off the road into a shallow ditch.

He limps forward into a cobbled yard and looks about him and then makes for a barn which lies at right angles to the house. Please God, the door will be unlocked and there will be hay and straw inside. Perhaps even a cow against whose warm flanks he can stretch his frozen limbs.

The door swings open to his touch and he discovers immediately that there is indeed an animal — two, in fact — but they are dogs, rushing madly from the shadows, teeth gleaming, ears laid back, barking like the hounds of hell. He hears the rattle of chains and prays that they will not reach him. But already teeth are closing around his bad leg and he cannot fully restrain a howl of agony as he hits the cobbles.

'*Qui va là?*' The door of the house has been flung open and a man is standing there.

'Anglais! Englander! British soldier! Can you call off the dogs?'

'Franz! Josef! *Couchez!*' The dogs subside into mutinous, growling hulks. The man moves forward and shines a powerful torch. 'You are really English?'

'Oh yes!'

'Then how . . . ?'

'Escaped from the Germans. Mo'bike,' he can hardly articulate, 'in ditch. See — I still wear British uniform.'

He tries to pull aside the wet ground sheet and the torch moves over his body. 'You are wounded?'

'Old wound — your dog — '

'What can you expect? Arriving like this in the middle of the night? But come, we will get you indoors.' The man turns to call over his shoulder but already a woman has come to join him.

They carry him into a stone-flagged kitchen, prop him, gently enough, upon a wooden settle. The woman places a cushion behind his back then turns to poke into life the embers of the fire smouldering on the hearth. As the flames leap up, she swings a blackened pot over the heat.

'*Sa jambe est blessée,*' her husband tells her.

Between them, they ease off his boot and Robert clamps his mouth tightly shut as the sudden release from its restriction and the consequent surge of blood through his veins causes even greater pain. He glances down and sees that his knee is hideously swollen.

Later, when he has drunk several bowls of soup and the woman is making up a bed for him in a room off the kitchen, the farmer hands him a glass of some fiery, golden liquid that burns his stomach but revives him sufficiently to listen carefully to what the man tells him.

It appears that sometime during the night he has turned northward towards the sea. Now, he is a bare five miles from the coast. While still behind enemy lines, it is an area that the Germans, other than to mount a series of observation posts above the sea, do not patrol regularly.

'So it's a place used by the Belgian Resistance,' the farmer explains. 'Men like you who have managed to escape are brought to my farm. But this is the first time one has arrived — 'under his own steam', I think you call it! Fate has been good to you, my friend.' He pauses while he fills Robert's glass.

'Now this is what will happen. You will remain here until your leg is better — or recovered sufficiently for you to be moved. Then you will be taken to the coast, to a small fishing village where you will await your turn to — go fishing! When the fleet is sufficiently far out, it will happen to mingle with the boats of another fleet from a village in a part of France not yet occupied by the Boche. You understand?'

'But don't the Germans ever notice that fewer men come back than went out?'

The farmer smiles. 'That, we have taken care of! Always, two escapees are included in the crew but only one is visible on deck, the other is below. Immediately the transfer is made, the one from below emerges on deck and so — should there be any Germans watching when we arrive back in harbour, the same number of men come back that went out.'

'And the man who comes back?'

'Is the one that goes next. But only when he has been joined by another man. That is important even though he may sometimes have to wait a long time.'

'It is a very brave and ingenious plan, m'sieur.'

The man shrugs. 'It is the least we can do.'

After Robert is in bed, having drunk the potion given him by the farmer's wife and which, she has assured him, will 'make better', he thinks back over the last twentyfour hours. He hopes the Brig is suitably chastened, but doubts it. But Major Matheson will no doubt still try to use his capture as a salutary lesson to his senior officer. And it will be he who will set in motion the procedure that will eventually cause a telegram to be delivered to his father. 'Missing' — but surely not 'believed killed'?

And then, inevitably, he thinks of Alice. Hoisted by her own petard, and no mistake! For there is no way he is going to be able to marry her soon enough to avoid gossip and speculation; he might have a long time to wait, the farmer had told him. It could be weeks, even months, before he sees her again. At least, he thinks as the pain in his leg eases and he drifts off to sleep, he won't be breaking any promises, for he never had written that letter.

* * *

'So you see, Nurse Frobisher, this puts a completely different light on the situation.'

'You mean you'd rather believe a servant than me, Matron?' Alice was outraged as she faced Lady Belinda Holker in her office.

'Emily is more than a servant, Nurse. She is a trusted friend. I have known her since she came here as a nursery maid to George and Robert.'

'Exactly! She is hopelessly biased. She'd swear black was white if she thought it would help Robert.'

While privately thinking Alice was probably right, Aunt Bella was equally as convinced that in this case, Emily was telling the truth. And she didn't think this opinion was influenced by her own vast relief when she'd heard Emily's story. While admitting that her nephew's morals were entirely his own affair and that if he wished to make love to a girl without 'benefit of clergy' then he was only doing what most young men did these days, it had been inexcusable that he should do it while a guest under *her* roof and with one of *her* nurses. The fact that, technically speaking, it was more his roof than hers, had nothing to do with it. For the duration of the war, Holker Hall and those within it, were under her care, and he was the visitor.

'Anyway,' Alice was still defiant, 'it doesn't make any difference. Daddy's already put an announcement in the paper.'

335

'Without Robert's permission?' If true, this was, indeed, a calamity.

'Oh, I've written to him. Explained the situation. You see — there's something you don't know, Matron. I'm pregnant!'

Aunt Bella was silenced — but only temporarily. She gathered her wits. 'You seriously expect me to believe that Robert is the father?'

Alice looked suitably shocked. 'You surely don't really believe there was ever anyone else?'

But Aunt Bella, gazing at her shrewdly, was quite sure there'd been someone else. Of course, all the patients loved Alice Frobisher a little, or at least, desired her, but Alec Gethin had been rather different. Had he not been sent on to another hospital for treatment she might well have had to take Alice off his case; and certainly would have done so now that Emily had told her what she'd seen. The moment, she decided, had come to fire her own broadside.

'You won't be aware of this yet, Nurse, because my brother has only just heard, but Robert has been reported missing.'

Alice's reaction was such that Aunt Bella hastily poured a glass of water from the carafe on her desk and pushed it across to her. 'Here, drink this!' The girl had gone white as a sheet.

Alice gulped it down. Then drew a long breath. 'But I thought Staff Officers didn't go near the fighting.'

Aunt Bella sighed. 'I'm afraid we all presumed that was the case. But I gather that Robert's Brigadier held rather different views.'

'I see!' Clearly, Alice was now seeing many things and in rather a different light. For a few moments, she continued to sit there and then slowly got to her feet. 'This is dreadful news. I must go and see Daddy right away.'

'You do that,' said Aunt Bella. 'And Alice, I think it would be better, under all the circumstances, to discontinue your nursing career at Holker Hall.'

'Oh, yes! Whatever happens, I shan't be coming back. Poor Robert!' she added belatedly, as Aunt Bella held open the door for her.

'Dear Brigadier O'Murphy,

I hope you will forgive this letter from someone who is a complete stranger to you; but I am hoping you will be able to spare a few minutes of your valuable time in order to set my mind at rest; or rather, my daughter's. She is engaged to be married to Captain Robert Holker, one of your 'aides', who has just been reported missing. Would it be possible for you to acquaint me with the circumstances of Captain Holker's disappearance? And would it also be possible for you to expedite matters with the Red Cross in order to establish if he has been taken prisoner? My daughter would welcome any information you can give her for, as you can imagine, the poor girl is distraught with worry.'

I bet she is! thought the Brig, but only because her little scheme has gone grievously awry.

He pondered. He wished very much that he could write and tell this Stanley Frobisher that he was well aware of the true nature of his daughter's worries, and that marriage to her, if *he* had anything to do with it, would be the last course of action Robert Holker would ever take. But he knew he could not say this. Robert had unburdened himself in confidence and at the Brig's own insistence. With a sigh, he picked up his pen and began to draft a reply.

'Dear Mr Frobisher,
Thank you for your letter. I fully appreciate your concern for Captain Holker's safety. He was captured in what was clearly a raiding party, made for the express purpose of taking a prisoner for interrogation. This is a common practice on both sides.
The chances of his still being alive are therefore very high; and I think your daughter can be reasonably confident that Captain Holker will eventually be returned to her safe and sound. However, I doubt very much if that will be before the end of hostilities; and when that will be is a matter about which it would be unwise to speculate.
When news of Captain Holker's whereabouts is received from the Red Cross, I will make sure that you are told immediately.'

The Brig re-read what he had written, placed it in the appropriate tray for his clerk to collect and type, then sat for a moment, deep in thought. What would the girl do now? Probably visit some obscure relative in the back of beyond until the baby was born. And then what? Adoption, he supposed. Or would she brave the disapproval of society, the virtual ostracism it would cause, and keep the child until Robert's return could legalise the situation? If she were to do that, then he thought it likely she would have Robert's support. Anyway, there was no more he could do himself, other than to badger the Red Cross. And this he would do, anyway, for his own satisfaction. For he couldn't quite ignore a niggle of guilt about the whole affair, especially with old 'Ma Matheson' gazing at him with those great, sheep's eyes of his. But war was war, dammit! All the same, he hoped to God the boy *was* all right.

27

'Are you sure you're warm enough?' Mrs Money-moon asked yet again.

Jamie Coleano grinned. 'You sound just like my Mom!' He was stretched out on a sofa in front of an enormous log fire in Mrs Moneymoon's little sitting-room; the heat was intense. Cushions supported his back and head and a table beside him held a pile of magazines, books, writing materials and a cup of coffee.

Mrs Moneymoon, seated on the other side of the fireplace, smiled back at him. 'Good! That's just how I want to sound. This is your home while you're in England, Jamie. And I know Kate agrees with me.'

'Are you sure of that?'

'Of course! It was her idea, after all, that you should come here to convalesce. And it's good for Prissy to have young company — and for you to be able to talk to her about life in America.'

'She's still determined to live there after the war?'

'Well, she's still convinced Hank will come back. Even though the Red Cross say we should have heard by now if he was a prisoner.'

'It's great that she's got Rosie May. Tell me, Mrs Moneymoon, would you mind very much if Prissy were to go and live in the States when the war's over, with or without Hank?'

'Not if that was what she wanted. And we'd still have Kate.'

'What if . . . ' Jamie hesitated. 'What if Kate were to go, too?'

'Well, naturally, she'd go to see Prissy. We all would.'

'But what if — she lived over there full-time?'

Mrs Moneymoon looked at him keenly. 'Jamie, are you trying to tell me something?'

'It's really the Prof. I should be talking to like this. Isn't that how it's done over here, when a guy wants to marry a girl? He asks her Pa first?'

'Jamie!' Mrs Moneymoon's face creased into a broad smile. 'But that's wonderful! I couldn't be more pleased! At least, there'll be one wedding I can plan for. When's it to be? Kate's next big leave? Before you go back?'

'Hold on, Mrs M.! There's still one big snag. I haven't asked Kate how she feels about it. And that's kind of important, I guess!'

'But surely she knows how you feel about her?'

'It isn't my fault if she doesn't! But I don't want to rush her. Prissy told me there was a guy she was keen on, a long time ago.'

The smile left Mrs Moneymoon's face. 'Robert Holker. A dear boy. Quite what went wrong there, I've never understood. But clearly, it wasn't to be. And as Prissy said, it was a long time ago. You ask her, Jamie.'

'I will. Just as soon as she can grab a couple of days off.'

★   ★   ★

Angela and Kate were drinking coffee outside a Boulogne café. Their wounded had been unloaded and now they could enjoy a few blissful hours to themselves. It was late March and the sun was burnishing the pale pink ruffs of the pigeons to gold as they pecked among the cobbles. But a breeze was lifting the corners of their table-cloth and they would normally have sat inside. However, until they had bathed and changed their clothes, they hesitated to inflict themselves upon the local populace, garlic and acrid cigarette smoke notwithstanding.

'Kate,' Angela asked suddenly, 'are you feeling all right? Because you haven't opened your mouth for the last ten minutes and then only to ask me to pass the sugar. Which I did. And which you still haven't touched!'

'Sorry!' Kate helped herself to sugar then went back to staring out across the square. 'I was just wondering whether I should marry Jamie Coleano.'

Angela spluttered into her coffee. 'You said that as

if you were trying to decide between one croissant or two! And I didn't even know he'd asked you.'

'He hasn't! Not yet! But I'm sure he's going to before he's drafted. He's made a remarkable recovery and now that the Germans have started their big push and the Americans are flinging themselves into the fray, they're going to need every man they've got.'

'It doesn't look too good, does it?' Temporarily diverted from Kate's love-life, Angela considered the progress of the war.

'Edmund doesn't think the advance will last,' said Kate. 'He says that now the German army is so much bigger because of the troops diverted from the Russian front, they simply haven't got the resources to maintain it.'

'Let's hope he's right! I don't fancy living under the German jackboot.'

Kate raised a quizzical eyebrow. 'Even if it belonged to Ernst?'

'Ernst doesn't wear jackboots! Either literally or metaphorically. And I certainly wouldn't be under them, if he did. Mutual respect, that's what my parents tell me is the secret of a happy marriage.'

'Mine, too,' Kate agreed. 'And I'd certainly get respect from Jamie.'

'But surely the important point is that you don't love him.'

Kate bristled. 'How do you know I don't love him?'

'If you did, you wouldn't be wondering if you should marry him. You'd have done it by now.'

Kate considered. 'All right! So I don't love him

342

like you love Ernst, or Prissy, Hank. And,' her voice wavered slightly, 'like I once loved Robert Holker. But life with Jamie could be good. I'd grow to love him, I'm sure of it.'

'Certainly living in the States could be fun,' Angela conceded. 'Nice for Prissy, too. When's your next pass?' she asked as the breeze intensified and they stood up to go.

'Two weeks' time.'

'So, jackboots permitting, you could be coming back a betrothed woman.'

'Could be!'

★ ★ ★

'It's worrying,' said Jacques to Robert. Jacques was not his real name. 'I change it for every new man who comes,' he'd admitted. 'It's safer that way. The less you know about me, the better.' The implication wasn't lost upon Robert. Clearly, if he were to be taken prisoner for a second time, he couldn't expect the leniency he'd received before.

'The Germans are advancing,' Jacques continued now, 'especially around the Somme area. Things don't look good. So the sooner you are away, the better for everyone. Perhaps tomorrow night. You must be ready.'

In many ways, Robert would be sorry to leave the farm. For several weeks now, as he'd conscientiously rested his leg, he'd spent many daytime hours in the farm kitchen, doing what jobs he could to help Jacques' wife, Madeleine, talking to Jacques when he was there, playing with their little daughter, Yvonne.

343

It was like living in a kind of limbo; powerless to do anything but wait, and entirely dependent upon others.

He thought a great deal; about his future if he survived the war, about his parents, about Alice. What was she doing now about the baby? Had she not told everyone, flaunted it almost, it would have been easy for her to have retired discreetly to some remote place for her confinement, and then to have had the child adopted. But the reaction of Robert's father to this was easy to imagine. The virtual 'giving away' of a possible heir would be anathema to him, especially since there was every hope that its position could be legitimised once Robert was home.

But things wouldn't seem that simple, of course. As far as they were concerned, he could easily be dead for there would have been no news of him through the Red Cross.

Although he usually managed to stop himself thinking of Kate while he was awake, it was impossible to keep her from his dreams. Night after night, she came to him and although it was soul-destroying to awake each morning and remember that she belonged to another man, his dreams of holding her in his arms, of telling her that he loved her, became infinitely precious. Once, he even dreamt that it was she who was pregnant and not Alice and that, miraculously, he really was the father. If only . . .

★   ★   ★

'Are you sure about this' Stanley Frobisher asked his daughter.

'Quite sure, Daddy.'

'Do Robert's parents know?'

'No, it's my own decision.'

'And Robert? What will Robert think of it?'

'He won't mind!' Alice was quite sure on that score.

★ ★ ★

'Kate, have you heard? The Germans have taken the château.'

Kate looked up from the valise she was packing for her seventytwo hour pass. 'Our château? Are you sure?'

'Deadly serious, I couldn't believe it either but it's just been confirmed by one of the M.O.s.'

'And what about the patients and staff?'

'I'm not sure, but Matron's definitely a prisoner of war. She refused to leave her patients.'

'Good for her!'

'She's a tough old bird and no mistake.'

'Should I still go on leave?' Kate wondered.

'Of course! There's still a fair slice of France left before they reach the Channel. And it'll probably be your last chance of seeing Jamie for quite a while.'

★ ★ ★

Apart from several Red Cross vehicles drawn up in the driveway, Moneymoon Manor looked reassuringly the same. Swathes of daffodils stood sentinel

345

beneath the trees and primroses were like clotted cream in the lane leading down to Toby's field. In Ma's little sitting-room, Kate and Jamie sat drinking coffee. Through the window, they could see Priscilla pushing Rosie May's pram down the drive. Ma, they knew, was busy checking a new delivery of stores.

'So, you're off at last,' said Kate.

'Yup! Day after tomorrow. But this time, it's going to be different. This time, I know what to expect.'

Kate wondered if he was right. Trying to repel a conquering army as it swept relentlessly on its way would surely be a different matter from playing the cat and mouse game of trench warfare. She wished that Edmund were there to make reassuring comments and perhaps put the German advance into perspective.

'And this time,' Jamie continued, 'I want revenge — for Hank.'

'You're still convinced he's dead?'

'Afraid so, honey. We'd have heard by now if he was a prisoner. And don't forget, I saw it happen.'

Covertly, Kate studied the face of this man to whom so much had happened during the last few months; now, there were lines of firmness and resolve where before there had been weakness and fear. Perhaps he was right, perhaps this time things would be different for him.

He caught her glance and smiled — a lopsided grin that caught at her heart. Beneath the tough veneer, the small boy was still there, needing love and reassurance.

'Kate,' he said, 'it would mean so much to me

knowing that you were waiting for me to come back.'

'But there are so many reasons for coming back, Jamie.'

'Only if you're one of them! If I do come back, will you marry me?'

It wasn't the proposal she'd longed for, but there was no hesitation in her reply. 'Yes, Jamie, I'll marry you. And *when* you come back, not if.'

★   ★   ★

Robert tries to ease his cramped limbs, but there is very little room to stretch out in the back of the cart that he is sharing with a load of swedes. The sweet, almost sickly smell of them fills his nostrils. If he has to lie there for much longer under the tarpaulin, he will be sick; all over the ancient threadbare jacket, the workman's shirt and trousers that he wears, but then his nausea vanishes like mist on a summer morning, blown away by the invigorating tang of the sea. Not far now!

He hears the rumble of the wheels over cobblestones and the cart jolts to a halt. Jacques calls out a greeting, another man replies and then comes the creaking of heavy doors and the horse begins to back, its hooves ringing on the cobbles. The tarpaulin is thrown back.

'You can get out now,' says Jacques.

Robert lurches off the cart, sweat pouring off him, swedes scattering in all directions. He is standing in some sort of stone outhouse, lit only by one grimy window set high in a wall.

'From now on,' says Jacques, 'Jacob will look after you.' He indicates a middle-aged man in dungarees who has already begun to shovel the swedes into a bin. 'Do exactly what he tells you. He speaks only Walloon but you will understand. Goodbye and good luck.'

He has gone before Robert has time to thank him properly. Jacob stops his shovelling long enough to indicate a ladder leading up to a closed trapdoor. 'Up! You go up! Then knock — two times!'

Robert does as he is told. He reaches the trapdoor and knocks twice. Immediately, it is opened and a hand comes through to help him scramble off the ladder. 'Come on in, buddy!' says Hank Shelton.

★ ★ ★

'Well?' asked Angela. Normally, she would have waited for Kate in their room at the hostel but today, she was on the quayside.

'Very well, thank you!' said Kate, poker-faced. 'Good crossing. And Prissy sends her love.'

'Don't be difficult! You know what I mean.'

But Kate was gazing around, deceptively innocent. 'No jackboots as yet?'

'Repelled them single-handed!' Angela decided not to mention, just at the moment, the German breakthrough on the Somme and the troop trains of 'doughboys' she's seen heading in that direction. 'Now, come on — tell! Are you or are you not an engaged woman?'

For answer, Kate put down her valise and extended her left hand for inspection.

'It's bare!' said Angela in disgust.

'Well, Jamie did give me this whopping great solitaire, but it was a bit too big and when I was pointing out a passing U Boat to a fellow passenger, it fell off into the sea. No! Pax!' as Angela extended both hands menacingly towards her throat. And she put up her own hand to loosen the neck of her cloak and pull out a silken cord. From it dangled a gold signet ring, flashing in the sunlight. 'We hadn't time to buy a ring so Jamie's given me his, but it would only fit on my thumb.'

'So it's all signed and sealed,' said Angela with satisfaction.

'All signed and sealed,' Kate agreed. 'And we're to be married on Jamie's next leave.'

★　★　★

They had talked for hours. Both, at first, had been speechless with shock and then unable to do anything but hurl insults at each other like a couple of overgrown schoolboys.

'You son of a gun!'

'You Yankee yellow-belly!'

'You boneless, blue-blooded Brit!'

They had ended by putting their arms around each other and clapping each other on the back, then drawing away to stare again in disbelief, finally pouring out their stories.

Hank, too, had been the victim of a raiding party. 'I was with a pal, Jamie Coleano. Don't know what happened to him but he may have been blown up by this god-damn shell. The blast must have knocked me out because when I came round, I was in the back of a truck — with just one Kraut to look after me. I lay doggo until we lurched around a corner and then I managed to get a neck lock on him. Probably strangled him. Hope so! And then I jumped for it and landed in a ditch. Only trouble was, my right arm got broken. By the time the Belgians picked me up, I'd gone a bit delirious. They had to hole me up for the winter in an old mill house. Then, when I was well enough, the miller passed me down the line until I got here a couple of days ago. Now, your turn.'

Briefly, Robert explained what had happened to him.

'We sure are the lucky ones,' Hank said when he'd finished. 'Now, how about some cold coffee? Not up to Moneymoon standards, I'm afraid, but it's the best I can do.'

Startled by this casual reference to the Moneymoons, Robert accepted an enamel mug of the bitter brew. 'You kept in touch with the Moneymoons, then?'

'If you count marrying Priscilla as keeping in touch, I sure did!'

Robert put down his coffee, very carefully, on the floor beside him; by now, they were both leaning, legs outstretched, against the bare, stone wall. 'You married Prissy?'

'Yes. If you remember, I was always crazy about her. And if all's gone as it should, I'm a proud Poppa by now.'

But Robert was still in a daze. 'The last I heard, you'd gone back home at the beginning of the war, toeing the parental line.'

'Yeah, that's right. But I joined the American Red Cross in 1916. Came over to France and married Prissy in '17. She and Kate were nursing in this French château. Hey!' He clapped a hand to his forehead. 'I remember now! Prissy told me how *you* turned up there — during the Battle of the Somme, wasn't it?'

Robert nodded. 'Between them, she and Kate saved my life. With the help of a French doctor, Pierre someone or other.'

'Montarial. Yeah, he was a great guy. Still is, I hope.'

Surely that was a very casual way to refer to a brother-in-law? Speaking very slowly, Robert said 'Let me get one thing clear. Did Kate marry this Pierre Montarial?'

'*Marry* him? Good God, no! He wasn't exactly the marrying kind — at least, not for a girl like Kate. Say, are you feeling all right?' Without ceremony, he pushed Robert's head down on to his knees. And Robert let it stay there for at least a minute until the dizziness had passed. When he looked up again, it was to find Hank staring at him with a broad grin on his face.

'You were really worried in case Kate was hitched, weren't you? But I thought — at least, *Priss* thought — that everything was over between you two. Something about not keeping in touch back at the beginning of the war.'

As if he had pressed a button in his memory, Robert suddenly saw the face of the young girl to whom he had entrusted his letter to Kate, all that

351

time ago. A girl about whom he knew nothing, who could have been the most unreliable creature in the world and who could have thrown it in the gutter the moment he was out of sight. Why had he been so trusting? So sure that Kate hadn't cared? And then panic gripped him.

'Is there anyone now? I can't believe that someone as attractive as Kate . . . '

'Well, I wouldn't really know about that,' Hank said. 'I've been missing for a long time now, remember. Jamie Coleano certainly had ideas that way, but he might be dead by now, poor devil!'

But he might not be! And then Robert took himself to task. He couldn't wish another man dead in order to leave Kate free for him. He forced himself to concentrate on some of the loose ends still to be tied.

'A silly question probably, but — Prissy hasn't dyed her hair has she?'

'Of course not! Still a beautiful blonde, I'm glad to say. Why d'you ask?'

'Oh, nothing. Just something someone said.' It was too complicated to go into now.

'Except when they wore those crazy wigs,' Hank suddenly remembered.

'Wigs?'

'Yep! Christmas before last. They all dressed up. Gave me a shock, I can tell you.'

So that was it! Relaxing a little, he suddenly grinned shamefacedly. 'Did you say something about being a proud father?'

'Thought you'd never ask! I just hope everything's gone all right. He — she — was due at the beginning of the year. Please God, I shall soon know.'

And he'd soon know about Kate. The next few days — weeks, even? — were going to be the longest of his life.

28

Their turn has come at last. The United States First Division flexes its muscles and waits for the command to attack. Until now, the Somme has been only a name — given to a stretch of countryside saturated with the blood of the French, British and German armies. Now it can only be a matter of time before its own blood is shed upon it.

Jamie Coleano fingers his rifle and reflects that now, more than ever, he has a reason for living — but also for dying if it proves him worthy of Kate's love. Fear is what he fears the most.

★　★　★

'Tonight,' Jacob says, pointing at Hank, 'you go!'

'And I?' Robert dares to ask, pointing at himself. 'When will it be my turn?'

'Soon!' says Jacob. 'Soon!' And with that, he must be content.

★　★　★

'No news from Jamie?' Angela asks. They know that the American losses have been heavy.

Kate shakes her head. 'Only one short letter written after he'd got to France.'

Angela seeks comfort in platitudes. 'No news is good news!'

But Kate shakes her head. 'Not necessarily. His father will still be listed as his next of kin. Jamie wrote to tell him we were engaged, so I'd hear eventually if anything had happened, but for the moment . . . '

★ ★ ★

'Well done! You have a lovely little boy!'

Just what Robert's father had wanted! Alice reflects as she gazes down at the bundle in her arms. Her feelings are mixed; pride, not only that the child is perfect and clearly adorable but also at her own part in the miracle of his birth. But with the pride, there is also humility; a rare emotion for Alice to feel. But above all, there is hope — that the difficulties that lie ahead will be overcome.

★ ★ ★

'Any messages?' Hank asks. He and Robert are saying goodbye in the tiny, evil-smelling cabin of the fishing boat. Within minutes now, the summons will come for Hank to go on deck, there to climb over the rail and let himself down into the oily darkness of the sea to swim the few yards to the French vessel whose crew will be standing by to pick him up.

'If you'd telephone my Aunt at Holker Hall, I'd be grateful. She'll tell my parents.'

'And Kate?'

Kate! If only he had the right to send her his undying love. To explain the cruel tricks Fate has played upon them. But there are too many unknown factors. She may already be married to another man. He, himself, may have had responsibilities placed upon him and even if he were to deny them, would Kate want marriage to a man whom society would inevitably condemn? Even *her* liberal views might not extend that far.

'Tell her,' he says, 'that I'll never forget her.' That, at least, is the truth, if only a small part of it.

★ ★ ★

Robert's partner — the man who will be his 'shadow' when it is his turn to go — is called Dennis Cooper and he is an aviator. He has been shot down behind enemy lines but, thanks to the Belgians, has evaded capture. He cannot wait to get back behind the controls of an aeroplane; most of his waking moments are spent telling Robert about the future of commercial aviation.

'The sky will be the limit in every sense when this bloody war is over. Planes will soon be crossing the Atlantic on scheduled flights. Maybe even the Pacific.'

'What if the Germans should win the war?' Robert asks. Not that he anticipates that Germany will, but he is intrigued to hear the young man's response.

'It won't make a blind bit of difference who wins,' he says confidently. 'The Germans are bloody fine pilots. I'd work with them any day.'

Which is probably a very sensible attitude to take, Robert reflects. He explains in detail how their escape route will work.

'No chance of our going together, I suppose?' Dennis asks predictably.

'Doubt it. And it's important we do exactly as they tell us.'

But next day, to his astonishment, it seems that Jacob shares Dennis's view. 'Both go!' he tells them.

'Both? Tonight?'

'Both — *now!*'

At first, they don't believe him. He has to push them towards the trapdoor.

'Why?' asks Robert.

'Germans — maybe come soon!'

So the Germans must be advancing — and at such a rate, the escape route is threatened; it must be so, for them to be evacuated in broad daylight. Before they leave the building, Jacob helps them into oilskin capes and sou'westers.

'Must be choppy out there!' says Dennis and is immediately motioned to silence as the door is swung open and they join a little group of men, similarly attired.

A fine drizzle is falling and as they walk down the street towards the quayside, they see that the sea is indeed choppy. Robert feels immensely vulnerable, especially when they see a couple of German soldiers walking towards them. But they have been well-placed in the middle of the little group and the soldiers barely glance in their direction.

Robert prepares to follow Dennis on to one of the vessels tied up in the little harbour, but is nudged along to the next. A sensible precaution, he supposes, in case the Huns are observing them, but he wishes that he and Dennis were still together.

'This way,' a man breathes in his ear and he follows him below deck. Once in the familiar, cramped quarters, the man turns. 'The Germans are moving fast, so fast we dare not keep you here any longer. That is why we risk the daytime. But it means we will have to go much further out to sea — beyond the range of their telescopes.'

'I understand,' Robert says.

'I think perhaps you do not understand — completely. There will be mines out there. You will have to swim.'

Robert swallows hard. He is not a strong swimmer. But he refuses to contemplate failure now. 'Yes — I see! But if *you* are willing then we certainly are.'

'Good!'

★   ★   ★

The Brig is secretly greatly relieved. Although he has appeared breezily confident about Robert's safety, he has inwardly begun to suffer serious doubts, and even twinges of guilt at his own part in the affair.

'Told you so!' he blithely informs Major Matheson after the report has been received from American H.Q. that a Private H. Shelton has

357

escaped from behind enemy lines, and has reported his meeting with a Captain R. Holker. Captain Holker, it is hoped, will shortly follow him. 'Alive and well!' adds the Brigadier triumphantly.

'But not yet back with us,' the Major reminds him stiffly.

'But soon will be,' the Brig refuses to be deflated. 'Says so here!'

'That is the *American* viewpoint, sir.' The Major's opinion of his American allies is still cautious.

'Have we informed Captain Holker's next of kin?'

'Not yet, sir. I thought it advisable to wait until we had more definite news.'

'H-mm! Perhaps you're right.' Might be as well, too, to wait before writing to the father of that fiancée of his. But then he brightens. 'Any chance of getting this Private Shelton over to tell us exactly what happened?'

'I'll enquire sir, although he may already have gone on leave.'

★   ★   ★

They know that he's on his way. Since early morning, Moneymoon Manor has been en fête, its façade festooned with the flags and bunting that Mrs Moneymoon has kept since the Coronation of their Majesties. Over the front door, the Stars and Strips — in reality, a square of linen on which Danny has been let loose with paint pots and brushes — flutters bravely.

'Don't tell me the war's over and I never knew!' says the postman, scratching his head.

So to make it quite clear, a banner has been stretched from one side of the Manor to the other with a slightly uneven 'WELCOME HOME HANK' — Danny's work again — emblazoned across it. All that is missing is the cause of the celebration.

Around one o'clock, Priscilla's eyelids begin to droop. She hardly slept a wink last night, what with Rosie May's midnight feed and the adrenalin of her excitement. She takes Rosie May into the nursery — it is more than time for her midday feed — settles herself and the baby into a nursing chair, bares her breasts and promptly falls asleep.

It is thus that Hank finds them. He tiptoes across the floor and sinks to his knees. It is the baby who wakes first, puts out a podgy hand and hits him on the nose.

It is his chuckle of delight that awakens Priscilla. Dreamily, still half asleep, she, too, puts up a hand and strokes the face that is so transformed with love and pride, she hardly notices how much thinner it is and, somehow, older.

'Oh, Priss! You clever, clever girl!' And suddenly they are both crying as they hug and kiss. And Rosie May, considerably put out at this trespass upon what, until now, has been exclusively *her* domain, opens her mouth and bawls in concert.

★ ★ ★

'And how's Kate?' Hank asks. It is half an hour later and he is being fed tea and home-made cookies.

'Fine! Still nursing. And,' Priscilla pauses for

359

maximum effect. 'engaged to be married to Jamie Coleano!'

'That's great news!' He's already been told, back at base, that Jamie is still alive. But pleased for his friend though he is, his heart goes out to Robert Holker. The man was so obviously besotted with her. He must try to see Kate and at least deliver his message. Home-coming isn't going to be all plain sailing, after all.

★ ★ ★

When the order comes, Robert is more than ready; if only to escape from the violent movement of the boat. Even so, he is horrified, when he emerges on deck, at the turbulence of the sea; a grey, heaving mass lashed by squalls of blinding rain. Only with difficulty, can he make out the blurred outlines of the rest of the fleet. And when his companion points into the murk, presumably in the direction in which he must swim, he has to peer for several seconds before he catches a glimpse of the boat that is standing by to pick him up. His heart sinks; the distance must be several hundred yards. And he has no idea how his wounded leg will react.

'We dare not go nearer,' the man at his side tells him. 'Look!' And now he is pointing out to sea, at a round metal object studded with the horns that mean the instant annihilation of any vessel that hits them. 'A drifter,' the man shouts against the wind. 'There could be others.'

And even as they look, they see another — and much nearer this time. Robert prepares to climb over the side; the sooner he leaves the better for the fleet, if not himself. But what of Dennis Cooper? And then a flare is fired from a nearby trawler and he sees Dennis diving into the sea. His head is down, his arms flail through the water in a racing crawl. Clearly, he is a strong and accomplished swimmer. At least, thinks Robert, one of them should survive.

'Good luck!' shouts his companion. He's going to need it!

He has covered perhaps half the distance when he realises without a shadow of doubt, that he can go no further. His leg is not only excruciatingly painful but has ceased to function, so that it now trails behind him like a heavy piece of driftwood which he cannot dispose of. And his lungs are at bursting point. Keel-hauling can be no worse!

It is then that he sees the mine, immediately ahead. Initial panic gives way to common sense. It needs the ramming of a steel hull or some other weighty object to set it off. Approached with caution, it can become a life line, a sort of halfway house. He reaches out and grasps one of the horns and hangs limply as he draws breath, then puts out his other hand to grasp the one above. And so on, until he is draped across its surface like a rag doll. The discomfort is infinitely preferable to the pain. He will just rest there, for a little while, he thinks. And then, inexorably, he drifts into unconsciousness.

★ ★ ★

'My Dear Kate, It is with great sadness that I write to tell you that our dear son, Jamie, has been killed in action on the Somme.

We are fortunate in that his Commanding Officer is also a family friend so we have had the privilege of hearing from him directly.

It happened at the end of May. Alone — for his companions had already fallen — Jamie continued to advance towards enemy lines until he was sufficiently close to hurl a grenade with perfect accuracy at the machine gun that had killed his comrades. Immediately afterwards, he fell, a victim of the German crossfire. His Commanding Officer, I understand, is recommending him for a posthumous decoration.

I will write no more now, other than to say how much we had looked forward to welcoming you into our family as a beloved daughter. Sadly, it was not to be, but it is still our fervent hope that one day we shall meet.

Meanwhile, I remain, most sincerely, Frank Coleano.'

Kate lets the tears fall unchecked. She is alone in the garden of Moneymoon Manor, enclosed between walls of sweet-smelling roses and tumbling vines.

She can imagine it all so clearly; Jamie's determination to conquer his fear driving him on against all odds. Not for him the coward's way of feigning death and lying comatose beside his comrades. Perhaps a hero's death is what, unconsciously, he has sought all along. But how his family will grieve! His father, his mother, his 'kid sister', his dog who will wait for him until the end of his days.

'Kate!' She turns her head as Hank pushes through the curtain of vines. He studies her face, then sees the letter in her hand. 'Jamie?'

She nods and hands him the letter. Hank reads in silence and then puts his arm around her shoulders, 'A crazy thing to say, but I think he would have wanted it this way.'

'I know!' Kate wipes away her tears. 'I shall always be so glad that I knew him.' She begins to rise. 'I must write to his parents straight away.'

But Hank's arm restrains her. 'Kate, this isn't the moment, but I must still use it. You'll be going back soon and I don't know when I shall see you on your own again. I have a message for you from Robert.' He has already told them all of the extraordinary coincidence of his meeting up with Robert behind enemy lines, but has thought it more appropriate to deliver Robert's message when Kate is alone. She says nothing but he thinks a look of intense longing has come into her eyes.

'He asked me to tell you that he will never forget you.'

The look fades. For the words have a ring of finality about them, a tacit assumption that memories are all that now remain between them. Certainly, that is how it sounds to Kate.

There is anguish in Hank's eyes as he looks at her. Somehow, the message has gone grievously awry. Clearly, he's useless as an intermediary. But before he lets her go, he tries to give her some small shred of comfort. 'At least, the tide's turning. The Jerries are on the run. Jamie's death wasn't in vain.'

Kate nods wordlessly, and attempts a smile that she hopes will hide the bleakness in her heart.

★ ★ ★

'There you were,' says the Brig, 'like a beached whale. They had to prise you off with a boat-hook. Two boat-hooks, to be precise. I only wish I'd been there!'

'I'm surprised you weren't!' says Robert, then adds belatedly, 'Sir!'

The Brig twinkles amiably. 'Believe it or not, I've learned my lesson. Not that I've admitted it to old Ma Matheson!'

Robert grins up at him from his hospital bed. He knows that that is the nearest the Brig will ever get to an apology. And besides, the part he has played in Robert's rescue has more than compensated for his involvement in the first place. Robert has already been told the bare bones of it by Dennis Cooper.

'Most impressive, it was! They'd hauled me in from the briny and were getting ready to leave until I told them there were two of us. And then I saw this minesweeper standing by. At first, I thought they were on a routine sweep but then this naval bloke came over to me and told me they were there for the sole purpose of ensuring *your* safety — didn't matter a twopenny damn about mine! — and when I said you should have arrived by now, they got into a frightful stew and the next minute a skiff was putting out from the trawler with three men on board. And it was a bloody long wait before they came back, I can tell you! And even when they did, there you were spread out on the bottom like a bloody starfish. We all thought you were a goner. So why all the fuss? Are you related to the King, or something?'

Now, the Brig fills in the gaps in the story. 'We had Hank Shelton brought over to Brigade. And he told us about the escape route. So we made it our business to contact the fishermen and find out what was happening. The rest was easy. I got on to old Mugsy Murgatroyd at the Admiralty — went to school with him — and the rest you know.'

'Thank you, sir!' said Robert dutifully.

'The least I could do! And by the way, I had a letter, way back when you first disappeared, from the father of your lady-love in Staffordshire. I said I'd let him know when we had news of you.'

'Don't bother, sir, I'll get in touch when they send me home.'

★ ★ ★

'Is that you, Aunt Bee?'

'Robert! Darling boy! Are you all right?'

'As ninepence! But it's good to hear your voice!'

'It's like a miracle to hear yours! Where are you?'

'London. At the War Office for a couple of days. And then I'll be up. How are mother and father?'

There is a tiny pause so that Robert is partly prepared for what follows. 'Not too well, I'm afraid. When you were reported missing it was like George's death all over again. And of course, Alice's defection didn't help.'

'Alice's defection?'

'Oh, Lord! Of course, you wouldn't have heard.'

'Aunt Bee, what . . . ?'

'She's gone off with Alec Gethin. You remember him? The officer who shared your room for a little while.'

'I remember.'

'He was the father of the baby. Mind you, I guessed as much after Emily had been to see me.'

'Emily?'

'Oh, you wouldn't know about that either! Robert, are you sure you can't come home *now*?'

'Quite sure, Aunt Bee! And I must go in a minute. So please, just spell it out to me. Do I take it Alice is marrying Alec Gethin?'

'As soon as his divorce is through. Once Alec found out about the baby — he came back to see me and I made sure he knew — he left his wife without a moment's hesitation. No love lost there, anyway, I gather. Once the war's over, they'll all be off to Australia to start a new life.'

'*All*, you say?'

'Yes — Alice had a baby boy a few weeks ago.'

'Aunt Bee, I love you!'

'And I you, dear boy! Come home soon!'

Robert replaces the earpiece on its stand and sits down abruptly. His first coherent thought is that he is a free man — that he has no obligations to Alice who, in the end, has shown surprising courage. Life in Australia will not be easy. He feels, too, a certain sympathy for his parents for he knows that they will have set great store by his marrying Alice.

But at last he allows his mind to dwell upon the incredible, wonderful fact that he can now ask Kate to marry him. Unless, he forces himself to remember, she is already married, or promised, to another man.

How can he find out? Telephoning Hank at Moneymoon Manor is out of the question. What was the name of the man Hank had mentioned? Jamie — Colabri? Coleato? Coleano! That was it! But Hank had thought he might be already dead. Who will know — or can find out?

He is suddenly aware that a sergeant is standing in front of him, coughing discreetly. 'Excuse me, sir. The Field Marshall will see you now.'

'Thank you, sergeant.' But even as he follows the sergeant into the vast room, and salutes the man who, until now, has been only a name and one to be mentioned with awe and respect, is actually coming forward to shake his hand, he is still wrestling with his problem.

'Well done, Captain Holker! My congratulations! Please sit down.'

'Thank you, sir!' And then, as he sits, he remembers and can only just stop himself from shouting the name aloud. Edmund Moneymoon! *He* will know! And he must be somewhere in this building.

★ ★ ★

'So there it is, I'm afraid, Robert. Killed in action — although in the bravest circumstances.'

'And Kate?'

'I haven't seen her but Ma tells me she's utterly devastated. Understandable, of course. They hadn't been engaged more than a couple of weeks. I gather she'll be going out to visit his parents as soon as hostilities end. Which shouldn't be long now. The Germans . . .'

But Edmund's opinion about the end of the war, falls upon deaf ears. Robert is far too occupied facing the unpalatable fact that Jamie Coleano, dead, is as much an impediment as Jamie Coleano, alive. For how can he suggest marriage to a girl whose heart has been broken?

29

As Edmund had predicted, the tide of war rolled inexorably onward, and this time in the Allies' favour.

Albert, Arras, Bapaume, Havrincourt Wood, all names that had once signified defeat, were recaptured. In September, the American First Army, supported by French troops, actually advanced five miles in one day in the area of St. Mihiel. Hank, prevented by his permanently stiff right arm, from returning to active service and now at American H.Q., met up with Edmund to celebrate.

'By the way,' Edmund said after they'd lifted their glasses to 'absent friends', 'Robert Holker came to see me. Wanted to know what had happened to Jamie Coleano.'

So he knew that Kate was now a free woman, Hank thought. He was relieved for he had wondered how to get in touch with him.

The Western Front was not the only area where the enemy was vanquished. There was victory in the Balkans, the Turkish 7th and 8th armies virtually ceased to exist and the Bulgarian army surrendered.

One of the sweetest victories of all came from the offensive by the Belgians and British in Flanders. Robert thought of 'Jacques' and his family and rejoiced.

Throughout October, the German rout continued. 'Not long now!' Angela exulted.

'Not long!' Kate was determined not to give way to the despair that had engulfed her since she'd heard of Robert's meeting with Edmund. For a little while, she had lived in hope that he would contact her but clearly, that was not his intention. And why should it be, when he was engaged to another woman; perhaps even married to her by now, although she had seen nothing in the newspapers.

At the end of October, Austria-Hungary capitulated, followed immediately by Turkey. At the beginning of November, Austria followed suit and, a certain indicator that it was all over, the Kaiser abdicated. The armistice between Germany and the Allies was signed at 5 a.m. on November 11th; hostilities would cease at 11 o'clock.

'All over bar the shouting!' said the Brig.

★ ★ ★

'So, where is he?'

Edmund frowned. 'Kate, the war may be over, but security still has to be observed.'

'You mean to say that knowing where one insignificant little P.O.W. is at this moment is going to bring down the Government?'

'Sorry, sister mine, I shall have to clear it before I can tell you. And remember, he'll still be a prisoner. It won't be a simple matter of just letting him go.'

'Angela understands that. She just wants to *know*.'

'She will — in the fulness of time.'

'The fulness of time!' Angela exploded when this information was passed on to her after Kate had returned from her pass. 'I shall only have 72 hours!'

'This is Edmund's phone number,' Kate tore a leaf from her diary. 'See what you can get out of him.'

'Sorry, Kate!' Angela relented. 'I'm a selfish cow, aren't I? It's just that I'm terrified we may have to fight our way through a tangle of red tape as difficult as any war.'

'You'll manage! And it won't be long now before you have all the time in the world to do it.'

'What will you do, Kate, when your services are dispensed with? Become a *proper* nurse?'

Kate grinned at the sarcasm in her voice. 'I haven't decided yet but first I shall go to the States.'

★ ★ ★

'What will you do first, Robert, now that you're demobilised?'

370

'Persuade Father and Mother to stay in the Dower House, for a start.'

'They'll huff and they'll puff but in the end, they'll see it's for the best. And then?'

'Well, once you've finished with it, I thought about suggesting we turn the Hall into a sort of housing co-operative. There'll be a great need for housing now that the men are coming home. What's left of them, that is.'

'It would need a lot of work doing to it.'

'Well, there should be enough tradesmen coming back to manage that.'

'It sounds a good idea. And what about you? Where will you live?'

'I wondered,' Robert looked at his aunt with great affection, 'if you'd consider setting up house with me in a couple of the farm cottages or there's the stable block. We could convert either of them. I intend to get more involved with the Pottery — run it, if I can — and I shall need to live somewhere close at hand. What do you say?'

'No!' said Aunt Bella firmly.

Robert was so startled by this unexpected rejection, he could only stare at her.

'It wouldn't be right,' Aunt Bella continued, 'for a good-looking — yes, you are! — eligible, young war hero . . .'

But at this point, Robert intervened. 'Aunt, I am *not* a war hero. I did nothing beyond the normal call of duty. Unlike some.' He thought, as he often did these days, of Jamie Coleano — the man was becoming an obsession with him. Aunt Bella saw the pain in his eyes and her resolve strengthened.

'That's as may be — it still wouldn't be right for someone like you to settle down with an old fogey like me.'

'You're young in heart, and always will be.'

'It still wouldn't be right.'

'So what would you like me to do? Advertise for a young, attractive, nubile housekeeper?'

'I'd like you to *marry*, Robert. To live a happy and fulfilled life.'

'*You* haven't married.'

But she waved him to silence. 'The man I should have married was killed at Ladysmith but I've been lucky, even so, in finding my niche. And I shall find something else to occupy me when I'm no longer needed here.'

She leaned back in her chair and gazed at him reflectively. 'What happened to that nice Kate Moneymoon?' she asked bluntly.

Caught unawares, Robert felt his colour deepen. 'She's at Moneymoon Manor, I imagine. Or perhaps in America. Her fiancé — an American — was killed on the Somme. She was devoted to him.'

As you still are to her, his aunt mused. 'How do you know all this?'

'I met her brother in town. He told me.'

'People recover from broken hearts, you know.' She leaned towards him. 'Nettles, my dear boy, are made for the grasping.' With which enigmatic remark, she left him. 'I'm in my office if you want me.'

She sat in her office for a long time, thinking hard. Then she reached for the telephone directory.

* ⋆ ⋆

'Robert when are you going to inspect the house in Oxfordshire? The one that nice General left you.'

'I thought I'd go down next week, Aunt. If that's all right with you.'

'Actually, dear boy, it would suit me far better if you went *this* week — tomorrow, in fact. I could use your room.'

'Fine! Tomorrow, it is.'

⋆ ⋆ ⋆

It is just as Kate remembers it. The same straight path between miniature, box hedges leading to a blue-painted door, the same sentinel bay trees. Perhaps the paint is flaking a little on the door but the brass knocker in the shape of the Prince of Wales' feathers is as bright as ever, and the diminutive rose-beds either side of the path are free from weeds.

Kate lifts the latch of the iron gate and walks slowly up the path, her heart hammering. Ever since Aunt Bella's telephone call she has been in what Ma calls 'a state', alternating between wild bursts of almost uncontrollable excitement and fits of depression when she has been convinced it would be far better not to do as Aunt Bella has suggested. At the same time, she has known that nothing would stop her from doing it.

'I am sure that to see you is what Robert wants more than anything in the world,' his aunt has told her. 'Forgive me, my dear, if I am speaking out of turn. I know that your fiancé has been killed and I know, too, what terrible grief the death of a loved one can cause.'

She hadn't tried to explain that it wasn't like that; that of course she was sad but only as anyone would be at the sacrifice of a young life; that she hadn't known Jamie for long enough or well enough to grieve for too long or too deeply. She had simply said that she would like very much to see Robert again — if he wanted to see her.

'I'd stake my life on that!' And Aunt Bella had gone on to tell her that Robert would soon be staying at Long Wittenham for a few days.

It was all very well, Kate reflects now, as she reaches the front door, for Aunt Bella to interpret Robert's wishes but how can she be so sure? As she lifts the knocker, she cannot help remembering the last time she had arrived unexpectedly at his house — or rather his father's house — and the reception she had received then.

But as before she straightens her shoulders and lifts her chin. And this time, she does not turn her back on the door. From the unguarded expression on Robert's face when he first sees her, she will know immediately what his feelings are.

The door begins to open and Kate holds her breath. And then lets it out in a long-drawn-out sigh. A woman is standing there, a woman whom she remembers as Miss Crawley, General Waver-tree's housekeeper. She clears her throat but the woman forestalls her.

'Miss Moneymoon! What a lovely surprise! You've come to see the Captain, of course. But I'm afraid he's out — gone for a walk to the top of the Clumps. Won't you come in and wait?'

But Kate shakes her head. 'Thank you but perhaps, if you would direct me, I could catch him up.' For she knows it would be unbearable to meet Robert again in the company of another person, no matter how pleasant.

'Of course, miss!' Miss Crawley is delighted to conduct Kate back to the gate. 'Turn left at the corner, then make for the church. The path to the Clumps is just opposite. It'll be muddy!' she warns.

But Kate doesn't care about mud. She follows the housekeeper's instructions, finds the church and the path opposite, looks up and sees two steep little hillocks, their crowns of elm trees skeletal against the grey winter sky. And then she sees Robert halfway to the top, standing with his back to her. Gathering up her skirts, she begins the steep climb towards him.

Robert has paused deliberately at the spot where he'd first met General Wavertree and Pugsie. He smiles to himself as he remembers them — the old gentleman leaning on his stick and the fat little pug panting at his feet. He remembers, too, the ease with which he, himself, had walked up the hillside. Today, he knows a little of how the General must have felt. He'll reach the top, there's no doubt of that, but it won't be with the same buoyant spring in his step. But at least, he is alive. Even if . . .

He lifts his head to gaze about him; down at the Abbey nestling in the serpentine curves of the Thames and then back to Long Wittenham church.

It is then that he sees the girl climbing towards him, a girl in a little green hat with a feather set rakishly over one ear, who holds up the folds of her long green skirt so that she can climb the faster, a girl whom he would have known anywhere. And then she lifts her other hand and waves and he begins to run, to stumble anyhow down the hill towards her. But the speed at which he is travelling is too great for his bad leg to control. He stumbles, grabs wildly at the air and falls heavily.

Within seconds, Kate is crouching beside him, cradling his head in her arms, telling him to be still until his breath returns. At last, he manages to sit up so that they are both half-lying, half-sitting on the wet hillside, their arms around each other.

'I should have done this years ago,' he says thickly, 'cast myself at your feet and never, ever let you out of my sight!'

'Oh, Robert! Darling Robert! It's not too late!'

And now their mouths are clinging as if they will never separate and they know that the years between are unimportant, a mere preliminary, in fact, to their future together.

Epilogue

They have chosen to meet at the same hotel where Kate, Prissy and Angela had taken afternoon tea during the war. This time, their waiter is young but not that much faster for he walks with a limp and has a row of medals pinned to his breast, as have many of his colleagues. And this time, it is Kate who is paying, not because she is wealthier than the others but because she is the one who has arranged the meeting.

It is the spring of 1922 and Prissy, Rosie May and James — her two-year-old son — are over from the States and staying with Kate at Holker Hall or, to be precise, the Dower House. For Robert's parents have died, his mother soon after the ending of the war when she had waited in vain for the return of her eldest son and his father, unable to accept the new order of things, a year later. Holker Hall, as Robert had planned is now a thriving housing co-operative.

Angela, now Frau Ernst Schreiber and living in Munich, is on a visit to her parents and Megan, the only one not present at that wartime tea-party, has come up from Hereford especially for the reunion. She lives there with her new husband, John Corben, Gareth's army friend. Throughout the war years, they have kept in touch and in 1919 when they had met again, friendship had rapidly blossomed into love.

At first, the tale is of children; Prissy's are with Kate's two-year-old son, Mathew, at Holker Hall, Angela's little girl, Lotte, is in Kent with her maternal grandparents and Megan's year-old daughter, Mair, is being cared for by her father in Hereford. It is because of Mair that Megan will be catching an evening train home. John Corben is a Baptist minister and easily able to arrange his working day around his daughter, but Meg cannot bear to be parted from her for more than a few hours.

'Wait till the next one,' Prissy tells her. 'Then you'll be glad to get away.'

But Meg cannot believe this is true. Nor is it a belief shared by Kate. 'You weren't too happy about leaving James this morning, even with Aunt Bella.'

'Nonsense!' says Prissy but she knows that her twin is right.

'How is Aunt Bella?' Angela enquires.

'As wonderful as ever. She does all the administrative work of the co-operative practically single-handed. And that means Robert's able to be at the Pottery full-time.'

'Has he thought any more about Ernst's suggestion of designing for him?' Angela asks.

Kate nods vigorously. 'He's very keen on the idea. And with Prissy and Hank selling for us in New York, the potential's enormous.'

For Hank has at last managed to convince his father that his interest in beans, be they canned, baked or in their natural state, is nonexistent. The tiny china and pottery store in Greenwich Village that he now owns and which is largely stocked by exports from the Werrington Pottery, is thriving. Ernst Schreiber's designs can only increase the sales potential.

The conversation turns to news of old friends. Abbie is not with them because the birth of her second child is imminent and Fred won't hear of her travelling even the short distance from the East End.

'He says his child isn't going to be born on top of a London bus and that's final!' Angela reports. 'Even when Abbie told him she couldn't possibly reach the top of one, even if she wanted to, he still wouldn't hear of it!'

Kate hears regularly from Pierre and Heloise. 'They're both fine and far too busy with their clinics to have children, Heloise says.'

Megan has kept in touch with Sister Hopkins who is now Matron of a cottage hospital in Norfolk. Sergeant Hopkins looks after the maintenance staff. 'She says she'll be happy to accept any of us as nurses if we ever get tired of family life!'

They know this will never happen but the suggestion unleashes a flood of reminiscence.

Time passes quickly and reluctantly they prepare to go their separate ways. 'Don't forget Wavertree Cottage is always there whenever you want a change of scenery,' Kate reminds Meg, for she guesses the salary of a Baptist minister cannot be large. 'Miss Crawley loves to have someone to fuss over and we can't get there every weekend.'

Before they go, Kate distributes the dregs of the teapot between their four cups. 'This should really be cocoa, but this will have to do.' She raises her cup. 'To four V.A.D.s who stuck it out to the bitter end. Well,' she smiles at Prissy, '*almost* to the bitter end.'

'To four V.A.D.s,' they chorus, chinking their cups.

THE GREENWAY
Jane Adams

When Cassie and her twelve-year-old cousin Suzie had taken a short cut through an ancient Norfolk pathway, Suzie had simply vanished . . . Twenty years on, Cassie is still tormented by nightmares. She returns to Norfolk, determined to solve the mystery.

FORTY YEARS
ON THE WILD FRONTIER
Carl Breihan & W. Montgomery

Noted Western historian Carl Breihan has culled from the handwritten diaries of John Montgomery, grandfather of co-author Wayne Montgomery, new facts about Wyatt Earp, Doc Holliday, Bat Masterson and other famous and infamous men and women who gained notoriety when the Western Frontier was opened up.

TAKE NOW, PAY LATER
Joanna Dessau

This fiction based on fact is the love-turning-to-hate story of Robert Carr, Earl of Somerset, and his wife, Frances.

McLEAN AT THE GOLDEN OWL
George Goodchild

Inspector McLean has resigned from Scotland Yard's CID and has opened an office in Wimpole Street. With the help of his able assistant, Tiny, he solves many crimes, including those of kidnapping, murder and poisoning.

KATE WEATHERBY
Anne Goring

Derbyshire, 1849: The Hunter family are the arrogant, powerful masters of Clough Grange. Their feuds are sparked by a generation of guilt, despair and illfortune. But their passions are awakened by the arrival of nineteen-year-old Kate Weatherby.

A VENETIAN RECKONING
Donna Leon

When the body of a prominent international lawyer is found in the carriage of an intercity train, Commissario Guido Brunetti begins to dig deeper into the secret lives of the once great and good.

A TASTE FOR DEATH
Peter O'Donnell

Modesty Blaise and Willie Garvin take on impossible odds in the shape of Simon Delicata, the man with a taste for death, and Swordmaster, Wenczel, in a terrifying duel. Finally, in the Sahara desert, the intrepid pair must summon every killing skill to survive.

SEVEN DAYS FROM MIDNIGHT
Rona Randall

In the Comet Theatre, London, seven people have good reason for wanting beautiful Maxine Culver out of the way. Each one has reason to fear her blackmail. But whose shadow is it that lurks in the wings, waiting to silence her once and for all?

QUEEN OF THE ELEPHANTS
Mark Shand

Mark Shand knows about the ways of elephants, but he is no match for the tiny Parbati Barua, the daughter of India's greatest expert on the Asian elephant, the late Prince of Gauripur, who taught her everything. Shand sought out Parbati to take part in a film about the plight of the wild herds today in north-east India.

THE DARKENING LEAF
Caroline Stickland

On storm-tossed Chesil Bank in 1847, the young lovers, Philobeth and Frederick, prevent wreckers mutilating the apparent corpse of a young woman. Discovering she is still alive, Frederick takes her to his grandmother's home. But the rescue is to have violent and far-reaching effects . . .

A WOMAN'S TOUCH
Emma Stirling

When Fenn went to stay on her uncle's farm in Africa, the lovely Helena Starr seemed to resent her — especially when Dr Jason Kemp agreed to Fenn helping in his bush hospital. Though it seemed Jason saw Fenn as little more than a child, her feelings for him were those of a woman.

A DEAD GIVEAWAY
Various Authors

This book offers the perfect opportunity to sample the skills of five of the finest writers of crime fiction — Clare Curzon, Gillian Linscott, Peter Lovesey, Dorothy Simpson and Margaret Yorke.

DOUBLE INDEMNITY — MURDER FOR INSURANCE
Jad Adams

This is a collection of true cases of murderers who insured their victims then killed them — or attempted to. Each tense, compelling account tells a story of cold-blooded plotting and elaborate deception.

THE PEARLS OF COROMANDEL
Keron Bhattacharya

John Sugden, an ambitious young Oxford graduate, joins the Indian Civil Service in the early 1920s and goes to uphold the British Raj. But he falls in love with a young Hindu girl and finds his loyalties tragically divided.

WHITE HARVEST
Louis Charbonneau

Kathy McNeely, a marine biologist, sets out for Alaska to carry out important research. But when she stumbles upon an illegal ivory poaching operation that is threatening the world's walrus population, she soon realises that she will have to survive more than the harsh elements . . .